# THE
# HANGING
# TREE

ISBN: 978-0692053591

**Cover Design:**
Giovanni Auriemma
**Book Developmental Editing/Manuscript Evaluation:**
Ann Castro
**Line Editing/Proofing:**
AnnCastro Studio with Ann Castro and Emily Dings
**Interior Design:**
Mallory Rock and Melissa Stevens with Rock Solid Book Design

*For Gar*

*My partner in crime*

*"Try to touch the past. Try to deal with the past. It's not real. It's just a dream."*

—Ted Bundy

# CHAPTER ONE

**EVIE**
**JANUARY 13, 2017**
**FRIDAY**

**FROM** the window in office 23B, I have a perfect view of the hanging tree. That's what I call it—only to myself, never out loud—even though I'm fairly certain no one ever hung themselves or anybody else from the oak's gnarled limbs. They stretch up and out like an old man's arthritic fingers, thin and gray at the tips. Surely, they'd snap like bird bones under the weight of a body.

Every morning before my 9 a.m. group arrives, I put myself in the exact place, rolling my chair to the well-worn indentions in the carpet that offer me the best, unobstructed view of the tree. From this spot, my clients can never tell I'm looking just over their shoulders at the place where those dark branches scrape the sky. And beyond, to the small, sad patch of weedy grass where it grows.

"Did you hear what happened there?" I'd asked the realtor, pointing with accusation at the tree when she'd shown me the office space years ago. *Perfect for an upstart professional,* according to the ad on Craigslist. That was me then—upstart, professional. Now, I was fast-tracking it to forty. Four more years and I'd have outlived my mother by a decade. I'd already lived nearly three times that without my dad. To be expected, I suppose, when your parents meet outside a methadone clinic in the Tenderloin.

"No. What happened?" Underneath her not-so-blonde roots and Botoxed wrinkles, the realtor had the face of a teenage girl stricken with morbid curiosity. The kind of girl I'd spent my entire adolescence simultaneously worshipping and loathing. The kind of girl who wouldn't have been caught dead talking to Evil Evie (that's me). She leaned in so close I caught a whiff of minty toothpaste. "Tell me." Her voice breathy, almost aroused.

And I did. The thing she couldn't possibly have known, the thing I'd never told anyone else. Because I had the inexplicable urge to please her. And silence her. This woman I'd met once and hadn't known at all. "Someone died there. A murder." I'd watched her face contort at the word. Listened to her gasp. It had satisfied me like I'd been waiting my whole life to say it.

"Who?" she'd asked, and my insides curdled. "When?"

I should've known there would be questions. Questions I didn't want to answer. Questions that loomed so large over my whole life, they cast a shadow I couldn't shake.

"I'll take it," I'd said, suddenly wishing I could snatch the keys from her and run.

"Huh?"

"The office. I'll take it."

"Oh. Are you sure? There are some other spaces I can show you." Her eyes had seemed to judge me, making me feel twelve again.

*Evil Evie stares right through me. Her eyes could kill with just one lookie. Evil Evie, please don't touch me. You are creepy, creepy, CREEPY!*

"That tree is a little spooky. I'd understand if you—"

"I like it." And with that, she didn't say anything else. A good thing, because I might've told her the whole truth about that night at the hanging tree. That I had been there. That I'd watched it happen. That it had been my fault. And that I need to see it every day to remind myself what's at stake if I get it wrong again.

****

Today, the tree looks positively nightmarish. It stares back at me from the dead of winter and the gloom of a cold, steady rain. Below its canopy, blowing in the wind, one of its brittle fingers amputated. A gust carries the small branch across the grass until I can no longer see it. At 9:01 a.m., New Guy clears his throat while the others watch him, territorial, sniffing him out like a pack of dogs. I print a word on the whiteboard behind me and face the circle, the men there.

"Intimacy," I say.

New Guy twitters, then puts a hand over his mouth, embarrassed. His bleary eyes flit up at me. Then down again. *Someone hasn't been sleeping.* I notice, because that's my job. To notice everything. To notice and make meaning.

"That's our topic for today. Healthy intimacy. What is it? And how do we get there? But first, introductions. We have a new member joining our group." I gesture to George, the veteran among them, and the only one who's here because he wants to be. He's been coming to my Mondays, Wednesdays, Fridays since I hung the sign on my door, claiming it as my own. Doctor Evelyn Maddox. "Go ahead. You know the drill."

George nods, solemn. He reminds me of a grandfather. Not mine, per se, because I never met either one of them. But someone's. With a kind face that's been softened by time. He'd let you eat all the candy you wanted and get away with anything, and he'd play with you. Hide and seek. Piggyback rides. You name it. Like a big kid himself. And he was. That was his weapon. "Well, alright. I'll go first, Dr. Evie. My name is George, and I'm here because I molested my neighbor's little girl. She was six."

"And?"

George has the look of a scolded puppy, and I almost feel sorry for him. Another one of his weapons, and I can't forget that. Remembering—that's my job too. "And I touched three other little girls, two I didn't get caught for. I served ten years in the pen, and I've been coming to this group since—"

"We don't need your whole goddamn life story," Vince interrupts. "Can't we just get on with it?"

Not for the first time and not likely the last, I feel the urge to throttle him. Or at the very least, to hurl the marker, cap off, at the lapel of his fancy suit. "Canali," he'd bragged to us last week. "Cost me…well, your weekly salary. Sorry, Doc."

I'd squeezed the marker between my fingers until my knuckles whitened. Using my feelings is another part of my job. But you can't use what you can't control. When I look up, New Guy is watching me. He turns his head so quickly, I know I've caught him. "If you can't be respectful to the other members of the group, Vince, I'll have to ask you to leave."

"Ha!" Scorn drips from Vince's lips, down his perfectly trimmed goatee, his blue eyes equal parts ice and heat. "I should be so lucky. I'm Vince Kincaid. And the only reason I'm here is some wannabe Chris Hansen moron in IT found porn on my work laptop when I took it in for service. He probably thought they were gonna give him a medal. Or at least a promotion. Those guys in IT don't make half—"

"What kind of porn?" It's necessary, my interruption, but it feels good too. To jab him like that. New Guy smirks, barely, but I notice. Of course, I do. And I start to feel uneasy. Like he knows what I'm thinking.

"C'mon," Vince groans. "I had no idea that was on there. It's not like I went looking for it. Do you really think I'm stupid enough to type *sex with teen girls* into Google? Puh-lease. Give me some credit. I've got a freakin' MBA. Magna cum laude too."

*Who's telling his life story now?* I don't say that though. I just nod. Vince's distortions are nothing new. Nothing I haven't seen before. And when you get right down to it, reality is debatable, elusive. It's all a matter of perspective, even for a jerk like Vince. "Tony, go ahead."

Tony barely looks up, eyes fixed on his work boots. The words, when they finally come, seem to drain something essential from him. It's always this way. "Antonio Estrada. I'm innocent."

"What were you convicted of?" I ask, trying to hide my mental teeth grinding.

"PC 288. Lewd and Lascivious."

"And your victim?"

"*Alleged* victim." Vince pipes up, just to irk me, no doubt.

"My stepdaughter."

"Alright," I say, already exhausted. I turn to New Guy. I'd forgotten how much I hate introductions. And New Guy would be the worst of them all. They always were.

"Uh…My name is Sebastian Delacourt. And…I—uh—do I have to say more?"

I nod, encouraging, but I want to do it for him. Save us all the trouble of this awkward dance. I'd read his file already, memorized his dirty laundry list. And that was enough to know why he didn't want to say it out loud. Even in here, with his own kind, he would be judged. They were already eyeballing the GPS monitor strapped to his ankle. I was judging him too for my own reasons. New Guy adjusts his glasses and runs a hand through his wavy black hair—as black as my own—and, just then, the hanging tree catches my eye. There's something in it.

The rain is nothing but a drizzle, but the wind has picked up, tossing anything that's not tied down. An unexplained dread stirs inside me, before I realize that's how it got there, whipping around with a life of its own, struggling to hang on or to free itself. I can't tell which. It's caught in the tree, just like I am. A child's birthday balloon.

****

It's dark outside, my office empty, when the rain finally stops. I bundle up anyway, pulling the hood of my jacket around my face, and descend the stairs to the parking lot. They still haven't fixed the street lamps like I'd asked—there's only one working now—and the edges of the lot dissolve into blackness. I can't even see the tree, but I head toward it anyway, knowing its place by heart.

I have to stand on tiptoe to reach the ribbon. One solid tug and I've got the whole balloon in my grasp. Wet and flimsy as a dead fish. I want to drop it, wipe my hands on my dress pants and leave it for someone else to find. But I don't. It feels like a sign meant for me.

Nobody gave me a balloon on my twelfth birthday or any birthday for that matter. If I had been the sort of kid worthy of a balloon, I wouldn't have been at the hanging tree that night. I'd like to think there's some other version of my life, a version where Friday, May 13, 1994, passed without incident. With birthday cake and paper hats and gifts wrapped by someone who loved me. A version where the hanging tree doesn't exist, spreading its black rot over my past, my future, and the brief speck in between.

I squeeze the thin flesh of the balloon between my fingers, close my eyes, and try again to remember. I start where I always do. Me in the tree, breathless.

The bark was as rough as calloused hands on my bare legs, so rough it scraped the back of my thighs. Cicadas screamed bloody murder from the branches above me. I'd never climbed that high before—*what am I doing up here?*—but had swallowed my fear in one gulp the same way Cassie had sucked down her Slurpee.

Fear had writhed in my stomach, desperate to get out. *Cassie.* I'd said her name then, but only in my head. My voice wouldn't work.

**12**

Hands either. They were useless stumps. But my eyes had registered her face, plain as day below me, with the full moon masquerading as a spotlight. Around her neck, laced tight—too tight—the man's fingers. And his face, his face, his face . . .

*C'mon, Evie, think.* But like always, I come up empty, his face just a shapeless hole in my mind, scribbled over with black crayon—even after one hundred and four sessions with Dr. Riley, supposed expert in trauma, grief, and loss.

But then, you can only get so far in therapy without the truth. Haven't I always told my patients exactly that? I understand now what I've been asking of them. To let loose of a string they've been holding tight, the one that held their seams together somehow. To pry open a part of the self they'd soldered shut. To do what seemed impossible. Maybe I don't want to remember.

"Dr. Maddox, is that you?"

It takes a few skips of my heart before I find myself again. I'm not thirteen anymore. My feet are firmly planted on the earth, not scrambling against the hard armor of the hanging tree, one misstep away from a fall. From him. The faceless man. Cassie isn't here anymore. Not her body anyway. Though I suppose I can't be sure of that. Still, I imagine it's buried in an unceremonious grave, somewhere it was meant to never be found, her bones biding their time—slowly, surely—rising to the surface.

"Hello? Dr. Maddox?" I recognize the voice—New Guy, Sebastian Delacourt—and then the skip in my heart becomes a flutter, frenetic as the beat of a moth's wings.

"Sebastian? It's late. What are you still doing here?" *Group ended eight hours ago.* That's what I don't say. Saying it aloud would only make it worse. And by *it*, I mean the blood whooshing to my head with the urgency of a siren.

"I could ask you the same. It's Friday night. Shouldn't you be home by now? With your...husband?" His voice lilts up at the end, but he doesn't give me a chance to dodge the question. "This isn't the best neighborhood, you know."

I do know. Even back then it was the kind of neighborhood two little girls could get lost in. Forever. "It's not so bad," I say, not wanting to offend him, because he's pointing up the street to one of the only halfway houses that accepts offenders like him. Rapist and murderer, both.

"I live up there," he says.

"How do you like it?"

"Not so bad. Short commute for therapy at least." He chuckles a little. "And there's this great park exactly 2,603 feet away." Any closer and it would be off limits to him and any other registered sex offender. But I couldn't imagine anybody calling it a park. The grass, what little there is, colored a dingy brown as if it sprouted from poisoned soil. "It's lovely, isn't it?" He gestures his hands wide and dramatic like he's sweeping them across Central Park itself. And for a moment, they could be *the* hands. The ones that wrapped around Cassie's throat. He's old enough, mid-forties, similar m.o. I nod at him, unease curling like a worm inside me. "I especially like that tree," he adds.

"Which one?" As if there's any doubt.

He looks at the balloon in my hand, and I feel caught. Like I'm holding a loaded gun. "The one you can see from the window in your office."

# CHAPTER TWO

**EVIE**
**JANUARY 13, 2017**
**FRIDAY**

*HITCHHIKING is usually very safe.* That line never fails to amuse me and punch me in the gut. I read it every other Friday on the Hitchwiki website before I call the taxi. It's part of my ritual, and tonight's no different. Except it's just my second time hitching from my new apartment. And it's Friday the thirteenth. My hands shake a little—my nerves still frayed from my run-in with Sebastian—when I fill up Samson's bowl to the very top just in case I don't return. He meows like a madman, flicks his tail, and darts through my legs as if to say, *I can be crazy too.*

"Don't judge me, Sammy," I whisper, prompting another, more demure meow. "Haven't I always come back to you?" He blinks at me before disappearing behind the sofa. If I was a cat, I'd look just like Samson, sleek black hair and eyes the color of swamp grass. That's what the lady at the shelter had told me when I'd pointed to his cage—"That's the one." I'm even more like a black cat than she knew, because nobody wants me. And because I'm cursed. Obviously.

I double-check my backpack to be sure I haven't forgotten anything. Well, the most important thing really—my keychain canister of pepper spray. Someday, it might be all that stands between me and a fate like Cassie's, between the milky white skin of my throat and *those* hands. I can't bring myself to carry a gun, not even a cute little number that could fit inside one of those fancy clutches that Jared's mother totes around.

I perch on the edge of the sofa in silence, staring at the shiny edge of the cellophane balloon I'd rescued—*Happy, Happy Birthday!* I'd pressed it flat between page 100 and 101 of *Memory: The Science of Recollection,* marking the passage I'd memorized since grad school. *Learning and memory are state dependent. The surest way to access traumatic memories is to return the brain to the same state of consciousness as when the memory was first encoded.*

State-dependent recall. That's the general idea. When my cell phone rings, I hurry for the door like always. Before I can change my mind. I wave at Samson, his eyes, anyway. They're shining from beneath the bookcase. Then, I steady myself—*this is for you, Cassie*—and make my way downstairs to the taxi waiting for me.

"Where to, lady?" He's probably expecting me to name some swanky new bar in the city even though I'm not dressed for it. Skinny jeans, a two-sizes-too-small Warriors T-shirt, and my favorite pair of Converse sneaks. Ponytail and no makeup. I want to look young and fresh-faced. But mostly, I want to feel young again. If I could, just for a moment, maybe I would remember.

"The Safeway in El Cerrito."

"Alright." He hides his surprise well, but it's there in his voice. Most people wouldn't, but I notice.

I crack the window, lean back against the seat, and close my eyes. With no traffic, it's a twenty-minute cab ride from Oakland to the

Safeway that wasn't always a Safeway, and I've seen every mile of it before. Two years' worth of every other Fridays, so many that the getting there is just a blur of stale cigarette smoke, talk radio, and the sound of the highway. When I open my eyes, the driver's sneaking a glance at my chest in the rearview mirror, and I pull my jacket tighter. The way this T-shirt fits me, I'm not surprised, and I wonder if I've gone too far this time. If Jared was here, he'd tell me I have a death wish. But he's not, and that's my fault too.

My throat gets achy and raw, the same way it does every time I think about Jared. To be fair, I had warned him. The curse of Evil Evie is real. When I'd said that, he shook his head at me, brown eyes crinkling, then kissed me hard, almost like a dare to the universe. Overconfident, because life had never kicked him in the teeth. With his invincible broad shoulders that could carry the weight of the world and an easy smile that told you he'd never had to. He graduated first in his class and was accepted into Stanford, early decision at that. He'd known nothing about Cassie or the faceless man, and it still unnerved me how easily I'd concealed an entire country inside myself without him—my husband, for God's sake—suspecting a thing. It was a lesson too. I had to notice. I had to remember. I had to go by feel. Because people lie.

"Ma'am, we're here."

I fork over the forty-dollar cab fare—a small price to pay for redemption, if it ever comes—and climb out, waiting until he's rounded the corner before I start walking. The same route Cassie and I took twenty-three years ago. I try not to think about it that way, because when I do, I know what a freak I am. Like the first time I'd twisted a few strands of hair around my fingers and pulled them out until there was a tiny bald spot at the base of my head. I heard the class snickering behind me—*creepy, creepy, creepy*—but I couldn't stop myself. Ripping hair from my scalp felt like scratching an itch I couldn't reach. And it's no different now, coming here. I'm compelled.

If I squint into the lights outside the Safeway, I can almost see it the way it used to be—the Port in a Storm Home for Children.

The peeling white paint, the wraparound porch that seemed to make promises it could never fulfill. Inside, the twin beds stacked side by side like matchboxes, and everything I owned in a garbage bag at the foot of mine. I wished I'd been there when they bulldozed it down, but by then, I was long gone, aged out of the system.

That night, a lifetime ago, I'd climbed out the second-story window and shimmied down a drainpipe like I had nine lives. I can't recall much of the walk, just Cassie by my side, but I imagine it wasn't so different from tonight. Except for the cold that's cutting deep as a blade through my jacket. I set a course through the parking lot, down the street, toward the freeway, grateful for the heat of the cars rushing past me. A man in a truck honks and whistles—"Hey, baby," he says as I turn—but he keeps driving. *It could be him*, I think. It could be anyone.

Past the gas station, the inky cave of the underpass looms up ahead, straight out of my nightmares. "You need a ride?" That was the first thing he'd said to Cassie and me while we stood in the shadows drinking our Slurpees. I see his hand in my dreams sometimes—his fingers as long and white and gnarled as the branches on the hanging tree—dangling out the window of a run-down pickup truck, tapping along to a song only he could hear. And we'd nodded, somehow already knowing he was the one who would take us where we wanted to go.

# CHAPTER THREE

**EVIE**
**JANUARY 13, 2017**
**FRIDAY**

I stand on a small patch of weeds just outside the underpass—my usual spot, near the freeway sign—squinting in the headlights of the passing cars. The oncoming high beams expose the rot and rancor Cassie and I had simply disregarded since we'd passed that way so many times before. Or maybe things just look different when you're thirteen (it's your birthday), when you're with your best friend (only friend), when you're on a mission (do or die). Empty beer cans and needles at the periphery now. Further in, where I don't go anymore, concrete walls defaced with graffiti. And further still, a lump of something—blankets? clothing?—that might be a person. Living or dead, it's hard to say. I focus on the blades of grass just under my sneakers, inhaling the heady smell of exhaust.

*Remember. Try to remember. It's safe to remember.*

"You need a ride?" The first thing he'd said, but not the last. Cassie had gone up to his window while I hung back, still tasting the wild cherry Slurpee at the back of my throat. His voice, what I could hear of it anyway, didn't sound so different from the older boys who lived with us at the group home. Cassie turned to me and smiled, her tongue bright red. "He can give us a lift. What do you think?"

I shrugged, looking past her, trying to make him out in the dark. Now I know the first rule of hitchhiking: If you doubt the ride, turn it down. But it wouldn't have helped me then. Because I didn't doubt the faceless man, even with all that had already happened to end me up there, orphaned and sneaking away from Port in a Storm. When you're thirteen, when you're with your best friend, when you're on a mission, there's no room for doubt.

"Al-right," my voice cracking midway through. If the faceless man had a reaction, I wouldn't have seen it anyway. We'd already climbed into the backseat, still holding tight to our Slurpee cups, though mine was nearly empty and sweating against my palm. I must've stared at the back of his head for the entire drive or close to it, but the smell of that truck—suntan lotion and sweat—is still the only memory I've got left. That and the morbid, old folk song he sung under his breath, faint as a whisper. *Hang down your head, Tom Dooley. Hang down your head and cry...poor boy, you're bound to die.* I'd heard Miss Cherice singing it in the mornings while she went room to room waking us up—that one and "Swing Low, Sweet Chariot." Two of the most depressing songs I'd ever heard. But Cherice's voice, warm and thick as honey, had made them seem not so bad.

In his voice though, the words sounded strange. Eerie. *Down in some lonesome valley. Hangin' from a white oak tree.* Now that was a sign, but I might've only imagined him singing about a hanging tree. The whole night was a riddle. A cipher. A puzzle, unsolved.

Sometimes, I stick my thumb out, old-school style, but not tonight. I just sit on my backpack and wait, cataloguing everything I know about the faceless man—white and young, but at least sixteen because he could drive—which is virtually nothing. Memory is a funny thing. I should know. As vast and mysterious as the universe itself, and that's why I'm out here with a death wish—*you're right, Jared*—because even if it kills me, I will remember.

****

"I've never seen eyes like yours." The man in the driver's seat—Danny, he'd told me—fiddles with the radio before he looks up at me. Other than his name, it's the first thing he's said since he pulled his black jeep to the shoulder ten minutes ago, introduced himself, and asked those infamous four words, "You need a ride?" He'd added *miss* to the end of it, probably trying to be polite. "They're so green—are those contacts?"

I shake my head no, taking note of the slight twist in my gut, the prickle that works its way up my spine like the buzz of a revving motor. Jared always told me that my eyes were my best feature. Actually the way he'd said it, they were springtime green. But then, he had a way with words. He is—was—a closet poet. My mom had said they belonged to my father, never hiding her distaste. Everybody else just called them creepy. Evil Evie with the glowing cat eyes.

"You get them from your mom? Was she as purdy as you are?" Danny doesn't turn his head from the road, but the way he says that word makes me uneasy, and I'm willing to bet he's side-eyeing me. His face is all shadow under the brim of his baseball cap—his hands tense as he grips the wheel a little tighter. I wonder what he's holding back. Because everybody's holding something.

My breath hitches a little—like a skip in a record—and I try to think of the right thing to say. It's not the first time a ride has hit on me, but Danny's different. Older. Fiftyish. With bits of gray in his beard. He should know better. I should've known better. I hold tight to the backpack on my lap, rethinking my reluctance to carry a gun. Along with my sanity. "Uh…I couldn't really tell you. I don't remember much about my mother." That part is true, so it sounds believable. To me, anyway.

"What happened to her? To your mama?"

Panic flashes like lightning and I freeze, caught in its glare. "I—I didn't say anything happened to her, did I?" Danny doesn't answer. He reaches toward me with stubby fingers, leathery knuckles, and the bare, tan skin of his forearm. "Anyway, she's dead."

He doesn't touch me—thank God—though I brace myself for it anyway. I consider the door handle, making a break for it, already anticipating the skin-ripping burn of the freeway at seventy miles per hour. I know the door opens, because checking is part of my hitching routine. But he doesn't touch me. I repeat it to myself like my words have power, and somehow they do. He doesn't touch me. Instead, he grabs an empty cup from the floorboard near my Chucks, puts it to his mouth, and spits into it. That's when I notice the bulge of tobacco in his lower lip.

"Nasty habit," he says, securing his spittoon in the cup holder. The brown liquid sloshes a little as the jeep traverses a pothole. I shrug at him, already feeling better. *I've seen worse.* "Sorry 'bout your mom."

"It was a long time ago," I say, like that makes it any better. Like time isn't amorphous, expanding and constricting at will, seconds stretched out like miles on the highway, years shrunk into a thimble. This drive has already lasted a century.

"So what do you do, Anne?" That's my hitching name. It jolts me to hear him use it. I assumed he'd forgotten. "When you're not accepting rides from strangers."

"I teach yoga." My hitching profession. I announce it matter-of-factly, hoping to quash the giddy lilt in his voice.

"I've always wanted to try that stuff. They say it makes you better in the sack. Any truth to that?" I laugh, because it gives him an out. He can still pretend he's joking. "Just teasin'," he says, obliging. But then, "I don't need any help in that department anyway."

His spit sloshes again, the brown sludge leaving its mark against the side of the cup, and I feel sick. "What about you?" I ask, fingering the outline of my pepper spray in the front pocket of my bag. "What do you do when you're not picking up hitchhikers?"

He turns his head from the road to smile at me, showing his stained teeth. "Librarian." I don't ask any more questions. We ride in silence until I point to the exit.

"This one," I say. "You can drop me at the Chicken and Waffles. I'm meeting a friend." That's my hitching story. The restaurant is a few blocks down from the hanging tree, and a quick bus ride back to my new apartment.

He takes the exit but taps the brakes a few times, jolting me forward then back, as if he can't make up his mind. "You wanna go somewhere?" he asks, his voice suddenly decided, already thick and husky with lust. I doubt the answer matters, but I give it anyway.

"I told you. I'm meeting a friend. He's expecting me."

He chuckles to himself, and I figure he knows I'm lying. "Your friend can wait."

I know this story. I've heard it a hundred times from the men in my groups. I know how it ends, but still. *He won't touch me, he won't touch me, he won't touch me.* He pats my knee once, then leaves his fingers resting there like I belong to him. My mouth gets dry. I stiffen. This is a first. No ride has ever put a hand on me, not like this. It's the precipice of terror, but I try to lean into it, knowing (as twisted as it sounds) this is what I've been waiting for.

The same state of consciousness.

Abject terror.

This is where I'll find it. The memory.

Streetlamps glow in the distance, but we'll never get there. Danny makes a sharp turn toward the Port of Oakland, then another down one of the long, dark, dead-end roads that look like the sort of place this would happen. A makeshift dumping ground with an overflowing dumpster and piles of trash bags vomiting their contents onto the street. But the worst, a bare mattress, stained and waiting.

"You don't want to do this," I tell him, addressing him like a patient. He's George, inviting a little girl onto his lap. Tony, ogling his stepdaughter in her short shorts. Vince, a finger poised at the keyboard. It's that moment, the one where he can still turn back. "You don't have to do this. Just let me out here. I won't say a word about it."

"Look at you." He practically spits the words at me. If I could feel them, they'd burn. "Standing out on the side of the road in that little T-shirt. You wanted this from Jump Street. Don't try to tell me you didn't."

Danny stops the jeep, and I'm a prisoner of whatever comes next. I'm not even surprised—how could I be?—just a dreadful combination of pathetic and ironic. This is what I get for helping sex offenders. No. This is what I get for letting Cassie die. But not only that. This is what I get for keeping quiet for twenty-three years. This is what it will take to be square with the universe.

I don't reach for my pepper spray. I don't open the door. I don't even scream. Because that's what fear can do to you. At thirteen. At thirty-six. Everything in me sucked out the way the tide draws out the water. And there it is—in that smooth, empty place—a new memory. The faceless man had touched my hand where it rested on the top of the seat, and I'd jerked it back like I'd been stung. He'd said something too, asked a question. "Are you down with that?"

But it's a flash I can barely hold onto, a tail that slips away in the underbrush. And I'm left with Danny and his hot tobacco breath and the knife he's slipped from his boot.

"It'll be easier if you don't fight." He actually has the nerve to say that. "Just close your eyes. I'll be quick." He giggles like a schoolgirl. "Not too quick though."

His hands crawl on me, and I think of Cassie with her eyes locked on mine, frozen. *Do something, Evie!* Had she said that? No, but she should have. Like the swell of a knock-down wave, my senses come rushing back—*crash!*—and I fill with life again, all of it. White-knuckling it in the backseat while my mom scored heroin; sitting with her cold body in our dumpy room at the Blue Bird, the needle still in her arm, until the cops showed up; elbowing Bobby Pierce in the stomach when he told everybody I'd killed her with my witchy stare; running from school with the girls behind me, chanting *Evil Evie*; squeezing Jared's hand on the last day he was alive, the day my curse—and his cancer—finally caught up to him.

All of that is fuel on a fire that had been burning long before I met Danny. It rises in my chest. "It's not going to be easy, asshole."

# CHAPTER FOUR

**EVIE**
**JANUARY 13, 2017**
**FRIDAY**

**ONE** of us is bleeding, I know that much. There's a smear of red on the dash, and my fingers are wet, so it must be me. But I feel nothing except the raw throb of adrenaline commanding my body. I'm sheer muscle—no brain—taut, instinctual, ready to strike, to destroy if necessary. And the way Danny's grunting and snarling, searching beneath the seat for the knife he dropped in the scuffle, destruction seems necessary. Imminent even, for one of us. Him or me.

I fumble for the door and scream again, louder this time. The noise that comes out of me is nothing I've heard before, but I imagine it's the sound Cassie would've made if those hands had let her. It's primal. Animal. And it scrapes my ears.

"Shut the fuck up!" Danny looks up from the floorboard, face flushed. A few jagged red lines mark his cheek, one of them deeper than the others. My handiwork, and I hope like hell it leaves a scar. "Where do you think you're goin'? You're not leavin' here till I get what I want. Till I give you what you deserve. Understand?" His hand wraps itself tighter around my calf like a tentacle and pulls me back toward him. The other hand behaves differently, caressing the side of my face, winding gentle fingers in my hair.

"I understand," I tell him, feeling the floorboard for something, anything I can use. The pepper spray's there somewhere, lost when Danny banged my head against the window. "Please just don't… don't hurt me. I'll do whatever you ask." I don't understand. He's already hurt me. And there's no way I'm doing anything he asks. Because we both know if it's up to him, I'm not leaving here. Not alive anyway.

"I knew you wanted it—"

I fling Danny's spittoon in his face. It's not the pepper spray, but somehow it's better, watching him recoil at the taste of his own polluted saliva. His grip softens, releases—for an instant—and I'm out. Free. And flying. With Danny behind me. I don't look, but I hear him. His heavy steps on the concrete, the huff of his breath. He swipes at my back, grabs a fistful of ponytail, and yanks hard. I fall against him, crumpling down his legs and onto the cement. He leans over me, and I see his teeth grinning or grimacing, I can't be sure which. I smell tobacco and sweat, taste the metal of my own fear as pungent as a gun in my mouth. He's got me pinned by my arms like I'm one of those frogs pickled in formaldehyde and tacked spread eagle on a dissecting board. I close my eyes—squeeze them so tight no light gets through. *Please don't let his face be the last thing I see.* And that's when I realize I'm not the girl in the tree anymore. I'm the one down below.

With his weight on me, it's too much to breathe. My chest burns, and my vision goes in and out, the darkness luring me, pulling me under. Telling me it's not so bad dying. Until I hear his voice in my ear, a rasp that comes straight from hell.

"Like mother, like daughter."

He lifts up a little, and I suck in a greedy gasp of air. *Like mother, like daughter? Is that what he said?* I must be hallucinating. Because he's quiet now, busying his lips on my neck.

Then, his mouth, parted and vicious as a barracuda, is mashing against mine. But at least his hands haven't moved—one secures each wrist, grinding the soft flesh of my arms into the wet pavement. As chances go, it isn't great, but it's the last one I've got. He groans a little as I kiss him back, luring him, and I read his thoughts. I've heard them before. Spoken by other men, different from him, but the same too. *She didn't stop me. She didn't fight. She was into it.* When the mocking voices in my head quiet—*this is it*—I bite down on his lip with all the force I can muster. He cries out and lifts up off me just enough. I knee him in the groin, roll from underneath him, and spring to my feet. He's scrambling behind me. Wild. Desperate. He can't let me get away. His fingertips slash the air like claws at my back and grab hold. *This is how it ends*, I think, detached. Like I'm watching us from a distance. These two frenzied, needful shadows grappling to decide each other's fate.

At the long end of the alley, just out of the glow of the streetlight, I see the tall silhouette of a man. With it comes the slippery feeling I've been here before. He's not moving—not at first—but I yell out anyway. He's just staring. And it's strange, inexplicable really, how fast he goes from standing statue-still to barreling toward me with the urgency of a man possessed. It's almost as if he's being chased himself.

# CHAPTER FIVE

I killed a girl. There, I said it. Best to be up-front from the get-go. After all, honesty is the best policy. That's what they say, isn't it? Whoever *they* are. I can tell you this—*they've* never done ten to life in Folsom and come out on the other side. Still, I killed a girl. Did you ever think to come up with one sentence that defines your entire life? Go ahead. Try it. *I killed a girl.* That's mine. Now you already know everything about me.

That's the conversation I have, mostly with myself, every time I go on one of these waste-of-my-time job interviews Agent McElroy sets up for me, and today was no different. Waste. Of. My. Time. Four and a half months on parole. Twelve interviews. And jobless, in spite of the degree I'd earned behind bars. Yep, I'm a college boy, but if it wasn't for the last of the settlement money, I'd be dead broke.

And that's a bitter pill to swallow since that money all but put me in prison. Now, here it is, saving my ass.

"Sorry, son, you're just not a good fit for us." The boss man had offered a tight smile, sort of like he was afraid of me, before he ushered me out the door lickety-split. "Best of luck to you though."

Nobody wants to hire an ex-con with a murder rap. Even if it was twenty-three years ago. Even if I recite all that mumbo jumbo I practiced about how I'm different now, reformed, a new man. Truthfully, I'm still Butch Calder. And Butch Calder ended somebody's life. Not just somebody. Her. Strange how a girl I barely knew in life would latch on to me close as my own shadow, how I've come to know her better than a lover, as well as my own hand. In one night, I'd linked us for eternity in some kind of sick death dance.

I take another bite of the waffle that's gone cold and pretend to read the newspaper some other diner left behind. It's empty in here now, just me and Brenda and a table of four, staring at their smartphones and fast-typing on those mini keyboards with their thumbs. They'd probably LOL—I'm learning the lingo—if they knew Agent McElroy had to help me decipher this ancient flip phone I picked up for twenty bucks.

"Didn't eat much today, hon." Brenda pats my shoulder as she clears my table. Per her usual formula of seduction, she leans forward as far as she can, letting her shirt gape open enough for me to catch more than a hint of cleavage. My half-eaten waffle slides dangerously close to the edge of the plate, threatening a syrup waterfall, but I doubt she cares. It's me she's eyeing. "You on a diet?" A shameless wink, then a toss of her bleached hair. I swallow the urge to tell her everything so she'll leave me alone. I killed a girl. Strangled her, if you want specifics. Now there's a conversation ender.

But I just shrug. "Not hungry today."

"Well, don't wither away. Biceps like that need fuel, you know." I'm pretty sure I'm blushing, because she laughs at me. Her laugh is amazing—it's freedom, the fast car on an open road kind—and it's been a long time since a girl…woman…looked at me that way, really saw me. As a man, not just a number. Young Butch would've been all over that. But now, geez, I'm forty-one, and I feel like an old man. My outside's okay, I guess. I've still got my sandy blond hair; I'm letting my beard grow to cover the unfortunate shank scar on my neck; and not to brag, but I'm in the best shape of my life. Solid muscle. Prison will do that to you with push-ups and burpees and running in circles on the yard. The inside of me though, that's another story. In there, it's all withered and dusty and gray. It's been so long I'm not even sure I'd know what to do with a woman. Frankly, I'm not sure I ever did.

"I'll keep that in mind," I tell her, careful not to flirt. "And I'll take the check whenever you get a chance." Not that I need it. I always order the same. A ten-spot doesn't get you much these days. Just a waffle, two eggs scrambled, and coffee strong enough to wake the dead. So Chicken and Waffles it is—every single night—but I don't mind the routine.

"Sure thing." She tears off the bill and lays it next to my hand. Her fingers graze my wrist. "Same time tomorrow?" Even though I saw it coming, I pull away. Fast.

"Sorry," I say. "It's just…uh…it's been a long…" *Time. Day. Life.*

"Don't be." She turns to walk away, and I figure the spell's finally been broken. Brenda's totally over me. But then, "You know my dad did a stint at Quentin. When he came back, he slept on the floor for two months. Said he just couldn't get comfortable out here in the real world. I know a fish out of water when I see one. So if you ever want to talk or…" She gestures to the bill, her name and phone number scrawled on the back.

I give her a polite smile, drop twelve bucks on the table, and beeline for the exit, my heart already off to the races, slamming against my chest like it wants out. It does that a lot lately. Like it can't quite figure out where we are, how we got here, what to do next. And Brenda's *or* isn't helping.

I lean against the wall outside and try to look cool. But really, I'm listening to my breathing, waiting for it to get quiet again. *Take it slow, Calder.* Agent McElroy's always saying that. As if there's any other way to take it when you're plopped right back down in the middle of all this. I tell ya, sometimes I feel like a squirrel that darted onto the freeway during rush hour.

It's a three-block walk to the remodeled warehouse I call home—me and thirty-one other fine, upstanding ex-cons—and I'm in no hurry. Transitional housing. That's what the brochure said, and to the parole board it must've sounded good enough. Personally, I prefer halfway house, because that's what it is. Halfway a home. Halfway a prison. But at least I've earned an extended curfew. And my roommate got violated—parole lingo for sent back to the clink—last week on a dirty test for coke, which means I'm flying solo in my one-hundred-and-twenty-square-foot lap of luxury. In a way, it sort of feels like I belong there. I haven't lived in a house, a real house, since the accident. The big rig that crossed the centerline and wiped out my whole family with one head-on thwack.

Two blocks to go, and I'm shoving my hands in my pockets, deep down, past the crumpled-up slip with Brenda's digits. *Don't get any bright ideas, Calder. That's going straight in the trash. Why'd you take it anyway?* It's colder than I expected tonight. Quieter too. And I spin around, paranoid, just to make sure I'm not being followed. It's another thing I do now. Too much open space, I suppose.

One block to go, and I'm thinking about my bed. How Brenda was right. It's too soft. And too big. And the room is way too still. Maybe I'll try the floor tonight. The scream comes out of nowhere… the shadowy nowhere at the dead end to my left, where people dump things they don't want anymore, do things they don't want seen.

I'm two places at once. I'm here, and it's a woman's voice shrieking, and I'm standing still, staring. *Don't get involved. Do. Not. Get. Involved.* I can't risk it. On parole, it's one wrong move, and I'm back in the slammer.

Also, I'm there, twenty-three years ago, the girl's eyes wide and white, and I've got my hands around her neck. I can't stop squeezing.

Before I've made up my mind, the woman screams again, and I'm running, sprinting, straight into nowhere. What choice have I got anyway with this ghost at my heels?

# CHAPTER SIX

**IT'S** been twenty years since I punched somebody, and damn, I've forgotten how good it feels. When you spend your nineteenth birthday in Folsom State Prison, you've gotta learn how to fight. Or somebody bigger is gonna teach you. It's trial by fire, especially with a crime like mine. Back there, trapped in Folsom's warped pecking order, my position was clear: One step up from the child molesters and rapists. I'd learned that the hard way when a skinhead sliced my neck with a sharpened piece of plastic and called me a sicko. It hurt like hell, and I bled all over the place, but I managed one good shot that flattened him.

Anyway, one good shot to the kisser is all you need to earn respect in the joint. Especially if it's the kisser of the biggest, baddest SOB you can find.

This punch—a fast left hook to the jaw—feels even better than that one. Because I've been saving up for it, but mostly, because it's not me I'm fighting for. The man wobbles back a step, and I hit him again. This time he doesn't get up.

"Are you alright?" I have to yell to the girl, because she'd run right past me. Or from me. Not that I'd blame her. She's sitting on the sidewalk, head down between her knees. She doesn't answer, doesn't even look up, so I jog toward her.

"Hey, miss. What happened back there?" Her hands are shaking. Bleeding too. There's a gash on her forearm I don't think she's noticed yet. "Do you want me to call the police?"

I pray to God she says no, because a yes means I've got to stick around. And that means explaining myself, telling the coppers I'm on parole. And that means they'll call McElroy, wake him up at—*what is it now, midnight?*—and he'll be pissed at me. The last thing I need is a cranky parole agent on my case. I'm sort of hoping she's a hooker—this is the neighborhood for it—because she'll send me on my way, and we'll both pretend this night never happened. But the way she's dressed I doubt it. What hooker wears Chucks?

"Is he…am I…who are you?" The girl finally speaks, even if it makes no sense, and she lifts her eyes to mine.

"Holy crap." I recognize her, her eyes anyway, and I think I might be sick. Waffles don't taste so good on the way back up, but I swallow anyway, my throat burning. She was a kid when I saw her last, but you don't forget eyes like that. "I mean, uh, you can use my phone if you need to. You should probably get that looked at." She follows my finger to the cut on her arm, and her whole body starts to tremble, but she doesn't cry.

"I'm okay," she says. She stands up, swaying a little, and I move to catch her before she falls. She grabs on to my T-shirt, leaving a bright red palm print that may as well be a scarlet letter. And I deserve it. I swear I've got the worst luck, because the sirens are coming this way. I couldn't have been the only one who heard her screaming.

"I'm on parole," I tell her. God knows why. Maybe I'm practicing. But she doesn't freak out. At least not any more than she already seems.

"I was hitchhiking." I guess we're both confessing, but she says it more to herself than to me. I nod anyway. Hitchhiking? Maybe she is a hooker. Great. I can add that to my guilty conscience too. Because one thing is absolutely certain. Whatever she turned out to be, it's partly my fault.

"Is he...?" She's pointing over my shoulder, her mouth slightly open in surprise. Behind me, an engine revs over the wail of the sirens, and the fervent growl of it hits me right in the ribs. I realize then the guy I decked is awake. And barreling toward us in his jeep, tires screaming the warning cry of a banshee.

"Watch out!" I yell, giving her a shove as he peels past us and takes a hard right onto the street, flooring it. It's the kind of thing Young Butch would've done. Did. Getting the hell outta Dodge. But now, I'm a cannonball. A sunk anchor, old and rusted and pinned down by the weight of guilt and fear. I'm virtually immovable. And apparently, so is she.

"Thank you," she whispers, still breathless from the shock of it all. "Thank you so much." I'm not sure what to say—I can't make her take it back—so I just keep my mouth shut and pretend it doesn't gut me to hear her say that.

The dark end of the street brightens in flashing shades of blue and red. It almost looks pretty, the way the colors glint against the wet pavement. Until I follow her eyes—Evelyn, that's her name, I remember it now—to the dingy mattress cast out with the rest of the trash. The red light washes it the color of blood, and I picture her there.

Her. The girl I saved.

Her. The girl I strangled.

Both of them. Interchangeable faces. I can't tell the difference.

"Show me your hands!" The cop barks, gun raised and pointed right at me. "Now, get down. Slowly, slowly!" I know what it looks like to him. And I wish I could tell you the way it feels. To be innocent but guilty at the same time. To be Butch Calder. On parole. Bloodied shirt. Bruised knuckles. And with a helluva lot of explaining to do.

# CHAPTER SEVEN

EVIE
JANUARY 13, 2017
FRIDAY

**I'M** not dead. I am not dead. I mouth the words as I glance down at my forearm. My skin—pale as ivory and cold to the touch—seems to belong to someone else. A corpse, perhaps. The gash on my arm soaked through three cotton bandages. But I am *not* dead. And it's just a flesh wound, according to the paramedic. It's up to me if I want stitches. Regardless, I'll have to go to the hospital. "Protocol in these kinds of cases." That's what the officer had told me.

"So…" Such a small word, but heavy with accusation, with judgment. The officer frowns at me as he speaks. "Dr. Maddox, I just want to be sure we've got this right. You were hitchhiking?"

The single nod I give him takes all the energy I've got left, and I start to wish I had just kept running.

"And that man over there…he just happened to show up at the right time? He didn't hurt you?" He's gesturing, but I don't look. I can't. There's something about that guy. The guy on parole. I think I know him from somewhere. And every time I let my eyes steal a glance, he's looking back at me from his undignified seat on the ground. The pavement is still damp, a minefield of puddles from the afternoon rain, and by now, I'm betting it's soaked through his jeans.

"I've already told you. He didn't do anything wrong. He helped me. You really should let him go home."

"We will, ma'am. He's not under arrest—not yet, anyway. He's been detained until we nail down what happened here."

I suppress a giggle at the image of the officer, hammer in hand, swinging away, but it bubbles up anyway, escaping from a dark place before I can contain it. The officer raises an eyebrow, my nervous twitter an apparent confirmation that I am most certainly unhinged. *The hitchhiking shrink*, I can practically hear him snickering about me over beers with his buddies.

"At least uncuff him then," I say.

"Ma'am, I don't tell you how to do your job, do I?"

That's the sort of question that's not meant to be answered. It's a statement. A warning, even. But I can't seem to help myself. The parts of me I usually keep tightly wound have come unloosed. "Thank God for that."

He snorts with contempt, and I continue.

"Did you catch him yet? Danny? The guy who attacked me?" I already know the answer, because it's not the first time I've asked. But it seems necessary to remind him the real bad guy got away.

He regards me blankly, but his jaw tightens. "We're doing the best we can. With the description of the vehicle and the plate number you gave us, I'm sure we'll find him. Plus, we might get a hit on the DNA if you scratched him good like you said. These perps are usually in the system. Repeat offenders, ya know?"

Of course I know, but I deny him the satisfaction of my agreement. "And my backpack?"

"Yes, ma'am, I'm getting to that. You said he drove off with it. What exactly was in your bag?"

I pack it the same way every other Friday—pepper spray, a book to pass the waiting time, and a picture of me and Jared—but I keep that to myself, pretend to be uncertain. I'd told the officer it was my first time. Hitchhiking on a friend's dare. "Uh, not much. Some pepper spray. A book, I think."

"Any valuables? Cash? ID? Cell phone?"

I pat my jacket pockets—the right, then the left—feeling smart for the first time in hours. In the middle of a satisfied smile, I realize something's missing. Left pocket. Driver's license. I pull at the thin fabric, turning the empty pocket inside out. Panic starts to seize my chest again, squeezing tight. I must've lost it in the struggle.

My eyes pinball across the shadows, the shimmering pavement, the old, waterlogged mattress, landing squarely on the man who saved me. Three officers lord over him like trees, blocking his view. Their mouths are moving in turn, but I can't make out the words.

"My license," I say. "It's not here."

Frowning, the officer turns away, and my stomach shrinks in the clutches of reawakened fear. *Danny has my license. My full name.* I head back toward the darker end of the street scanning the ground with desperation.

"Hey, Calder," the officer yells. "You take this lady's license?"

*Calder.* My brain sticks on his name, repeating it with each step, but I still can't work out the puzzle. *I know him, but how?* The officer stalks toward him in a huff.

"I asked you a question. Did you—"

"No, sir." I can't help but feel sorry for him. He has the look of a dog kicked too many times. I've seen it before from the men in my group. "That's what the big house will do to ya," George would say, the other men nodding at his sage wisdom.

A few feet from the mattress, black rubber marks the road where Danny made his hasty exit. I prod a half-emptied trash bag with my foot, and something small and fast scuttles into the shadows near the place he had me pinned. The concrete there is bare, expectant. Like it's still waiting for me. And the wound on my arm is beginning to throb. Tangible proof. But the whole night feels like a dream. A dream I've had before. A dream upon waking with a new reality. Danny knows who I am. Danny will find me. And worse—I let him get away.

**\*\*\*\***

The officer motions me over to his patrol car, and I trudge past poor Calder, still handcuffed on the sidewalk. I feel the urge to speak to him, to ask him how I know him—at the very least, to tell him I'm sorry for dragging him into this—but the words stick in my throat.

"Do you live alone?" the officer asks me. Assuming attack-cat Sammy doesn't count, I nod bleakly. "Is there someone I can call?"

"There's no one." A hard sentence to hear and worse to speak it. "Then I'll drive you to the hospital myself. Do you have someplace you can stay tonight?"

"Other than my apartment you mean?"

"It's probably best if you stay somewhere else until we get this scumbag. Especially since he seems to have driven off with your license."

Feeling reprimanded all over again, my cheeks burn, and I press my cold fingers against them. "My mother-in-law's, I guess."

"You're married?" The question prods at the dull ache in my chest, the one that never really goes away.

"Not exactly." *Widow.* I hate that word—it makes me think of a spider, small, black, and deadly, spinning cobwebs around my heart—and I won't say it. Not for him. "But I'll need my car for the morning. Could you give me a ride…after?"

"Your car. Your car." Repeating my words, the officer smirks at his buddies as they pull Calder to his feet and free his hands. "You might want to use your car from now on, Dr. Maddox. Like when you come to the station tomorrow to talk with the SVU detective."

He juts his chin in Calder's direction. "And you. Go home. Your PO will call you in the morning."

The officer holds his door open for me. "Give me a minute," he says, shutting me inside. I expect it to be warmer in here, but the air bites my skin, and I shiver. Calder walks past, head down and hurried, fists clenched. I'm sure he's wishing he never met me...again?

*I know him, but how?* I ask myself for the second time, groaning at the certainty of another misplaced memory. I start to open the door, to call out to him, to thank him once more, but I think better of it. It's raining again, and the clock on the dash reads 1:13 a.m. Thirteen. My unlucky number.

# CHAPTER EIGHT

EVIE
JANUARY 13, 2017
FRIDAY

**MY** fingernails have been cut and bagged and carted away for evidence. My clothing is gone too. They let me keep my Chucks at least, but I left in a donated sweat suit. My bruises have been catalogued. Photographed. All of them. And my mouth swabbed for the saliva Danny left behind.

Tonight can't get any worse. I've been convincing myself of that for the last fifteen minutes, the entire winding drive up into the Oakland Hills. "Where the rich folks live." That's what my mother always said when I'd asked her, pointing up at the houses stacked like dominoes on the edges of the hillside. "You're gonna live there one day, baby girl." She'd said that too, when she wasn't too stoned to make sense. Her noticing me had felt so good, I'd never told her I didn't want to live there, lost in the thick fog where it seemed the whole world could slip right out from underneath you.

*Like mother, like daughter.* Danny's in my head again. But he didn't say that. He couldn't have. And I wonder how something imagined can seem so real.

I make the turn, and I know she's waiting for me. A single light—an unblinking eye—watches me from the window. Margaret Maddox is awake. And angry no doubt. This is what she's left with. A sad sack of a daughter-in-law who she never wanted anyway. A daughter-in-law who takes rides from strangers. And nearly gets herself killed. A daughter-in-law who seduced her precious baby boy for his money. Never mind that Jared approached me at Claremont Country Club the spring I'd turned nineteen and wouldn't take no for an answer from the girl who waited on snooty tables to put herself through college. Never mind that Jared insisted he pay my way through grad school with his ample trust fund. Maggie owned my PhD. She just didn't know it.

The curtains stir, and I imagine her there, the anticipation of my arrival bitter in her mouth, sour as a lemon. She'd never said it to my face—"That girl's a stray puppy, Jared. Be careful she doesn't bite you"—but she had no qualms telling Jared just loud enough for me to hear every chance she got. Even the night after we got hitched on a beach in Mexico, thumbing our noses at the fancy Napa wedding she'd planned. And honestly, she hadn't been wrong. Deep down, I am a stray puppy, and now she's stuck with me.

I tug my duffel from the backseat, and Sammy lets out a low growl from his carrier. "It's okay, buddy. We're almost there." My words are no comfort to either one of us, and by the time I mash the doorbell, he's howling. I know exactly how he feels—there's no place like home—but I couldn't leave him behind. In two years, we'd never spent a night apart.

"Evelyn, my goodness. You look awful, just awful." *See what I mean.* "What were you thinking, dear? Hitchhiking. Really?" I want to hate her, with her coifed hair the color of a fox and her acrylic fingernails, long and red as claws. But she has Jared's face, Jared's fawn brown eyes. Strong dislike is all I've ever been able to muster.

"Can I come in?" I raise my voice to drown Sammy's meows, so plaintive I wonder if he's channeling my soul.

"Of course, dear. But does that thing have an off switch?" She taps the carrier, provoking a hiss, then opens the door and beckons me inside. "Jared was always partial to dogs, you know."

I swallow hard. "I know." The house is different than I remember—cold and vacuous. Two years since Jared's been gone, and longer since Bill, Maggie's grief feels as permanent and palpable as the polished hardwood under our feet. "It's been a long time," I say. "Thanks for letting me stay on such short notice."

"Well, you're still family. Even if I haven't heard from you in… what's it been? Six months?"

"I'm sorry, Maggie. It's no excuse, but I've been really busy with the move." It had been harder than I'd expected leaving the place where Jared lived…and died. Like losing him all over again.

"I still don't understand why you left that house. It was beautiful—a little modest for my taste—but all those windows. And so close to the Claremont. You know how I like to play tennis there."

I hang my head. "It was too…" *Lonely.* "Big. For just one person. And a cat."

"So, moving…that's your excuse?" She's joking. But not.

"And work, of course."

Maggie makes a noise from her throat, half-understanding, half-contempt. "I imagine so. Is that what you were doing tonight, Doctor? Recruiting a new patient?"

It stings, but I laugh, because it sounds like something Jared would say. "Touché."

"So, why *were* you hitchhiking?" she asks, raising her manicured eyebrows. Maggie will never buy my I-did-it-on-a-dare story. And the truth? *I've been hitching rides from strangers since your son died, hoping I'll remember a murderer from twenty-three years ago, a murderer nobody knows exists. Nobody but me.* That sounds even more preposterous.

**44**

"Is it okay if we don't talk about it right now? I'm exhausted."

"Well, are you alright? At least tell me that. Your arm. It's…"

"A little worse for wear." I show her the bandage. "But not that bad, all things considered. This bystander sort of saved me. He saw the guy trying to…" I couldn't say it. Years of sex offender treatment, and I'm the one in denial. "…hurt me, and he intervened. If it wasn't for him, I don't know…" I want to tell her I recognized him. I know him. But that would make me sound completely certifiable.

Maggie puts an arm around my shoulders—like me or not, her mothering comes hardwired—and I don't have the energy to resist. I lean into her, suddenly tearful.

"I made up one of the spare rooms for you, dear. You and Sammy." *She remembers his name.*

****

I let the shower run until it goes cold and the steam drips from the mirror in long streaks, distorting my reflection. It's better that way. The bruises I can see are bad enough. Barefoot, I pad down the hallway, barely breathing, past the room Maggie made up for me, the room where I left Sammy curled like a snail at the foot of the bed. I carry my journal with me.

The knob is ice, but it turns easily in my hand, as if it's been anticipating my return. I open the door, and my knees buckle a little. I can almost smell nineteen-year-old Jared. Hints of the fancy Tom Ford cologne I teased him about and his soccer cleats, clogged by fresh-cut grass. I want to call out to him, as the moon makes strange shadows on the wall. A unicorn. A wolf. A witch's hat. Shapes that change as I move, blocking the light.

Unlike the rest of the house, Jared's room is preserved exactly the way I recall it. A shrine to him, erected the day he matriculated to Stanford. I pull back the sheets and slip beneath them, cocooned in the past. We had sex in this room once—fast and sweaty and desperate—while his parents cooked dinner downstairs. I'd laid here, naked and content, giggling with my boyfriend about his stodgy mother, his trophies, his perfect life. And by default, my perfect life. I'd almost started to believe that kind of perfection could belong to me. *The curse of Evil Evie is real.* I'd said those words in this room, partly joking, in this bed, a lifetime ago. I touch my lips, half-expecting them to be wet with Jared's kiss.

But my mouth feels sore, raw. *Danny.* His shadowed face, angry and wanting, thrusts its way in, poisoning everything. *Like mother, like daughter.*

I squirm under the covers, unable to escape myself, the thought that all this—me, nearly raped and murdered for God's sake—means nothing. I still can't remember that night. The faceless man is as faceless as ever.

The sheets twist and ball in my hands, and I squeeze instead of screaming. It's not like I misplaced my keys or forgot the lyrics to my favorite song. It's an entire episode, the most important thing, and it's a blank. Just like most of my journal. The one I'd bought years ago to record snippets of memory from that night, hoping someday the parts might form a whole. Even now, everything I know fills just one lined page. At the bottom, I add a few sentences.

*He touched my hand. I didn't like it. He asked me a question—"Are you down with that?" And I wasn't.*

Whatever it was, I definitely wasn't *down* with it. The word makes me feel hollowed out, scooped clean like the inside of a melon.

I don't intend to, but I fall asleep right there, imagining Jared's arms around me, him whispering in my ear. *I don't believe in curses.* Then, even softer, and for the first time. *Plus, I love you.*

How can one memory stay so close to the surface, shimmering as if I could touch it and another float away, away, away, like a birthday balloon lost in space?

# CHAPTER NINE

**OLD** habits die hard, and I'm beginning to think some of mine are immortal. Like this one, for starters. I shower in three and a half minutes flat. Any longer than that in the big house, and one of three things could happen. Some prick CO shuts the water off midstream, leaving you sudsy and mad as a hornet. Or, the biggest, baddest SOB you slugged plots an ambush and pummels you back. And let me tell ya, getting hit in the face is even less fun when you're stark naked and the guy's got a shiv in his fist. Or, you drop the soap, so to speak, and become somebody's girlfriend. Yep, three and a half minutes and I'm out, dripping water on the freezing-cold floor, and wondering how this day got so turned upside down.

I'd booked it back to the halfway house thirty minutes ago—practically running—knowing I'd already missed my 1 a.m. curfew.

*Let's just get this over with,* I thought. Explain myself to Mr. Richert, the counselor on duty, shut my door, and get my bearings. But the spare bed in my room wasn't empty anymore, and Richert was disappointed in me.

"I'm telling you, sir, my PO will be here in the morning. He'll verify the whole story."

Richert had nodded, as if he'd heard it all before. He had a war story too. He'd been drunk as a skunk when he stabbed a man in a bar fight. "Listen, son, I've been there. I've been exactly where you are. Keep that in mind. Imagine you fifteen years ago and black at that. The cops had me on my toes every day, watchin' like hawks, just waiting for that one mess-up. That one reason. That's all they need."

"But, sir, I was trying to—"

"I know. I know. But now you've given them a reason to look closer, and that's the last thing you want. Cause ain't nobody perfect. And for the love of God, please call me Frank. *Sir* makes me feel like a goddamned correctional officer." I'd nodded at him, chuckling. "Now, I'm gonna let you slide tonight on the curfew, but I need you to pee in the cup for me."

He'd handed over a small plastic container, pointed to the bathroom near the front door, and followed me inside. *This is what it's come to.* I couldn't even be trusted to pee on my own. But I supposed it was one rung up the dignity ladder from a daily strip search.

Then, he'd said the worst part. "We assigned you a new roommate. He's a lifer like you, fresh off the boat."

I look in the mirror, wipe the toothpaste from the corner of my mouth, still bristling at the thought of those words. I'm just one of the friggin' club, the Lifers' Club, bonded together by the sheer despair of all the years we wasted. I throw on the KISS T-shirt and sweats I bought at the secondhand store around the corner—where I bought most of my wardrobe—and slog back to the room I now share with Sebastian Delacourt. His fancy-schmancy name makes him sound like a real punk. He probably got busted for conspiracy or some other hands-off, thinking-man type crime. But who am I to judge? A

*Butch Calder* should be beer-bellied with a mullet and a Confederate flag hanging from the back of his pickup. I know my mom had a thing for Paul Newman, but I still wonder what came over her, giving me the name of an outlaw. *Good one, Mom. Good one.*

Sebastian is asleep. Or playing possum. And I'm grateful. I give him a quick once-over. Hair, black as a crow's feather, sticks out haphazard from beneath the covers. A pair of glasses rests on the nightstand, alongside a worn copy of *Lord of the Flies.* Seriously? It's not the sort of book I'd want my PO to catch me reading, even if it is a classic.

I grab the jacket I'd shrugged off earlier, lie down, and turn away from him. Even if he wakes up, he won't be able to see over the broad wall of my back. I reach into the inner pocket and pull out the one thing the officers missed when they patted me down within an inch of my life. Like I was the bad guy. But maybe I am. Because I don't know why I took it. And doing something without knowing why is a very bad thing. Years upon years of psych evals for the parole board—"But why did you do it, Mr. Calder? Why did you kill her? Why? Why? Why?"—drilled that into my thick skull.

The license feels like a hot coal in my hands, and I toss it on the bed before it burns me, brands me a liar and a criminal. It tells me nothing really. Less than nothing, but it seems essential. I know her. Knew her. Evelyn Allcott—Maddox now, apparently— but they called her Evie. Evil Evie. Kids sucked, even back then, before the invention of the internet. Information highway, my ass. More like Pandora's box, if you ask me. Which nobody did, of course, because I was busy rotting away in a six-by-eight box of my own.

I scour her details like there's a test at the end of this. DOB 5/13/81. HGT 5'6." WGT 130 lb. She's a donor. Hair, black. Eyes, green. Green like the first patch of grass I walked on barefoot. That green. She looks younger in her picture, different than she did today, and way different than the last time I saw her. *What did you expect,*

*Butchy? A twelve-year-old girl?* She's a woman. A beautiful woman. A damaged woman, more than likely. And seeing her tonight—*I still can hardly believe it*—it's like I paid some kind of debt to the universe. A whopping cosmic IOU. Of course, it doesn't work like that, and I know it. I owe more than I can ever repay and not just to Evie. I feel sick again, so I slip the license under my mattress before I upchuck.

What was I thinking taking it anyway? *That's the point, man. You weren't thinking.* I'd seen it there half-submerged in a puddle near that lowlife's grubby paw, and I'd snatched it up lickety-split like Young Butch would've done. The same kind of act-first-think-later nonsense that landed me in prison. I stare at the ceiling, listening to the steady patter of the rain, and wait for my stomach to settle. But I know it's going to be a while, because I've got the answer to the *why* and I don't like it. It's spinning and spinning in my head like a hamster on a wheel. I want to see her again. I need to. And this license is my ticket to the show.

****

I'm eighteen again. I know it by the way she looks at me—part confusion, part fear, part jealousy—like I'm a hot rod racing down the freeway, blue lights in the rearview. She wishes she could be so alive. I know it, too, by my hands. They're strong and smooth and unsullied, not yet marked by sun or scar. Her neck is lovely, delicate as a stem under my fingers. And right now, it's a stem I want to snap. To pulverize. I'm not angry. No. I'm pure heat. Rage personified. And it builds and builds and builds. My thumbs root into the small hollow above her clavicle, and I squeeze. It always ends the same. Like sex. What little I know of it anyway. The mindless rush gives way to sweet release. And it's just the two of us forever and ever.

I sit up straight, gasping for air. Sweet Jesus. It's back. The dream I'd had every night for three years straight. The dream that followed me like a beggar until I banished it by doing the one thing I swore I'd never do. Admit guilt. The dream that's not a dream. I wipe the sweat from my face, but it does no good. My T-shirt is soaked all the way through, and my throat feels raw like I was screaming bloody murder. Great.

"I'm sorry, man," I say, searching in the dark for my new roomie. But his bed is empty. Like he was never there to begin with.

# CHAPTER TEN

EVIE
JANUARY 14, 2017
SATURDAY

I open my eyes to a thin stream of sunlight. *Where am I?* I blink against the bright ray piercing through a space in the blinds. I feel raw and exposed—a peeled grape plopped in a vat of acid. I've never been a drinker, but I imagine this feels a lot like a hangover. One pure moment of white noise and nothingness before last night comes spewing back. All of it. And with it, literal pain. Fingertip bruises on my upper arms. The bandaged gash. A dull ache in my lower back. And shame corroding in the back of my throat. *Shame is a soul-eater.* That's what Carl Jung said, sort of. And that's what I told George in group when he said the world would be better off without a sick perv like him.

I know where I am now. Who I am. Jared's perfect smile mocks me from his senior photo, and I toss off the covers, anxious to get out before Maggie catches me in here. She'd never told me his room was off-limits, but the shut door always felt like a warning. I crack it open and peer into the hallway, checking before I scamper back to the guest room where Sammy is—big surprise—still sleeping. I don't bother with a shower or breakfast. Just run my hands through my hair and throw on jeans and a sweater. It's still early, and I want to get back there before the rest of the world wakes up. I tell myself I need to find my license, that it's probably hidden under someone else's trash in the alley, but really I want to see it in the light of day. That place where karma wrapped itself around my throat and almost ended me. I feel drawn to it, almost harried, as I fish around in my purse in search of my keys and come up empty-handed.

"Looking for something?" Maggie stands in the kitchen doorway. She's effortlessly casual. Or casually effortless. Either way, her high-end workout gear costs more than the lone suit hanging in my closet at home. I know, because she'd left the tags on the leggings she gave me two Christmases ago. "For that price, they should do the workout for me," I'd told Jared, wanting to see him laugh. We were days from the end then.

"My keys. I swore I dropped them in here." I'm scavenging again, tossing my purse one item at a time. "But I wasn't exactly thinking clearly. Have you seen—"

"Evelyn." I stop and look up at her. "I took the keys. For safekeeping. I thought it was best."

"Safekeeping? What do you mean?"

"I mean that I don't think it's wise for you to be driving around on your own right now in your state of mind."

"And what state is that exactly?" My voice trembles a little, confirming her diagnosis, but I keep my eyes on hers.

Maggie clears her throat with purpose. As if the answer is obvious. "Whatever state is required for one to accept a ride from a complete stranger. As a mental health professional, you would probably know better than I do."

*It's none of your business, Maggie. I'm not your daughter, Maggie. Bite me, Maggie.* "I understand your concern, but really, I'm fine. Okay?"

Leaving me unanswered, she steps into the kitchen, opens the fridge, and pours herself a small glass of green liquid. "Wheatgrass," she says. "Would you like some?" I shake my head as she drinks it in one gulp. I watch the hollow of her throat expand and contract, the skin there sagging and spotted. Her neck is the only part of her that shows her age.

"What would Jared say?" she asks. His name, spoken aloud again, pins my lungs shut. "Would he agree you're just fine?"

"Jared trusted me. He would believe me if I told him so."

"Like the time you told him your mother was a roadie for a rock band and that was the reason she was never around to meet him?"

"I can't even believe you remember that. I was nineteen, Maggie. I was just a kid. And I was desperately trying not to scare your son away. Or you and Bill, for that matter. Besides, it all came out eventually." Meaning Maggie and Bill had dug and dug until they'd unearthed my mother's bones. And mine by association. Most of them anyway. Some bones were buried so deep even I couldn't find them.

There's pity in Maggie's sigh, but not just that. Frustration. Resignation too. "Where are you driving off to, anyway? Let me come with you."

"Actually, I need to go to the police station. So…I guess you're tagging along? To downtown Oakland? I can show you the spot of the drive-by where that kid got shot last week."

With that, I know I've won, but I try not to gloat. She drops the keys on the counter and flees the kitchen. Then, only then, I smile.

\*\*\*\*

After descending the narrow, snaking roads of the Hills, the drive is mindless, and I don't let myself think. I blast the radio to deaden the

**54**

sound of my own voice in my head. Still, I can hear it nagging. *What were you thinking hitchhiking? You almost got yourself killed, moron. And for what? You're exactly where you started. Worse actually. What would Jared say to that?* Funny, the voice in my head sounds a lot like Maggie.

I take the exit and plot the same route as Danny, even matching his hairpin turn into the alley. A split second later and I would've driven right past. I park alongside one of the buildings and trudge toward the dumpster. The infamous, yellowed mattress, disemboweled and bleeding foam. A discarded bicycle tire. A child's ball, deflated and cracked. A half-eaten hamburger. A book, splayed open and waterlogged. In the stark daylight, there's something forlorn and unceremonious about it all. These things had been brought here to die. Like me.

I find the spot—as best I can tell anyway—where Danny yanked me down by my hair. *It hurts back there,* I realize, rubbing the aching place at the base of my head. Kneeling down, I run my hands over the concrete. It's cool and damp and grimy, and it smells sickeningly sweet like gasoline and rot and wild cherry Slurpee. When I look down, my hands aren't my own. They belong to thirteen-year-old Evie. A friendship bracelet loops the wrist, chipped pink polish colors the little nails, but I take a breath and they're gone again, sunk back into the past, that murky swamp from which they came.

"Dr. Maddox?" I look up at him, Sebastian squinting into the sun. "If I didn't know better, I'd say you were following me." He purses his lips and laughs from his throat.

I jump to my feet, brushing my hands off on my jeans. "Sebastian. Hi." *Hi?* I sound like I'm still thirteen. And I'm fidgeting too, shifting my weight onto one leg, then the other.

"What are you doing here? If you don't mind my asking."

*What am I doing here?* I'm a complete blank. My neck feels hot, feverish, and it must be scarlet red, because he's staring. "Um…" License. *License, Evie. That's what you're doing here.* "I…" *But don't tell him that.* "I'm…" I used to be better at this.

"Is it to do with the police?"

My chest tightens. There's no air getting through. *How could he possibly know about Danny? About last night?* "What?" I manage. "Police?"

"Are you alright, Doc? You look like you've seen a ghost." He reaches out to me, but I step back. And his eyes meet the ground, a smirk passing across his face as fast and fleeting as a shadow. So fast, I wonder if I'd imagined it. Maybe I'm seeing things.

"I'm fine. Just stood up too quickly is all. Now what were you saying?"

"The police. I thought you knew. They're outside your office building. There's yellow tape everywhere." The sky starts spinning again. A blue-and-white kaleidoscope. I try to keep up with it, but I can't, so I look away at the flat gray of the nearest building instead. "I think somebody got…hurt."

"Outside my office?" My voice is far away like the distant splash of a pebble thrown down an old well. I'm hearing things too—I must be.

"Sort of," he says. "At the tree. The hanging tree."

I'm halfway there, Sebastian tagging behind before I realize. Nobody's ever called it that before. Not that I remember anyway. Nobody but me.

# CHAPTER ELEVEN

**BUTCH** *Calder goes to the library.* It sounds like the name of a corny kids' book. But in the last four and a half months, I've spent more time in the library than the first forty years combined. I did most of my degree sitting on my bunk, watching my cellie guzzle pruno and tattoo himself. I warned him not to ink his girl's name on his face. But you can't fix stupid. I should know. Still, *Linda* with a heart for the *i* smack dab above your eyebrow is a hard lesson to learn.

And before prison? The only productive thing Young Butch ever did in a library was rounding third base in the stacks. With her. Gwendolyn Shaw. Dammit. I let myself think her name again. It's that dream that's got me all mixed-up today. That and Evie and my missing roommate. He must've reappeared sometime during the night—I'd lain awake for at least thirty minutes waiting—but

I didn't hear him till the morning, snoring like a chain saw. Me, I couldn't even attempt breakfast with this gnawing in my gut. I grabbed a banana and caught the bus before most of the house was awake.

Libraries are different now. They're all modern and fancy and lit up inside. No more atmosphere, that's for sure. And the public ones don't open till noon. That's why I'm here—Horizon University. Because even on a Saturday, they open at 8 a.m. sharp. I choose the computer in the back, take a seat, and plug in the user ID and password from the kid I'd bribed out front. No one's watching, but I pretend I'm job hunting anyway. Just in case Agent McElroy tailed me. After last night, I'm definitely on his radar and not in a good way. "I understand your wanting to help and all, but watch yourself, Calder." His exact words.

I pull out my list, the one with *Companies that Hire Ex-Cons* printed in big letters at the top. I've already scratched through five of them. Then, I type her name into the search bar. *Evelyn Allcott Maddox*. I don't know what I'm looking for. Scratch that. I won't *find* what I'm looking for. Closure. Forgiveness. Absolution. You can buy a grilled-cheese sandwich with the face of the Virgin Mary, Britney Spears' chewed-up bubblegum. Hell, you can probably buy a goddamn vital organ. But some things—the ones that really matter—you can't find online.

My finger hovers over ENTER. *Why did I never do this before?* I tap the button. 503 results. I read the first one without breathing. It's worse than I thought, knowing this much. *And that's why you never did it before, jackleg.*

### OBITUARIES

**Jared Dean Maddox passed away at his home in Oakland, California, on December 28, 2014, at the age of 32. A Bay Area native, Jared graduated with honors from Stanford University and served as Director of Marketing**

**at MDX Global, the San Francisco-based management consulting and strategy firm. He was preceded in death by his father, William "Bill" Maddox. Jared is lovingly remembered by his wife of five years, Evelyn, and his mother, Margaret, both of Oakland.**

It doesn't get any better. There's the post-wedding announcement, picture and all (apparently, they'd eloped to Cancun) without a single mention of Evie's parents. Just the proud Mama and Papa Bear Maddox of MDX Global flanking the happy couple outside of city hall when they made it official. It's only a photo, but Evie's smile looks forced, as fake as Margaret's ample chest. I know what it's like to stand next to money. She has that look.

"You're not good enough for me, Butch. You'll never be good enough." I hear it as plain and clear as if Gwen is over my shoulder, and I spin around expecting to see her there. Blonde and long-legged and perfect and smacking watermelon bubblegum. She always smelled like too-sweet watermelon. Tasted like it too.

"Jesus Christ." I mutter it under my breath, but it's so church-mouse quiet in that library, I feel like everybody can hear me. I wait for a beat—surely, they're about to kick me out—then turn back to the screen for the pièce de résistance, no less than twenty hits for Dr. Evelyn Maddox, sex offender treatment provider.

"Sex offender." I don't realize I've said it out loud until the mousy girl at the desk across from me tosses her books into her bag and hightails it for the exit, looking scared out of her wits.

"Sorry," I call after her. I guess the real world's not so different, because you can't say that word in prison either. Unless you want to wind up on the wrong end of a shank. I figure I'm on borrowed time, so I jot down Evie's office address fast and prepare for a hasty exit. But there's something sticking in my craw, and I just can't shake it. I have to check or it's gonna bug me all day.

Thanks to the vocational computer class I took in the joint, I know exactly what to do. Even though I'm pretty sure this is not what they had in mind by functional technology skills. I type her address into a maps application and wait for the answer. The one I already know in some dank and unspoken place within me.

Yep. Evie's office is near my Chicken and Waffles, but that's not all. It's right across from the spot where I left her twenty-three years ago.

**** 

I'm a zombie, a dead man walking as I plod away from the bus stop toward the halfway house. A single thought beats like a black heart inside my head. *I wish I could take it back.* Of course it's not the first time I've thought it, but it feels new again. Freshly colored with a punch that knocks the wind right out of me. Like it just happened. *I wish I could take it back.* But what exactly? Where would I begin?

A dog snarls from the cover of a fence, and I feel myself come alive again, pulse quickening. I check behind and around me. Nobody lurking, but I've missed the turnoff for home. My feet are setting a course to Evie's office, to that godforsaken tree, though I won't admit it to myself. Up ahead, I can see the building, and I stop cold. It's two stories, nondescript. The sort of building you wouldn't notice, wouldn't remember, even if you passed it a hundred times. But there's something going on. And it's bad. I duck behind the nearest tree, my knees wobbling a little. I didn't do anything wrong. Still, I feel the need to remind myself. They don't bring out this many cop cars and the yellow tape for anything less than murder. And then there's the van—Alameda County Coroner.

I peek out from my hiding place, desperate to get a look at the tree, convinced I'll see Evie up there. That I've wandered into a wormhole. That I'll relive it all again. Instead, I find my reflection in the nearest car window. I'm relieved at the sight of my face, the strength of my jaw, the salt-and-pepper stubble, the crinkles around my eyes. Old Butch.

"If you could change things, where would you start?" A psych doctor had asked me that once, years ago, and I'd pretended not to know. I probably shrugged in that aw-shucks-ma'am way I had back then. Truth is, I know it to the day, to the hour, to the minute, to the second. I also know there's no going back. What's done is done.

## BUTCH
## APRIL 29, 1994
## FOURTEEN DAYS BEFORE I KILLED HER

I bought a car. But not just any car. My first car. The car every guy dreams about. A 1971 Plymouth Barracuda convertible. Hemi engine. Ebony black. And damn, I looked wicked in it. Top down, hair blowing in the wind, I would've given Clint Eastwood a run for his money. I drove it off the lot of Emeryville Classics at exactly 3:15 p.m. The dash clock told me so. Who knows why some things just stick in your mind? But I'm pretty certain there's only one reason I remember: Girls. Lots of them—tan skin, bared in sandals and sundresses—getting out of Berkeley High at 3:30. Just enough time for me to cruise by in my new ride. I couldn't have planned it better if I tried. Which, let's be honest, I had.

I hit the freeway doing ninety-five, revving the engine every chance I got. A guy in a minivan flipped me off when I rode his ass and screeched around him because he didn't get out of my way fast enough. But I didn't care. Didn't he know I had someplace to be? I felt good. Damn good. Like Fourth of July fireworks exploding in my brain. Like a home run over center field, bases loaded. That good. And free. So free.

I'd spent the last six months in juvie on a commercial burglary, and I needed to make up for lost time. For Young Butch that meant drinking like a fish, smoking like a chimney, and sucking face with as many hot girls as possible. Or trying to. And spending the blood money, of course. Now that I'd turned eighteen it was all mine. Three-hundred-thousand big ones. That's how much Y-Trax Trucking figured they owed me for Mom, Pop, and my little brother, Jesse. Even with my splurge on the 'Cuda, I still had a cool hundred thousand left, and damn if it wasn't already burning a hole in my pocket.

When I took the exit toward Berkeley and slowed to a crawl on the MLK, I turned on the radio—KISS—and cranked it up, half-belting the lyrics, half-watching everybody watch me. "I wanna rock and roll all night…and party every day…I wanna…" And let me tell you, I was a sight to behold. By the time the end-of-day bell sounded, I was parked half a block from the school, and that shrill little ring thrilled me to my core.

The double doors opened, and out they came. Tall ones, short ones, blondes and brunettes. A feast for my senses and my raging hormones. I checked myself in the mirror, smoothed my shaggy blond hair, and grinned. In this car—my car—I felt unstoppable. It was almost unfair. Like shooting fish in a barrel. Straight off, I spotted a cute redhead, giggling with her friends. She kept glancing back at me over her freckled shoulder with a shy smile.

"Hey," I said, pulling up alongside her, idling, when her friends walked on without her.

"Nice ride."

I shrugged like it meant nothing to me. "You wanna go for a spin?"

Her cheeks pinked, and I was already counting my chickens, imagining my hands on her tight body. "I can't," she said. "I've got a boyfriend."

"No, you don't."

"Are you accusing me of lying? That's rude. Who do you think you are?" She put her hand on her hip and frowned. "His name is Jason, and he plays football, and he has a car too. I'm waiting for him."

"I'm just sayin'. I don't see a ring on your finger, so…what's the harm in a ride, huh? I'll bet he doesn't have a whip like mine."

"Did you steal it?"

"Now who's being rude? Hell no, I didn't steal it. Do you wanna go for a ride or not?" I sounded pissed. But I got the feeling this little snob was about to burst my balloon, and I didn't like it one bit. All the fireworks fizzled, leaving ash and embers crackling in my chest.

When she didn't answer, I tried again. "What's your name?"

"I've gotta go." She turned back toward the school, and I shifted into reverse and followed.

"You won't even tell me your name?"

Hell, she wouldn't even look at me. "Please, leave me alone."

"What if I guess it? Will you tell me then? Is it—"

"I'm going to get the principal. He'll call the cops." *Cops.* She might as well have doused me with ice water.

"Bitch." The car lurched forward as I threw it in drive, leaving a trail of rubber behind me.

Next stop, UC Berkeley. College girls wouldn't be so damn uptight. I drove three blocks, steaming, before I caught my reflection in a building as I passed and let out a whistle. *Worth every penny,* I thought, feeling revived. I shouldn't have even bothered with those prissy high school brats. They had curfews and rules and parents to contend with. What I needed was a woman.

And that's when I saw her. Yellow dress the color of lemonade, swirling around her thighs. Honey-blonde hair and legs for days. She sat on a guitar case, chin in her hands, crying. I slammed the brakes, and she flinched. *Way to play it cool, Calder.*

"You okay?" I called to her.

She wiped her eyes with the hem of her dress and gave me a curious once over. "Not really. I'm late for practice."

"You play that thing?" She nodded at me, her lips hinting at a smile. *Jesus. Her lips.* "Me too. I play." I would've said anything to get her in my car.

"My dad forgot to pick me up again, and I thought I'd walk. But then…" She slipped off her sandal, broken strap dangling. "This happened. My favorite shoes too."

"I can see why. They're great shoes. Not exactly my style, but…" She actually laughed. And it was the best sound I'd ever heard. "I'm Butch, by the way, but my friends call me Calder." *Like I had friends.*

Her eyes lit up. Even from here, I could see they were blue. The color of a robin's egg. "Hey, Calder, could you…"

"Could I what?"

"This is going to sound weird. But could you maybe give me a ride?"

"Uh, well…I'm kind of in a hurry, but…is it far?" *Please let it be far.*

"UC Berkeley. Not far at all. And I'm Gwendolyn, but my friends call me Gwen." I imagined she had throngs of them. I wanted to be her friend.

I reached over and popped the door handle, inviting her, and she slid into the passenger seat like she belonged there. Like she'd been riding shotgun with me her whole life. "So you play the viola, huh?" I heard the singsong in her voice. Definitely flirting.

"I thought it was a guitar. What the heck is a viola?"

"Don't worry. Everybody mixes them up. It's a string instrument too. Just a bit bigger than a violin. It's like the violin's big brother." I nodded, even though I knew jack about string instruments. "How long have you played the guitar?" she asked.

Me and my big mouth. "A couple years." One hand on the wheel, I pretended to strum with the other. "Electric guitar," I added, because it sounded like something that might make her want to have sex with me.

"Like Slash from Guns n' Roses?"

"Exactly." *How cool could this girl possibly be?*

"Is this your car?" she asked, grinning. "It's a classic." *That cool.*

"I bought it today. It's mine."

A small crease formed between her brows, and I worried I messed it up. I'd said the wrong thing. "How old are you?"

"Just turned eighteen. You?"

"Seventeen." So she was a high school girl after all. But nothing like the others. In a crowd of dull pebbles, she sparkled. "I'm a senior at Berkeley High. What about you?"

"Graduated early." I left out the GED in juvie part.

She reached into her purse, pulled out a pack of watermelon bubblegum, and unwrapped one small, pink square. *Keep your eyes on the road, Calder.* But that was impossible. She opened her mouth, and the gum disappeared inside. "Do you work or…never mind, I'm just being nosy."

"If you're wondering about the car, my parents are filthy rich. It was a graduation present," I joked, but she didn't crack a smile.

"Sounds like something mine would do. They're always trying to buy me with stuff. I know I sound like a spoiled snot, but don't you ever just get tired of it? I mean, this is like the tenth time this year my dad forgot about me. Literally, just forgot I existed for an entire afternoon. And every time, he says the same old stuff—*I got so busy on this call or in that meeting, blah, blah, blah.* It makes me feel…oh my gosh, I'm so sorry. I'm just rambling." She points up ahead, then hides her adorable face in her hands. "You can let me off there. I don't know what got into me. I guess it's nice to feel like somebody understands."

I stopped the car by the sidewalk and said the first prayers I'd uttered in about ten years. *Please God, let me see her again. I'll be good. I'll be a goddamn choir boy.* "I don't mind. You can ramble with me anytime, Gwen. It was nice to meet you. Beyond nice."

She cracked the door and climbed out without a word, still smacking her bubblegum. The air around me shifted, and I felt cold in the middle of spring, like somebody just stripped off my blanket. Then she lifted her viola from the backseat and sighed. "Aren't you going to ask for my number?"

## BUTCH
## APRIL 30, 1994
## THIRTEEN DAYS BEFORE I KILLED HER

A lie is like a cat. A feral cat. Like the ones Mom used to feed table scraps outside of our apartment in Richmond. You might think you've got it under control, that you know exactly what it will do next, but when you least expect it, it will unsheathe its claws and scratch you right in the face. And it's your own fault for thinking it could ever be something other than what it was. A bald-faced lie.

Last night, I called Gwen. I'd meant to play hard to get, but who was I kidding? I wanted to be gotten. Listening to her smile—*I could tell she was smiling*—I had no choice. I kept feeding the lie I told her, and it kept getting bigger and hungrier and wilder. Just like one of those cats.

"What're you doin' tomorrow? Do you wanna do something— together?" I'd barely taken a breath. *Cool your jets, dude.*

"I can't. I've got this thing."

"A thing? Sounds mysterious."

"Trust me. You wouldn't be into it." If she was involved, I was definitely into it.

"Try me."

"It's for school. For citizenship class. We have to volunteer. I've been helping out at a children's home in El Cerrito. Port in a Storm— that's what they call it. It's just for a few hours on the weekends."

"A children's home."

"Yeah, that's where they send kids who don't have anybody to take care of them." *Kids like me.* But she can't know that. To her, I'm Butch Calder, son of the filthy-rich Calders.

"I know what it is." I grew up in one. I thought that was as bad as it got. Until they shipped me off to the foster-care mill. Until I started taking the things I wanted—candy, sneaks, bikes, cars—and graduated to juvie. "What time do you have to be there?"

"You actually want to go?"

*I would clean toilets with you, Gwendolyn Shaw.* "Uh, sure. It'll get me out of the house at least. Plus, I can break in my new ride."

"Now we're getting the real story." I pictured her with the phone pressed to her ear, the cord curled around her fingers, a smirk playing on her lips. The lips that would be mine. "Pick me up at eight. Grizzly Peak Boulevard…" I jotted down the address, gleefully. I knew that street. I'd egged a house on it once. Okay, three times, and the eggs had been more like rocks. That's where Francis Conway, the CEO of Y-Trax, laid his pathetic little cue-ball head. Smack dab on one of the wealthiest streets in the Oakland Hills, where the other half lived. The half that included the most beautiful girl I'd ever laid eyes on. "Unless you'd rather I come to you. My dad can drop me off before his tennis lesson."

"Nope. I'll be there eight o'clock sharp." As if I'd ever been on time for anything. Mom always teased I'd be late to my own funeral. My social worker, Maria Rodriguez—the first in a long line of social workers—had made sure I'd been on time to Mom's. They'd been buried on the same day, my family. Three deep holes side by side in the earth. Pinned in place by Maria's tight grip on my arm, it was the first time I'd felt the need to run. To keep running.

"Oh, hey, where do you—" I hung up fast, like the phone was on fire, before she could finish, my face hot with shame. I knew what was coming, the question she would ask, and I shouldn't, couldn't, wouldn't answer. Because I still had a chance, and I wasn't about to blow it with the truth. *Where do I live, Gwendolyn?* In the Blue Bird, the no-tell motel where I've been staying since I turned eighteen and the group home kicked me out. Like there was some kind of voodoo—a visit from the responsible adult fairy—that happened between seventeen and 364 days and that magic number, eighteen.

"Sorry, Butch," my social worker, seventh after Maria, had said, patting me on the shoulder. "As unfair as it seems, you're responsible for yourself now. Try to make good decisions." What she meant: I was too young to have a clue, and old enough to screw it up. Too old to stay.

I flopped back on the bed and reached for the remote. Free cable. A perk of motel living.

Next door, Wade and Peggy were already going at it. Whether they were killing each other or making up, it was usually hard to tell till the next day. Wade always left his mark, but I kept my mouth shut since he let me bum cigarettes and beer whenever I wanted. Something heavy thudded against the wall, and I ratcheted up the volume, ogling a half-naked blonde in a music video. If I squinted my eyes a little, the picture blurred just enough I could pretend she was Gwen. Dancing just for me.

****

And that's how I ended up fighting a serious case of déjà vu on the porch of Port in a Storm. If I'd been there before, I didn't remember it. I'd laid my head in so many places by then, I couldn't tell them apart. They'd blurred into an ugly smear of well-meaning smiles and empty promises. Hot tears and holes punched in walls so thin I could hear that nobody wanted me. This place was no different than the others. It felt familiar. But also, unfamiliar. Because for the first time—standing beside Gwendolyn Shaw—I was winning.

"Thanks for coming with me," she said as we headed toward the front door, its white-washed wood chipping and peeling like even the paint couldn't stand to be there a second longer. I took her viola case from her hand, trying to prove I was a gentleman. She rewarded me with a sweet smile. "It'll be fun. You'll see."

I shrugged. Casual, devil-may-care Butch. That's the face I wore then. She couldn't have known it was all an act—*could she?*—but she slipped her fingers into mine and squeezed my hand, reassuring me. My whole body thrummed as if it didn't belong to me anymore. *Just like the lyrics of that KISS song, "Love Gun,"* I thought, grinning wide as a hyena. Back then, everything was a KISS song. I might have even hummed a few bars under my breath as we walked inside. *No place for hidin' baby, no place to run.* Gwen had me locked and loaded, her red-polished finger on the trigger...*of my love gun, love gun.*

I followed her inside, watching her skirt swish as she walked. On the ride over, the wind had caught the hem, almost blowing it up, and she'd yanked it down just in time. But not before I'd glimpsed the paleness of her thighs, the soft white hair above her tan lines. And a single freckle, a sprinkle of cinnamon, I longed to touch. A solar eclipse of a freckle that obliterated any trace of buyer's remorse. *That car was so worth it.*

"Come on," she said, tugging me inside the door—she knew the way—and to a room just off the entrance with polished hardwood, wall-to-wall bookcases, and an old piano where a woman sat, singing. The kids, a room full of them, sat wide-eyed, transfixed by the woman or the singing. Or both.

"That's Cherice Currey," Gwen whispered right up against my ear. The tickle of her watermelon breath jolted my groin like a cattle prod. I tried to think of something to say—and fast—so she would do it again.

"Curry? Like the spice?" Young Butch at his finest. And an epic fail, because Gwen only nodded. No whispering. No watermelon. No electric shock to my junk. I settled against the wall and listened.

Cherice was a beauty in her own right—the anti-Gwen—older, with chestnut skin and eyes so brown they were almost black. A scar ran the length of her cheek, raised and dark as a leech, out of place on a face that seemed otherwise unmarked. She had mystery and grit and a voice that came from pain. And the whole room, Gwen included, couldn't look away from her. But that day, I'd hardly noticed her. Because Gwen had something I needed but couldn't name and couldn't have.

When Cherice finished playing, Gwen clapped, so I did too. Then Cherice stood in front of the piano, waiting for quiet. "Alright, kids, it's the weekend, and you all know what that means." She paused, and cast a conspiratorial smile in Gwen's direction. "Our special friend, Gwen, is here to play the viola. And it looks like she's brought a guest. What's your name, young man?"

*Loser. Just call me Total Loser.* I didn't speak until Gwen nudged me with her elbow. Nobody told me I had a speaking part. "Butch... uh, Butch Calder." I'm not sure if Cherice replied. I was too busy hiding my beet-red cheeks, calculating how many cool points I'd lost. But I perked up when I heard Gwen addressing her audience.

"Butch plays the guitar. You have a guitar, don't you, Miss Cherice?"

The Butch I am now could've talked his way out of it. Damn if prison didn't make me a better liar. But Young Butch, poor sap, did all he knew how to do. He turned tail and ran. Out the door with its peeling paint and around the porch to the rear of the house. I had no clue where I was going. Just away from perfect Gwen who would figure I lied to her. Hell, maybe she already knew. Away from those eyes—at least twenty pairs of them—that would see me for who I was. More like them, castoffs, runaways, delinquents, than Gwen with her swishy skirt and her viola. I could've headed for the 'Cuda, and I still can't say for sure why I didn't tear off in a cloud of dust. I didn't see it then. The fork-in-the-road moment. I chose, like we all do, unknowing.

Nobody came after me. But I wasn't alone.

I stopped short of the backyard when I heard a man's voice. Even now, when I think of it, he sounded like the devil himself. Raspy and cruel and full of fire.

"Do you really think anybody is gonna believe you, Evelyn? You're a little freak. Evil Evie. Isn't that what they call you?" The man who spoke looked familiar to me. Then, I'd wondered if I knew him and how. Now, I know he was a type. The type of guy I'd grown up with in juvie. Tatted, long-haired, skinny as a rail, but mean. The type who'd coldcock you for an accidental bump in the chow line. The type who cut his teeth on boys like me.

"Well? Isn't it?" He flicked his cigarette right in the girl's face, sending a spray of ashes to the ground. She followed them with her eyes. "Cat got your tongue?"

"Just leave me alone, Trey." She didn't look at him when she said it, but her voice had gumption.

"Just leave me alone, Trey," he mimicked, then guffawed like he was a real Jim Carrey. He ground out the ashes with his boot, still chuckling to himself. "Make me," he oozed, moving closer to her, reaching out his long, bony arm with its skeleton fingers and grazing the side of her cheek. "You look just like your mama. Real purdy."

I stood there frozen for longer than I should have. Truth, I was afraid.

"The kind of purdy men pay for. But you already know that, don't ya?" His hand rested on her small shoulder. Jesus, she was just a kid. Twelve. Thirteen at most.

"Hey," I said, finally, wincing at the way my voice cracked. "She said to leave her alone." I stepped out from the side of the house and showed myself. Butch Calder, wannabe bad boy. Hair gelled within an inch of its life. Levis and Doc Martens that I'd dropped another Benjamin on last week. And the knowledge I'd never be good enough for Gwendolyn Shaw sitting like a rock in the pit of my stomach right next to that other unpleasant reality. I was completely and utterly alone.

"And who the fuck are you?"

No matter Trey's demand, the girl drew my attention. She stared at me with eyes I wouldn't forget—big and bright and green, but scared as a rabbit. "I'm nobody," I said. "Nobody."

# CHAPTER TWELVE

EVIE
JANUARY 14, 2017
SATURDAY

**THE** officers stop me a block from the office—"I'm sorry, ma'am. Police personnel only"—leaving me to fend for myself in the quicksand between the past and the present. I listen to the sound of my own breathing, the ragged push and pull of it, to keep at least one foot in the now. Sebastian stands next to me, quiet. Watching. I want to ask him why he called it the hanging tree, but the more time that passes in silence, the more I think I imagined it all.

"Looks like a murder scene to me," he says, finally. Which is obvious with the coroner's van parked in front. The crime scene tape hanging loosely around the trunk of the tree, as if it can contain all the evil in the world inside its happy yellow lines. And the draped white sheet that conceals one thing. I study its shape—what I can see from here—measure the length of it in horror. It's small enough to be a child. But not too small. *Cassie's height*, I realize. The height of a soon-to-be, never-to-be adult.

"Do you think they'll want to talk to us?" Sebastian asks. His voice registers. Barely. Then, his question.

"Of course not. We've done nothing wrong." *What does he know? What could he know?*

"I mean *us*. Your group. Of sex offenders." *Nothing, Evie. He knows nothing.*

I feel awful for making him utter the word, say aloud what he is, within earshot of the reporters circling like buzzards at the periphery. "Oh. Right. Um…I imagine they'll probably be looking at everyone in the building." After the words are spoken, I realize how ridiculous they sound. Like I've already decided somebody is dead. A homicide has occurred. A sexual homicide no less.

But I'm not the only one. "We'll be the prime suspects. Who am I kidding? I'll be the prime suspect," Sebastian adds, in a flurry. "Obviously. Unless there are other convicted murderers meeting up once a week in your building, I'm totally screwed. I'm so, so…"

He's talking fast under his breath, shaking his head like he's ridding it of something. But when our eyes meet, I see focus there. Stillness. Like mirror-smooth water. I wait and watch, trying to make sense of him—even, it seems, as he's watching me.

Finally, a reporter pushes by us, and Sebastian jumps, the still water broken and rippling. "Sebastian, you've got to calm down. We don't even know for certain what's happened here. Don't work yourself up."

"Right, right. You're right."

"You should probably go home. Being here will only make it worse."

His face is stricken. "Wait. Wait a minute. You don't think I had something to do with this, do you? Do you, Dr. Maddox?"

Another part of my job is lying. Or should I say, the avoidance of honesty. And in only twelve and a half years, my mother had made me an expert.

"Of course, I'm clean, Evelyn Anne."

"No, Evelyn Anne, I didn't take your money."

"I can stop anytime I want, Evelyn Anne."

She'd always used my full name when she lied, and by the time I graduated middle school, I'd earned my PhD in deceit. Of course, they don't call it lying in grad school. "Wait until the client is ready to hear the truth," they say. So, I do.

"You're worried that I suspect you. It makes complete sense. You must be feeling vulnerable right now. But the reality is, neither of us have enough information to make a judgment."

He bites his lip, nods. "I'll see you on Monday then. I hope."

I follow Sebastian with my eyes as he skirts the crowd and takes the turn toward home. He doesn't look back. Not once. And when he's finally out of view, I let myself think it. It washes over me like the tide—slow and secret—until I'm neck-deep in it and drowning. Whatever happened here, it could be him. Not Sebastian, per se. Or George. Or Vince. Or Antonio. Or even Danny. But him. The faceless man. Whoever he is. I spin around, scanning the crowd for a sign. He could be right here, right now. The hair on my neck prickles at the possibility.

And if it is him, then it's also me. Because I'm to blame.

****

I hover near the media vans, my nerves a steady buzz under my skin. I've ignored three calls from Maggie. It's been at least two hours since I left the house, but I can't go until I know.

"What happened?" I direct the question to a man with a camera bag slung over his shoulder, but the woman next to him, a reporter, answers. Her heavy makeup cracks as she frowns, but her voice is as flat and colorless as the mud-puddled sidewalk beneath my feet.

"It's a kid. A girl."

"How old?"

She shrugs. "They're not saying."

"Murdered?"

A single bob of her head, and my mouth gets dry.

"Was she...you know...?" That word still won't come out. Instead, it festers inside my mouth like an open sore.

"Raped, you mean?" *Rape.* I wince. "Probably. I heard she was half-undressed."

I mumble a thank you and retreat, willing my legs to move. My car is back in the alleyway where I left it, probably towed or broken into by now. Before I take the turn around the corner, before the hanging tree disappears, I look over my shoulder. Two policemen are loading the coroner's van. The white sheet is gone, replaced by a sturdy, black body bag. I imagine Cassie inside it. She would seem, at first glance, to be sleeping. But she's too still, too pale for that. Her skin too cold. If you looked closer, which they would, you'd know something wasn't right because of the marks on her neck. The tiny red petechiae where the blood vessels burst under the force of his fingers. Her eyes—opened by a gloved hand—also red. The hyoid bone, delicate as a bird's wing, fractured.

I never saw Cassie dead, but she died. I'd watched it. From up there in the crook of the tree, still as a magpie, I'd taken it in. The hunger for air. Her small, wild hands reaching out and up toward me. Though by then, I imagine I was just a shadow to her. She'd stopped moving, but the man kept on. Fumbling with the button of her cutoff jean shorts, the ones we'd exchanged like sisters so that I couldn't remember if they were hers or mine. I'd heard him grunting with effort. With pleasure. My last memory of Cassie is that vile sound.

"Excuse me, ma'am."

I must have stopped walking, because I haven't moved. That's what the past will do to you. Fix you in one spot like a stone statue. I meet a pair of familiar eyes. Brown and uncertain. Tired like mine. His stubble is still there, thicker now, but it doesn't hide the razor-thin scar on his neck.

"I'm not sure if you remember me," he says, "but I..."

"Mr. Calder, right? You're practically my guardian angel. Of course, I remember. I hope your PO wasn't too hard on you." He lowers his head, kicks at an invisible pebble. I think I've embarrassed him.

"I didn't want to bother you. I just saw you walking, and I thought I'd ask if you were okay."

I catch him looking at the bandage on my forearm, and I fold my arms across my chest. "I'm alright, I suppose. As alright as I can be."

"Did the cops catch that creep from last night?"

"Not that I've heard." My gaze trails back to the yellow tape, and his eyes follow.

"Are you sure you're okay?"

"It's just…" The coroner's van pulls away with someone's body— not Cassie's—inside. "That's my office across the street."

"I'm sorry," he mumbles. "I mean, it looks bad. Whatever happened."

I intend to walk away, but there's an urge. An impulse I can't ignore. "Do I know you?" His breath catches, or maybe I imagine it. "I mean, from before last night?" He doesn't reply. His face is blank, so he's not thinking. Whatever the answer—yes or no—he already knows it. He's known it. "Calder," I say. "What's your first name?"

"Butch."

Remembering is a revelation. What's gone one minute, lost and not even missed, is there the next. In splendid color. I remember Butch Calder. It's a kind of miracle.

# EVIE
## APRIL 30, 1994
## THIRTEEN DAYS UNTIL MY BIRTHDAY

*I wish I could disappear.* That's what I thought the first time I laid eyes on Butch Calder, though I didn't know his name then. He was just a boy—an older boy, and cute too—standing on the porch with his fists balled and his face sort of scrunched up. Like he was tough or trying to look it. I fell for his act until he opened his mouth.

"I'm nobody," he'd said to Trey, and you could tell deep down, he really believed it. Big mistake, letting Trey Waters see inside you. I knew that from experience. Trey's hand was on my shoulder—it fit all the way around—and squeezing tight. Sometimes, I thought Trey was the devil with his red-rimmed eyes, his long, bony fingers, and his nails that looked like claws, stained yellow from his cigarettes. You never let the devil know who you really are.

"Well, Nobody, if I want your opinion I'll give it to you. Now scram." Trey didn't even look at Calder—that's what his friends called him, he told me later—but I wanted him to, desperately. I wanted him to look anywhere but at me. Because I swear, it felt like he could see through me. Right down to my bones and further, where I'd buried my secrets. The ones he could never know. Trey's thumb brushed my neck, and I shivered. "Now, where were we?" he asked, all slick and slimy, the way he used to talk to Mom.

"Not until you let her go. She's a kid, you pervert."

This boy was braver than I'd figured. Or stupid. But his courage made me bold, and I shrugged off Trey's devil claw. I wondered if it left a mark. "I'm going inside," I told him, the words sticky in my dry mouth. I didn't move though. It was one thing to say it and another to do it. Trey had that kind of power.

"You get one free pass, Nobody, because I'm such a nice guy. And I don't feel like gettin' your blood all over me." Trey slipped his knife out of his back pocket and pressed the little button—*click*—that revealed the blade. I was acquainted with that knife. I'd held it in my hand before. Tomahawk brand with a gold alligator on the case and the initials *B.A.*, for Bruce Allcott. Trey's knife had once belonged to my father. "But next time, I suggest you mind your own fucking business." He made a show, polishing the length of it with the hem of his shirt like the star of a gangster movie.

Calder didn't answer, and he didn't look scared. At least he wouldn't have to most people. But I noticed the way he held his body rigid as a board. I knew fear when I saw it.

"And don't think I'm gonna forget about you, Evelyn. You owe me, and you know it. Your mama knows it too, God rest her soul."

Trey slunk away through the woods at the back of the house. I watched his oily brown ponytail until I couldn't see it anymore. Then I turned to the boy, suddenly feeling nervous. I didn't talk to older boys. I didn't talk to boys period. But he seemed different. Safe. And did I mention, cute? Cassie would be so jealous. "Thanks," I mumbled. "He's a jerk."

"I was gonna say psychopathic asshole, but yeah. Jerk. That too. Do you want me to tell somebody he's bothering you?"

I shook my head fast. That was the last thing I needed. Everybody already thought I was a freak. *Evil Evie with her mutant-green eyes.* Someday, I'd get contacts. Turn them brown as mud.

"Alright. Mum's the word then, but be careful." He paused for a second. "Wanna come back inside?"

I headed up the stairs. From the porch, I could hear Gwen playing the viola. I liked her, though I couldn't say why. I just knew she wasn't like the girls at Port in a Storm or even Cassie. She was beautiful and smart and nice and different. But that day, her playing sounded sad, and I wondered if this boy knew her. "So what's your real name, Nobody?"

# CHAPTER THIRTEEN

**BUTCH**
**JANUARY 14, 2017**
**SATURDAY**

EVIE remembers me. Or at least she thinks she does, and I'm not about to tell her otherwise. That she doesn't know the real me. That the Butch she met that day at Port in a Storm—the Butch who hadn't killed a girl yet—is a ghost. A shadow. I recall him fondly, bittersweetly, like a long-lost friend. But I don't pretend we're the same person. Ending a life, her life, ended him too.

"I wasn't sure you'd remember me," I say. "Or want to be reminded. It was a long time ago." My heart is doing that thing again. Thumping like a goddamn snare drum. She's going to ask me where I've been the past twenty-some odd years. She's going to ask what I did to land myself on parole. She's going to ask why I've got her license in my pocket.

"A lifetime ago," she says. That's all. Then, she goes quiet, just standing there back-dropped by the past. Our past. I can't look at that tree, but I can't *not* look at it. And the silence grows as wide as a frozen lake. Before I know it, I'm yammering to fill it.

"I guess you turned out alright, huh? A doctor. Wow. That's pretty impressive considering..." Insert foot in mouth, Butchy. "I mean...you had it pretty rough. I'm sorry. I hope that wasn't rude." That's another thing about prison. It really does a number on your social skills.

"It was honest," she says, looking up at me with those eyes. And the weight of pain in them, the beauty too, nearly bowls me over. Because I'm light-years from honest right now. "How have you been?"

This is my chance to spill my guts. I realize now, she won't ask. It's one of those taboo questions like asking a woman if she's pregnant or asking your boss how much he makes. "I've been..."

"It's okay if you don't want to talk about it. I understand. I work with offenders. A lot of them were in prison too."

I nod at her, grateful, but I can't leave it at that. *Can I?* I owe her something. Everything really. She doesn't know the half of it. *Think twice, speak once.* That's what they taught us in anger-management class. So, in my mind, I play it out like I always do.

"I killed someone. A girl." The words will collapse the universe. I'll wait for them to suck us into a black hole, the kind of place nothing could escape from. Not even light.

"Oh." Not a horrified *oh*. Shocked, yes. But she won't run. So it won't be a complete disaster. "That must've been hard to say out loud."

"Yeah." She'll be in full therapist mode by then, but I won't mind. I know the rules of that game, and it feels safe. "But I've had a lot of practice. Eight psych evals before they let me out. Not that I counted or anything."

She'll laugh, and for a moment, I'll remember her as she was, as she used to be. A kid and already smarter than I was. Just for that moment, I'll let myself pretend to be Young Butch again. Hero. Rescuer of young girls. Not the villain. The destroyer.

I open my mouth to do it, to get it over with. I've done it so many times, performing like a trained monkey for those parole commissioners judging me from their ivory tower. But I've never said those words to someone who knew me before. Someone like me. And it feels all wrong. Like meeting your doppelganger.

"I got my bachelor's degree in Folsom." That's what I come up with. Of all things.

"What did you study?" As if we're just two old buddies at a high school reunion, shooting the breeze. And I'm not a murderer. And she's not a hitchhiking shrink.

"Sociology. Go figure. No wonder I can't get a job to save my life." We both laugh, and it feels good. But then, I feel guilty. Again.

"You know, my office building manager is looking for a custodian. You're probably overqualified, but…"

"I'm interested. It's the best offer I've had yet. Heck, it's the only offer."

"I can't make any promises, but I'll put in a good word. It's the least I can do, Butch? Or is it Calder? What should I call you?"

Creep. Liar. Cold-blooded killer. Among other things. "Well, as I recall, it was always Calder for my friends."

"Calder it is then." She smiles at me, a smile with a twist to it. A secret I want to know. And I realize I'm in more trouble than I thought. Trouble, with a capital *T*. Because Evie remembers me, and she's not a little girl anymore.

****

Sebastian is sitting on the bed, reading, when I get back. Apparently, Lord of the Goddamn Flies is so engrossing he can't be bothered to say hello.

"Hey. I'm Butch. Your roommate."

He studies me over the rim of his glasses, then extends a hand. "Sebastian Delacourt. Nice to meet you." His grip is as weak as a dead fish, and as soon as I let go, he's back in his book.

"*Lord of the Flies*, huh?" I flop down on my mattress, wondering why I can't stop talking. But with Evie's license still in my pocket and everything I didn't say spinning in my head, I've got to move my mouth to stay sane. "I was always partial to Piggy myself. How 'bout you?"

"Jack." Well then. Heartless savage it is. As if this guy wasn't spooky enough with his disappearing act last night. "Jack's misunderstood, you know. The officer sees it at the end. He's just a little boy who's in over his head."

I'm not sure if I should laugh or run. "That's one way to look at it, I suppose."

Sebastian closes the book and chuckles, shaking his head at me. "I'm totally messing with you. I like Piggy too. I mean, look at me," he says pointing to his glasses. "I practically am Piggy."

I put a pin in that one. It would be downright uncivil to agree. "Did you hear what happened up the street?" I ask. "I'm surprised this place isn't crawling with cops ready to give us the shakedown."

"Uh, yeah, sort of. Some of the guys were talking about it at breakfast. Why? What did you hear?" I'm surprised this guy lasted one day in the joint. He's a ball of nerves, the way he's tapping his fingers against the cover of that book. But then again, maybe he's got reason to be.

"They're saying murder. Of a kid. A girl. Probably happened early this morning. Maybe around 4 a.m."

I wait for my bluff to sink in. For Sebastian to crumble, to dissolve into a murky puddle, leaving only his glasses and his copy of *Lord of the Flies* behind. Instead, he raises the leg of his jeans, showing me a GPS monitor strapped to his pasty-white ankle. "It's a good thing I've got this to vouch for me then."

I play it cool, but I'm losing my edge. Clearly. It's the size of my cell phone. *How could I have missed it?* In a house like this, that

**84**

gadget can only mean one thing. My roomie is a high-risk sex offender.

**** 

Mr. Richert's door is open, so I don't bother knocking. But I close it behind me, carefully, quietly. I don't want anybody to know I'm here. And by anybody, I mean Sebastian.

"What's up, Calder?"

"I need a new roommate."

Richert leans back in his chair, rubs his baldhead, and smirks. "Does this look like a college dorm to you? It doesn't work like that. Now, what's this all about?"

"You know what it's about."

"Enlighten me."

"He's got a bracelet, Frank. Don't mess with me."

"And?" He shakes his head, dismayed. "Everybody's the same in this house, Butch. Anything that happened before you got here is confidential. That's for your protection too, ya know." It hits like a grenade, but it's not a shocker. That's what he's thinking. We're the same. Sebastian and me.

"I'm not a goddamn perv." It feels good, spitting it at him like that, but I want to take it back. It sounds like prison talk. I suck in a deep breath and count to ten just like I'd been taught. "I'm sorry. That came out wrong. I mean, I'm not a sex offender."

Richert considers me with a blank stare. "Remind me again why you went to prison."

I sigh, accepting complete and utter defeat. "Murder. I killed a girl. I know it's not any better or any worse. But Sebastian left his room the other night. Last night." Murderer and now a snitch. Real classy, Butchy.

"You're better than this." Richert points to the door, sending me on my way. "Now get a grip and deal with it like a man. Okay, cupcake?"

## BUTCH
## MAY 1, 1994
## TWELVE DAYS BEFORE I KILLED HER

"**I** think I'm in love. And my life's lookin' up." That was the song playing on the clock radio when the alarm went off at 9 a.m. Like Eddie Money read my mind. "I think I'm in love. Because I can't get enough." *That's right, Eddie.* I couldn't get enough of Gwendolyn Shaw. Which explained why Young Butch was up at the butt crack of dawn on a Sunday. And hungover, no less.

I lay there—head pounding and thirsty as hell—but snug as a bug in those scratchy two-dollar motel sheets, because Gwen had kissed me. No. Gwen had made out with me. Definitely first base. Tongue and everything. And as sick as it sounded, I had a little girl to thank for that.

"Evelyn Anne Allcott, we've been looking for you everywhere." That's what Cherice had said the moment she'd seen us walk in together. Me with my tail between my legs and Evie hiding behind me. Gwen had stopped strumming the viola, and all twenty pairs of eyes turned to take us in. The silence stretched out long and as taut as a rope.

"Calder found me," Evie had said, finally, clinging to my hand like I was her big brother, and she wanted to show me off. And just like that, three words, and The Unfortunate Incident of Butch and the Guitar (otherwise known as Butch is a Filthy Liar) was completely forgotten. Well, almost.

**86**

"So why did you lie about playing the guitar?" Gwen had asked, hours later. We were parked up at Grizzly Peak, sunning ourselves on the hood of the 'Cuda. And I was already half-drunk on the bottle of Patrón Gwen had stolen from her dad's liquor cabinet. The good stuff. Not the crappy tequila Wade always puked up in the Blue Bird parking lot.

"Why do you think?" I'd tilted my head to take her in. The curve of her shoulder, where—*have mercy*—she'd pulled down the strap of her tank top. The cute upturn of her nose. Her lips, the palest pink, like rosebuds. *Geez, Butch.* This girl had turned me into a poet, a goddamned Shakespeare.

"I don't know why, Calder. That's the reason I asked." She'd taken a lazy swig from the bottle and licked her bottom lip. Then, she'd laid back and closed her eyes. *Who is this girl?* This girl who looked like an angel and played the viola. This girl who drank tequila straight from the bottle.

My head buzzed—maybe I was drunker than I thought—and the whole world went a little gauzy. I couldn't think hard enough to come up with a good excuse. "I wanted to impress you. That's why."

I'd felt the heat of her body beside me. Closer. And closer still. But not as close as I'd wanted her. Her fingertips had brushed mine, and I'd held my breath until she spoke. "Kiss me."

Horndog I was back then, it sounded like an invitation, a request. A demand even. *Kiss me, Butch! Do it now, before I spontaneously combust from wanting you!* But looking back, years later, I wondered if it had been more of a dare. Whatever it was, however she meant it, she didn't need to say it twice. I'd sat up, taken her face in both my hands, and pressed my mouth to hers, hoping Lydia O'Connor had been right when she'd told the entire fifth grade I was a good kisser.

"I think I'm in love! It's gotta be love!" I belted out the final chorus into my toothbrush, laughing at myself in the bathroom mirror. Then, I froze, leaned closer. Blinked and blinked again.

Mom's chestnut brown eyes, Dad's hawk nose—plus the bump I'd earned in juvie—and Jesse's goofy grin. My face belonged to the dead. The eyes white with terror. The nose—and the ribs and the spinal cord—shattered on impact. Jesse's head nearly cut clean off by a mangled shard of metal. It all flashed in the mirror like I'd been right there when it had happened. I should have been. But I'd convinced Mom that thirteen was too old for a dollar-store Halloween costume and old enough to be left home alone.

"Batman." That's what Maria had told me when I'd asked her what costume they'd found in the wreckage. "Batman and the Joker. There were two, Butch. One for your brother, and..."

That wasn't meant to make me feel like the worst kid in the history of the world, but it did anyway.

I started the shower and stuck my whole head under the ice-cold water, still wearing my boxers. It hadn't happened in a while, but sometimes my brain needed a hard reset. A CTRL-ALT-DELETE like the dinosaur computer in juvie, where they'd let us play PAC-MAN. I figured the shower was better than punching my face like I used to. And when I looked back at the mirror, shaggy hair dripping, my face was my own again. Except for my lips. Those were Gwen's now. They were chapped and sore to the touch. A small sacrifice to the make-out gods.

Humming again, I stripped down and waited for the water to warm. At the Blue Bird, you never could tell how long that might take. And usually, I didn't give a damn. My schedule was wide open. But not today. Today, I had somewhere to be, and a girl—*the* girl—who was waiting for me.

❄❄❄❄

Picture this. I pulled up to Lake Anza in the 'Cuda—top down, *duh*—blasting track 1 of my KISS cassette tape, "I Was Made for Lovin' You," and outfitted in my all-new swag. Black board shorts with orange flames licking up my thighs and Ray-Bans propped on my head. When I saw Gwen sitting on the bench in an itty-bitty red bikini, I thanked God I'd been doing a hundred pushups a day since foster home number two, where the dad was hardcore ex-military. I was no Schwarzenegger, but I'd won the pull-up contest in juvie last year.

"Hey," I said, swaggering toward her like I owned the place. I watched her eyes linger on my pecs. But I cut her some slack, because my own eyes were fixed to her chest like a hawk hunting field mice.

"I like your shorts."

"Thanks. I got them 'cause of the flames." Great. I sounded like a third-grader.

"You're a KISS fan, right?"

I nodded, my tongue suddenly thick and useless. *Why am I so nervous?* I tried to remember that very tongue had been inside Gwen's mouth less than twenty-four hours ago.

"I figured," she said with a grin. "Gene Simmons is my favorite. He's so wild, ya know. Like he doesn't care what anybody thinks of him."

"Cool." I hoped I sounded distant. Smooth. But inside, my heart flip-flopped like a fish out of water. *Gwen liked KISS?* She'd obviously wandered straight out of one of my wet dreams. "I just bought an autographed *Love Gun* LP," I bragged.

"Awesome. I love that album. Maybe I could see it sometime." I just shrugged, noncommittal. What she didn't know—and wouldn't ever—is that it hung above my bed at the Blue Bird.

"Alright, well I got a spot for us down there." Gwen pointed toward the small beach, where the mossy green lake met the shore. Then she dropped her hand to her side and linked it with mine as we walked. "I hope it's okay that I invited Cherice and—"

"Cherice?"

"Cherice from Port in a Storm. From yesterday. We hang out sometimes. She's twenty-one, so she can buy us alcohol. She doesn't like to do it, but I can usually convince her."

"Oh, right. That Cherice." The Cherice who'd seen me run out of a room full of kids like my pants were on fire. The Cherice who Gwen told me had grown up in an orphanage herself. The Cherice who'd probably seen right through me, recognizing me as one of her own.

"And her new boyfriend, Matthias."

"Matthias," I repeated, making a face. "Sounds biblical."

"Yeah, and don't call him Matt or Matty. He hates that. Cherice says he's kind of uptight about it. I guess some of the kids at school used to tease him or something."

"Got it. No Matt. No Matty. No Matthew." I gave her a little joking salute. "Any other instructions, ma'am?"

"One more thing." She lowered her voice. "They don't exactly know that my family is well-off. So can we keep that our little secret?"

She didn't wait for me to answer, just tugged me along, already waving to Cherice. I tried to hide my disappointment. I'd been hoping to have Gwen and her red bikini all to myself. But, seeing Cherice, splayed out on a towel and slathered in baby oil—her body curvier, more womanly than Gwen's—I started to think I *had* died in that crash. And this, this place was heaven.

****

Gwen was right. She'd easily twisted Cherice's arm—*C'mon, don't be a stick in the mud. It'll be fun*—and the four of us were back at Grizzly Peak, sucking down Bacardi and sharing my pack of Marlboros on the hood of the 'Cuda. Even in the dark, Matthias' secondhand pickup truck seemed pathetic parked beside it—a hunk of scrap metal—and I felt bad for him. His ride was lame, and he had to deal with all the guys side-eyeing him for dating a black girl. But, then again, he looked tougher than me with his white-blonde buzz cut and that iron-cross tattoo between his muscled shoulder blades. And the way Cherice ogled him, they'd definitely done it. Plus, he was the assistant manager at Barky's Pet Store, whereas I had no plans beyond the Blue Bird. And Gwen. In less than seventy-two hours, she had become my plan. The shining star where I'd hitched my wagon.

"So, Calder, a lot of the girls have a crush on you now," Cherice said, snickering as she elbowed Gwen. "Since you rescued our little Evie yesterday."

"I wouldn't call it a rescue."

"Well, she did. She told everybody you scared off a big, angry Doberman that had her cornered in the yard."

"She did? Uh, yeah. I guess. It was more like a Chihuahua though." I felt satisfied imagining that asshole, Trey, as a tiny yapping dog I could've kicked across the yard if I'd wanted to.

"That's what I figured. Evie has a loose relationship with the truth. That's why the other kids pick on her. Well, that and…"

"And?" It wasn't my business, but I liked that Cherice was talking to me. That she noticed me. She'd spent half the afternoon with her nose in a book and the other half dog-paddling in the lake with Matthias. And to be honest, I hoped Gwen would notice her noticing me.

"I shouldn't really be talking about this. I could get in trouble at Port in a Storm if anybody found out. They fired the last house manager for breaking confidentiality."

"My lips are sealed. Tight." I heard the alcohol in my exaggerated whisper.

Gwen kissed me, then, without warning, right there in front of them—sloppy and open-mouthed—like she was marking her territory. Maybe she *was* jealous. And she tasted amazing. Like rum and watermelon and a hint of smoke. "Did someone say lips?"

"Get a room," Matthias said, rolling his eyes in her direction.

She rolled hers right back at him and kissed me again, harder this time. "Apparently, Matthias is kind of a prude."

I started to rib him—*what guy in his right mind wouldn't want Cherice all over him?*—but he looked too serious for that. Besides, his eyes were set on Gwen. And now *I* was jealous.

"And Gwen is kind of a…" He smirked at her, daring her to fill in the blank. And I took another swig to quell the heat in my chest while she draped her arm around my shoulder and fired back.

"Bombshell? Stunner? Knockout? Goddess? What do you think, Calder?"

*All of the above.* But I only nodded at her, feeling out of place. Like I'd stumbled into somebody else's party.

Mercifully, Cherice ignored them both. "Anyway, don't say anything, okay? About Evie." I nodded. Whatever Evie had been through I doubted it was any worse than anything else I'd heard. Than the things I'd lived through myself. "Her mom was a junkie and a prostitute. Evie found her dead with a needle in her arm. She sat with the body for a whole day in a motel room till somebody found them."

No wonder I'd felt like she needed protecting. Like we were kindred spirits somehow. "Jesus. Kids tease her about that?"

"You know how kids are. They think it's weird she didn't go for help. Like she wanted her mom to die. They call her Evil Evie."

"Is she the one with the spooky green eyes?" Matthias asked Cherice, freakishly widening his own baby blues with his fingertips. "They were practically glowing at me from the porch the other day when I came to get you. If you ask me, the name suits her."

Cherice scowled. "That's not nice. The poor girl literally has no friends. I think that's why she's always sneaking out. Besides, you know how I feel about name-calling, Fatty Matty. Stop being a jerk."

"Fatty Matty?" Gwen's laugh—sudden and cruel—made Matthias' face blaze red, but he said nothing. Just slunk away to his pickup, brooding and lighting another cigarette.

With an over-it sigh, Cherice turned away from him. And Gwen. Back to me. I dug that more than I should have.

"Fatty?" I mouthed, disbelieving. The guy was ripped.

"He was a chubby kid, apparently." She pointed me to the scar on her cheek. "Scarface. That's what they used to call me."

"The Schnoz," I said, tapping the nose I had my father to thank for. "Before I grew into it. At least I hope I did."

"You're funny, Calder. I think your nose is—"

"I'm bored," Gwen whined, grabbing me by the hand and pulling me toward her. She silenced Cherice, her opinion of my nose destined to remain a mystery. "Let's get out of here." Gwen breathed the words into my ear, and you already know what that did to me.

"Okay." I was way too drunk to drive, and I had no clue where we'd go. Her parents were entertaining guests on the veranda. That's how she put it. *What the hell is a veranda?* I wanted to ask. And my place? Completely out of the question. Gwendolyn Shaw would not set foot—or any other part—in the Blue Bird. Still, it was all small potatoes to me. Because I had my eyes on the prize, and I couldn't tell her no.

**\*\*\*\***

Gwen kneeled on the passenger seat as I drove, arms raised in the air, wind whipping across her face. "I'm not drunk enough," she yelled.

"Um...really? Cause you had a lot of the—" I bit my tongue. I sounded like a goddamn camp counselor. I wanted her drunk, didn't I? Hell yes, I did. *Drunk girls are easy.* That's what Wade always said. And I believed him, because the farthest I'd ever gone with a girl—Jackie? Jill? Julie? with the red hair—she'd already downed half my beer and two of her own.

"Do you think Cherice is pretty?" Her eyes were closed; she faced straight ahead, making it impossible to tell what she was thinking. Her hair flying behind her like the mane of a wild mustang. I'd wanted her to be jealous but that question wiped my brain clean. Totally clueless. The way I'd felt in continuation school when Mr. Whitecotton asked me to identify three major themes in *To Kill a Mockingbird*. The book had sat in my locker all weekend while I'd gone MIA from group home number two. "It's okay if you do. I just wondered with her scar and all..."

"Uh...she's alright, I guess. Why'd you lie to her about your family being rich?"

"Oh, you know how it is. Once people find out, that's all they can think about you. That one thing. Like they already know everything about you."

"Right. You're totally right. I hate that." The hole I'd dug was halfway to China, so why stop now? "Did you tell them that I'm…that my family is…?"

She grinned, sliding one hand along the 'Cuda's smooth black paint while the other—*God help me*—rubbed my thigh. "I'm pretty sure they figured it out."

I would have said anything to keep her hand moving, true or untrue. To feel it rest on my knee, each of her fingertips points of heat. "You're amazing, Gwen. Cherice has nothing on you." True and untrue.

"What about Matthias?" she asked.

"What about him?" Her hand restless again, slipped under the hem of my board shorts. I gulped a breath, and she giggled.

"Do you think he's really into Cherice? They're kind of a mismatch."

I shrugged, censoring the truth as I saw it. *He's into you.* Because I was afraid she'd like it.

"Pull over there." She pointed to the all-night mini mart at the base of the Hills. "I've got a plan to get us drunker if you're game."

I followed directions like a schoolboy, parking the 'Cuda in the empty lot, and letting the engine idle. The gray-haired cashier spotted us through the window, and Gwen waved to him. I tried to see her as he must. A carefree girl out for a ride with her boyfriend. *Boyfriend!* I could be Gwen's boyfriend. I was definitely game.

"Stay here." I watched her walk to the door, hips swaying in her little cut-off jean shorts, the way a man would eye a tornado. Or a hurricane. Some kind of fearsome natural disaster that awes you and scares you shitless at the same time.

When she returned, she held a pack of watermelon bubblegum—already opened—and flashed a cat-that-ate-the canary grin that left me weak in the knees. "He wouldn't let you buy it?" I asked.

She chewed quietly, saying nothing, until we were flying down the freeway, speed limit be damned. "I didn't ask his permission." I saw it then, in her purse. A bottle of Hennessy. Pilfered by the girl who looked like an angel and played the viola. I'd stolen before—under the cover of darkness, sneaking in through a broken window, jimmying a lock—but never like that. Blatant. Right in that old man's face.

What I could've said: "I'm not seventeen anymore. That means I could go to jail—real jail—for a stunt like this."

What I should've said: "It's been great knowing you, Gwen. Have a nice life."

What I actually said: "Sweet."

# CHAPTER FOURTEEN

## EVIE
### JANUARY 14, 2017
### SATURDAY

I circle the block again, waiting for a spot with a view of the police station. I can hardly stand the tightness in my chest, the grip of anticipation. But what am I expecting? The faceless man flanked by police, hands cuffed behind his back? The body—so much like Cassie's—wheeled into the morgue? My thirteen-year-old self running past on her way to God knows where, scattering the memories of that night behind her like breadcrumbs? I finally concede there's nothing to see here. I'm just delaying the inevitable. That being Detective Olivia Munroe and the questions I don't want to answer. Another thing about my job—I'm always the one asking the questions. And that's how I like it.

I sit in the waiting room folding and unfolding the corner of Detective Munroe's business card until it's worn thin enough to tear and watching the minute hand slog around the face of a clock that looks about as old as I feel.

"Evelyn Maddox?" My name comes out in a burst of breath, and she wipes beads of sweat from her forehead on the wrinkled sleeve of her shirt before she extends her hand and introduces herself. "Sorry to keep you waiting. It's been one of those mornings." I imagine her under the hanging tree, hunched over, examining the victim, the body small and broken. Combing the wet grass for clues. Skirting the media vultures circling outside. To get to me. The Hitchhiking Shrink. God knows what the officer already told her. No wonder she looks exhausted.

I follow her down the hallway marked Special Victims Unit. That's what I am. A special victim. Special in the worst way. Because I can't censor myself, even when I should. "I think someone was murdered outside my office. This morning." It feels necessary to specify, though there's no way Detective Munroe could know about Cassie. "Do you think it could be connected to what happened to me last night?"

She doesn't answer, just directs me inside a nondescript office with no signs of life. "Sit," she says, pulling out a yellow notepad that can't possibly contain the entirety of my story. "I've reviewed the report from last night, but I'd like to hear it in your own words. Tell me what you remember."

*What do I remember?*

*What do I remember?*

I remember waking up in the last seat of a Greyhound bus— woozy—the morning after I'd turned thirteen. I'd stumbled to the bathroom, retching in the toilet, until the world stopped spinning. Then I'd stood to examine the sore spots on the backs of my thighs, scrapes chafed red from the bark of the hanging tree. My throat just as raw, like I'd spent the whole night screaming. Irrefutable proof it had happened. Cassie was…dead. But the rest of the night had slipped away like a dream. "Where are we going?" I'd asked the lady across the aisle, ignoring her irritated frown. She'd waved her ticket in my face. "Oh. Right. Los Angeles."

"Dr. Maddox? Are you with me?"

"I'm sorry. I'm with you. I was just…"

"I know how difficult this must be. Especially in your line of work. It's tough to be on the other side, I'd imagine." So she'd Googled me. Great.

"I just feel so silly," I say. "Hitchhiking, I mean. It's certainly not one of my finer moments." I hand her the same half-truths I gave the officer, hoping she'll go easy on me. Feel sorry for me, at least. The pathetic doctor. The cautionary tale. She nods along through most of the story, listening like I would if the tables were turned.

"So what's your friend's name? The one who dared you?"

"Melanie Lee." I came prepared. Melanie rents 23A, the business suite below mine—Melanie's Massage—and she owes me one for lying to her husband the last time he came looking for her and her new boyfriend. "She can call you if you need to check out my story."

"Is she thirteen?" Detective Munroe pauses for a beat then chuckles, oblivious to my silent freak-out. Cassie's bright smile, her dancing brown eyes—*I'm thirteen going on thirty*—mocking me from the day I'd met her at the Willow Court swimming pool, which was really just a giant concrete hole that served as a makeshift dumping ground and a spot to do the sorts of deeds you weren't supposed to be doing. "I'm kidding. It just sounds like something a teenager would do. A double-dog dare, you know?"

"Yeah, Melanie's like that. A little unpredictable. This is the kind of crazy thing that usually happens to her. I'm the normal one. But, we've been friends forever." I almost laugh when I say it. I hardly know her.

"We'll call you as soon as we have any information, Dr. Maddox." Detective Munroe stands and heads for the door while I sit gaping at her back, her dark wiry hair escaping from a braid at the nape of her neck.

"That's all?"

"For now."

"Can I go home? Do you think it's safe?"

"I wouldn't," she says. "Not yet. We've got an officer patrolling your apartment complex, but I'd prefer if you stay elsewhere, at least for the time being. Leave the address at the desk so we can reach you."

She opens the door, ushering me out, but I feel stuck to the chair, weighed down by all the things she doesn't know. "What about the hanging tree?"

I don't even realize I've said it. I've spoken it aloud—blown up the wall between now and then, the one I worked so hard to build—until she tilts her head at me, confused. "Excuse me? The what?"

"I mean, the tree outside my office. Something happened there, right? This morning? Or last night? It's just a few blocks from where I was attacked. That can't be a coincidence."

"I can't discuss any other investigations with you, but suffice to say, we're looking at all angles. DNA can take a while, but I'm pretty sure the lab will rush those samples we got from your fingernails given recent developments. Now, if you'll excuse me…"

That's my cue, and I know it. I walk out the door, trailing behind her. "Detective Munroe? Can you just tell me one thing? How old was she?"

Her face is stern, her voice a hammer. "Dr. Maddox, you know a bit about confidentiality, don't you? Things like jeopardizing an investigation? Now, unless you're hiding a badge under that sweater, I have no idea what you're talking about."

\*\*\*\*

*Went to yoga. Be back soon. Eat something! And call me, please.*
*—Maggie*

The note on the counter stares at me, speaking in Maggie's disapproving tone. Regrettably, I am hungry. Starving actually. I ignore the quinoa salad she left for me, packed in Tupperware with my name written on a sticky note, and head for the pantry where she keeps the good stuff. And I don't call. Not yet anyway.

"Don't even think about it, Sammy." He sniffs at the bowl of chips on the counter before he saunters away, tail flicking, as if he's too evolved for junk food anyway. Maggie would be proud. I shovel in a handful, crunching shamelessly, as I open my laptop and type *murder Oakland today* in the search bar. 180,000,000 results. *Really?* But, it's right there at the top, beckoning like a door ajar in a horror film. *Body of unidentified female found in park*. I remind myself to breathe.

**At approximately 7:15 a.m. this morning, officers responded to the report of a female body in a small park in the 1500 block of Jackson Street. Officer Gillian reported that the unidentified female victim appeared to have been the victim of foul play. No other information was immediately available.**

*Foul play.* The rest of the article—useless anyway—blurs until those words are all I see. Until I'm in the hanging tree again, watching, mute. Until I'm in the bus's bathroom, splashing grimy water on my face, with no clue how I got there. Until I'm standing outside at the bus station, heat rising from the asphalt, brain buzzing with fear, only knowing one thing for certain. I couldn't go back.

Sammy bounds up the stairs, an imaginary foe in hot pursuit, and I jump. In the tense quiet, I expect Danny. He's here, stalking toward me, wielding his knife. Having found me at last, he'll give me what I deserve. But nothing happens. Sammy sits on the top step, calm but vigilant. My furry sentinel.

From the kitchen window, I see the sky darkening. The sun from the morning vanished behind a thicket of clouds. The rain is coming again. And Maggie is too. She'll be back soon, so I hurry. Another search. One I've done before, always in secret, and too many times to count. Hiding like a common criminal in the bathroom while Jared slept. Deleting my history, as if the name would mean anything to him. As if it was a lover I sought. But it was more corrupted than that, my betrayal. Withholding the most essential part of myself, the cracked foundation on which I was built.

And now, even with Jared gone, the guilt nags in my stomach, but I can't stop myself. That's the power of the unknown. It hooks you, leads you around by your nose. Demands things from you, things you don't want to give.

I type the one name I can't forget. Ironically. *Cassandra "Cassie" Garrett.* And I wait to see her returned to me. To see her face. On a missing poster. A Facebook page. A newspaper headline. An obituary. But it always ends the same. With nothing real. Leads that go nowhere. Like the one I'd followed years ago. Donna and Edward Garrett. Rang them up. *Do you know a Cassie Garrett?* I'd asked, certain the voice on the line would choke back a sob, gasp in recognition. But there was only this: *Sorry. Never heard of her.*

So, the person I can't forget doesn't exist. Not according to the internet. And what I know—*remember?*—about Cassie wouldn't fill half a page in that empty journal of mine. She'd told me she'd hitchhiked from Phoenix to Oakland after her mom went off her meds again. That she'd been looking for her real dad, but he'd already moved on. Texas maybe, according to somebody who thought he'd remembered him. "I'm savin' up for a bus ticket to Houston," she'd told me, counting out the few bills stuffed in her bra. I can still picture it, can still hear the soft swish of the money in her fingers.

I stare at the computer screen like it's a portal to the past. It's supposed to tell me what I need to know. Unless...I imagined her. And imaginary friends can't be raped and murdered. Sometimes, it's a relief to think it. Today, though, it feels like a curse. Like in twenty-three years' worth of silence, I obliterated her myself.

I shut the laptop, suddenly wanting to be rid of it and the secrets it knows—*surely, it knows*—but won't let me see. I tuck it inside its case and drag myself back up to Jared's room. It's barely afternoon, but the weight of the last twenty-four hours is too much to bear. And

I'm bone tired. I don't even care if Maggie finds me in here, curled up with her son's T-shirt, one of a dozen still folded in the top dresser drawer. I have just as much right to him as she does.

****

It's Saturday. I remember that much. And I'm at Jared's house. But he's dead now. I remember that too. It's my fault that he's dead. My curse.

I shouldn't be in this room. His room. Maggie wouldn't like it. She doesn't like me. But she's good at pretending.

I get up fast—too fast—and the room starts to spin.

When it stops, I'm somewhere else. Some place I don't remember. A long, dark hallway that seems to go on forever. And doors. So many doors. The only light comes from beneath them.

I try the first knob. It's warm in the palm of my hand. Like someone's just opened it. This is where I need to go. Now.

But it's locked.

*Don't panic.*

I walk to the next door, a little uneasy. It feels right too. This could be the place. The right place. That's what I think. Until I turn it.

Locked.

*Don't panic.* But . . .

There's someone following me. Don't ask me how I know. I just do. It's a feeling. A feeling I've had before. So I run.

Locked. Locked. Locked. They're all locked!

"Evie! In here, Evie! Please!" It's someone I know. It's my mother. It's Cassie. It's Jared. Someone who needs me. Someone whose life depends on it. On me.

The door won't budge—*I twist, I pull, I fight, I scream*—no matter what I do. And whoever's in there, whatever's happening to them, it's my fault. It's all my fault.

I crumple to the ground, sobbing. And time ticks by. The voice in the room goes quiet. The lights beneath the doors flicker off and on and off again.

**102**

There's a hand on my shoulder. It doesn't mean me any harm. It belongs to a boy…a man…a boy I've seen before. It holds a key. Butch Calder has the key. I remember that much.

****

When I open my eyes, Maggie stands over me, frowning the way she did just before we lost Jared—afraid, not mad like I expected.

"Are you alright?"

I nod. "I'm sorry. I had a really weird dream."

"You were breathing strangely," she says. "Panicked. I could hear you from the hallway."

"What time is it?" It could be two in the afternoon or the dead of morning. That's how I feel. Lost. Disoriented.

"It's just after five." Her frown deepens. "Saturday," she adds.

"I know. I know it's Saturday." My dream-self nags at me, mocking me from the boneyard of my brain where she's hiding out.

I follow Maggie downstairs in a fog, listening to her chatter over the drone of the four o'clock news. About yoga. And why I didn't call her. Or eat the quinoa salad she made especially for me.

"Isn't that near your office?" she asks, breaking the cadence of her prattle. She points to the television screen, mouth open. Sure enough, it's the scene from the morning. Crime-scene tape, body bag, and all. "My goodness. What is the world coming to? Do you really think it's safe for you—"

"Wait. I want to hear this."

A reporter delivers the update from behind the safety of a news desk. Still, she makes it sound harrowing.

**The Oakland Police Department has not released the name of the female found deceased early this morning and has not yet specified a cause of death, though foul play is suspected. Sources close to the investigation tell us she was underage. Authorities have asked for the public's**

**help in finding a person of interest who may have been the last to see the young girl alive. Detectives would like to speak to Oakland native Trey Waters, but emphasized he is not a suspect in a crime at this time. If you have any information…**

I make a small noise—part gulp, part whimper. It's the sound of my past, exhumed. Undead and staggering behind me, step for step. I'd never forgotten Trey—I only wish I could—but I'd shoved him into a cobwebbed corner of my mind like a box hidden in the attic. A box you'd just as soon incinerate.

"Anyone you know, dear?" Maggie asks, reaching for the remote. She doesn't wait for an answer. She's half-kidding in that insulting way she has. "But really, we should find you a new office. Rockridge, maybe? People need psychologists there too, you know."

I stare at the screen. They've put up a photo of Trey. It's a mug shot. The only kind of picture the Trey I'd known ever took. When I see him—the stringy brown hair, now threaded with gray; the pockmarked skin; the eyes, soulless as a tin can—I think of myself. Who I was then. Who I am now. And it's like no time has passed at all. Hate is like that. Love too, I suppose. And I can't look away while the fire of hell burns through me.

"Mind if I change the channel?" Maggie asks. And then he's gone—she's already flipping—and my heart cools like a dead star. "Dr. Phil is on."

## EVIE
## MAY 1, 1994
## TWELVE DAYS UNTIL MY BIRTHDAY

**TWO** days after I first laid eyes on Butch Calder, I became a woman. At least that's what Cassie called it when I told her that night. Me, I just considered it further evidence of my freakdom. None of the other Port girls my age had their periods yet. And worse, I was motherless. Not that she would've been much help anyway. Arlene Allcott was always too loaded to do mom things like fix a button on my sweater or practice multiplication tables. Still, it would've been nice to have a *real* woman to talk to or at least to save me the total humiliation of uttering those four words to Wally, the residential counselor on duty. Just my luck, Cherice had the night off.

"I got my period."

Wally was hunkered over the kitchen table, and I watched the thick folds of his neck turn red as a tomato skin. *How was I supposed to know he'd just bitten off a hunk of fried chicken?* He choked down a gulp of water, coughing and wiping the runoff from his chin.

"Are you okay?" I asked, my mortification complete.

"Uh...yeah. Think so." Two more coughs. And another swig and swallow. "Do you have the...uh...equipment that you need?

*If I did, I wouldn't be asking, moron.* That was the look I gave him.

"Alright. I think the girls keep some extra..." His voice was so low, I had to strain to hear him. "...pads in the hall closet. Do you

**105**

need help finding them?" *I'd rather poke out my eye with this greasy chicken bone.* That was the look he gave me back.

I shook my head, wishing I'd thought to check there first, and scurried into the bathroom with a flowery, pink package that resembled a tiny diaper. This was worse than I thought. When I emerged, hoping to make a break for my room (the one I shared with three other girls), Wally stood there. I waited for him to say something, do something. I'm not sure what I'd expected. An apology. A high five. A handshake. Just something. Some middle ground between a blank stare and what came out next. "So you know you can get pregnant now, right?"

I nearly fell over. Cassie warned me guys were stupid. "And the older they get, the dumber they seem," that's what she'd said. But this took it to a level I never expected. "I'm twelve, Wally."

"Don't worry, Mr. Wally." Bobby Pierce leaned against a doorway, grinning. And behind him, his little crew, Sarah and Cindy and Melissa, already giggling. *How much did they hear?* "Nobody will ever have sex with Evie. Heck, I don't think she could pay any boys to touch her."

Everything. They heard everything. "Get out of here, Bobby! You too, girls!" But I was the one who took off running. Straight out the front door. I didn't even bother to sneak out the window like I usually did. I ran until I stopped crying—a whole two blocks—because what good did crying ever do me? I couldn't blame Bobby for what he said. After all, I'd landed a solid elbow to his stomach last week.

And I didn't want to have sex anyway. Not now. Not ever. My mom thought I didn't know why she painted her lips blood red. Why she wore patent heels she could barely walk in and snuck out with Trey every time she needed a fix. But I'd seen *Pretty Woman.* The trouble was my mom was no Julia Roberts. She'd wasted away to nothing. Skin as gray as an oyster. Twig legs scabbed with needle sticks. If she hadn't died, I would've figured she had just disappeared. Like old bones that turned to dust. And there were no Richard Geres in Oakland. Only desperate, gross old men who paid my mom to touch them.

*So, take that, Bobby. It's usually the boys doing the paying.* Maybe I'd let one kiss me someday—maybe—but only if he looked like Butch Calder. And didn't stink like sweaty socks the way Bobby did. Even then, it seemed like a gamble.

Some nights when I snuck out, I'd shimmy down the drainpipe, jog to the mini mart, and buy a Slurpee—wild cherry—then get punch-drunk on its sugary sweetness. Other nights, I'd troll the aisles of Wal-Mart until closing time. It sounds silly, but I'd feel safe there. Happy even. With those bright, buzzing lights and the neat corner displays and the man with a beard like Santa Claus greeting all the customers.

But tonight, like most nights, I went through the underpass—the cold tomb beneath the freeway—fast-walking to the other side. I kept my eyes straight ahead, pretending the moving lump in a grimy sleeping bag at the edge of the shadows was just a stray dog keeping warm. I'd already made up my mind where I was headed, and I figured Cassie would be there. But I wasn't going for her. I'd been mulling it over since Trey slithered out of his hole and showed up at Port in a Storm, reminding me who he was. The things he was capable of. As if I'd forgotten.

He would never find it. I knew that. He couldn't even be sure I had it. But the way he'd asked—"Where is the goddamn money, Evelyn? And the ring?"—with his claws hooked in and his eyes drilling tunnels right through me, I couldn't take any chances.

**\*\*\*\***

Willow Court, at twilight, was a nightmare come to life. My mom and I had lived there once, before the whole place was condemned. Before it became sad and dark and abandoned with things you couldn't see skittering in the shadows. And boards on the windows that looked like mouths waiting to swallow you whole. It wasn't much better in the daytime.

"This is where I hang out," Cassie had announced the day I'd met her, almost two months ago when I'd first arrived at Port in a Storm.

**107**

She'd been sitting on the edge of the Willow Court pool—the one with no water—dangling her feet and smoking a cigarette. "What're you doing here, little girl?"

I'd sized her up. Older than me, but not by much. A little taller. And curvy enough to wear a bra. Homeless, maybe, judging by the dirt on her hands and blue jeans. And her attitude had runaway written all over it. "None of your business," I'd said, relieved I'd already hidden the money. Unless she'd seen me. *Had she?*

Her laugh was a proclamation. "I figured you'd say that. That's why I was watching you."

"Liar."

"Alright. If I'm a liar, then how do I know you stashed something in 136?" I'd rolled my eyes, relieved. Obviously, she'd thought I was an amateur. "Hope you hid it well, because…" She'd tapped her fingers to her thumb one by one. "…sticky fingers."

"How old are you?" I'd asked.

"Thirteen, but I'll be fourteen next month. My mom says I'm thirteen going on thirty."

"I can see why."

After stubbing out her cigarette on the broken concrete, she'd hopped down into the shallow end of the pool and pretended to swim to the other side and back, making a clumsy trail through the trash. "I'll take that as a compliment. And you?"

"Almost thirteen." I'd sat down and watched her, captivated. I didn't want to leave.

"Wow," she'd said, looking up at me from below. "Your eyes are fierce." *Fiercely freakish.* I'd waited for her to add something mean the way Bobby and his band of idiots would have. "Like Tyra Banks fierce." She'd grabbed a trash bag from the heap and ripped it open. "Wanna help me look for stuff to sell?"

I'd nodded and jumped in, making a soft landing on a stained sofa cushion. She'd had me at Tyra. Since then, we'd been thick as thieves. Or scavengers. That was more like it.

But I didn't see Cassie by the pool tonight, and it was getting late, so I headed straight for Apartment 136, sliding the graffitied plywood from the window and climbing inside the jaws of the beast. I had to stretch to step over the broken glass into the room someone once called home, the room where Cassie slept nights now. The only sign of life, the skeleton of a mouse I'd nicknamed Cheesy. And look how he'd ended up. In front of the hall closet with a toothpick cross I'd made, marking his gravesite.

So I didn't waste time there—136 was only a stop along the way, a trick to fool spying eyes. I slipped out the bathroom window into a small courtyard that was hidden from the street, the access gate grown up with weeds thick as a curtain.

In the middle of the lawn, an old swing set, the chains rusted and swaying a little as the breeze picked up. Their soft clanging reminded me of an old Christmas movie my mother loved, Jacob Marley dragging the weight of his past behind him. Cherice had let me rent it a few weeks ago, even though it was practically summer. I'd watched it alone while the rest of the house went swimming. I'll admit that I'd lain in bed that night, holding my breath, listening for the sound of my dead mother's footsteps on the stairs and the rattle of her chains. Surely, they'd look like needles, filled with my mother's tainted blood, sharp little points at their ends.

*I'm not a scaredy-cat.* I skirted the swing, trying not to look at it, afraid the tiny seed of fear would start to grow. The door to 201 was propped open, the way I found it the first time. The way I left it the last time. Still, I hesitated. It was so dark in there, and what little daylight was left wouldn't last much longer.

I could've turned back right then. Run home to the Port—the only home I knew—breathless with the thought of a shapeless monster at my heels. But the vent was so close, and I needed to touch it. Just once. To prove Trey wrong. To show him I could win. To take something away from him, the way he'd done to me.

Sideways, my body fit through the space between door and frame without touching, and I stood there for a heartbeat on the other side of the threshold, letting my eyes adjust. Once the kitchen counter took shape, I climbed up and dragged my fingers along the ceiling until I felt the slats of the heater. One hard tug and it snapped free, and I slipped my hand inside, feeling for the smooth surface of the envelope. The one my mom must've snagged from the front desk of the Blue Bird, the cheap motel where we'd lived for a while. The motel where she'd died.

"Hide it," she'd told me, shoving the envelope inside my backpack and pushing it against my chest. "Whatever happens, don't let that asshole take it from you." She hadn't specified. Didn't need to. There was only one asshole. "Do you hear me, Evelyn? Trey never touches this. Or you." It scared me to see her like that—stone-cold sober. Heroin softened her, dulled the edges until she was a slurring skeleton in the bed without a care in the world. But at least I could manage her. This wasn't my mother. She shook my shoulders so hard, I bit my cheek. "Evelyn. I need to hear you say it. Promise me."

"Trey never touches it, but—"

"Or you."

"Or me."

"Ever."

"I promise."

She'd laughed then, at herself. "God, baby, I'm sorry. I got carried away. Your mama needs a fix, doesn't she?" I'd almost sighed with relief. *That* was my mother.

I laid my palm against the thick envelope, still safe in the vent. Trey had never touched it. *At least I'd kept one promise,* I thought, rubbing my arm, achy from his grip. I wedged the vent closed and headed out the way I'd come. Past the swing set, through the bathroom window, and into 136, where I greeted Cheesy's remains.

*I'm not a scaredy-cat.* This time I believed it. Until the front door creaked opened, and I let out a scream that could've awakened the dead.

"Shh. It's me." Cassie sauntered in, a half-eaten ice cream cone in one hand, a twenty-dollar bill in the other. "Chill."

"Where did you get that?"

"I don't know. Some guy." She stepped toward me, nearly crunching Cheesy's bones under her sneaker. "He drove by asking about you. Said he'd seen you here before."

"What did he look like?" My heart thumped so hard in the curve of my neck, I wondered if Cassie could hear it. But she was too busy taking big bites from the melting chocolate scoop. She wiped her chin with the hem of her T-shirt before she answered.

"Like a grungy scarecrow."

"That's Trey. The one I told you about."

"The evil pimp?"

I nodded. Although that was the very least of what Trey was.

"He didn't seem so bad." Chomping the last of the cone, she tucked the twenty inside her bra. "He said I was pretty. Too pretty to be hanging out here. And he gave me his pager number. Said I could call him anytime."

"Seriously?" I rolled my eyes at her. "Did he buy you that ice cream?"

She shrugged. "It's no big deal. We just drove to the Mickey D's around the block."

I saw myself, two years ago, the first time I met Trey. He'd lingered in the doorway of our room at the Blue Bird, flashing me a sleazy smile while my mom had rattled on about him. "He wants to take us out to dinner, baby. At the Red Lobster. His treat."

"Cassie, that guy is trouble. Trust me. He's trying to butter you up. Like a Thanksgiving turkey. If you let him, he'll take a knife to you and gobble you up."

"Geez, Evie. That's gross. It was just an ice cream."

"For now." Two weeks post-lobster, my mom had started walking the streets for him. "C'mon, Arlene. Just this one time. For us." They'd thought I was asleep.

"He's got girls working this area. You think he's being nice—he's recruiting you, Cassie."

"You're such a worrywart. It was just—"

"I know. I know. It was just an ice cream. But be careful, okay?"

Cassie groaned the way Bobby did at school when the teacher asked him to go to the back of the line. "So, he wants the stuff you hid?" she asked.

"Did he say that?" I imagined Trey's ear pressed to the door, my father's knife in his hand. "That stuff belongs to me, Evelyn. You owe me." That's what he would've said.

"No." Cassie frowned at me. "You told me. He didn't even mention it. Just said he was worried about you and wanted to talk."

"What did you tell him?" I whispered.

"Nothin'."

"And he just left?"

"He said he'd be back."

"Crap." I made a beeline toward the door, heart scampering again. "I've gotta get out of here. Do you want to come back with me? To the Port? You'll be safe there." It wasn't the first time I'd asked, but it was the first time I needed her to say yes.

"Heck no. They'll make me stay. With all the other castoffs and misfits. No offense." She lowered herself to the floor and sat cross-legged. I could barely make her out in the dark, but she looked like a little girl. Not the badass I'd gotten used to. "Can't you hang out a little longer? He said he had to drive to Oakland to visit a friend, so…I'm sure he's got better things to do than pester you anyway."

"Just a few more minutes." Only because Trey had the patience of a two-year-old, and I figured he was long gone, busy marking all the other twisted errands off his list. I joined her on the floor, pulling my legs close to my chest. We sat there, not speaking, until the quiet itself stood my hair on end.

"I got my period today," I said, finally. "And apparently, I can get pregnant now, according to Mr. Wally."

Cassie's laughter came out in a whoosh—like letting go of a balloon before tying it—and once she got going, neither of us could stop. I laughed so hard my stomach cramped, and inexplicably, I started to cry.

"Welcome to the club," Cassie said, putting her arm around me.

"What club?" I blubbered.

"You're a hormonal mess. And a guy said stupid shit to you. Congratulations, Evie, you've become a woman."

****

You can't underestimate the devil. I saw my mistake right away. Careless and stupid—like forgetting to carry the one on the chalkboard in math class—but it was already too late. Trey pulled up alongside me, halfway back to Port in a Storm, and whistled to me out the window. Head down, I kept walking.

"Been lookin' for you." He tossed his lit cigarette in my direction, but it fell short, dying on the dewy sidewalk. "Hey, I'm talkin' to you, Evelyn."

I wanted to flip him off, to say every curse word I knew, to take my fingernails and make long, deep scratches on his ugly face. At the very least, to run as fast as a jackrabbit.

"You ain't gonna look at me? Didn't your mama teach you to respect your elders, little girl?"

I spotted the fluorescent glow of the gas station up ahead. Just beyond it—so close—the one place Trey couldn't touch me. It was the best thing about the Port. If only I could get there.

"I'm not givin' up, if that's what you're thinkin'. That money don't belong to you. The ring neither. And don't start gettin' any bright ideas about takin' off on me."

Dumb as he looked, Trey could be cunning as a fox. And he could smell fear. I was sure of it. "That ring belonged to my dad. Just like the pocketknife you took."

"Evie, one day you're gonna learn that dead folks don't have no claim to nothin'. And your daddy is deader than a doornail. 'Sides, your mama gave me that knife as a present." More than likely she had.

*And that stung.* "Your mama was an Indian giver. A thief. A liar. And a whore." Stung worse than any insult he could've hurled at her. "And now, she's dead too."

"That was *her* money. She earned it."

Trey's laugh came straight from the pit of hell. Part rasp. Part hyena. "By spreadin' her legs. Yeah, she earned it alright."

"She was saving it. For me." I only hoped it was true. She'd never said it out loud. And now that I had, I barely believed it.

"More likely she was savin' it to slam straight up her vein. You know your mama. She never could hold on to money. But think what you want if it makes you feel better. Either way, that money is rightfully mine, and I intend to collect it. The easy way or the hard way."

Trey swerved his car toward the sidewalk, a near miss, and I flinched. Then I cursed myself for giving too much away. I kept moving, faster now.

"I guess it's gonna be the hard way then. Your friend, the brunette. Cassie." He made her name sound like a dirty word. "She's older than you, ain't she? More womanly. I've been thinkin' she's the right age to be one of my girls. She can work off the money for ya. The ring too. Shouldn't be nothin' to it with a bangin' little body like hers—"

"Leave her alone. She's not interested."

"Is that what she told you? Because seems to me, she needs money real bad. She wants to find her daddy. And she ain't no thief like all you Allcotts."

"I told you I don't know where it is. Have you checked the room at the Blue Bird? That's the last place Mama was alive…" I stopped before I got too close to it. The thing Trey knew I had on him. Even though I couldn't prove it. The thing I kept locked up tighter than any treasure, because I could only use it once.

"Well, there's an idea. I'll just mosey on over and knock on the door. I'm sure whoever's renting that room will let me right in—hiya sir, I left five grand and a ring in here somewhere—and it'll be sittin' right where she left it."

"She had a few hiding places. I could tell you where to look." That laugh again. I would've rather made out with Bobby Pierce than listen to that soul-grating noise for one more second.

"Oh, you're gonna do better than that, Evelyn. You're gonna show me." I looked at him for the first time that night. His eyes were black as coal. "Get in."

# CHAPTER FIFTEEN

**MONDAY** morning, I put on my new collared shirt. The lady at the secondhand store had said the color made my eyes pop—whatever the hell that meant. Anyway, I bought it. Even though I promised myself I'd never wear prison blue again. I shave for the first time in two weeks. Heck, I even borrow some hair gel from the guy next door.

As promised, Evie had come through for me with the hookup, an 8:30 a.m. interview with her building supervisor, Gary Vinetti. And I'm not about to blow it. Plus, she'll be there, and as boneheaded as I am, I want to impress her. Because one day soon, she's gonna figure me out. And then she'll never want to see me again. But at least there's a chance she'll remember me this way. In my eye-popping shirt and pressed khakis. *He lied through his teeth, but he sure did clean up nice.*

"Mornin', Butch," Sebastian says, grinning at me from his seat at the breakfast table. To the right of his plate, it's that damn book again. "You look spiffy." We're the last two out the door today—with Mr. Richert standing by—but I've got too much on my mind to make small talk. So I reach for the *Tribune*, a handy excuse to be antisocial.

Richert clears his throat in a way that can only mean I better open my mouth and say something. "Thanks, man. Big day today. Another job interview."

With that taken care of, I proceed with the usual morning routine. Open the cabinet. Review my choices. Cornflakes, Raisin Bran, Rice Krispies, Cheerios...*Jesus! How can there be this many cereals?* Shut the cabinet, overwhelmed. Feel my heart start to flutter in my throat like I swallowed a damn parakeet. Look over my shoulder. *Phew.* Nobody's noticed. Gulp the lump down, and grab a banana for later.

Richert pats me on the shoulder. "Lucky number thirteen, huh?" The knot in my gut twists a little tighter. May 13, 1994. The day I killed a girl. *Her.* I put my eyes back on the *Tribune* to distract myself as Richert keeps talking. "Thirteen interviews. This is the one, Calder. I feel it."

I nod, but I can hardly focus. Not with thirteen spinning in my brain and Trey Waters' ugly mug on the front page of the newspaper, staring at me. **Police seek person of interest in murder of teen Jane Doe.** I'd nearly lost it when I saw his photo on the news Saturday night. Because sometimes you close the door to the past, and other times you nail a board over it. And I've hammered as many nails as I could find to keep Trey where he belonged. In. The. Past. That night, I'd had the dream again. Woke up with my sheets wound around my hand, like I'd been squeezing the life out of them.

"You okay, Calder?" Richert raises an eyebrow. "Wanna practice some interview questions?"

"Nah. I'm as ready as I'll ever be." I'm more nervous to see Evie. That she'll ask about Trey and what I remember.

"Well, you two can head over together then."

117

That snaps me back to reality faster than a toupee flies in a hurricane. "Together?"

Sebastian's already up—book in hand—and heading for the door. Like he's known all along. He holds it open for me. "Yeah, Butch. I thought I'd mentioned it. Your interview is in the same building as my therapy group. I told Mr. Richert we could walk over together. That maybe you could give me some pointers on the free world. One lifer to another."

"Group?" I could only manage one word at a time now, apparently.

"The group with Dr. Maddox. C'mon, I'll tell you about it on the way." But he doesn't. We take the whole ten-minute walk in silence.

****

Gary Vinetti takes a long swig of coffee from a mug that reads: *You don't have to be crazy to work here. We'll train you.* He chuckles when he catches me reading it. "It's true. Our training program is top-notch."

Encouraged by his toothy grin, I take my chances with a little prison humor. "With all due respect, sir, I've had about two decades of crazy training myself. I'd say I'm an expert."

"Touché, Mr. Calder. In all seriousness, your resume is pretty impressive. Considering." *Considering I'm a murderer. Considering I've spent the last twenty-three years mooching off the state.*

"Thank you, sir. I tried to make good use of my time. As you can see, I took a couple of vocational courses relevant to the position. Porter and building maintenance."

"Sure did. College too, right?"

"Yes, sir."

"And you don't feel you're overqualified? This is a custodial position. Sweeping the floors, taking out the trash, fixing what's broken—"

"I need a job, sir. Any job is a good one. I want to support myself again. To be a productive member of society."

118

"You know, you don't have to call me *sir*. We're informal here. Gary will do."

"Yes, sir. I mean, Gary. Thank you."

Gary leans back in his chair and considers me. Like he's trying to solve a riddle. "So, what did you do to wind up in prison, if you don't mind my asking? Twenty-three years is a long time."

Here we go again. "Well, sir. Gary. There's no easy way to say this. I was a different person back then, and I—"

"On second thought, I don't want to know. If Dr. Maddox trusts you, that's good enough for me. In her line of work, I figure she's got to be a pretty good judge of character."

That's a dagger right to the heart. "I'd say she knows me about as well as anyone." Which is to say, not at all.

"Great. Can you start today?"

\*\*\*\*

In fifteen minutes, it's official. I'm hired and in uniform. It's not blue, which I consider the first perk of my first job on parole. Not counting proximity to Evie, of course. Because I can't tell yet if cleaning her floors and emptying her trash cans every day is a blessing or a curse. All I know is every time I see her, it's like taking a long, hard look in the mirror. And after a boatload of psych evals and a whole lotta self-help mumbo jumbo, you'd think I'd be an expert in self-examination. That I'd recount every scar, bruise, and defect—all my sins—with no shame. But it doesn't get any easier. It's not supposed to. A parole commissioner told me that once, just before she'd laid down a five-year denial. *Talking about what you did should never be easy, Mr. Calder. Remember that.* Still do. Every single day.

"Did ya hear what happened over the weekend?" Gary asks as I jot my details onto an application form. Just a formality, apparently, because we've already shaken on it. And Gary has the handshake of man who doesn't go back on his word. "Some sicko…" He catches himself. To him, I've got something in common with said sicko. It hurts how right he is. And how wrong. "Well, anyway, some of the tenants are a little on edge, as you can imagine. Could you do a check of the exterior lights? I want to make sure they're all in working order."

"Sure thing."

He pats me on the back and leaves me alone in a room full of wrenches, hammers, and screwdrivers. That's a treasure trove of weapons in the joint, and I stand there for a second, waiting for him to change his mind. To tell me I'm out of bounds. That I don't belong there. But we're in the free world now, where men don't spend hours whittling a toothbrush to a point, so sharp it could cut through a steak. Here, tools are just tools.

Still, I can't shake that sticky feeling I'm doing something wrong, so I hurry. I pull on the khaki jumpsuit I've been issued, grab a toolbox, and step into the hallway—as uncertain and enthusiastic as a kindergartener—with the first assignment of my first job on parole. And I nearly smack heads with Evie. She goes left. I go right. She goes right. I go left. *C'mon, Butchy, you clumsy ox.* I stand still as a board, my face burning. And we both laugh.

"Sorry, Evie. Or should I call you Dr. Maddox? What're you—uh—are you looking for Mr. Vinetti? I mean, Gary." Smooth. Really smooth.

"Actually, I wanted to say hi. And congratulations. Gary just told me he'd offered you the job." She smiles at me, and I let out the breath I've been holding. "*Evie* is fine, by the way."

"Well, Evie, I owe you big time." I run a nervous hand along the front of my uniform, smoothing imaginary wrinkles. "But I've gotta say, it feels a little weird to have a real job. In the real world. Not that prison isn't the real world. It's as real as it gets, but…" *Shut up already.* "I guess I'm just starting to feel human again. Sane. Or at least I think so. I guess you'd be the one to ask." *Seriously, Calder. Stop talking.* "I'm gonna stop talking now."

She laughs again, but not at me. Her eyes are too kind for that. "Were you always this talkative?"

"Definitely not. Come to think of it, I might've just broken my own record for the most words I've strung together at one time. Maybe it's a shrink thing." *Or an Evie thing*, I think to myself, remembering the second time I saw her. Way back when. Caught in Trey's clutches in the parking lot of the Blue Bird. "I better get to work before I start spilling all my secrets. Gary's got me checking the lights…with what happened the other day."

"Good idea. I've been complaining about the broken street lamps for years." But her thoughts are somewhere else. I can tell by that faraway look she's got. It's the look of a lifer like me. The look of somebody tethered to the past. The kind of rope that chokes every move you make. "I assume you've seen the news."

At first, I'm not sure how to answer, but her hard swallow gives it away. And I don't hold back. "I probably shouldn't be saying this, but I sort of hoped that guy was dead. I mean, I've met a lot of lowlifes in my day. But Trey Waters was probably the lowest. The way he bullied you—"

"Not here," she says, backing away so fast you'd think I took a swing at her. "I can't talk about it here. Not now."

"I didn't mean to upset you." I raise my hands in surrender. "I shouldn't have said anything."

"No, it's not your fault. I shouldn't have brought it up." She puts her palm on my forearm—for a moment—and I don't pull away like I've been bitten by a snake, not the way I did with Chicken and Waffles' Brenda. "I should probably head over to my office. Group starts in a few minutes, and I can't be late."

"Sure. I've gotta go too. Last thing I need is Gary catching me slacking on my first day."

I wait until she's gone. I watch her raven hair disappear around the corner before I look at my arm. The spot where she touched me. Then and now. Touch has a memory, I think. Because even though her hands are different, a woman's hands, the intention is the same. Like she's giving me the sort of comfort I need but sure as hell don't deserve. And it feels like absolution.

## BUTCH
## MAY 2, 1994
## ELEVEN DAYS BEFORE I KILLED HER

**TURNS** out, drunk girls are not easy. Drunk girls—Gwen, anyway—are just drunk. And they puke. A lot. After we'd downed most of the Hennessy she'd swiped from the mini mart, she upchucked twice in the bushes and fell asleep in the front seat of the 'Cuda before I drove her home. I'd parked outside the gate and watched her stumble inside the back door of the Shaw family mansion. Then, I'd hightailed it outta there, expecting her dad to come storming out with a shotgun, but the house stayed dark, and I'd lived to fight another day.

By the time I got back home, it was after midnight. I parked the car, straddling the two spots facing my room, taking no chances with my baby. A blind man could park better than most guests at the Blue Bird, and the last thing I needed was a door ding. When I went inside, the phone's red message light blinked at me like an accusation, and I knew what it meant. Simon Merriwether: Coffin-chaser, shyster, attorney-at-law. Since I'd dropped most of the blood money on the 'Cuda, he'd been hounding me.

I kept the phone a good six inches from my ear—that guy's voice was nails on a chalkboard—but I could still hear him droning. *Irresponsible, foolish, impulsive.* Me apparently, in a nutshell. Couldn't argue with him there. I hung up, my buzz long gone, and flipped on the TV to drown out Wade and Peggy going at it like cats and dogs. Right on schedule.

"I saw you starin' at him, Peg. Don't try to deny it."

"I wasn't. I promise, babe. I've only got eyes for you and you know it."

"Are you callin' me a liar?" Without two pennies to rub together—and the motel rooms were sparse—Wade always found something to throw. Where there's a will, there's a way, I guess. Whatever it was, clock radio, ice bucket, leather Bible, or Peggy herself, thudded against the wall.

I cranked up VH1 and closed my eyes. Drunk girls talk a lot too. And Gwen had spilled a secret I kept replaying. A secret louder than Wade and Peggy. It ached in my stomach, pounded in my ears. "I need to tell you something, Calderrrrrr," she'd said, slurring the end of my name into a sexy growl. "I did something really bad. I'm a bad girl." She'd put her head in my lap, post-vomit. Pathetic, but I still got turned on.

"I doubt that, Gwen. What did you do?"

"I'm not a volunteer at that kids' home. I have to be there. Cause the judge said so."

"The judge?"

She'd sighed. "Yeah. I'm a common criminal. I stole some stuff from the drug store. And Russ says I'm a klepto. His parents hate me. They think I'm a bad influence."

"Who's Russ?" I'd asked.

She'd gazed up at me with those baby blues, and I'd had to steel myself. "I lied to you, Calder. Are you mad?" *How could I be?* I had no right. And yet, there I was, a hypocrite hiding sparks of hellfire in my chest. Because if I'd been caught shoplifting—which I had, of course—they'd have carted my ass off to juvie and left me there for a while. Because Butch Calder never met a judge who knew the words *community service*. Because I only stole things when I was poor, things I needed. Because—who the hell was Russ?

"Who's Russ?" I'd asked again.

"A doofus. A big, ugly doofus." Her eyes had glistened when she'd said it. Like she'd been about to cry. "I think I'm gonna be sick again."

The slam of a door brought me back to the Blue Bird. Wade, probably. Gone off to drown his sorrows in the bar down the street. He'd sulk back in a few hours, sleep it off in his truck, and wait for Peggy to wake up so they could start all over again. Sure enough, I could hear her wailing through the wall. Just another day on the crazy train.

I propped two flat-as-a-pancake pillows behind me and leaned back against the headboard, trying to think of one good thing. It was a game my mom played with me when I'd had a rough day at school. And then, it was a game I played with myself, mostly in juvie, when the best things I could come up with were pizza in the chow hall and my counselor's boobs busting out of her too-tight uniform.

One purely good thing. One. Just one.

Gwen was a good thing. But also not, because I wasn't Butch Calder of the Filthy-Rich Calders like she thought. And mostly, because of Russ—whoever he was. With an uppity name like that, he must be loaded. I already hated him.

The 'Cuda was definitely a good thing. But also not, because Merriwether wasn't wrong. I'd pissed away half the money that my family died for. Even though I did look damn good in it.

The Blue Bird was a good thing, a roof over my head, but also not. Peggy punctuated that one with a sob, desperate and whiny and—

Cut mercifully short by a sharp rap at her door. At least it sounded like her door. But it couldn't be. Wade was too stubborn to come crawling back that soon. I muted the TV and pressed my head to the wall.

The knocking came again, louder this time. "Hello? Is anybody home?" A girl's voice. Definitely not Wade. "Please open up. I need help."

Peggy didn't answer. She was as quiet as I'd ever heard her. I hopped off the bed and put one eye to the peephole. *Holy crap!* I jumped back. Stunned. I thought I might be dreaming. Or worse, hallucinating. Maybe this was what happened when you drank way too much cognac. Stolen cognac, at that.

But then, I looked again, and I knew I wasn't dreaming. From this angle, I couldn't see Wade and Peggy's door, but it didn't matter. He was real and lounging against the hood of my 'Cuda like he owned it.

All these years later, I can feel the cool knob in my hand as I opened the door. And I still wish I hadn't.

****

"Well, hell, if it ain't Nobody. You live here, man?" Trey flicked the ashes of his cigarette, and they tumbled like dirty snow onto the hood of my car. I gritted my teeth. "Figures Nobody would live in a dump like this. Ain't that right, Evelyn?"

If Evie was surprised to see me, she didn't show it. She just stood there, eyes darting between me and Trey and Peggy's unopened door. Looking like somebody about to make a run for it.

"Get off my car, Trey."

"Trey? You think you know me? Funny, I don't remember ever tellin' you my name. Or givin' you permission to use it." He stalked toward Evie and grabbed her wrist, circling it like a noose with his long fingers. "You didn't tell Nobody my name did you?" She shook her head and tried to pull away, but he just squeezed tighter. "Good. Cause that would've been real stupid. Even for you."

"Listen, man, I don't want any trouble. Wade and Peggy aren't home right now, so you should probably scram before the front desk clerk calls the police."

He let Evie go and pushed her away from him. Then he took one step and another toward me till I could smell him—nicotine and sweat and pure meanness. "Thanks for the advice, Nobody. But I don't give a fuck about Wade or Peggy or the goddamn clerk. Something that belongs to me is in that room, and I need it back real bad."

"What does she have to do with it?" I nodded my head at Evie. "Doesn't she have school tomorrow?"

**125**

"Today actually," she said. The corner of her mouth twisted into a smirk so faint if you blinked you might miss it. "It's one in the morning."

Trey flinched in her direction, and she sucked in a breath, silenced without a word. Then, "Damn, Nobody. You're a regular boy scout, ain't ya?"

"She's a kid, dude."

"What's it to you anyway? You got a thing for kiddies? I can help you out, you know. She's got a little friend, Cassie, I can hook you up with. Or maybe Evie here will give it up for free if you ask real nice." Her ears went beet red, the color spreading like fire across her cheeks. "Seems like she's taken a real likin' to you."

"You're sick."

Trey shrugged like I'd offered him a compliment. "I like to think of myself as a businessman."

"You mean a pimp?"

"More like a salesman. I can sell you whatever you want if the price is right. Or we can settle this the hard way." He held up the edge of his T-shirt, showing me the knife case in his pocket. "And I seem to recall you already used your free pass."

"How much to leave her alone?"

Trey guffawed, slapping his knees so hard I thought his skinny legs might snap in two. And Evie, she just shook her head at me—fast—like I'd made a deal with the devil.

"It's okay, Calder," she said. "I'm okay. Just go back in your room."

"Evelyn, Evelyn, Evelyn. It seems you've made quite the impression on Nobody. Or Calder, is it? I'll leave her alone, buddy. For the keys to *this*." He ran his stained fingernails across the side of the 'Cuda.

Me and my freakin' big mouth. *How're you gonna talk your way out of this one, Butch?* "That thing. It's not mine. I mean, I wish it was. But I was just bluffing. I can give you cash though."

"You can have my ride, if that's what you're worried about." I grimaced at the purple Buick Grand National idling in the spot next to mine. An eggplant on wheels, he'd probably spent his last nickel on that custom paint job.

"No offense, but your car is a hooptie."

Evie giggled, and Trey didn't like it. I heard him hiss something at her under his breath. He reached in his pocket, pulled out the knife, and opened it. "Better yet, how 'bout you give me the keys and the cash, and I keep Evie? You see, she took something from me, and that ain't right. Kids these days, ya know? No manners."

"I told you. It's not my car."

"Well, then I guess you won't care if I do this." He poised the tip of the blade on the driver's side door, and I felt dizzy. The Hennessy burned my throat on its way back up.

"Don't do that, man. Please."

Evie reached for his arm, but he batted it away. "Stop, Trey. You're being a jerk."

He grinned as he dragged the knife, slicing an inch-long wound on the door of my baby. I died a little inside, half-expecting her to bleed red from the gash on her smooth black paint.

"Here," I said, scrambling through my wallet to produce a wad of cash. "Take this." The money disappeared inside his bony fist, but he kept his blade on the 'Cuda. And I saw how it would go from here. I'd rush him like a pissed-off rhino, taking his legs out from under him, but somehow he'd get the upper hand—Trey didn't strike me as the kind of guy who took his licks lying down—and once he did, it would be lights out. Game over. A knife to the gut. He'd sooner stab his own mother than lose a fight. But I couldn't punk out now. I already looked soft, coughing up my money like that, begging him. "Touch my car again, and I'll make you wish you were never born."

"I'll touch whatever I damn well please. And I'd like to see you try."

We squared off. *I hope my life doesn't end like this, shanked in the Blue Bird parking lot by this lowlife.* That was all I could think, when the door to Wade and Peggy's flew open. Peggy stood in the threshold in her nightgown—a modern-day Annie Oakley—pointing a pistol right at Trey's chest. "Get the hell out of here, Waters! Don't make me use this thing."

"C'mon, Peg. I thought we were friends."

"Ha! I'd sooner be friends with a crocodile. Now I told you last time to stop coming around here making trouble for these young girls. You're not welcome. Haven't you put Evelyn through enough?"

Trey grabbed at Evie, pulling her under his arm, the knife blade dangerously close to her cheek. "This girl. *This girl.* You know I practically raised her. Took care of her and her mama. And she said her mama might've hidden somethin' of mine in there. You remember how sneaky Arlene could be. Didn't she steal somethin' of yours one time? Just let us take a look. A quick one. Then we'll get outta here and leave you fine folks to your—"

Trey never saw it coming. Wade clocked him from behind with a half-full bottle of cheap wine, and he hit the deck hard, Boone's Farm and blood running down his forehead. The knife skittered on the pavement and underneath his Buick. "That'll teach you to run your mouth to my old lady."

"You tell him, honey." Peggy's chest puffed up, proud as a peacock, and she winked at him. Wade was definitely getting laid tonight. So that made one of us.

Trey groaned and rolled to one side, clutching at his head. His fist opened like a flower. "I think that belongs to you," Peggy said, pointing at the cash on the concrete.

Old Butch would've let it go—just watched Trey slink away with my blood money, knowing that I'd won—but Young Butch had already lost so much. He had to make somebody pay. So I loomed over him and snatched up my money. Pressed my boot to his hand. Stomped down with all my might till I felt his bones crack like eggshells. Till he writhed and squealed like a stuck pig.

I'm embarrassed to tell you how good it felt. Better than kissing Gwen. Better than walking out of juvie. Better, even, than flying down the highway in the 'Cuda. How it warmed something cold inside me. How once I started, I didn't want to stop. How I probably wouldn't have if I hadn't spotted Evie and her watchful green eyes.

Still, I had to get the last word. "I would've given you a free pass, Trey. But then I remembered you're a scumbag loser. Now get the hell out of here."

Trey crawled back to the Buick and fished underneath till he found his knife. He cradled it in one hand, the other limp as a dead fish. "Get in, Evelyn."

"She's not going anywhere with you," Peggy said. "And if I catch you at my door again, I'll shoot first. Got it?"

After Trey backed out, tires crunching over the broken glass, he rolled down his window and pointed to me with his good hand. "You're dead, Nobody. Next time I see you, you're dead." And in a way, he was right.

****

Evie rubbed her goosebumps and shivered. "Are you sure you want the top down?" I asked. "It's gonna be a while before I get you back to Port in a Storm."

"I told you. I've never been inside a convertible. It's like flying, Calder."

I laughed for the first time since I'd watched Trey burn rubber in the Blue Bird parking lot, giving us the bird before he'd made the turn to the street. "He should be happy he can still move his finger," Evie had said, and I'd chuckled along with Wade and Peggy, trying to shake off Trey's threat. "You're dead." No one ever said those words to me before. Not even the baddest badass in juvie.

"I guess it is like flying. I hadn't thought of it that way. Maybe that's why I like it." I sped up a little and did my best Frank Sinatra. "Come fly with me. Come fly away." And Evie shrieked with delight. I turned my eyes from the road to watch her for a second, wishing I could feel that free. "Is Trey your stepdad or something?"

"God no. What made you think that?"

"Just that he said he raised you. I wasn't sure what he meant by that."

"Trey says a lot of things. And none of them are true. My real dad got shot in a drug deal. He was in a coma for a while. Or at least that's what my mom said. He died when I was five."

"My dad died too." The words tumbled out before I could put on the brakes. Before I realized I didn't want to stop them. It felt good to say it out loud. Finally. Not to some bleeding heart who got paid to feel sorry for me. To someone who understood. "My whole family actually. Truck driver on speed crossed the center line." I kept my eyes on the little stretch of blacktop lit up in the headlights' glow and said the one thing I'd never told anybody. "I was supposed to go with them that day. Sometimes, I wonder what would have happened if I had. Like maybe it was my fault."

"I know what you mean. I was there when my mom died, and that's even worse."

"It wasn't your fault though." I said. "Just like it wasn't mine."

She touched my arm, and her hand felt cold as ice, but it warmed me somehow. "We're both orphans then," she said. Like it was a badge of honor. And I guess, in some ways, it was.

"So, how do you know Trey?" I asked.

"He used to stay with us sometimes—me and my mom—at the Blue Bird. In the room that's Peggy's now. He mooched drugs off my mom. And then, when she couldn't afford them anymore, he... you know...found other ways for her to make money. Before long, she was just another one of the girls on his roster. He thinks I stole something from him, but it was never his to begin with."

"What did he mean about you and your friend? He hasn't tried to get you to—"

"He's all talk. Seriously." But I didn't fall for it. Not for one second. Because I could tell she was afraid of him. When she talked, she wound a strand of her hair around and around and around her finger. Tight, like she was about to pull it right out of her head. "He swore to my mom he'd never touch me. Not *that* way."

"Well, he sounds worse than I thought. And I already thought he was a piece of—never mind."

"Excrement?" Her hair fell loose again, and she giggled. "We learned that word in science last week. Did you know animal poop is part of the Earth's nutrient cycle?"

"I can't say I ever thought about it. But it makes sense. I guess Trey will serve some purpose after all."

"You're funny, Calder." For somebody who'd been through as much as Evie, she sure laughed a lot. I wished I could be like that. "Is Gwen your girlfriend? She's really pretty."

"She is pretty. That's for sure. She's not my girlfriend, though. I'm not sure she ever will be."

"Why?"

I didn't even think to lie. "I kind of let her believe my family was rich. She just assumed, because of the car and all. But I got the money from the trucking company, and it's already half gone. You know how sometimes you tell a story for so long it's too late to tell the truth?"

Evie *tsked, tsked* at me, wagging her finger, the way my mother would have. "It's never too late to tell the truth. Besides, I think she likes you. Why wouldn't she?"

"Are you sure you're only twelve? Because I think I'm talking too much."

"It's okay. I don't mind. Cherice says I'm a good listener."

"You are. You turned me into a Chatty Cathy, and that's a damn miracle. Ask my social workers. All eight of them."

She shook her head at me, chuckling. "If I'm good at listening, it's only because I don't have to talk about myself. It's a lot easier to let other people tell me their problems. Besides, sometimes I feel like nobody cares anyway. About me. About what I have to say. You know?"

That was the truest thing I'd ever heard. And the saddest. "I care, Evie. I'll be your friend. As long as you promise not to tell anybody I can't sing worth excrement."

"Deal."

Back then, a promise didn't mean much. I'd promised Mr. Whitecotton I'd do my homework. I'd promised Jackie? Jill? Julie? I wouldn't tell anybody that she'd let me get to third base. I'd stood over my mother's coffin and promised I'd make her proud.

And that promise I made to Evie? I broke it. Of course I did. With friends like me, who needs enemies?

# CHAPTER SIXTEEN

**EVIE**
**JANUARY 16, 2017**
**MONDAY**

**THEY** don't teach this kind of thing in grad school. There's no *How to Lead a Sex Offender Treatment Group across the Street from the Scene of a Sexual Murder* course. With the guys giving me their hangdog faces and the gash on my arm throbbing like a steady drumbeat, I feel like a total amateur. Even if the police haven't come out and said the words *sexual murder* yet.

I know Trey's involved, so I'm sure of it. And if Trey had something to do with Jane Doe, then…*I can't do this now. Focus, Evie. Focus.*

Maggie had done her best to convince me to play hooky. "You need a mental health day. Your patients will be fine without you," she'd said this morning, cajoling me with promises of yoga and a movie. But she didn't get it. It was me I was worried about, and slowing down had never done me any good. I'd learned long ago that when you slow down, your problems catch up. And they hit you smack in the face like a Mack truck. Not to mention I rarely get sick. If I called in—today, of all days—the guys would be suspicious. They'd start asking questions.

Resigned to the day ahead, I turn my chair from the window so I can't see the hanging tree. *Better.* Its long, spindly branches look even more ominous than usual against the gauzy sky, its soft blue an unexpected color in the middle of winter. And there's been a steady stream of reporters all morning. The last van pulls away, leaving a puff of exhaust and a few discarded coffee cups.

*One hour*, I tell myself. I can leave the past outside for just one hour. And then, I need to find Butch. I have to talk to him. Again. Since I chickened out the first time. Problem is I'm not even sure what I want to ask him. *Just one hour, Evie.*

"Alright, gentlemen. We're going to pick up where we left off last week. Healthy intimacy. Did everyone get a chance to do the homework?"

The rustling of paper is a familiar comfort, and I sit back in my chair, allowing myself a deep breath. *I'll get through this after all.* But then, Vince puts his hand in the air like a petulant child. I want to pretend I don't see him, because I know where he's headed. And it's nowhere I want to go. "Do you have a question?" I ask, seeing no other option.

"Uh, yeah. I do. This is a process group, right? Well, I've got some shit I need to process. Are we seriously going to pretend there wasn't a homicide right there? This weekend? Of a teenage girl?" He points out the window, like he's accusing me of something, and I can't help but look. The tree is the same as it ever was. Unmarked by recent events. Unscarred by the past. Unmoved by Vince's tirade. I wish I could be so stoic.

"It sounds like you have strong feelings about it. Would you like to share with the group?"

"I'm freaked the fuck out. That's how I feel. C'mon, guys. Back me up here. Anytime something like this goes down, who's the first one to get the blame? Who's the first one they stick it to? The sex offender, that's who. How long do you think it'll be before the police want to talk to us? To *you?*" He launches the word from his mouth like a poison dart aimed right at the heart of me. "You know nothing we say in here is confidential. I'd be surprised if they weren't listening outside this room right now."

"Hey, that sounds like one of those whatchamacallits…" George scrunches his face, thinking hard. "Cognitive…cognitive…cognitive distortions!" He turns to me, desperate for approval, and I nod.

"Can you explain what you mean by that, George?"

He beams. "Well, Vince is just working himself up over nothing. As long as he didn't do nothin' wrong, there's no reason to freak."

"Bullshit." Vince glares at George. "That's easy for you to say. You don't have a probation officer riding your ass. You're here vo-lun-tarily." More poison darts, spit at George this time. "Besides, you prefer 'em younger, don't you? Bet if that had been a little girl's body out there, you'd be pissing your pants right now."

"Vince. Respectful language, please." I should stop this right now. Put an end to it. Before the group veers completely off the rails. I should ask them about their homework. Redirect them. But I don't. Because Sebastian looks distracted. He's got a death grip on the book in his hands, and I follow his eyes to the tree and back. To the tree and back.

"What I meant to say is that George might not understand how the rest of us feel because his preferred choice of victim is a goddamned kindergartener. Is that better, Doc?"

"It sounds like you're feeling blamed already," I say. "And misunderstood. But don't take it out on—"

"Hell yes, I am. Tony gets it." Vince nudges Antonio with his elbow. "Tell me you get it. You get it, don't ya, Tony?"

But Tony is a statue, per usual. He doesn't agree. He doesn't disagree. He doesn't speak at all. And somehow that's more unnerving than Vince's outburst.

"Tony?" I try to encourage him. "Do you want to share your feelings with the group?"

He shrugs, barely looking up. "Man, I just want to do my six months of treatment and get out of here."

"But do you have any thoughts about—"

Sebastian clears his throat. Like he's shaken off his nerves—an old dog shedding fleas—just for this moment. He talks over me. "I thought you didn't have any victims, Vince. That you were innocent..."

"Who hit your buzzer, New Guy? Out of all of us, I'd say you have the most to be worried about. And technically, I don't have any victims. I had teen porn on my computer. What guy doesn't? I didn't make it myself."

"But someone did. Someone made it," George says. "You paid to download it. I'd say that's just as bad as holding the camera yourself. And none of us have anything to worry about as long as we keep our noses clean. Right, Dr. Evie?"

Vince shifts in his chair, tightening his fists. I wonder if I've lost control. I can see the headline: *Sex offender group ends in brawl.* But I let them go, too tired to care. That's what happens when you get one hour of sleep. In the childhood bed of your dead husband. And you have the dream again. The locked doors, the panic. Butch.

"Well, I'm not worried," Sebastian says, holding up his pants leg. "If my PO wants to know where I was Friday night, this will tell him."

"Pshh." Vince leans back in his seat, exasperated. "You're not fooling anybody, dude. We all know there's ways to get around that thing. Like tinfoil and jammers and—"

"Not everybody breaks the rules like you."

"I don't break the rules. I make the rules."

I hold up my hand, finally spurred to action by the white heat in Sebastian's eyes. The blatant arrogance in Vince's. "That's enough, guys. We're moving on now."

George waves the worksheet I handed out last week when life was still in proximity to normal. The page is covered in blue ink and his block print. It's almost childlike. "Time for homework," he says.

**** 

The men file out, silent. Even Vince. "Sebastian, can I talk to you for a sec?" I ask, before he reaches the door.

"Sure." He keeps his eyes on that book. His hands too. Like it holds him together somehow. The cover is worn at the edges, the spine cracked, and the green color faded. He secures it with one arm against his chest. He looks diminished, hardly the guy who took Vince head on.

"This is for you," I say, handing him a blank urge card. "It's for you to fill out and use anytime things get difficult. And I'd like to schedule some time to talk one-on-one."

"Oh. Okay. Is that because…" He gestures to the homework on my lap—*What I Learned about Intimacy (Healthy or Unhealthy) from My Family.* The one he'd read aloud. The ink so dark on the page, his pen strokes seem violent.

*Shame. Secrets. Hate. Sex. Rage. These are the things that go together in my family. Not that any of them would ever admit it. As far as they're concerned, I'm the devil's spawn. They don't even claim me. So there is no such thing as healthy intimacy. Never will be. Not for me. They made sure of that.*

I glance up, not wanting him to catch me reading it. "No. It's something I do with every new patient. I'd like to get to know you better. But, what you shared today…well, I'm sure it's something we can discuss more in our session if you'd like."

"I don't want to. But I know I need to. Does that make sense?"

"Perfect sense. Talking about the past can be painful. But keeping it inside, that's even worse." And don't I know it. "Does Wednesday morning work for you? After group?"

"I'll have to check my schedule." He makes a show of pretending his well-worn copy of *Lord of the Flies* is a day planner. "Yep. Booked solid." Waiting for my reaction, he twitters. "Just kidding. That works for me."

"Good. And don't let Vince get to you. He can be a bit of a bully."

Sebastian meets my eyes. "Yeah. I can't stand bullies. Reminds me of my stepdad. I'm sorry if I got a little heated."

I wave off his apology—Vince can push anybody's buttons—but Sebastian pauses at the door. "What happened to your arm, Doc?"

I don't look at it—the angry mark Danny left behind. It's hidden anyway under a gauzy white bandage that must've peeked out from under the sleeve of my blazer. I tug it down and stare straight ahead. "Cat scratch."

"Ouch." He blinks a few times. Three to be exact. I count them in my head. *Liar. Liar. Liar.* And then, he's gone, leaving me alone to wonder if he'd believed me. And why I felt certain he hadn't.

I turn my chair to face the hanging tree and sit down. A little girl appears in a bright blue dress and tiny black rain boots. She skips along the sidewalk, carefree and so alive, and the tree watches. As if nothing has changed. As if it hadn't borne witness to death. Twice now. At least.

"Dr. Maddox?" The voice startles me, even though I know it by now.

"Sebastian? Did you forget something?"

He cracks the door and peers in at me. "Uh, no. I found this outside." He passes me an envelope. Once white, it's dirtied with mud and folded and folded and folded again. Like it's traveled a long way in someone's pocket or bra or shoe. "It was under your mat. Not that I was looking or anything. I tripped and the corner turned up and there it was. It's got your name on it." Sure enough, printed on the outside: For Evelyn Maddox. I regard it like I do the tree. With complete suspicion.

"Thanks. I'll take a look."

I count to thirty to be sure he's gone. Then I slice open the corner with the engraved letter opener Jared bought me when I'd rented this office. The paper inside is pulled from a cheap motel notepad, a single line of text written in the center.

*I need to talk to you about Cassie. Meet me at Willow Court. Monday, 9 p.m.*

I'm not sure how long I stand there, gaping at it. But when I look up again and out, the little girl runs toward the tree, laughing. She looks over her shoulder, toward the window, and my heart stills. Her brown pigtails, her sassy grin. She could be Cassie's daughter or Cassie herself years ago, before I knew her. Before life ended her up here, the place where she'd disappear as cleanly as if she'd slipped through a seam in the fabric of the universe.

I toss the letter on my desk and move toward the window, panicked now. Because the little girl has disappeared. And it's silly—crazy, really—but I don't trust the tree. Or myself.

Where is she? *Gone like Cassie*, I think. *Gone. Gone forever.* My forehead bumps the cool glass. That's how close I am, how close I need to be. *I have to find her.*

I race out the door, not bothering to lock it behind me. I want to run, but I settle for a fast walk in case someone sees. Crazy hitchhiking shrink. But I'm not crazy. Because somebody knows about that night, somebody knows about Cassie. Somebody knows what I can't remember.

"Evie? Where are…" Before he can finish asking, I brush past Calder who's tinkering with a light at the end of the hallway, then I speed down the stairs to the parking lot, where I can see the tree and everything around it. I need to see it. Now.

My breath is coming way too fast, and I worry I might fall down. Like I'm spinning in circles on a giant merry-go-round and barely holding on.

But there! There she is. The girl appears again at her mother's side. And she's grinning. I try not to stare, but from here it looks like she's smiling right at me. Like she knows my secrets. Even the ones I can't remember. Then, she raises her tiny hand and waves.

****

"Are you alright?" Calder peers down at me from the second-floor railing, and for a second I'm not sure if I am. *Or who I am.*

"I'm fine," I call up to him. I make my feet move back toward the building, pretending I don't need to catch my breath. *Why does everyone keep asking me if I'm alright?* Because you're running around chasing a ghost. That's why.

"Do you know them?" He points out toward the tree, the little girl and her mother a block away, almost vanished.

I shrug, already halfway up the steps. "Uh, no. I—I don't think so. *Maybe.*"

"Oh. You were moving so fast I thought you saw...well..."

"Saw what?" I climb the stairs carefully, focusing on each one. A step at a time, Evie. Slow and steady. "Who?"

"That guy. From the other night."

*Danny.* The merry-go-round starts up again, and I freeze on the top step, bracing myself. I hadn't even considered he might find me here. "Why? Did you? Did you see something?"

Calder's eyes widen—I must sound crazy—so I suck in a gulp of air and attempt to act a little less like a lunatic. "He has my license, you know."

He nods and opens his mouth to speak. Then, shuts it again. I know how he feels. The past is like an ocean between us. And I'm starting to have second thoughts about him working here. *What was I thinking?* He knows too much about me. About who I used to be. Maybe I was right. I don't really want to remember. But tonight, 9 p.m. *What choice will I have then?*

**140**

"Hey, I didn't mean to scare you. You just looked real pale…like you saw…like you saw a ghost." He chuckles, but his eyes seem serious. Worried. Concerned even. Exactly like the Calder I remember. The Calder I trust.

"Butch, I need to talk to you. Could you meet me after you get off work? Someplace quiet."

If he's surprised, he doesn't show it. "Sure, I know a spot."

\*\*\*\*

Melanie opens late afternoon on Mondays, and I pace outside her door like a caged tiger. Waiting. Right at two o'clock, she hurries around the corner, head down in her cell phone. I'd forgotten how blonde she was. How perky. Detective Munroe would never believe we were friends.

"Hey, Melanie."

She clutches the phone to her chest, her bright eyes popping. "Oh. My. God. For a second, I thought you were Nick checking up on me."

"Sorry. I didn't mean to scare you. Is he still bothering you?"

She shrugs and reaches elbow deep into her designer handbag, fishing out a Pi Beta Phi key chain. A single shiny key winks at me, and my dream comes back in a flash. Of Butch. The locked door. The key in his hand. "Just until he signs the papers. Then, I'll officially be a divorcée. I hate the way that word sounds, don't you?" *It's better than widow*, I think. But she doesn't wait for an answer. "So what's up?"

"Have the police talked to you?"

"About Nick?"

"About me."

"Whoa. No. Why would they? Did you do something bad, Doctor?"

Her giggle reminds me of champagne bubbles, and my chest tightens. *Nice one, Evie. You've staked it all on this nitwit.* "Listen, I need a favor. If they ask, you dared me to hitchhike on Friday night. You dare me to do stuff all the time." She unlocks the door and stares at me blankly until I add, "You owe me. Remember?"

"Alright, I dared you. I'm always daring you." She gazes down to the end of the hallway where Butch is tightening a light bulb. It flickers on and off and on again. "In fact, I dare you to chat up the new hottie in the building. Before I do. I double-dog dare you."

He's too far away to hear, but I cringe anyway. "I know him," I say. Like that's an answer.

"Even better. Then you can introduce me. You know I can't resist a man in uniform."

As she opens the door and flips the sign to OPEN, I force a smile and peek back at Butch. Try to see him as she must, like it's the first time. Tough as nails. A little worn around the edges. But better for it, like a beat-up leather jacket. That's Butch alright. "Don't you have a boyfriend?" I ask her.

"The more the merrier." She gives me a playful elbow and a perfect grin, and I follow her inside. "Totally kidding. Dangerously handsome maintenance guy off limits. I got it."

"I'm not...we're not...uh...I'll introduce you if you want." I feel thirteen again, desperate not to say the wrong thing. It comes hard-wired, this inexplicable need to impress girls with names like Melanie. Or Jessica. Or Holly.

"Whatevs." She tosses the whole conversation away with a flip of her hand. "Before you go, a gal stopped by on Friday evening asking about you. I think she got mixed-up with the whole 23A, 23B thing. I told her you'd probably left already, but—"

"What did she look like? Did she tell you her name? Did she leave something for me?" My voice is rushed and breathy, the same desperate woman who went running through the parking lot chasing...what? A little girl.

"Easy, killer. I didn't give her the Spanish Inquisition. But I do remember one thing. I thought it was pretty ironic actually. You doing therapy with pervs and all." I sigh hard to make a point, but Melanie hardly notices. "The way she was dressed, she had this look about her. I'm not one to judge, but I'm pretty sure she was a hooker."

# CHAPTER SEVENTEEN

**BUTCH**
**JANUARY 16, 2017**
**MONDAY**

**MR.** Vinetti let me go half an hour early with a pat on the back and an attaboy. "Great job today, Butch. Really nice work." I ate it up, even if it seemed like overkill. I'd changed fifteen light bulbs, fixed a clogged toilet in the first-floor bathroom, and laid a handful of mousetraps. Hardly rocket science or world peace. But hell, I had a job—one that paid more than twenty cents an hour—and that was progress.

Still, sitting here in my usual booth way back in the corner, drinking my usual coffee, something feels off. Brenda's here too, flashing her cleavage and her crooked smile. Otherwise, the place is deserted. Like I said, the usual. So, it must be me. I'm off. And I know why. But I couldn't tell her no. Correction—I didn't want to tell her no.

I watch the door, half-scared, half-excited. These butterflies in my stomach feel more like goddamn bats. That feeling, it reminds me of...

nope, don't think it. She'll be here any minute. But in my head, I'm back at Folsom in the boardroom, midway through my last parole hearing.

*Mr. Calder's prison record is exemplary, that's true. But, as Dr. Jeffries noted in the psych report, he's never been tested outside of a controlled environment. He's had limited opportunities for relationships with women, and we remain cautious about his ability to manage rejection, abandonment, and other strong emotions.*

And they were right. Because the last time I was completely alone with a woman—a girl, really—I killed her. That sits like a rock in the pit of my stomach. A goddamn boulder. There's no getting around it. I don't trust myself.

Not with her.

Not with any woman. But especially her.

I'd looked her dead in the eye and lied today. A lie of omission. The parole board would have a field day with that one.

"Hey," Evie says, sliding into the booth across from me and taking off her jacket. Perfect timing. "I'm sorry I'm running a little late. I had to stop by the DMV, since that creep got my license, and you know how that goes."

The last time I went to the DMV Bill Clinton was president. But I nod, feeling guilty as hell. And every bit the creep I am. "Do you want anything? Coffee or…the apple pie's pretty good."

Brenda circles, hawk-eyeing Evie and the white bandage on her forearm. I stare at it too, feeling slightly off-kilter, like a kid's top spinning toward the edge of a table.

"Hi. I'm Brenda. Welcome to Chicken and Waffles." But her voice—flat as a zombie's drone—says the complete opposite. "Can I get you anything, ma'am?"

"Um, the pie?" Evie grins at me, and I feel better, righted again. "Two pieces, please. À la mode. And a coffee for me as well."

Brenda stabs the pen against the pad, jotting our order. "Coming right up."

"Geez, what's her problem?" Evie asks, after Brenda stalked away, muttering under her breath. Young Butch would've totally gotten off

**144**

on that—a woman jealous over him. But, what can I say? I'm old. My ears get hot, and I stare at my coffee. "Oh. I see. Brenda thinks I'm competition. You must come here a lot then."

"A fair bit. I guess I'm a creature of habit. That or I really like waffles."

"They say it's good to have a routine, right? I mean, it makes the transition a little easier. Or that's what the guys I work with tell me anyway. How long have you been out?"

That boulder rolls in my stomach, and I feel nauseous. So I keep talking. Anything to tamp it down. "Almost five months. But it seems like nothing. Every day I learn something new." I hold up my flip phone for her, and she laughs. "Like this thing. I'm still trying to figure out how to program my damn voicemail."

"Does anyone even use voicemail anymore?" she teases. "I'm pretty sure you should just send a text."

"LOL."

"Yep. Welcome to 2017. Where we can't be bothered to write out words anymore."

Brenda approaches, pie in hand, and I say a silent prayer she didn't spit in Evie's ice cream. "Here ya go, Butch." She winks and grazes my shoulder, putting both plates smack dab in front of me. "Enjoy, sweetie."

"Um, what about my coffee?"

"Oh, sorry, ma'am. I totally forgot you were here. One coffee coming right up." By the way she says it, I'm willing to bet that means sometime next year.

Evie's giggle makes her sound young again. "You've really done a number on her, Calder. I hope she doesn't poison my coffee."

I roll my eyes and chuckle. "Maybe this wasn't the best place to meet."

"It's perfect. I get why you like it."

She forks a bite of pie—like we're just two girlfriends catching up—and I can't help but stare at her mouth. It's kind of perfect, the way Gwen's was. And I'm a total prick for asking when I know the answer—*thank you, world wide web*—but what the hell. I go for it anyway. "What about you? Are you married?"

"I was. My husband, Jared, died two years ago. Cancer." She's been asked before. I can tell. Because her face doesn't show what I find in her eyes. What I've known myself too well. Loss undergirding everything. Immovable as the rebar beneath the foundation of Folsom itself.

"I'm sorry. That must've been hard."

"Yeah. It was. But I don't have to tell you that. It's funny—well, not ha ha funny—but I think the first loss is the hardest. Nothing compares to it. You can only live through that kind of pain once."

"Your mom?" I ask, and she nods. Forks another bite of pie and smiles through it.

"So speaking of the past," she says. "This might sound strange. But I've been having these dreams lately. And you're in them."

I hope like hell I'm not blushing again. "Okay."

"Do you remember that time at the Blue Bird? When you stomped Trey's hand?"

"Yeah. That was stupid. I don't know what I was—"

"Are you kidding? That was awesome. Nobody ever stood up for me like that. Did you know that place—the Blue Bird—is still standing?" I shake my head, even though I'd taken the bus there once, just after I got out. Just to see it. "And then you let me ride in your convertible. A Barracuda, right? Whatever happened to that thing?"

*Fuck me.* This is worse than I thought. Worse than I could've imagined. Worse than the psych doctors in prison, scribbling on their notepads. Worse than the commissioners. It's even worse than Peter and Janice Shaw showing up at every single parole hearing until she died and he followed a year later. "Crashed it. It was a total loss." And so was I. "I'm not in any hurry to get back behind the wheel."

Her face contorts—she's confused—and it hurts. I'll bet she's trying to reconcile the two Butches. The one she knew and the other one she didn't. Good luck with that. "Is that how you ended

**146**

up in prison? Motor vehicle homicide or something? I know I said I wouldn't ask, but…"

"You really don't know? I assumed you might've heard. That it got around that kids' home…Port in a Storm, wasn't it?"

She nods. "I left there. I stayed in LA for a while. Years actually. A few foster homes. You know the drill. So, no, I didn't hear."

My sigh comes out shaky, louder and more pathetic than I intended. This is really happening. *Now*. At the goddamned Chicken and Waffles. And it feels like I've been waiting so long to say it, I'm not ready anymore. But, here goes nothing. "I killed—"

"Excuse me, Butch. Don't mean to interrupt, but I've got that coffee you ordered." My mouth hangs open, and I stare blankly at the flirty waitress. *Brenda*. That's her name. *Brenda at Chicken and Waffles.*

"Over here," Evie says to her, saving me. "I ordered that."

"Oh. Right. You."

Brenda deposits the coffee and slinks away, but she's just background noise. I'm only watching Evie. She wraps her hands around the cup, puts it to her lips, and blows softly. Little ripples break the surface, and she raises her eyes. Offers me a sad smile. And I savor it—that moment—because I know she'll never look at me the same.

"I killed someone. A girl. Gwen." I swear to God, the words collapse the universe.

# CHAPTER EIGHTEEN

**EVIE**
**JANUARY 16, 2017**
**MONDAY**

**"GWEN?** The pretty blonde?" I picture her bowing her viola in a room full of orphans and throwaways, her flowy skirt blowing in the breeze from the open windows. I see it like it was yesterday. That much I remember. My dream-self mocks me again, and Calder makes a guttural noise I take as a yes. There's so much pain in his eyes, I can't look at him. But I can't look away.

"When?" I ask, wishing right away I could take it back. *When?* Who asks that? First. Before why. Or how. Someone who can't remember a whole chapter of her life, that's who.

He swallows hard. "When?"

"I just—I thought I saw you two together a few days before… *"Before I watched my friend die and forgot it all.* "…uh, never mind."

"May 13, 1994."

He's so sure I wonder if it's tattooed on him somewhere, but I ask him anyway, because I can't believe it. "Are you sure?"

His bottom lip quivers. And I notice, even with that date whirling in my brain. The letter burning in my pocket. After I'd come unglued in the parking lot this afternoon, I'd hightailed it to the bathroom, planning to flush it to oblivion. But I couldn't let it go. It was proof—the only proof I had. Cassie was real. Cassie had existed. And it was the loss of her that I'd been thinking of. Not my mother, who was so strung out most days she was an in-between person. Halfway here, halfway gone.

"That's my birthday," I say.

"Oh. Weird. Yeah. I'm sure. That was the day. I'll never forget it."

"Wow, Butch." I take another sip of the worst coffee I've ever tasted—maybe Brenda really did poison me—and try to center myself with both feet in the present. To think of the least awkward, least awful thing to say. An acquired skill in my profession. "It takes a lot of courage to admit something like that."

He chews on his bottom lip. "You called me that night, didn't you? Left a message for me at the Blue Bird?"

"I did?" But, I remember. *I did.* And my cheeks flush.

"I think you needed a ride or something…you and your friend… Cassie." His mouth stops moving, and I stare at it, the dark cave between his lips. "I wish I'd picked you up that night. Then everything would be different."

Scared of what I might say—*I don't remember. Can you help me remember?*—I say nothing, and he sighs again.

"Are you still in touch?" His eyes buried in his lap like he might find the answer there, I don't understand the question at first. And then I do, and it's like a knife between my ribs. A sneak attack.

"With Cassie? No." *What more is there to say that can be said aloud?* Only this, "I wish you'd picked us up too."

Solemn, he nods. "Thanks for not hightailing it out of here. You can, you know? Leave. If you want."

Maybe I should. But I'd trusted Butch since the first day we met, the day he stood up to Trey for me. Nobody'd ever done that before. Not even my own mother. "I'm sure you know this—and I'm not trying to sound like a shrink—but a man can do bad things and not be a bad man. The Butch I remember wasn't a bad guy. You're kinda the same, you know. But different."

"You definitely sound like a shrink. But I appreciate it. And I know what you mean. You're different too. And the same." He leans back against the booth, runs a hand through his shaggy blonde hair, and lets out a long, slow whistle of a breath. "So is that what you wanted to ask me? What I did?"

Truth is I've been stalling. I'm afraid to say it out loud. To make it real. *Somebody knows.* After all this time, somebody knows. "Not exactly. Did you see anybody hanging around my office today? Maybe this morning?"

"I don't think so. But, I can't be sure. Once Gary put me to work, I was all over the place. Why? Did something happen? Is that why you seemed shaken up?" *Shaken? More like a massive earthquake at my very core,* but I don't admit it.

"Is there somebody bothering you? I can keep a look out." He studies my face closely, and I know I'm not as good at faking as I used to be. "Is it Trey?"

My whole body tenses at that name. Like one of Pavlov's dogs, I hear it and I expect to be punished. "Trey is the least of my worries."

"Good, because…" He points over my shoulder at the oversized TV screen hung in the corner of the diner. "Looks like he's somebody else's problem for a while anyway."

The television's on mute, the closed caption streaming at the bottom.

**Person of interest, Trey Waters, was arrested today on charges of human trafficking. Police believe he may have information on the murder of an underage female discovered in downtown Oakland early Saturday morning.**

**Though police officials have not yet confirmed the manner of the victim's death, sources close to the investigation revealed she was strangled and likely sexually assaulted. The same source cautioned that Friday night's rainstorm has complicated investigative efforts by compromising much of the forensic evidence.**

And there he is, so real that I shudder. He's shielding his ruddy face from the camera, one hand raised. Like he's signaling right to me. And on one skeleton finger, my father's ring.

****

Butch takes his pie—and half of mine—to go. "Lost my appetite," he says, holding the door for me. I catch Brenda watching us through the window. She jerks her head away and wipes the table down. Again.

"I'm sorry for dredging it up. The past, I mean."

"It's not that." I cock my head at him, disbelieving. "Okay, so it is. You're the first person I've told out here. And I know it sounds strange, but I feel like I let you down."

"Why would you say that? We were just kids. Both of us."

He shakes his head, closes his eyes. He's got a haunted look about him. Like something's sunk its claws in him, took hold, and refused to let go. "I'd like to tell you more…about Gwen…about everything. If you're up for it."

"I'd like that. It's nice to talk to somebody who knew me back then. Somebody who doesn't expect me to be Dr. Maddox." Or a Maddox at all, I'd add, thinking of Maggie. "Coffee with an ex-con?" she'd ask, incredulous. *No, Maggie. Pie with a murderer.* And what would she say if she knew Butch Calder was my first…crush? That word seemed appropriate for what I'd felt. The way it had come on—sudden, fierce—threatening to squash my heart like a grape.

"It's a date then. Let's do it." His brown eyes crinkle with mischief, and he laughs at himself. "I didn't mean it that way."

*Date.* That word kicks up the two years' worth of dust that covers my heart. And I realize today was the first time I'd shared a meal with a man—even if it was just half a slice of pie—since Jared. It doesn't feel as unnatural as I'd thought it would.

"Careful, Calder, Brenda's already out to get me. Next time, she'll sprinkle arsenic in my cup. And the way that coffee tastes, I'll hardly know the difference."

He's still smiling as I drive away. A melancholy smile, but it suits him. It reassures me somehow, and I stop to wave at him in the rearview. He stays there, waving back at me, until I turn the corner.

Butch's lopsided grin almost makes me forget about the ring on Trey's finger. The one my mother swore he'd never touch. "Over my dead body," she'd told him. And then she'd wound up exactly that— dead—leaving it to me. All these years, I'd failed her without even knowing. The devil prancing around with my father's ring like he'd earned it.

But Butch's smile, it nearly makes me turn around and ask him to come along. I don't though. Willow Court 9 p.m. is a pilgrimage I have to make alone.

# CHAPTER NINETEEN

BUTCH
JANUARY 16, 2017
MONDAY

**ON** the walk home, I pass Murphy's Tavern, a hole-in-the-wall bar I'd barely noticed before. But, tonight, the door is propped, and I catch a whiff of molasses and vanilla. The unmistakable scent of gin. And just like that, I'm back there. Kissing Hennessy off Gwen's lips. Her perfect, pale-pink lips. Twelve days before I'd killed her.

*I killed someone. A girl. Gwen.* My own voice haunts me—the inadequacy of those words—but so do Evie's eyes. Clear and bright, she'd looked at me without a hint of judgment. But, I'd held back. Because killing Gwen was only half of it. The half I'd been locked up for. The half I'd learned to stomach somehow. The rest I'd never spoken to a living soul. *You had your chance tonight, Butchy. And you blew it.* You keep something inside for so long, it becomes a part of you. An unnatural appendage. Like those objects—I'd seen a bicycle once in a magazine—that grow into trees. To cut it out would be fatal.

I pause outside Murphy's and peer in the window, tempted. The parole board always gave me hell about my relapse prevention plan—a fancy way to say *you've gotta stop drinking forever, moron*—and I fought them tooth and nail. After all, twenty-plus-years sober has to count for something, right? Even in prison where the pruno is about as tasty as dog pee. Turns out, those damn commissioners were spot on. Tonight, all I really want is a stiff drink. Or five.

But I keep walking. Take a breath. Remind myself of what's at stake. Of what I've lost already. Damn if I don't recite the Serenity Prayer under my breath the rest of the way back to the halfway house. *Relapse prevention, Mr. Calder. You can't white-knuckle it out there.*

I book it straight to the common area and grab a seat just in time for the weekly house meeting. It's mandatory for the new guys, like Sebastian. I spot him hovering at the back of the room, reading his usual. Or pretending to.

"Hey, Butch. Glad to see you here." Mr. Richert nods at me. "We've got some new faces with us this evening. Do you want to start us off?"

My dumb luck, he'd call me out tonight. Of all nights. "Uh, yeah. Sure."

I give a halfhearted wave to the group. "I'm Butch, but you can call me Calder. If you don't know me, I've been out for about five months now. And I got a job today. On my thirteenth interview..." I wait for the applause to quiet down, feeling like a total pretender. "Which is great, but...I also had to tell somebody about my crime. Somebody I care about. It was harder than I thought it would be."

The guys are all watching me, wary—especially the newbies. Hard-won freedom, like mine, is a bitch. You hold your breath. You bide your time. You wait for the other shoe to fall. I've been there.

"Honestly, for the first time since I've been out, I wanted to drink tonight. But I came back here instead to talk to all of you. That's what I want to say. You can't do it alone. And you don't have to."

**154**

Jesus. I'm turning into goddamned Oprah, but at least Richert's happy. He's got a satisfied grin on his face like he just cracked a code. The Code of Butch Calder. But really it's Evie who did the cracking. She makes me want to be better. To do better. Next time I see her, I'll give her the license. I'll tell her the whole truth. And nothing but.

"Thanks, Mr. Calder. I'm proud of you for using your support system. That's what this group is for. We can all help each other succeed. And Butch is right—we speak from experience—you can't do it alone." He gives me a wink before his smile flattens. "I know you're all probably aware of the crime that took place a few blocks from here this weekend. I don't want to worry anybody, but it's best to be prepared. The police may be stopping by to question some of you. Make sure you give them your full cooperation. Now, where were we?"

We go round the circle until there's one man left. The one I've been waiting for. He runs a hand through his jet-black hair, adjusts his glasses, and grips his book like a life preserver.

"Hello, everyone. I'm not really good at this sort of thing." Richert nods at him, encouraging. "My name is Sebastian Delacourt. I've been out on parole for about a week. It's going okay, I guess. I started group therapy last Friday, but I'm not sure if I like it. In prison, you get so used to hiding what you did and why you did it that it feels unnatural to talk about it even when you're supposed to. Even when you have to." He puts his eyes dead center on me, and my mouth goes dry. "I'd like to ask you, Butch, how...how...did you do it? Any words of wisdom?"

I can't tell if he's messing with me. But the stutter in his voice makes me doubt it, and I feel a little sorry for him. The answer rolls off my tongue like I've practiced. Which I have. But nobody has to know that.

"Best to be up-front from the get-go. After all, honesty is the best policy. That's what they say, isn't it? Whoever *they* are, I can tell you this—*they* have never done ten to life in Folsom and come out on the other side. So shoot'em straight. They'll respect you for it. And if all else fails, just pretend like you're talking to the damn parole board."

****

I'm showered and in bed by 8:30. Like I said, I'm old. And after today, I'm whipped. Drained. Like my confession came with a bloodletting. I still can't believe I'd said it out loud. To her. And the world didn't collapse after all. But it shifted. Words like that, spoken, change things. Irrevocably.

*You're not good enough for me, Butch. You'll never be good enough.* It's Gwen again, and she's in my head. *You're not good enough for Evie either. She married a Maddox. And she's a doctor. So don't go getting your hopes up. Loser.*

I stifle a groan. Roll onto one side, then the other. It's Princess Butch and the goddamn pea tonight. And the pea is that driver's license. *Tomorrow*, I remind myself. But it's more of a promise to the universe.

"Mind if I shut the lights?" I ask.

The only answer is a soft hum. Sebastian's staring blankly at the cover of *Lord of the Flies* on his lap, headphones in. It's the stare of somebody looking but not seeing. Not hearing either, apparently. So, I try again, louder this time. "Hey, man. Can I shut the lights?"

He blinks twice. And the corner of his mouth turns up like he's thinking about something good. Like chocolate cake. Or cool grass under his bare feet. Or the touch of a woman.

"Sebastian?" I tap the edge of his bed, and he jumps to attention so fast I expect him to salute.

"Sorry. Didn't hear you."

I point to the light switch, and he nods. "Sure, lights out. I've got my reading lamp if I need it." I quash the urge to laugh. Because, by now, he could probably recite that entire book from memory.

"Whatcha listenin' to?"

"Oh, you probably wouldn't like it."

"Try me."

He shrugs as he passes the headphones across the slim space between our beds. *This is gonna be good.* I've got him pegged for a Yanni diehard, and I smirk a little as the music starts. One of my cellies had a thing for electronic rock, so I recognize the song right away. With the heavy breathing at the start, it's unforgettable and creepy as hell. *Seriously.* Like stalker-level shit.

*I want you now, tomorrow won't do. There's a yearning inside and it's showing through.*

"Depeche Mode, huh? Cool, man. Wouldn't have figured it."

*Reach out your hands and accept my love. We've waited for too long. Enough is enough.* Like I said, stalker-level.

His laugh is jittery, quick as the cockroaches in Folsom. "It's my favorite song. Reminds me of being seventeen again. You know, when sex was all you could think about."

I pretend I'm not totally skeeved out when I return his headphones and shut the lights. In the joint, nighttime was a luxury, a little slice of heaven when I got to count my blessings I'd made it another day. Eight whole hours not looking over my shoulder. Not waiting for a shank to the back. Or some crazy cowboy CO to mess with me just to get his rocks off. Eight whole hours when I didn't have to be a goddamn number. Or a man with a stone face. I could just be Butch. In my T-shirt and boxers like any ordinary free fella.

But now, here, the darkness is different. This may sound certifiable, but I felt safer in that six-by-eight box. Tonight, I'm on edge, so I listen to Sebastian's breathing and follow the shadows beneath the door until my eyes get heavy.

"So how'd she take it?"

I flinch awake, stunned. Wonder, for a moment, if I'm still dreaming. But Sebastian's eyes glow like an owl's in the faint light from the window, and he's looking right at me.

"Who?" I ask. "Take what?" As the words leave my mouth, I know. And that stuns me even more.

"Dr. Maddox. Evie. She's the one you told, right? I saw you on my way home, sitting together at that restaurant."

*Is he fucking following me?* Young Butch (he's still in here) goes from zero to sixty in 5.8, same as the 'Cuda. But I quiet him down— *easy, boy*—and keep him in his cage. "Uh, yeah. We knew each other as kids. I guess she took it alright. But, she's a shrink so it's hard to tell."

"Poker face?"

"Something like that." Say as little as possible. Then, feign sleep. That's my plan, until—

"Have you told her you've got a thing for her?" Until Sebastian punches me in the gut. Or at least that's what it feels like. "You were talking in your sleep just now. Evie. Oh Evie."

I sit up, half ready to clock this punk. But I don't. Because the other half knows where that leads. Bars and fences and prison blues. *Been there. Done that. Bought the flippin' T-shirt.* "What? Man, you've got the wrong idea. We're just friends. Like I said, I knew her when she was—"

"Alright, alright. I'm just messing with you. You do snore though. Like a freight train."

I settle back on the mattress in self-imposed silence. I can't get a handle on Sebastian, and I don't like it. One minute he's got ice in his veins, the next he's a goddamn comedian. But twenty years in the pen will teach you patience. Among other things. Like how to needle a guy where it hurts him the most.

"Hey, where were you the other night?" I ask, casual as a heart attack. "I woke up and you were gone. For a while."

He doesn't show it. He doesn't bleed. Still, I know I stuck him. Especially with Richert's warning about the police sniffing around here. "Bathroom probably. Weak stomach. 'Night, Butch."

I wait for a beat—let him suffer—before I answer. "Goodnight, Sebastian."

# CHAPTER TWENTY

**THE** last time I'd come here, to Willow Court, I was eighteen and fresh off the bus from LA. I'd hitched a ride from the station with a family headed up north to Tahoe. "Are you sure you want to get out here?" the mother—so different from my own—had asked me, grimacing out the window at my preferred destination.

"I'm sure," I'd told her. But I wasn't. I wasn't sure about anything then. Except that the girl I had been—twelve days from my thirteenth birthday—left something behind here and I owed it to her to look for it at least once. Besides that, I could've used the cash. My scholarship to Berkeley didn't cover living expenses. And living in Berkeley was not cheap.

The last time I'd come here, to Willow Court, the place was still standing. If you could call it that. And I'd lingered by the pool half-expecting Cassie to turn up with her crooked smile and smart mouth. Like no time had passed. Like I'd skipped across five years as fast as a pebble skimming the water's surface.

The last time I'd come here, to Willow Court, I'd left empty-handed. 201 had been covered in graffiti, the floor ankle-deep with trash and God knows what else. To stomach the stench, I'd had to cover my mouth with my T-shirt long enough to hoist myself onto the counter and crack the vent. A light shower of grime had dusted my face like snow. And I'd reached a tentative finger inside the space, sure it would be bitten off by some creature—all teeth and fur and claws—that lives off the flesh of stupid girls. But nothing had happened. And the thing I'd left, it was gone. With no evidence it had ever existed at all. Not unlike Cassie herself.

And now, so is Willow Court. Gone without a trace. I park my car across the street and gape for a moment at the empty lot. The field of tall, weedy grass that waves to me as the wind picks up. The toppled LAND FOR SALE sign, its upended post sharp and threatening. I'm not sure what I'd expected—it's been nearly seventeen years after all—but it wasn't this. The sheer emptiness of it, the way an entire part of your life can just disappear, scares me. Like the ground opened right up and swallowed it whole. All of it. The dilapidated buildings, the mice skeletons, the old pool, Cassie, my memory.

I sit in the car until it's nearly 9, letting the heater blast my feet. Until it's so warm my eyes get heavy and I feel weighted to the seat, unable to move even if I wanted. Sleep threatens to pull me under, and I jolt awake a few times, my head falling sideways then snapping to attention like I'm sort of a string puppet, subject to someone else's whims. In the fuzzy space between, I keep thinking of Butch, what he'd said. "I wish I'd picked you up that night. Then everything would be different." He's right. I would be different. A whole Evie. Not this one, the girl with a dead friend and a missing piece.

Finally, I can't take it. I crack the door and let the cold rush in. It's 9:03—the minutes slog like hours—and the lot is just as empty.

**160**

Whoever it is, isn't coming. They've been swallowed too, straight down to the belly of the earth with all the other lost things.

But then, I spot her. She's on foot at least a hundred yards down the road, a small figure hunched against the chilly January wind. A truck speeds by, blaring its horn at her, but she doesn't change course. As she comes closer, my stomach starts to knot. I fight the urge to get back in my car and drive away.

She's not dressed for winter. Even the mild Bay Area winters that are more wet than cold. Her thin legs are bare and white as bones. They look strangely disconnected from the rest of her body, which is mostly hidden in an oversized sweater that hangs down to the knobs of her knees. And she's young. How young it's hard to say, because her hair—dyed fire red—is whipping across her face.

She doesn't approach, but I see her watching me from where she's sitting. On the curb, just in front of the field that swallowed Willow Court. She takes off her shoes—tall black stilettos—and rubs her feet. Then she tucks her knees toward her and stretches her sweater over them.

The light from the street casts strange shadows on her face. I know it's a trick, but her eyes look hollow. Two holes, empty and bored straight through. Her cheeks are sunken, and her        mouth is set in a hard line like she hasn't smiled in years. There's something wild about her, something dangerous. Something sad too. And it hits me like a wave. She reminds me of my mother.

"Doesn't your mama look purdy?" That's what Trey used to say when she'd strut around for him, bones sticking out of a secondhand dress and makeup, caked on her sallow skin. Once I'd corrected him—*pretty, not purdy*—and he'd told me he ought to slap my face for back talking him. He didn't though. Because my mom had already done it, my face stinging with the kind of shame that festers like an angry blister. "He would've hit you ten times harder," she'd explained after he left. And I hated her, because I knew she was right.

Even after that last day, when I watched her suck in one last rattling breath, anger—pure rage, really—is the only thing I've got left for my mother. I guard it like a precious stone, hot and hard, rooted at the center of me. That's what fuels my walk toward the girl. "Well, I'm here," I say. "I'm Evie."

Her eyebrows lift just a little, like she can't be bothered. Up close, her face is ashen and mottled with scabs. "Bitch, I don't care who you are. This is my spot. Get your own."

I stare at her, absorbing the words—their meaning—the way a fighter takes a punch. Silent. Stoic. Unwavering. "I'm not competition. I was supposed to meet someone here." I lower my voice and take another step toward her. "Maybe you?"

She snorts. "You a cop?"

"Of course not." Though shrink isn't much better, and I know it. "What happens in this house is nobody's business." That had been my mom's warning when the school told her I should see the counselor once a week. "Keep your mouth shut. That uppity broad doesn't know shit about our family." But that's what happens when the teacher finds a clump of your hair—black and balled and dusty, like some kind of vermin—under your desk. "Did you leave me a note? At my office?"

"Lady, I don't know what you're talkin' about. And you're cramping my style, okay?" I follow her dead gaze across the street where a car sits idling, a man watching from the window, eyes fixed and hungry as a wolf.

"I'll leave. If you tell me why I'm here."

Her sigh is heavy, beleaguered. Like I'm too dense to bother with. "I told you I have no fucking clue who you are. But I've gotta get paid."

"I've gotta get paid, baby." My mother again, on the nights I'd beg her to stay. Once I'd emptied my pockets onto the table, the few dollars I'd earned cleaning rooms at the Blue Bird, and she'd laughed at me. "That's sweet, Evelyn. But your mama needs real money." I'd shut myself in the bathroom until she left. When I'd finally summoned the courage to peek out, the table was bare.

"Here," I say, handing the girl a twenty. She snatches it up, so eager I can't meet her eyes.

"You'll leave then, right? If I tell you what I know." She stands and straightens herself. Through the thin fabric of her sweater, I see a lipstick-red bra and a snake tattoo above her breast. The tail of it loops upward across her collarbone. There's a bruise there in the shape of a thumb. It makes me think of Danny with his hands on me. Of Cassie too.

I nod at her, feeling like I might be sick. "If anybody told you to meet up here, it was probably Violet. She was stupid like that, always thinking she was better than the rest of us."

"Violet?"

"Yep."

"Is she around?"

"Ha!" The noise comes out sharp like the cry of an animal, and I feel my heart race. "Only if you believe in ghosts. She went and got herself whacked Friday night by some freak. Had it comin', if you ask me. This ain't no place for a teenager. Especially one like Vi. Too big for her britches, you know? I tried to tell Trey she was gonna get herself..."

She stops herself there—she's already said too much—and stubs out her cigarette on the sidewalk while I struggle to swallow. Like there's something alive in my throat, scratching its way out.

"Trey Waters?" Saying it out loud casts a spell, and I wait for him to materialize in a plume of smoke and fire. To press the blade of my father's knife against my cheek. Sink those devil claws into my arm. To whisper to me. "You look just like your mama. Real purdy."

"What's it to you?"

"Nothing." I step away, suddenly scared to turn my back to her. "Thanks for your help."

I hurry to the car and lock myself inside it, cracking the window an inch. Just enough so I can hear the man call to her. "Hey, Ruby. You wanna take a ride?"

**** 

Somehow, I manage the drive back up into the Hills. Until a deer darts out just before the last turn of the road—bounding across two lanes and disappearing into the brush—and I realize I've been somewhere else all along. Trapped in the past like a fly caught in amber. Only my body had been driving.

The house is all lit up, and there's a black sedan parked in front. A cop car. There's no doubt. I picture Maggie tending to the officers, plying them with coffee and cookies and stories about me. "Evie always was a good liar. Probably runs in the genes. I don't know what my son saw in her." But if I know Maggie, she's thinking those things. Not saying them. She'd never sully the Maddox name.

I feel numb, and I move like I'm in last night's dream, plodding through the cold fog toward the front door, turning my key in the lock. I half-expect it not to open, but it does. And the sound of it jars me, like I've unlocked the portal to another universe.

"Well, there she is. I told you she'd be back soon." Maggie's eyes glare at me from the sofa, her teeth bared in a forced smile. "Would you like more coffee, Detective? Another madeleine, perhaps?"

"No, thank you, Mrs. Maddox. But, if you wouldn't mind, I'd like to speak with your daughter-in-law alone."

"Absolutely. I understand." She gives me a pointed look before she disappears into the kitchen, leaving me alone with Detective Munroe. Seeing her here, among Maggie's things—a delicate vase, a coffee-table book of Richard Misrach photos, her leather slippers—I realize how imposing she is with her broad shoulders and wide hips. Just a hint of a smirk that makes me think she knows something about me. But then, she wipes a trail of cookie crumbs from the corner of her mouth, and I feel less afraid.

"Did you catch him?" I ask, hurrying to speak first. Before I lose my nerve.

"Still looking. We've got a name though. Danny Dunaway. Ring any bells?" I shake my head, seeing his shadowy face inches from my own. Smelling his hot tobacco breath. He'd told me his real name. Which meant he hadn't planned on letting me go. Not alive anyway. "I'm sure it won't surprise you to learn he's a registered sex offender. He did five years on a rape case, and he's had about twenty charges for soliciting since then. Hasn't checked in with his PO in over a month. And we had a tip about a black jeep. Somebody spotted one over by your office later that night."

"So, is he a suspect in that murder?"

"We're not ruling anything out. He wasn't a client of yours, was he? Maybe a while back? Someone you might've forgotten?"

"I wouldn't forget." I silently cackle at the irony. "Not that."

"Okay. But that's not why I'm here." She pauses, and I forget to breathe, suspended for a moment in complete uncertainty. "Ever heard the name Violet Kurchell?"

For the second time that night, I take the blow like a champ. A little woozy, but I don't show it. I don't even think before I lie. "Uh, no." Like mother, like daughter indeed. "Should I know her?"

"When you came to see me on Saturday you'd asked about what had happened outside your office. Why?"

*Because of Cassie. Because I watched her die right there. Because I can't remember.* "I guess I thought that it might have had something to do with Danny. Or even one of my group members. The whole thing seemed like a strange coincidence."

"I agree." Again, she waits for me to fill the silence. I know this trick. I've used this trick. And I want to tell her everything. "We identified the victim. Her name was Violet Kurchell. A fifteen-year-old girl who'd been in and out of the system. She had your address in her pocket. We think she may have stopped by your office the night she was killed."

"My office? Why?"

"I was hoping you might be able to shed some light on that. You and Violet have something in common, don't you?" I see the crack in the kitchen door, Maggie's shadow just inside it. She's not moving. She's listening. And the room starts to shrink around me. "Trey Waters. He knew your mother, right?"

I'm not in Maggie's house anymore. I'm back at the Blue Bird motel, hiding out in the bathroom, on the day my mother died. It was Saturday, but she'd told Trey I was at school so he wouldn't bother me. I couldn't decide who was more pathetic—my mom for saying it or Trey for believing it.

I'd cracked the door just enough to see the sofa. It was a hideous, urine-colored yellow (that Mom had called *happy*) with a huge tear in the cushion. She'd found it in a dumpster and lugged it back to the room with Peggy—like it was some kind of prize, a beast she'd hunted and shot herself. Never mind that the manager didn't allow it. Who brings their own furniture to a motel? And secondhand furniture at that? Arlene Allcott apparently.

Shirtless, Trey had loomed over her. And I'd stared at his back—a disgusting canvas of acne, hair, and ink. My mother was perched on the edge of the sofa, pointing at him, the muscles in her neck tensing in anger. She'd taken off the ring he'd given her, the one that turned her finger green, and chucked it in his direction.

Trey was yelling at her, and she was yelling back, saying the words I'd been waiting on for years. Like waiting for the cicadas to tunnel back to the surface, to begin their short lives above ground. The way I'd seen it, my mother was just like those cicadas. And her life above ground lasted just under five minutes.

"I'm done, Trey. Do you hear me? Done. I've got a girl her age, you know." *Her* being Brandy. Trey's newest recruit. "What's next? You gonna put Evie to work too?"

"Like mother, like daughter. Ain't that what they say? Besides, the young ones, that's what the johns like anyhow."

He stalked around her, and my stomach clenched. I should have closed the door right then, but I couldn't turn away. "You see this sofa you drug back here? It used to be real nice, real fancy. Sittin' in some gal's livin' room. Then she got a little careless. Spilled her wine on the cushion. Her kid puked his guts up on it. And the dog pissed right there in the corner. A few times. Now it's all used up. Just like you. Ain't good for nothin' no more."

"Fuck you. I'm through tricking. I've been saving my money. And I'm gonna make something of myself. Get my own damn sofa.

My own dog. And a house. Maybe up in the Hills somewhere. Get off this junk. For real this time."

He kicked at the cushions with his boot, upending one, and my mother tensed. "You can get all the sofas you can carry, bitch, but you owe me that money. It ain't yours to keep."

"Like hell it's not."

Just then, Trey's head swiveled toward the bathroom, and his eyes were like two black holes. Like tiny graves dug deep in the earth. I wasn't sure if he'd seen me, but I'd shut the door fast. Turned the cheap lock, though it was useless against someone like him, and climbed into the bathtub. It was still damp, but I was too scared to care. *Like hell it's not.* I'd repeated it to myself, indignant, not knowing then those were my mother's last words.

## EVIE
## MAY 4, 1994
## NINE DAYS UNTIL MY BIRTHDAY

I stood at the board, listening to Bobby Pierce giggle at me from the front row.

"Evil Evie," he hissed, just quiet enough that the teacher couldn't hear him. "You've got something on your pants. Looks like blood." The girls seated around him snickered. As if multiplying fractions in front of the class wasn't bad enough, I had to contend with period humor now.

I tried to focus on the numbers, to hold the nub of white chalk steady in my hand, but I couldn't keep my mind straight.

Cassie was missing. I hadn't seen her since Sunday night when Trey had all but kidnapped me and driven me to the Blue Bird in his hooptie. God, I loved it when Butch had called it that. To his face! And even more when he'd stomped Trey's weaselly little hand. I only wish I'd had the guts to do it myself. But I'd only ever had the nerve to hurt Trey in my daydreams. I'd sunk a knife into his shriveled heart, tiny as a raisin; punched him until his head floated off like a runaway balloon; and my personal favorite, the gators halved him with one sickening, glorious chomp. But now, Cassie was missing—she hadn't been at Willow Court for two nights straight—and I had a sick feeling it had to do with Trey. Because everything awful in my life began and ended with him.

**168**

"Evelyn, do you have the answer? The class is waiting." Mrs. Hildebrandt tapped her watch and raised her caterpillar brows at me expectantly.

"Yes, ma'am." My whole body got hot in an instant. Like I'd swallowed a burning coal. I knew the answer, but I couldn't make myself write it. And the room started to shrink around me until it was the exact size of the Blue Bird bathroom. I watched the chalk drop from my hand and splinter against the floor, sending a poof of white powder into the air. Bobby's cackle sounded like a scream, and I grabbed my backpack and took off running. Out the door. Down the hallway. Past Principal Masterson's office. I didn't stop until I reached the edge of the lawn that separated Burton Junior High from the rest of the world.

I'd never played hooky before, much less sprinted off school grounds, and I could hear them calling me. "Evelyn Allcott, get back here!"

I dipped one toe onto the street, then the other, and I felt a rush. Like zipping down the highway in Calder's Barracuda with the wind in my hair and him singing Sinatra. All my life, I'd wanted to be that free—to fly away from it all like a bird catching the breeze—but I'd never realized until that very moment, I was the only one who'd kept me tethered to the ground.

I didn't waste another second. I took off running and didn't look back.

**\*\*\*\***

At three o'clock, Willow Court was still deserted. No Cassie in sight. So I packed up my books—only I would do homework on a skip day— and began the trek back to the Port. I'd hoped Cherice was there. The school surely had called them, but at least she'd go easy on me.

The buzz of freedom had worn off, and I walked slower than usual, dreading tonight's lecture. And the teasing tomorrow. *I'm cursed*, I thought. *Evil Evie is cursed.* The sun was brutal and my armpits started to sweat through my T-shirt. By the time I'd reached the gas station, I was so desperate for a Slurpee, I could taste that first shot of sweetness at the back of my throat. But as I pushed the door open, the cold air hitting me like a slap, the taste turned bitter. Sour as death.

"Cassie?"

"Hey. What's up?" As if she hadn't disappeared. As if she didn't look like an entirely different person. Clean, for starters. And all dolled up in a yellow sundress, her fingernails glossy red, and her hair as shiny as a horse's mane.

"Where have you been?"

She shrugged. "Around. You weren't worried, were you? Trey said you wouldn't be worried."

"Trey?" My eyes darted. "Where?"

Cassie grabbed my hand and tugged me to the back of the store, whispering. "He's nothing like you said, Evie. He got me all this." She did a little twirl, flashing a lipstick smile. "He said I looked like a model."

*Purdy.* "I'm sure he did. Is he here?"

"I'm supposed to meet him outside in twenty minutes. He had some business to take care of."

*Business.* I rolled my eyes. Trey was a regular Edward Lewis. Not. He'd never pull off Richard Gere in *Pretty Woman.* "Are you staying with him?"

"No! Don't be silly. He put me up in a motel in Oakland for a few nights. The Blue…something or other."

"Blue Bird?"

"Yeah, that's the one. Just so I could shower and have a nice bed to sleep in. And he told me that once he's saved up enough money, he's gonna get me a bus ticket to Houston so I can find my dad."

"You can't honestly believe that. After everything I told you about him." But she did. I knew she did.

"He said your mom was sick, Evie. That she liked being with those guys. He loved her, you know. He even cried about it."

**170**

She spun around, away from me, and headed for the Slurpee machine. Stunned, I followed—dragging my legs like lead anchors— and grabbed her wrist. I let myself think it, the thing I never thought of, the thing I couldn't bury deep enough. Me huddled in the bathtub. Trey pounding on the door until I came out, slowly. Like I'd been asleep a thousand years, and the world had gone on without me. *Your mama finally did it.* That was all he had to say before he left us there. One dead with a needle in her arm, one wishing to be.

"Cassie. He killed her. I never said that to anybody. I don't know how, and I can't prove it. But I know he did. Whatever he does for you, it has a price. And you're going to have to pay it."

Her body stiffened, but she didn't look at me. Just filled up her Double Gulp like nothing, spearing the cup with a bright-blue straw. "You're wrong. Plus, it's not like I've got any better offers. I can't stay at Willow Court forever."

"Come back with me. They'll let you stay."

She didn't answer, and for a moment, I believed I'd convinced her somehow. But then, I caught her eyes looking past me and out the window. "He's here," she said.

I ducked behind the shelf of potato chips and rifled through my backpack, scrawling the number for the Port on the first sheet of paper I could find—my notes from third-period science. The process of photosynthesis. "Here. Just in case it doesn't turn out the way you hope."

She took it in her hand, stared at it. "I wish you could just be happy for me. Trey warned me you'd be jealous." Then she pointed to the heart I'd doodled in the corner during class. "Who's Calder?"

I hated her then. "My boyfriend. And he can kick Trey's ass."

# CHAPTER TWENTY-ONE

**BUTCH**
**JANUARY 17, 2017**
**TUESDAY**

**MY** alarm goes off at 5:30 a.m., coldcocking me from a dead sleep, and I hit the floor. Literally. I assume the prone position and await further instruction like the well-trained inmate I am. Was. Twenty-three years of alarm procedure will do that to you. Nose to the hardwood, I can't help but laugh at myself. I lift my head and peer up at Sebastian's side of the room, concocting a story to save face. *Pushups.* He'll buy that.

But his bed is empty, the sheets carefully smoothed, like he ran his hands over them more than once. Something about that—knowing he did it while I slept—makes me shiver. Or maybe it's just this block of ice they call a floor. I crank out a hundred pushups just for the hell of it to get my middle-aged blood pumping. Then I plunk down at the edge of the bed, breathing hard and listening to the steady brag of my heart. *Still here…still beating.*

I catch a glimpse of my face in the cheap mirror Sebastian stuck to the back of our door like we're college freshmen. Apparently, I slept hard. So hard my pillow creased the side of my forehead and did a real number on my hair. I lick my hand and smooth it down—what can I say, I'm a regular Vidal Sassoon—but it springs back up, as stubborn as I am. Anyway, I'll take it. Because a hard sleep is a dreamless one.

*Today's the day*, I remind myself. I'll give Evie her license. Fess up. And let the chips fall. "A man can do bad things and not be a bad man." That's what she'd said with those earnest eyes telling me she'd meant it. I'm just not sure I believe it. Sometimes, I feel like the baddest apple in the bunch. Rotten to my very core.

I slip my hand under the mattress. And come up empty. *Still here. Still beating.* I try again, reaching farther this time, shoving my hand in, shoulder deep. Nothing. And now, my chest is pounding. *STILL HERE! STILL BEATING!* I drop to my knees and lift the mattress, exposing the cheap box springs. Peer underneath the bed. Not even a respectable dust bunny. *STILL HERE! STILL BEATING!*

"Butch? What the hell are you lookin' for?"

I blink at Richert, hoping I don't look as mental as I feel. "My cell phone. I think I dropped it."

"You mean this one." He taps the phone on the top of my dresser, chuckling at me. "C'mon. Your PO called. He wants to see you before work."

"Yes, sir—I mean, okay, Frank. Just gimme a sec to…" *Freak out.* "…to, uh, get dressed."

"Hey, where's your roomie?"

"I was hoping you'd seen him. I need to ask him something." *Like who the fuck he thinks he is. And what kind of punk he's mistaken me for.* As usual, Young Butch is first out the gate and hitting his stride before Old Butch gets himself going.

"He must've taken off before I got here this morning. Early riser, that guy." Richert pauses at the door, takes a second look at me. "You okay? You look a little peaked."

*Breathe, Butchy.* "I'm alright. Probably just worn out from yesterday."

"Well, keep it up, man. I'm proud of you."

"Thanks. I plan to." And just like that, Old Butch is back in the running, threatening to edge out the odds-on favorite by a nose.

****

Agent McElroy reminds me of my dad. What I remember of him anyway. A no-nonsense, straight shooter with the uncanny ability to see right through my bullshit. Like the time Dad had caught seven-year-old me red-handed outside the dollar store with a Matchbox car in my pocket. He'd had a way of making me fess up without saying a word. Just his eyeballing that pocket—so hard I'd swear his eyes had burned right through it—and I'd given it up. Marched back to the store myself and placed the tiny 1957 Corvette back on the shelf, my heart breaking a little as I'd left it behind. "Calders work for what they have," he'd told me on the way back home. "And you're a Calder, son. Don't ever forget it." That memory comes with a heaping dose of guilt. All the times I'd let him down, even if he wasn't around to see it.

"Butch, I heard you got a job." McElroy runs a hand across his rust-colored beard and sizes me up. He's got his cop face on today, and it makes me nervous that he can tell what I'm thinking. An impromptu meeting with your PO is a lot like being called to the principal's office. Sometimes you get lucky and end up with detention. Other times, you wind up with your pants around your ankles, getting paddled by Mr. O'Shaughnessy.

"Yes, sir. Those interviews finally paid off." That can't be the only reason he'd asked me here. So I match his face with my own. My prison face. "Maintenance and custodial at the building off Jackson Street. I started yesterday."

"Well, it's about damn time. Anything else you need to tell me?" A pure Dad line right there. Making you think he had something on you. And damn if it didn't work.

"Actually, sir, I think you should know that the lady from the other night...Dr. Maddox...Evie. I know her—knew her, I mean—before I got arrested. She's the one who got me the job."

"How about that? Quite a coinkydink. Evie, huh? She pretty?"

*I'm so screwed.* This guy is good. "Uh…"

"That's what I figured. You remember what I told you, don't you? Drugs and—"

"Drugs and women. A parolee's kryptonite. The two things most likely to send me back to the joint. I remember, sir."

"Good. Just checking." He finally cracks a smile. "So Jackson Street...isn't that building near the spot where that girl was killed this weekend?"

*Now we're getting to it.* I steel myself. "Yes, sir. It's right across the street."

"I assume you don't know anything about that."

"No, sir. I went straight home after the thing with Evie. You can ask Mr. Richert. He drug tested me."

"Alright, alright. I believe you. It's just...well, the similarities. You might get some questions from the boys at the station."

"Similarities?" My blood runs hot under my skin, and if I could, I'd crawl under the table. Anything to stop him from looking at me like that. Making me feel like I'm eighteen again. *We know you did it, Calder. We just don't know why. But these things happen. It was an accident, wasn't it? You'll feel better if you come clean.*

"Teenage girl. Strangled. You know." I do know. I killed a girl. With my bare hands. It wasn't an accident. And I'm reminded again it's the most important thing about me. The only thing that matters. It's colossal. The eclipse that blocks the sun.

"Was she raped?" I fire back. It's all I've got left. Because there's no defending who I am—a bad man who's done bad things. Not who Evie thought.

"What kind of question is that, Butch?"

"Just wondering. I mean, Dr. Maddox runs a sex offender group in that building. I was thinking maybe the cops should talk to those guys."

He gives me a funny look. Like I've surprised him. "You looking to take my job, Detective? You know something you're not telling me?"

"No, sir. I'm just trying to be helpful."

He pats me on the shoulder the way Mr. O'Shaughnessy did after every one of those whippings. It's more control than comfort, but I don't squirm away like I used to. I just sit there and take it. "You stay in your lane, alright? Stick to fixing leaky toilets. And don't go falling in love."

****

It takes me an hour and a half on the bus to get to work from the parole office in Berkeley. And for half the ride, I'm holding on for dear life to a handgrip while another man's sweaty armpit is smack in my face. Public transportation. Just another perk of life as an ex-con. What's worse, I can't stop thinking about Sebastian. And Evie's license.

Why he took it and when. What his plans are. For me.

What my plans are. For him.

"Fear and anger, Mr. Calder. Do you know how they're alike?" Parole hearing number three, and I still had been clueless. Now the answer beats inside me like a second heart. *They're both about one thing. Control.* I'd been hunting for that nearly my whole life, since the day I'd lost it. Like some kind of demented old man with a scrawled treasure map that has *control* marked with a big red X. Because control's the first thing to go when you become a ward of the state.

I look at my hands, clenched tight above me—imagining them instead around Sebastian's scrawny neck, wringing it like a chicken. Until his face purples and his eyes bulge. However long it takes.

**176**

*Control.* I allow Young Butch that one wicked indulgence, then I push the thought away gently like sending a paper boat into a stream. I watch it go, but it makes my skin crawl. Because I know that by just thinking it, I've crossed a line.

It's another ten-minute walk from the bus stop to the office, and I book it, running from myself. I fling open the door to the office and clock in like a man possessed. It's gonna take a helluva lot of leaky toilets to fix the level of crazy going on up in this f'd-up noggin. Oblivious, Mr. Vinetti pokes his head in and waves.

"Hey, Butch. You busy?"

"Not yet. What have you got?"

"23B. Dr. Maddox's office. She said the door's been sticking. Can you check it out?"

"Sure." What else can I say? But I can't help but feel the universe is tailing me again, breathing down my neck, waiting to punish me for all the sins I haven't confessed. Or at the very least, having a roaring good laugh at my expense. "I'll go up right now."

It's still early, and the sunlight—what little there is on a gray day like this one—hasn't reached the hallway yet. It's cold and deserted. The stillness of it all gives me hope. Maybe she's not here yet.

I jiggle the knob to 23B. It's locked. And the relief is so intense my eyes well. Moving as quickly as I can, I let myself in with the spare key. Sure enough, a sticky door. *That* I can fix, and it feels good to be useful. I grab the Phillips from my toolbox and start to tighten the screws on the top hinge. With any luck, I'll be out of here in five minutes. I know I'm a coward, but what am I supposed to tell her now? *I stole your license so I could see you again. Pretend I found it and return it to you. Be the hero. But I'd hid it under my bed for days, carried it with me too. I'd chickened out. And then, Sebastian took it.* She'll never believe that. It sounds like a bad Lifetime movie, the kind the OGs were always watching in the dayroom. Besides, she's already been to the DMV. She's got another one anyway.

"Butch."

I don't bother to shut the door so I can see around it. The voice, I know. I've been hearing it in my head all morning. Hearing it. *Silencing it.* "Hi, Sebastian. I don't think Dr. Maddox is here yet."

"Oh, I know." He steps around, and we're face-to-face. He looks tired, harmless. And I start to second-guess myself. "She's not expecting me."

"You left early this morning," I say, finishing the top hinge. When I test the door, it opens and shuts with ease. But I'm too mixed up to feel good about it.

"I couldn't sleep." He rocks from one foot to the other. Then stops. Smiles. "But you were out like a light. You've gotta be careful when you sleep that hard."

I cock my head at him, and my chest tightens in a familiar way. It turns out anger is a lot like riding a bicycle. "What's that supposed to mean?"

"Relax, man. I was just joking with you."

"Is everything okay?" And there it is. The universe's well-timed punchline. Evie's appearing next to Sebastian, and she's staring at me. At my hand, specifically. And the screwdriver in it. I'm holding it with purpose, like a weapon—without even realizing—and my fingers start to tremble. Before she notices, I bend down to my toolbox and pretend I wasn't just fantasizing about driving the thing straight into Sebastian's gullet.

"Yep," I say, chancing a look up at her. "All good. I fixed your door." Evie nods at me, and there's something behind her eyes, a kind of urgency, but it disappears as soon as she speaks to him.

"What are you doing here, Sebastian? You know we don't have group today." She skirts around me into the office as I gather the broken pieces of myself—my pride, my sanity—and prepare to flee.

"I know." He's talking to her. He's looking at her. But it feels like his words are meant for me. "I was hoping we could chat. Just for a minute."

"Your individual session is tomorrow. Can it wait until then?"

He pauses, glances back at me, before he answers. "It can't wait."

## BUTCH
## MAY 5, 1994
## EIGHT DAYS BEFORE I KILLED HER

**I'D** spent the last three afternoons in the stacks of the Berkeley Public Library finding my religion. Or losing it, depending who you ask. Gwen had told her parents we were studying, and I had no one to tell. Which made it not count somehow. Like the tree that falls in the forest with no one around to watch it go.

Anyway, it wasn't a total lie. Making out with Gwen, I *had* studied every inch of her body—her pouty pink lips when they'd pressed against mine; the spools of her silky blonde hair I'd fisted in my hands; and the miles and miles of long, tan legs, she'd wrapped around me, pulling me closer with the kind of desperation I didn't know I could inspire in anybody. Certainly not a girl like her.

And then, holy mother of God, this afternoon Gwendolyn Shaw, Goddess of the Stacks, had dropped to her knees, unzipped my fly, and taken me to heaven. Right there in the religion section of all places. A-*freakin'*-men.

"So what're you doing this weekend?" she'd asked me as we walked toward the library's exit. She'd given a fluttery wave to the woman at the front desk. As cool as a cucumber. That was Gwen. Like she hadn't just rocked my world.

"I dunno." Me, on the other hand. I was still weak-kneed, and my brain wasn't working right. "Nothing really."

**179**

"Wanna come to a party with me? On Saturday? It's at Matthias' house."

"Yeah. Okay." Two words. That seemed about all I could manage right now.

We usually split up there, at the double doors. Gwen would go first, sashaying past the book drop to Daddy's awaiting chariot, ready to whisk her up to her tower in the Hills. I'd hang back and count to fifty before slinking out to the double-parked 'Cuda and driving home to my Blue Bird dungeon. But that day, Gwen didn't let go of my hand, sweaty as it was.

"My dad wants to meet you."

My stomach lurched with the kind of instant panic I reserved for officers of the law. "Right now? Are you sure? He's probably in a hurry. Doesn't he have work to do?"

"Relax, Calder. He won't bite." She raised my hand to her mouth and sunk her perfect, pearl teeth against my skin. Instant boner. But at eighteen, that's how it went. Lust, grief, rage—everything boiled so close to the surface, it didn't take much to trigger an eruption.

I ducked into the nearest aisle, eyes darting from shelf to shelf, desperate for the anti-Gwen. Not just the most boring book I could find, it had to be next level. Like watching paint dry during a calculus lecture in church. Finally, I found it. *The History of Farming in Central America in the 1900s.* That'd work.

Gwen giggled at me as I stared at the words on the mud-colored spine and waited it out.

"It's not the biting I'm worried about," I told her, finally allowing myself a glimpse in her direction. Just in time to watch her set a square of watermelon bubblegum on her tongue. *History of. Farming. Central America.* Do not think about Gwen and her sexy—*tractors, crops, ploughs*—mouth. "It's the brutal murdering that's definitely going to happen when he sees how much I like you."

"How much do you like me?"

"A lot. Obviously." I let out a long breath, wondering if it would always be this way. Girls had it easy. Nothing about them was obvious.

"Well, the thing is that he has to meet you before he approves. And he has to approve before I can invite you over." She tilted her head at me, coyly. "And I was thinking of inviting you over after the party on Friday night since my parents will be out late at a charity thing. But, if you don't want to—"

My fairytale was already spun, unfurling like Gwen's golden hair down her back. Her, the virgin princess, begging to be deflowered. Me, the unworthy commoner, with a fire in my loins. Alone in her room without the watchful eyes of the king. "Say no more," I teased, jogging toward the door as she laughed. "Let's go find him right now."

**\*\*\*\***

Peter Shaw was the human equivalent of steel. Sitting in his black Rolls Royce, polished, solid, and ice cold. He had the first cell phone I'd ever laid eyes on—and the only one I'd see up close for the next twenty-three years—pressed against his ear. When Gwen knocked, he held up a finger, and we waited.

"Is that a mobile phone?" I asked, gawking at the IBM Simon I'd nearly spent a grand on to reserve for myself last month. Until I'd realized I had no one to call and bolted from the store like I'd been shot from a cannon.

She rolled her eyes. "Don't be a smart aleck. I'm sure your dad has one too."

*Busted.* "Not the Simon though. That one's cutting edge. I heard they haven't even released it to the public yet."

"My dad went to Harvard with the CEO, so he's—"

The Rolls' window began its slow descent, an unveiling of sorts. "Gwen, are you ready?"

"Daddy, this is Butch Calder. The boy I told you about." He didn't blink. Didn't need to. Automatic bodily functions were clearly beneath him. When I extended my hand, prickly and hopeful, he stared at it for an eternity before he took it in his own.

"It's uh—really, really great to meet you, sir. Really." I couldn't have sounded any more pathetic if I'd tried.

"Good to meet you as well." Mr. Shaw's mouth smiled, but it never thawed his eyes. He patted the leather seat next to him. "C'mon, Gwendolyn. I have a call with Tokyo in thirty minutes. I can't be late."

"Butch's family is in oil, remember? They're remodeling that big house on Drury Road. It's going to have an infinity pool." My own lies parroted back to me in Gwen's voice—soft and cajoling—sounded ridiculous. And I readied myself for the Shaw firing squad.

"Congratulations." A curt nod, a raise of the brows, another smile. All covered in a thin layer of frost and disinterest. Not at all what I'd imagined, and suddenly I felt sorry for Gwen.

"Sir, I'd like to ask your permission to date your—"

"Fine. It's fine." He waved me off like a fly at a picnic. And in that flick of the wrist, I saw the truth. Meeting her dad wasn't about her getting permission. It was about her getting noticed. My fairytale crumbled. Mr. Shaw was no king, and Gwen was no less on her own than I was.

"He plays the guitar too, Daddy. He's really talented. I've heard him," Gwen said, insistent. Confused, I frowned at her—*damn if she hadn't co-opted my lie*—but she was fixed on her father, doe-eyed. And I decided right then. I loathed him.

"I'm alright," I said, playing along. What the hell. I'll do it for her. For Gwen. At least maybe he'd acknowledge her existence. My existence. But when Mr. Shaw's lips pursed tight with impatience, I upped the ante. For me. "Actually, my music teacher told me I remind her a lot of Gene Simmons. I might play some gigs in the city this summer. Maybe even start my own rock band. Gwen could come on tour with me."

"Good for you, Mitch."

Gwen's face fell, crumpled. "It's *Butch*, Daddy." And I started to wonder if I hadn't missed out after all. If my parents would've turned out the same. A never-ending well of disappointment. But

**182**

then I thought of my mom, carefully cutting the crusts off my PB&J. My dad, teaching me the perfect spiral. I hated Mr. Shaw even more for making me doubt them.

"Of course, honey. Butch. That's what I said. Now, get in the car. You don't want Dad to be late do you?" *What a prick.*

I watched the Rolls pull around the corner. Only Gwen looked back—beautiful as ever—and her cheeks flamed red. Peter Shaw had already forgotten me. No doubt about that. In fact, if I hadn't murdered his daughter, I don't think he would've remembered me at all.

****

The peeling blue paint of my dungeon awaited me as I tore into the parking lot blasting KISS's "Not for the Innocent." The ugly throb of the guitar drowned out Mr. Shaw's indifference until all I could hear was Gene. And he was on fire and singing just for me. *I'm mean and I'm dirty, like none you've ever seen. Bad habits drip like honey, no tongue can lick me clean.*

I put the top up on the 'Cuda and sat inside, sipping from the miniature bottle of Jack I'd stashed under the seat. Tuesday afternoon, I'd slipped two in my pocket at the liquor store a block down from the library while Gwen had lounged on the counter, flirting with the clerk. We were a team now. Partners in crime. A regular Bonnie and Clyde. She'd want me to save her some—it was only fair—but I swigged the whole thing before I could stop myself, belting out the lyrics with an exaggerated rasp in my throat. *I'm not of royal blood, I've never been discreet.*

That's right, Mr. Shaw. I'm not a goddamned royal. And neither are you.

The more I sang, the angrier I got. And the angrier I got, the more—the louder—I sang. *I've been damned, I've been cursed, I've been guilty and abused. I spit the hangman in his face and hung him on his noose.*

Halfway through the chorus, a girl burst out from the corner room. Her yellow dress was the first thing I noticed. Mainly because it looked too fancy for the Blue Bird with lace the color of a runny egg yolk. One of the straps dangled, broken, exposing the tan line above her breast. She didn't bother to cover herself—like it was too late somehow—and that made me look away. The rest of the dress was twisted on her body, mangled as a car wreck, with a gaping wound in the fabric.

"Get back in here, Cassie. Please." Trey Waters materialized in the doorway, a demon I'd conjured from the dark side. His eyes shone like black marbles against his pasty skin, and his hair hung freely past his shoulders, shrouding his face. I shivered when he ran his hand down the girl's arm, my eyes following hers to where his pants hung loose on his hips, his belt buckle undone.

"Don't you wanna thank Trey for all the nice things he bought you?" She stayed motionless as he fingered the broken strap, tying the two ends together, and fixing it on her shoulder.

I waited for Peggy to show herself, to make good on her promise. *How dare he come back here!* Then I waited for my own legs to carry me out of the car and into Trey's personal space, where I'd punch him so hard he'd never call me Nobody again. Maybe it was the alcohol, as potent as snake's venom, that left me paralyzed. Or some other poison coursing through my veins. I can't say why I did what I did. Only that I did it—hunkered down in my seat so I couldn't be seen. Turned down the music. Cracked the window. Watched.

"C'mon, baby. I won't hurt you. I promise it'll feel real nice."

The girl—Cassie—fixed herself, tugging and straightening what was left of her dress and rubbing her fingers underneath her eyes until the black smudges were nearly gone. And I understood her completely. Whatever was about to happen, it had to be on her terms. She wanted to decide. That's the thing about life—usually, you don't get to choose how it screws you over. Or when. It's just one bad surprise party after another where you're the guest of honor. Live that way long enough and the options mattered less than the fact you've got to pick between them.

184

"You're my girl now. Purdy as a damn picture. Come back inside, and let me take care of you." He slid his belt from beneath the loops with a swish and a crack that sounded like the world splitting open. "Now."

She didn't speak. Her face was a blank where you could've written any answer you wanted. Her chest rose and fell once, before she stepped back inside and the room swallowed her. I must've known then who she was—that she was Evie's Cassie—but I didn't let myself think it till I locked the door to my own private hell and slithered beneath the covers feeling slimy as a snake. By then, whatever happened already had.

**\*\*\*\***

I see it plain as day, looking back. How much I'd wanted to take something from someone the way things had been taken from me. How I'd envied Trey for all the taking he did. But what I knew then came in a single vile thought. Hot and white like a meteor, it burned through my brain. *I will fuck Gwendolyn Shaw. If it's the last thing I do.*

# CHAPTER TWENTY-TWO

**EVIE**
**JANUARY 17, 2017**
**TUESDAY**

I watch the clock above Sebastian's head and wait for the minute hand to move, wondering how the day has already gone so wrong. Not even nine o'clock, and I already want a do-over. To begin with, Maggie had tricked me, nudging me awake at 5:30 and luring me out of bed with a steaming cup of coffee and a slice of her organic banana bread.

"You're coming to yoga with me," she'd said, before I was caffeinated enough to launch a proper protest. Turns out yoga was code for interrogation. Which she launched the moment she'd trapped me inside her BMW with NPR and the cloying stench of Chanel No. 5 acting as her own personal torture rack.

"What was that all about last night? That detective?" I'd pulled my sweatshirt tighter around me, wishing I could disappear beneath the seat.

"Just an update. They have a suspect. Danny Dunaway. He's done this sort of thing before. He might've even been involved in that murder near my office."

"Shocking," Maggie'd deadpanned. "Imagine that. A repeat sex offender."

"Some of them do change, you know. They're not monsters." *Christ, I was defending Danny.*

"Of course. Why didn't you offer your services, dear? I'm sure he would've been interested."

"You know what I mean." Really, I'd been defending myself. Maggie thought the notion of a rehabilitated sex offender was an oxymoron. And me, by association, just a moron. "Not everyone is a Ted Bundy."

"Well, I'm just glad you're okay." I'd felt a twinge in my stomach. Maggie never gave up that easily unless…unless she had something better. "So was that all the detective wanted? I could've sworn I heard her mention your mother. That she'd been arrested with that Trey person once. Not that I was eavesdropping, but you know how thin the walls are."

"Uh, no. You must've misheard her." And just like that, I'd started the morning with a lie, followed by an amazingly awkward hour of yoga.

Thing is, it wasn't just any lie. It was the worst kind. The pathetic kind. The kind that doesn't fool anyone. Like the one I'd told the detective last night. "I don't remember Trey Waters, but my mother knew a lot of shady characters." She hadn't bought it any more than Maggie had.

The minute hand finally moves, advancing one small step, and Sebastian clears his throat. Again. Over his shoulder, the hanging tree waits, and I try not to look at it, focusing instead on the file in my hand. DELACOURT, SEBASTIAN.

"I'm sorry to just barge in like this, Doc. But I needed to talk to someone." He taps his fingers on that book of his, the sound of a tiny heartbeat drumming, and I fight the urge to strangle his hand with my own.

"You seemed upset out there. Did Butch—uh, the maintenance man—say something to you?" I replay the scene in my mind, but I get stuck at the same spot. Poised at the top of the stairs, Butch at my door. I'd been flooded with relief. I needed to talk to him. I had to tell someone—*him*—though I wasn't sure what exactly or where to start. Only that I'd become too full with the past, brimming. Overflowing. And only then I'd noticed Sebastian, hovering like a shadow, the tension between them taut as a bowstring and threatening to snap.

"We're roommates. Butch and me. Did he tell you that?" Sebastian smiles without showing his teeth, like he's holding in a secret.

"Butch is an employee here. We don't talk about that sort of thing." *Liar.* His eyes say it. They speak it for him. Or maybe I'm projecting. But still, it is the truth. He didn't tell me.

Sebastian leans forward in his chair, resting his elbows on his knees. The book sits—quiet now—sleeping in his lap. "Oh, you don't have to worry. I won't tell, Doc."

"Won't tell what?" And I hate the way my voice goes up an octave.

"About you. And Butch. I saw you guys together at the Chicken and Waffles. If you ask me, you make a cute couple." He's playing me—I see it clearly. Yet, I'm powerless against it. My nerves thrum like tight threads, already so close to the surface.

I peek at the tree, the place where it all began. My unraveling. But today, somehow, I find strength in its indifference. "Is that why you came to the office? To talk about me and the custodian?"

His eyes widen, and he sits back, securing the book in both hands. I've rattled him, I think. "So…it's my birthday. Kind of a rough day for me, if you remember…"

I grip his file tighter, thinking of the words inside. "Of course, I do." Sebastian had one of those cases. The kind you don't forget. The kind that would've sent Maggie into a tailspin. "How can you work with those people?" she'd asked me once, directing a pointed glance at Jared. "It'll be different when you have children. What will you tell them?"

**188**

That was before Jared got sick, before the possibility of a pregnancy, a child, a long life together evaporated like smoke.

"She'll tell them she helps people who did something bad learn to do something better." And I'd fought the urge to cheer for Jared. "Geez, mom. She does therapy with sex offenders. She isn't one."

But looking at Sebastian, with his book and his red-rimmed eyes, I knew how Maggie felt. Some people are contagious. Before you know it, you've got whatever it is and you'll never be well again.

"It's just that…it happens to be her birthday too. A twisted coincidence, I know. She's three years older than me."

"Sasha, you mean?"

"Yes, Sasha. My stepsister. And it makes today doubly worse. I wish I could tell her how sorry I am, but…it's not fair, that restraining order. I would never hurt her."

"Try to see it from her perspective. If you were in her shoes, how would you feel?"

His face contorts in pain, as if I'd poked him someplace soft. "I'd want to see my brother. Stepbrother. I mean, it's been twenty-something years. I know they want to see me. Her and my mom. It's my stepdad. Even now, he's the one feeding them lies about me. Telling them what a pervert I am. All the while, he's having an affair. I'm sure of it."

"I hear how difficult it is—that you love her—but you hurt her very badly. Her and someone she cared about. You murdered—"

"I know what I did!" His fists clench and his book falls to the floor. The edge of a picture peeks between two pages, but he snatches it up before I can see. "But I didn't mean to hurt her! I never would!"

"You're angry," I say, ignoring his blatant denial. I'm suddenly aware of how vulnerable I am. Here, alone with him. And his rage. That feeling—the slimy, hot-breathed Danny feeling—squirms in my stomach. And part of me eyes the door, plotting an escape. The other part remains cold and clinical, a distant observer.

"Hell yes. It's bad enough you made me say it out loud in front of everybody last week like I'm some freak show on display."

"It's about accountability, Sebastian. Not judgment."

"Did you see the way Vince looked at me? Pure judgment from that asshole. I think about what I did every day. Every time I see myself in the mirror, I see her. With him." He claws at his face, tears already streaming. "I'm sorry," he says. "I just hate birthdays."

I nod grimly. I can relate to that. "What can you do to make today more bearable?" I sit, silent, as he sniffles. This is also my job. To hold the space. To let him fill it.

"I need to be alone."

"Okay. Where will you go?" More sniffling. More silence. And my eyes dip to his file and the article I'd clipped at the top, the one his PO faxed, along with the therapy referral form where he'd scrawled, *Got a doozy for you!* I read it with renewed horror.

> **Sexual predator wins habeas corpus suit against State, awaits January release**
>
> **In 1995, seventeen-year-old Sebastian Delacourt sexually assaulted his stepsister, Sasha, and murdered her boyfriend, Roland Dermot, at the stepsiblings' birthday party in Pacific Heights, one of San Francisco's posh neighborhoods. Today, twenty-two years later, he is about to be a free man.**

Sebastian's voice is heavy and dull, and it cuts like an axe. "The tree," he says, finally. "The hanging tree. It's a good place to think."

I can't help but look at it—the tree. "Why do you call it that?"

He's calm again, eyes serene as lake water. "Oh. Hmm...I don't know really. An old wives' tale I guess. Before my mom met my stepdad we used to live here in downtown Oakland. There were rumors about that tree."

"Rumors?"

He shrugs. "They said a guy was hung there back in the 1800s. For murdering a little girl. And that if you climbed up high enough, you'd find the noose still tied there, all weathered and gray. Of course, we'd all get wasted and make our best attempt." He points to a crooked scar on his elbow. "Five stitches."

"You know, I've had this office for a long time and I've never heard that story." Even as I say it, I know it's not true. *I have heard it before, but where? From who?*

"Probably a good thing stories like that die." He shuffles to his feet, tucking his book under his arm. *Die. Die. Die.* The word echoes, and I have to speak to stop it.

"Probably. So, I'll see you tomorrow…"

I go through the motions, telling him goodbye. But before the door shuts behind him, a wave of nausea washes over me, leaving a memory, perfect as a polished pebble.

\*\*\*\*

The smell of beer had bitten at my nose, and I'd pretended to take a sip from the bottle. "C'mon, Evie. You can do better than that."

I'd shaken my head at Cassie, and she'd groaned, gulping down half of hers in one swallow. What was she doing? This wasn't part of the plan.

"Yeah, loosen up, Evie." The faceless man had laughed when he said my name—I wished Cassie hadn't said it—and I'd felt my stomach drop. Still, I'd put the bottle to my lips and tipped it back, letting the bitter liquid trickle down my throat as he spoke again. "Atta-girl. The hanging tree's more fun if you're drunk."

## EVIE
## MAY 6, 1994
## SEVEN DAYS UNTIL MY BIRTHDAY

**CHERICE'S** singing woke me up that Friday morning, and I was lying there, eyes closed and still half-asleep, just listening.

*Hang down your head, Tom Dooley. Hang down your head and cry... poor boy, you're bound to die. I met her on the mountain. There I took her life. Met her on the mountain. Stabbed her with my...*

"Knife!"

I sat up, straight as a board, and let out a shriek as Bobby Pierce jabbed me in the side with his grubby fingers.

"Gotcha, Evil Evie!" He scampered away with his entourage, but I could hear him shouting. "She looked at me! She looked at me!" The sound of their maniacal laughter followed them down the stairs until it grew faint and disappeared.

"Are you alright, Evie?" Cherice's voice floated into the room before she did. "I'll give him a good talking to after school today."

I felt the tears start to well, but I willed them away. "What is that song about? The one you're always singing?"

"Tom Dooley?"

I nodded at her, swallowing the sob still caught in my throat.

"Well, my grandma used to sing it to me when I was just a kid. But she told me it's not for little girls...unless they're very, very brave." Cherice sat on the edge of the bed and patted my leg. She smelled like coffee and cinnamon, and I leaned into her, wishing she was my big sister. Wishing I had a sister at all. "Which you are, of course. Very brave."

"Hmph. If I'm so brave, then why does everyone pick on me?"

"Sometimes being brave isn't about how loud you can shout or how big you can stomp your feet or even how unafraid you are. Sometimes, it's just about sitting still and getting through it. No matter how hard it is." She tucked my hair behind my ear and lifted my chin with her knuckles. "You're the bravest girl at the Port. One day you'll see."

When she said it, I could almost believe it.

"So, about that song…it's the story of the murder of a woman, Laura, and her baby. They thought Tom Dula did it—he was her boyfriend—and they hung him for it." She lowered her voice and brought her face next to mine. Her scar—waxy and brown as an earthworm—was close enough to touch, and I wondered about the rumors. That her own father had done it with a broken bottle when she'd stepped between him and her mother. Now that was brave. "Just between you and me, Tom Dula didn't do it. It was another woman who was jealous of Laura, but Dula took the fall for her."

"Why would he do that? Let himself get hanged if he was innocent?" The injustice burned as sharply as if I'd known him myself.

"He felt guilty. Thought he still deserved to be punished. Because he'd been at the heart of it all. Between two women who loved him."

"That settles it. I am never falling in love. Ever." *I'll make an exception for Calder though.* But I couldn't say that out loud.

Cherice's soft laughter bubbled from her throat, velvety and soothing as the sound of a stream. "We'll see about that," she said. "It doesn't always end in a hanging. Now, go on and brush your teeth and get dressed for school. You'll be late. And you're already skating on thin ice after that little stunt you pulled Wednesday."

"Do you have a boyfriend?" I blurted, desperate to keep talking to her. I couldn't have said why—not then—but looking back, she made me feel cared for. Mothered. Loved, even. Besides, I was pretty sure I already knew the answer. I'd seen a guy pick her up from the Port a few weeks ago, and I'd heard Wally teasing her about it. At twelve that seemed like proof of an epic romance.

"Evie. School. Now."

Minutes later, I stood in the mirror, baring my sudsy teeth and mulling over Cherice's story. Mid-floss, I realized I didn't believe it. Tom Dula was guilty as sin, just like that old song said. I knew it.

I let the memory creep in, just for a minute. What Trey had told me the day after they'd incinerated my mom's body—since we couldn't afford a funeral—and presented her to me in a small wooden box. The day he'd shown up with a new tattoo on his wrist—*RIP*—red and raised as a blister above my mother's name. I'd walked to the edge of the water at Oakland Marina and dumped her in fast, horrified at the tiny shards of bone that sank like pearls in the murky ocean. Then, Trey had driven me to Port in a Storm, his lips loosened with Jack Daniels and the white powder he'd snorted up his nose.

"Your mama . . .she just ended it, Evie. Just gave up on you. On me. On life. She saw me out with my new lady friend. And she was always real jealous. You remember that, right? But you were at school. You didn't hear us fightin' about it. You didn't hear us fightin' about nothin'. She wouldn't have wanted you to hear that. And you didn't. You didn't."

He'd paused then, putting his pothole eyes on me. I didn't look, but I could feel them making their demands, telling me to believe their lies.

*I didn't*, I'd said, hoping that would satisfy him. As if the devil was ever satisfied.

"Them pig cops might say somethin' different. Might try to convince you. But you listen to Trey now. She just slammed too much this time. Enough to kill a goddamn horse." He'd laughed then,

**194**

sudden and sharp like the cry of a bird. "Guess life just ain't worth living without me."

****

I remember everything about the first time I hitched a ride. After the school bus dropped me off at the Port, I'd walked to the underpass and stuck out my thumb like I'd seen people do in the movies. I tried to feel brave. The sky was as blue as a jewel that day, and the clouds that floated by took the shape of turtles, dolphins, elves. All happy things. Good things. Because I had pure intentions—to rescue Cassie—and fate was on my side.

I didn't wait long. The car that stopped for me smelled like French fries, and the man inside offered me one dipped in ketchup from the bag on his lap. He wore a blue mechanics jumpsuit with the name Elmer stitched on the pocket, black smudges down the front from the cars he worked on every day at the shop. He told me he was a dad to two boys, grown now. And a husband, though he'd lost his wife a year before. Breast cancer. So really, he was alone. Like me.

Elmer knew the Blue Bird. He'd stayed there a time or two when he was down on his luck. And he took me right to it, letting me out just where I'd asked. A block away.

"Do me a favor," he said, before I got out. "Don't hitch any more rides. It's not safe. Especially at your age." He reached in his back pocket, pulled out his wallet, and forked over a twenty-dollar bill. "Take a taxi next time. This should cover you one."

I shook my head at him. "Keep it. There won't be a next time." I fully intended on riding shotgun back to the Port in the 'Cuda, the wind catching my hair and Calder grinning at me from the driver's seat with that smile of his. The one that could make me forget just about anything. And Cassie would be there too. Wedged into the space between us. Or she'd sit on my lap, and we'd laugh the whole way back.

"Take it anyway," Elmer said. "Just in case." So I did. And that was that. He drove away—probably to his empty house—and I strutted to the front desk at the Blue Bird, a girl on a mission.

The day shift clerk lifted her eyes from *Cosmo* magazine and waved at me. "Hi, Nanette," I said, waving back. "I like your hair. You're letting it grow long again."

She flipped one of the magazine's articles toward me—Top Ten Ways to Get Him to Notice You—and pointed to number five. *Toss your hair over your shoulder.*

"Can't flip it if it's too short. And Mac likes somethin' to grab on to when we…uh, well…never mind. How you been, Evie girl?"

"I'm okay. I'm actually looking for Trey. Have you seen him?"

She raised her eyebrows at me. "You mean you *want* to find him? Most people that come through here are trying to lose him. Can't say I blame 'em for that. I'd rather pet a rattlesnake."

"I think he's here with a friend of mine. Cassie. She's in trouble."

"Well, if she's mixed up with him, then I'd say you're right. He checked into 157 a couple days ago, paid for two weeks. That's the one on the corner. You want me to come with you?"

"I can handle it."

"You go, girl." She chuckled as she directed my eyes to number one on the list. *Act confident even when you aren't.* "Call me if you need me."

Trey's car wasn't in the lot. Neither was the 'Cuda. But Cassie opened the door when I knocked, keeping the chain latched so all I could see was a sliver of her face. Impossible as it seemed, she looked older. Like a woman. Or maybe, just sadder. Like something behind her eyes had deflated, had lost its color.

"What're you doing here?" she asked.

*I came for you, dork. I figured you might need rescuing. But I'm still mad at you, in case you were wondering.* That's what I'd planned to say, but it didn't come out that way. Not at all. "My boyfriend lives here. In 145. Calder, remember?"

"He's not your boyfriend, Evie."

**196**

"How would you know?"

"I just do, okay. For one thing, I've seen him. And he's at least eighteen. And you're twelve."

"I'll be thirteen in seven days, and you're one to talk. Do you even know how old Trey is?"

"Thirty-one," she fired back, sticking out her tongue at me. And I felt my heart crack just a little. Like a fracture on the surface of the ice. "Besides, I'm almost fourteen and way more mature than you."

"Seriously? How?"

"I'm not a virgin." The crack in my chest widened and ached.

"Congratulations. I'm sure it was a beautiful experience. Trey's such a romantic. Is he your pimp now too?"

"He doesn't do that. Not with me. He wants to take care of me. He gave me this." She held her hand up, and my whole heart broke in two. It was the same kind of ring he'd given my mom. A band of fake gold crowned with a fake diamond and wrapped in fake promises. I imagined he had a whole drawer full of them. He'd probably gotten a discount for buying in bulk. "When I turn fourteen, we can get married in Utah."

"Did he say that? Did he ask you?"

"He will."

"You've known him five days, Cass."

"Whatever." She waved me off. "By the way, Trey wasn't my first."

"Oh really. I didn't realize you were so experienced. So who was the lucky guy?" The moment I saw her face, I wanted a take back. She was broken too. More broken than I was. Her outer shell was brittle as an egg's. *How had I missed it?*

"Dave something. I don't even know his last name. He was my mom's boyfriend before I ran away. But now I have Trey, and I don't have to run anymore." She shut the door softly. It barely made a sound. I wished she'd slammed it. That would've made it easier to leave her there. In that room, five down from where Trey ended my mother.

I stood outside Calder's door for thirty minutes waiting for his 'Cuda to come roaring into the lot. Waiting for *my* rescue. I even practiced my hair toss in the window's reflection. But no one came and nothing happened. And the clouds that floated by looked like snakes and devils and diamond rings. Finally, I gave up and called a cab from the pay phone, thankful that Elmer had insisted.

# CHAPTER TWENTY-THREE

I watch Sebastian scuttle out of Evie's office and down the stairs like a prickly little insect, and I follow, seething. Young Butch is at the helm, the screwdriver wedged in my back pocket. The last time I got this angry, I'd nearly blown it all up. My reputation. My twenty years of clean time. My goddamn parole date. I'd been walking a tightrope with a stack of fine china balanced on my head. Because that's how it feels when you're in Folsom, ten days pre-release—with 7,843 days behind you—and even breathing feels like a gamble. I'd been minding my own business in the chow hall when this young skinhead, Rusty, had smacked me from behind.

"Heard you got a date, asshole. I didn't realize they were lettin' out sickos too…girl killers like you going free. Imagine that." I'd scrambled to my feet with rage coursing through me, thick and hot as my own blood. "Now what?" he'd said, stepping toward me, his jaw jutting like a bulldog. He'd been strapped, the shiv glinting in his boot.

The whole place got real quiet. And I'd felt the world grind to a halt. This was it. My defining moment. I'd like to tell you I'd heard Gwen's voice or caught a flash of the anguish in her parents' eyes or even used the deep breathing I'd been practicing to get right again. But in truth, it had been Rusty himself who'd saved me. I'd stared at the nick on his baby face where he'd probably cut himself shaving with the safety razor. Saw the muscles in his neck tense like a snake swallowing its prey. Followed his eyes to the brand-new, biggest, baddest SOB on the block, perched on a table with his cronies, watching it all with cool disinterest. And it hit me.

How Rusty was me. *Then.* Scared shitless.

How I was different. *Now.* A man.

The circle of life, prison style.

"If you're gonna shank me, go on and do it, Rusty. But unless you kill me, I'm gonna be out there in ten days." I'd pointed toward the barred windows, so grimy you could barely see the sky. "I'll be sinking my teeth into the fattest, juiciest steak you can imagine. I'll be a free man. And you'll be spending the next twenty-five to life in Folsom. Gobbling the slop that passes for food, tattooing swastikas on your forehead, and whittling weapons in your spare time. So, go ahead, stick me. Add on another twenty-five. Either way, I win."

*I won,* I mutter, tossing the screwdriver into the bushes at the edge of the parking lot with disgust. I'd won my freedom, and there was no way in hell I was going back. I repeat it to myself again and again and again, slowing my pace until I'm just standing there. Motionless. With my heart racing and my head spinning ninety miles a minute. This is one of those high-risk situations the psych doctors were always talking about. "What are your triggers, Mr. Calder?" Rejection. Abandonment. Inferiority. Powerlessness. Fear.

And I have to admit it, I'm afraid of Sebastian. He's halfway across the parking lot when he stops on a dime and spins around.

**200**

"Are you following me?" He's so far away it's hard to tell if he's angry or scared or just amused with himself. I close the distance between us but leave myself an out. Enough room to think twice before I do anything stupid.

"It depends," I tell him. "Did you take something that belongs to me?"

He cocks his head to the side, scrunches his face in put-on confusion. "Does it? Belong to you?"

The nerve of this guy. "I'll take that as a yes. You did take it, didn't you?"

"Well then, I'll take that as a no, Butch. It doesn't belong to you."

It's a damn good thing that screwdriver is out of my reach. Because this—Sebastian's mocking, his smug little voice—is beyond high risk. It's a four-alarm fire. "Doesn't belong to you either. So why'd you take it?"

"Insurance. CYA, you know?"

"What's that supposed to mean?" I know good and well what it means, but I want to hear him say it. I need to see him squirm.

"It means I keep it until you do something for me."

"Oh. I see. Blackmail. That's a great way to start your parole." And I brand myself a hypocrite. "What exactly did you have in mind?"

His eyes dart around the lot, but it's still early and mostly empty. Evie's car is parked back by the stairs, the ones that lead straight up to her office, and I wonder if she put it there—close like that—because she's still on edge, thinking Danny is after her. That he has her name. That he has her license. That he can find her. *My fault, goddammit.* And I can't let her down again.

"Go on. Say it." With the thought of Evie, the urge to throttle Sebastian subsides, and I allow myself a small step forward.

"If anybody asks—and by anybody, I mean the cops—I was in my bed the other night. Friday night. I need you to do that for me."

"And if I don't?"

"Then you'll have to explain to Dr. Maddox how her driver's license ended up under your mattress. Now, there's a real non-starter."

"How do I know you didn't tell her already?"

He shrugs, one side of his mouth smiling. "You'll just have to trust me."

"Now, *that's* a non-starter. No way. I'm not lying for you."

"Alright. Have it your way, but…thieving isn't such a great way to start your new job either, is it? I wouldn't want you blamed if anything else goes missing. Say from Evie's office. After thirteen interviews, it'd be a shame to get fired."

I let out a long, slow whistle. Because cojones like that demand respect. Even if Sebastian is a few cards short of a deck. My first cellie, Jimmy, was just like that. J-Cat, they'd called him. Which meant a special kind of crazy. The straight-up 5150 kind. He'd snitched on the shot caller for the Mexican Mafia and told him so right to his face. Mendez was so shocked, he'd waited a whole day to toss him over the tier. They'd ruled it a suicide. And in a way, they were right.

"Damn, Sebastian. I've gotta hand it to you, man. You're not what I expected. I'll consider it on one condition. You tell me the truth about where you were. I'm not covering up for a murderer."

He shakes his head rapid fire—like he's trying to free himself from something—but he doesn't say no. He doesn't say anything. And Mr. Vinetti's voice stops us both.

"Hey, Calder. I'm not paying you to shoot the breeze. Get up here. And bring the mop and the Super-Sorb. A kid puked in 55B."

Sebastian shrugs at me. "Sounds like the call of duty."

\*\*\*\*

When the day starts with barf and blackmail, it can only go up from there. Or at least you'd think so. But by five o'clock, I'd tossed three dead mice, their spines snapped in two, and hammered my thumb… twice. Not to mention, I reek of vomit. So it figures, I run into Evie on my way out.

"Rough day?" she asks, following me down the stairs into the parking lot. The sky is the gloomiest shade of gray, the exact color of Folsom's walls, and a cool drop of rain splashes onto my forehead.

"Is it that obvious?" I wipe my face with my sleeve, catching an unfortunate whiff of myself.

"Gary told me about the incident at the clinic. Projectile vomit? That sounds awful."

I groan, reliving it all again. "Yeah, it was exorcist level."

She laughs, and it's the best sound I've heard all day. Like the tinkling tin-can wind chimes my mom hung on our front porch. They'd always given me butterflies. The good kind. "So I take it you won't be heading straight to Chicken and Waffles then?"

"I've gotta hit the showers first. Unless you think Brenda likes the smell of day-old puke." It strikes me then—dumb ox that I am, dumb ox twenty-three years out of practice. *Is she asking me out?*

"Something tells me Brenda wouldn't mind."

*Is she flirting?* The rain falls faster now, and I put up a hand as cover. Evie opens her umbrella and holds it high, inviting me underneath, but I shake my head at her. "Brenda might not, but you will…mind. Trust me, you don't want to get too close."

"At least let me give you a ride back. You'll get soaked."

"It's probably for the best." But I'm dreading the walk. The cold that will seep straight through my bones, soggy clothes clinging to me like a second skin. My feet sloshing around in my brand-new work boots, a welcome gift from Mr. Vinetti. And worst of all, knowing I passed up a ride from Evie. Because I'm too chicken to be completely alone with a woman.

"C'mon. It's really coming down now." She's right. And the wind is picking up too, mercilessly splattering drops against my pant legs.

"If you insist."

I run for the passenger side. It's warm and dry and still inside, and I sit there, dripping like a drowned rat. Evie reaches for the door, but I can barely see her through the foggy window. Only the shock of her blood-red umbrella, eerie against the dark sky, like a child's balloon floating through a graveyard. The rain beats against the roof—hard and hostile—like the beanbag rounds the CO gunners fire in a riot. The *rat-tat-tat* insistent as the pattering of my heart. It's doing its usual thing—straight up panic.

*I'm in Evie's car.*

*What am I doing here?*

*What did Sebastian tell her?*

I feel trapped. By the weight of my lies. My guilt. My shame. It's a goddamn elephant sitting on my chest. And I think of making a break for it until Evie gasps, sharp and sudden. The thwack of her palm against the glass sends a shot right up my spine.

"Oh my God. It's him." Her words—the fear in them—is unmistakable, even muffled by the rain and the window between us. "It's Danny."

I open the door into the pouring rain and follow her shaky hand to a truck idling in the corner of the lot. Not the black jeep Danny tore out in like a bat out of hell. Its lights come on, and I squint into the brightness trying to make out a face. But it's all blur and shadow.

"Are you sure?" I ask.

As she nods her head at me, the truck's wipers start to swish against the rain, building to a frenzied beating. I wonder if she's seeing things, getting paranoid the way I did in the joint. Because seeing J-Cat Jimmy go over the rails with a splat was just the beginning.

"Okay. Get in the car. I'll check it out."

I wait until she's tucked inside, safe with her red umbrella, before I slog toward the truck, fully expecting to find a hipster early for his acupuncture appointment. But I don't get more than a few steps before the engine revs and it rolls out of the lot, sending a spray of water into the air.

"He's gone," I tell Evie, hurrying back inside the car, wet and breathless. Her wide eyes find mine. There's worry there but something else too. Determination. And I can guess at what she's thinking. "Should we follow him?"

She answers with a turn of the ignition, a jerk of the gearshift. And I remember something I read once. Locked in Folsom with a thousand of my own kind, it always rang true. *Sometimes paranoia is just having all the facts.*

# CHAPTER TWENTY-FOUR

EVIE
JANUARY 17, 2017
TUESDAY

"**HE** took a right out of the lot. That way." Butch's voice comes out flat and steady—calmer than mine—but he fastens his seat belt and grips tight to the door.

I smash the accelerator, jolting us forward, and my stomach nose-dives. Half of me thinks I've lost my mind. That I'd dreamed the shadowy face in the truck's rain-streaked window. That I'd imagined the familiar feeling of dread cold as a blade to my throat. *It isn't Danny. It couldn't be.* But the other half is amped up on fear and adrenaline, running with laser focus toward the truck's rear lights. They stare back, taunting us, like the eyes of a demon.

*The hanging tree's more fun if you're drunk.* The words come from the past, from the tree itself, taunting me as I leave it in my rearview, where the smaller branches look like kite tails whipping about in the wind. I wonder how many will be strewn about by morning. Sometimes, I imagine the whole trunk uprooted—lying on its side like a beached whale. Dead. I'd like to take an axe to it. Chop it into blocks and send it through the mulcher. But it wouldn't bring me peace.

Up ahead, the truck makes a right and coasts down the hill toward five o'clock traffic, and I follow.

"I forgot to charge it last night," Butch says, frowning at his phone. "But we should probably call the police."

I nod at him, wondering when an ex-con became more sensible than me. *Probably when you started hitchhiking, Evie.* But really, who can trace the crooked path back to the beginning, to that first flawed decision? Long before I'd snuck out to meet Cassie, I'd sealed our fates, paved our road with bad intentions. I'd lived up to my nickname. Evil Evie.

*This road is just as treacherous*, I remind myself. I have to stay alert. Keeping my eyes fixed on it, I point Butch to my purse at his feet. "Get my phone. It's in the side pocket."

He slips it out and stares at it, tinkering and tapping, then banging, before setting it onto his lap with a sigh.

"It's locked," I explain. "Let's be sure it's him first. The cops already think I'm crazy." *And a liar.* "With the hitchhiking and all."

Butch doesn't disagree. Or agree, thankfully. He's too busy rummaging through my bag. When he finally looks up, his mouth turns into a rueful smile. "Do people still use pens? Paper? Or am I a total caveman?"

"Zipper pocket, Mr. Flintstone." And I let myself smile back at him, feel the muscles in my shoulders unknot. My hands unclench the wheel.

"Watch out!" Butch yells. I slam the brakes as a wet mass of black fur darts across the road and vanishes into a storm drain. I speed up to catch the truck, already two blocks ahead. "Sorry," he says, head hanging. "You get kind of skittish when you haven't ridden in a car in twenty-something years."

I wave off his apology with the truck back in my sight. "Was that a rat?"

"Biggest rat I ever saw outside of Folsom." He jots the license number onto an old receipt. "I don't think he's made us yet. Try to pull up alongside if you can."

Three blocks down, a stoplight flashes green. To yellow. To red. Casting its colors on the soaked pavement.

The rain hasn't let up, doesn't slow down, as the drops pound themselves against my windshield in a sacrificial fury. My wipers are working double time, pushing sheets of water so fast, too fast to get a clear view of the truck or the driver. I zero in on his lights and floor it, moving past him and into the left-hand turn lane at the last second.

Now that he's so close—a head's turn away—I have to force myself to look. Beyond Butch, with his tousled hair still dripping in rivulets down the back of his neck. Beyond my passenger's window, where he's wiped away the fog for a clearer view. Beyond the chaos of the rain and the charcoal sky. And when my eyes finally get there—*to him*—my body knows first. A sickening shiver works its way up my spine.

Danny stares straight ahead, waiting for the light to change. Oblivious it seems. Then he reaches toward the floorboard, searching its innards, and spits into a cup he holds to his lips. My neck prickles.

"Unbelievable," Butch mutters. "You were right. That's the guy." He tosses the phone to me and moves toward the door. "I'm getting out."

I grab his arm—*wait!* caught in my throat like a burr—and time does its trick. Slows to a creep. To a crawl. To a stop. And Danny's eyes, cold as a dead fire, meet mine through the streaked window. A sound comes out of me, somewhere between a yelp and a scream, and the spell shatters. The world spins ahead. Flying. At breakneck speed.

Danny zooms straight through the intersection—red light be damned—swerving left, then right, dodging a taxi and a minivan. I grit my teeth at the high-pitched screams of brakes screeching against the pavement. The grate of metal on metal.

**208**

One crash, then another. Somehow, Danny slips through unscathed.

And I'm frozen in my seat, helpless and staggered.

The stoplight turns an urgent green. *Go!* But there's nowhere to go and nothing moves. Except Danny—he takes a hard right at the next block and disappears—and the rain. Slowing as suddenly as it started, it matches the beat of my heart.

I wait for Butch to speak. The silence between us becomes uncomfortable, thick and heavy as a wet blanket. I cast it off as if my life depends on it. "Are you okay?"

Butch expels a breath that it sounds like he's been holding. And I realize I'm still latched to his arm. As if my hand had a mind of its own, wrapping tight to him, clinging like a dismembered claw.

"Holy shit," he says, finally. Returning from wherever he was. A million miles from here. "How the hell did that guy find you?"

I release my grip, avoiding his eyes, and return the offending hand back to its place on the wheel. "My license. Remember?"

"Oh yeah. I forgot. He took it, but…" His voice trails, and his gaze follows. Out the window to the stoplight. To the aftermath of Danny, where a small crowd has gathered. "How did he find your office?"

"Google, I guess. He must've looked me up." *Like Violet.*

"Why?"

*To finish what he started.* I can't say it out loud, so the question settles between us, unanswered, until I shrug.

"You should go," I say. "The cops will be here any minute, and it'll just be a hassle for you. Again."

"No way. I can't leave you here alone. This is my fault anyway." He lowers his head like he really means it.

"Your fault?"

"I told you to pull alongside him, didn't I? I spooked him. And I—"

"Seriously, Calder. This whole thing was my idea. And a stupid one at that. I should've just taken you home and called the police.

I don't know what's gotten into me. But I'll be okay. I don't have a parole agent to answer to. Just my former mother-in-law and an old tomcat."

There's a laugh, but I have to strain to hear it. It's more of a snuffle. "Alright. You win."

"Good," I tell him, passing him my umbrella and forcing the most reassuring smile I've got. "You might need this." He opens the door and climbs out, pausing to look at me just before he shuts it. If eyes are a window, Butch's are shuttered tight. "And, Calder…thank you."

The shutters fly open. The windows crack. "Stop saying that. Stop thanking me."

"I mean, I haven't done anything worthy of thanks. That's all."

"Okay. I'll never thank you again." I mean it as a joke, but it's serious business to him. I can tell in the set of his jaw. His teeth are clenched. "I promise I'll fill you in tomorrow morning. 7:30. Does Brenda do breakfast?"

"It's her specialty." Finally, he grins, and his face softens. But his fists stay balled up tight even when he answers. "As long as you don't mind your coffee with a side of arsenic."

# CHAPTER TWENTY-FIVE

I fling open the door to my room at the halfway house and charge in like a bat out of hell. "Get out."

There are things you learn in prison, things you can't learn anywhere else. When to take a man seriously. To follow orders even when you don't want to. Even when you don't understand. Even when you're a smart-ass like Sebastian. He leaves without a word, shutting the door softly behind him.

I toss Evie's red umbrella on the bed, cursing myself. *Real gentlemanly, Butch. Take the girl's umbrella and leave her there.* But I'd had to get out. I was losing it. She'd been so shaken herself—grabbing onto me like that. So I hoped like hell she hadn't noticed.

I pull out the bottom dresser drawer. Reach in the back under a stack of clean boxers and find the plastic bag they'd given me when

I'd left Folsom State Prison nearly five months ago. In it, the relics of a lost civilization. The personal property I'd had on me the night I'd been arrested. The night I killed Gwen. It's not much, but it seems precious. Like a touchstone or a talisman. And I need to see it. Now.

I open the bag and lay out the contents on my bed.

One Zippo lighter. Black. I flick the wheel a few times until the flame comes to life. Twenty-three years later, the damn thing still works.

One leather wallet. Five pennies and a condom inside.

And a blue box the color of a robin's egg. I remove the lid and drop the necklace in my palm, the sterling chain so delicate I could snap it without even trying. That chain had been meant for Gwen. For the neck I'd squeezed the life from with my own hands. I curl my fingers around the tiny music note and collapse on the bed, my wet clothes dampening the sheets.

It takes me a minute before the tears come. Hot and heavy and aching in my chest. Like I'd been storing them up for twenty-three years. Which isn't far from the truth. You can't cry in prison. Scratch that. There's a time and a place for tears. Take the parole board, for example. They expect you to cry on cue. No matter how many goddamned times you've said sorry, it can't sound rehearsed. And a dry eye won't help you plead your case. But real tears? Those will get you killed. You show the soft spots, the mushy underbelly, and somebody's bound to stick a shiv in it.

I give myself five minutes. Then I wipe my face on my shirtsleeve and sit up. *Think it through. Don't judge your feelings. Understand them.* These are the kinds of things they teach men in prison. And I'd programmed with the best of them. So I use my deep breathing and my positive self-talk—and replay the drive with Evie to find the exact moment when I'd lost it. When I'd checked out completely.

Danny exploding off the line when the light turned, like a maniacal drag racer. That was it. And hearing the crunch of metal he'd left in his wake. It had brought me right back there. All the way back. To that last week with Gwen. And the lying. *Jesus.* I was lying again. Too much and too easily. Because Evie didn't know I'd had the license the whole time—well, at least until my weaselly roommate snatched it. Which meant Danny had found her on his own. Or worse, he'd known her all along.

My body feels heavy. Too exhausted for a shower. So I gather the remnants of Young Butch, return them to the drawer, and slip into my pajamas. I am officially a forty-one-year-old grandpa, getting ready for bed at 7:30. But that's what happens when you work eight hours, tail a psychopath, and dive head first into a flashback. All while you're riding shotgun with—and completely deceiving—the only person in the world who seems to give a damn about you. Being a free man is exhausting.

I lay back against the pillow, anticipating Sebastian. Because I'm getting that license back tonight. Whatever it takes. I let my eyes close—just for a minute—and I'm eighteen again.

I know it by the way she looks at me like I'm a hot rod racing down the freeway. But everything is different. My hands are life worn, my left thumbnail blue from the strike of a hammer. The neck is lovely, porcelain, but it's not Gwen's. And yet, I can't stop myself from touching it. Soft at first, as tender as making love, but it builds and builds and builds. Because everything is different, but I'm still the same. My thumbs root into the small hollow above her clavicle, and I squeeze.

It could be the sound of my own breathing that wakes me. Because I feel like I'm drowning. Like I've been underwater all night. But the clock on my phone says 7:37, and it's still dark outside. I turn on my side and see it. What woke me. Sebastian's precious book is lying on the floor beneath his nightstand, duct tape around the edges where he must've tried to secure it underneath for safekeeping.

I listen for a beat then scramble to it and waste no time flinging it open. My heart is still thwacking away like it has a life of its own outside of my body, and it wants out. And the photo doesn't help. It's dated on the back. *June 22, 1991. Our new family. Sebastian, Sasha, Mom, and Dad.* There's a girl in it. A vivacious girl with freckles and shiny auburn hair pinned into a fancy updo. Her eyes look just past the camera, bored. Like she's got better things to do. There's a boy too. A young Sebastian, paling next to her with his pimpled skin, wiry glasses, and headgear. A tux hangs loosely on his awkward frame. Damn. Teen Sebastian must've had it rough. Behind them, the middle-aged bride and groom. *Is this what he's been looking at?*

But not just looking. Because the groom's face is marked through. Obliterated, more like it. With strokes so intense, the paper is nearly worn away.

I want to be rid of it, so I slip it between the book's end pages, where the heathen boys are rescued from the island, and turn my attention to the other thing he's been hiding. This I recognize. Alcoholic that I am. Was. Am. It's an urge card. Like a to-do list for addicts. Except Sebastian's is still blank and I'm guessing his habit has nothing to do with booze or pills. And everything to do with sex, in some twisted form, since he's wearing that GPS bracelet on his ankle.

I flip through the rest of the book, looking for Evie's license, but no luck.

My ears prick at the sound of anxious voices outside the room, and I hold my breath to listen. "...cops...downstairs...everybody..." Anticipating Sebastian's return, I drop to my knees to hide the book, pressing the tape against the underside of the nightstand until it holds its secret from prying eyes like mine.

I open the door to find Sebastian standing outside, flush to the wall, his breathing shallow. A backpack rests between his feet. "The cops are here to talk to the house." He slinks inside and paces, agitated, like a caged animal.

"I heard."

"So, do we have a deal?"

"Maybe," I tell him. "But I need the license back first, and—"

"I can't give it to you now. It's not here."

"Then, I can't help you man. No license, no deal. I'm sure the cops will be interested to hear about your little night escapades...and your reading habits." He blinks his wide eyes in shock, and I shrug. "It fell. And, given the circumstances, I figured it was fair game."

"Butch, please. I swear to you I had nothing to do with that murder. I'll show you. I'll show you where I go."

We both startle when Richert knocks. "Hey, you two. Get downstairs."

Sebastian's eyes are desperate, darting. He looks fresh off the boat. A regular fish. And I must be a real sucker, because I give him a nod. "Tonight. Or else."

****

It's 2 a.m., and I'm officially breaking curfew. With a creepy-as-hell ex-con who'd just disabled his GPS monitor by jerry-rigging it with aluminum foil he kept folded in the bottom of his shoe. *Go big or go home, right?* We're only a block from the house, and I'm sweating bullets even in the unforgiving cold that's chased out the rain.

"They say those ankle bracelets are tamper proof," I tell him, wishing I had eyes in the back of my head. The smallest sounds become the clink of handcuffs, the footfalls of a cop waiting to put a knee in my back. "Are you sure that thing won't go off?"

"It hasn't yet."

The ground is still wet, the streets emptied. And the air is thick and gauzy with fog. Like I'm walking in a dark, dark dream. And I can't help but think of Evie. Because it was her neck I'd strangled in my sleep. I hadn't seen her face, but I knew it as surely as I'd known those were my hands—*these hands*—with the purpling, half-moon bruise on my thumb. My nightmares about Gwen made sense at least. But Evie? That scared me. Like the old me was waking up a little at a time. A diabolical butterfly splitting its cocoon after twenty-three years' rest. Hungry and desperate and full of rage.

"Butch. Earth to Butch. Did you hear anything I said?"

"Just trying to figure out how I'm gonna explain this one to Agent McElroy when we get busted."

"Well, my PO hasn't figured it out yet. I doubt yours is any smarter. Besides, the GPS signals are pretty iffy anyway. So I wouldn't worry about it. We'll be quick." He gestures up ahead to Broadway, and we jog across the street. Jaywalking. The least of my problems.

"That's really comforting, Sebastian. My ass is on the line here."

"Yeah, well. You wanted to be here. And believe me, I won't fare any better."

"Hell no. You're not blaming this on me. You started it."

"We'll have to agree to disagree on that. But thanks for covering for me back there." The cops and a lady detective had gathered us downstairs and given us a talking to—that's what my dad would've called it. A stern warning. If we had any information, we'd better cough it up now. And they'd saved the worst for last. The cattle prod meant to spur us to action. Fliers with the victim's photograph: Violet Kurchell. Only fifteen, her eyes had already looked sad and weary, like she'd known her fate.

"Just remember, my silence is temporary. And it's certainly not free."

He holds up a hand and points to a bus stop that's covered in gang graffiti and smells about as rank as the dorm at Folsom, where I'd finished my last five years. "This is where you wait."

"Lovely. And where exactly will you be?"

"You'll see."

Sebastian opens his backpack and takes out a pair of surgical gloves and a dark-colored T-shirt. He wraps the shirt so that only his eyes and nose show through. Then he pulls his hoodie down as far as it will go. Until he's virtually faceless. Just a shadow man. Next, come the cans of spray paint he loads into the front pocket of his sweatshirt. Finally, he stretches the gloves over his hands. "Enjoy the show."

He sprints across the street and down a block, lithe. Almost graceful as he lines up his target. The front window of Merrill's Motors. Then, he fires. Hot-pink paint shoots out the camera above the door, and he goes to work.

I should run. Hide, at the very least. The cops are gonna show up any second. But I don't. I'm transfixed. Awestruck, really. And in less than two minutes, he's done. The cans are wiped clean and tossed into the trash, and he's booking it back across the street. Like nothing happened.

Me, on the other hand, I can't swallow the lump in my throat. It's my heart. I'm sure of it. It's finally figured its way out. Because my chest is as hollow as an empty barrel.

"You alright?" he asks, after we'd fast-walked for two blocks with only the sound of my ragged breathing between us. He drops the mask and studies me. "I thought you'd be..."

"What?"

"A little less square, I guess."

His brutal honesty earns a laugh, but it's more of a gasp than anything. Like the sort of sound that sputters out when you've been kicked me in the gut. "I'm too old for this. Aren't you?"

"My prison shrink said a lot of guys stop growing up when they come to prison. So technically, I guess I'm still seventeen."

I can't argue with that. I know exactly how he feels. Stunted on the inside. Like the world just kept going on without me. "Yeah, well, I thought you were gonna blow a gasket when the cops showed up earlier."

"Revenge will steel anybody's nerves. Mine anyway. It makes me feel alive."

His eyes are lit up from within, and I wonder if I'd been wrong about the urge card. If anger is his demon. Or something else. "Piggy, huh?"

"Told ya. I *am* Piggy."

"So what did Merrill ever do to you?"

"The list is long, my friend. Merrill is my stepdad. And the proud owner of twenty-five used car dealerships throughout the East Bay. And a complete swine."

"Let me guess. You plan to tag them all with a giant, hot-pink pig?"

"Something like that. I figure it's better than slitting his throat."

I sit with that one and follow him through the parking lot of Evie's office building, feeling like a thousand years have passed since this afternoon. That's another thing you learn in prison. Time is a bitch. Always thumbing her nose at you, doing the exact opposite of what you want. Speeding up when you need her to go slow. Or making you feel every goddamned second of those twenty-three years.

"You know you're gonna get caught," I tell him, sounding every bit like the square he thinks I am. "Are you sure it's worth it?"

I recognize his arrogant chuckle. I've heard it before, tossed in my direction. "He'll never turn me in. I know too much, and he knows I know. Besides, I only want to see my mom and stepsister. Is that too much to ask? I'll stop when I get what I want."

"That sounds familiar. Speaking of which…"

Sebastian waves me away. "I'll meet you at the tree in five. With the license."

He heads to the woody corner of the lot, back where the trash gets emptied into a row of dumpsters. I turn and pretend to leave, peering into the dark long enough to watch him crouch beneath the trees. Before he catches me, I hightail it out of there and into the park.

I try not to look at the tree. I hate it. As silly as that sounds— hating a tree. But I do. Its gnarled limbs that look like a witch's fingers, the grey-brown bark, thick as rotting skin. The way it had kept growing, flourishing while I'd been locked away. And most of all, the silent judgment I feel every time I pass. Because it knows the last of my secrets.

I press my hand against it. Hold my breath. And I swear I feel a heartbeat. I'd read an article once that plants have a memory, and right now, I believe it. "I'm sorry," I whisper. "I'm so sorry."

"Nothing to apologize for, man." Funny, the tree sounds a lot like a smart-ass. A lot like Sebastian. "Here." He passes me an envelope— covered in dirt from his hands—a hard rectangle tucked inside it. "Your precious license. Just don't get busted jacking off to it, okay?"

I snatch it from his fingers and shove it into my pocket like it's my last chance at redemption.

"Well, aren't you gonna look at it?"

"I'm going back to the house."

"So, you believe me now?" He's right behind me, so I quicken my pace, anxious to put him and this night—the whole day, really—behind me. "I didn't murder anybody. But, if you want to know the truth, I think I saw her. Violet."

"What?" That stops me. I have to see his face. And when I do, I'm sickened with dread. He's not joking.

"I can't be positive. I went through the parking lot of the building just like we did tonight. To stash my stuff. And something caught my eye—I thought it was a prowler. But there was this girl, and she put something under Dr. Maddox's mat. I swear she looked just like the girl in the picture. The one that got killed."

"Did you tell Evie…uh, I mean, Dr. Maddox?"

"Not exactly. But I made sure she got the envelope. It was still there on Monday. Under the mat. I don't know if she ever would've found it."

"Sebastian, you have to tell the police."

"So, what exactly am I supposed to say to them, Mr. Upstanding Parolee? I tinfoil-cheated my GPS monitor so I could graffiti one of my stepdad's dealerships—and oh-by-the-way, I just happened to see a girl who turned up murdered the next morning. I'd be on my way back to Quentin faster than you can say *rapo*."

I cringe at that word, though I'd probably used it a time or two. It sounded different in the free world. With hard edges that would cut when you spit it out. I'm trying to think of what to say—he does have a point—when we round the corner and spot the house. The police car out front, lights flashing. High beams aimed straight at us. *Oh shit.*

The last time I had this feeling I'd been holed up in my room at the Blue Bird, puking my guts out and shaking like a leaf. *Butch Calder, we know you're in there. Come out with your hands up.* Just like a Bruce Willis movie. Except that Bruce usually played the good guy.

I'd seen them through the small sliver of light between the motel curtains, their barrels aimed at the front door. And I'll tell you this much—it didn't feel real. I don't even remember opening the door or taking my last steps of freedom. That whole first year I'd wished I had. That I'd counted those steps, relished them.

The last time I had this feeling, I hadn't known yet what it meant. What it would cost me. I was still young and stupid and filled up with hope, fat as a tick. Now, I know. Prison will leach out every drop of a man's hope until his soul is nothing but a shell. I can't go back there. But I walk toward the blue lights anyway. Like a man headed to his own funeral.

\*\*\*\*

Well, this is familiar. My legs splayed, rough hands patting me down, digging through my pockets. Two cops with the same face, somewhere between tired and angry. *You've seen one cop, you've seen 'em all.* That's what Wade used to say. And after the hundreds I'd dealt with in the joint—tall ones, short ones, fat ones, skinny ones, bad and good—I can say he wasn't wrong.

Cop One takes the envelope and lays it on the hood. I stare at it, wishing I could set it on fire.

"You boys missed your curfew. Two hours ago. We tossed your room."

I know better than to say anything. And when I look at Sebastian, his eyes are as hard as mine. Two dark stones, unyielding. We've both put on our prison masks, and his is better than I thought.

"Which one of you is Delacourt?"

"Me." Sebastian's voice sounds a little off, like a flute, out of tune, and his mask slips a little. "Me," he says, again. Bolder this time.

"You tamper with that thing?" Cop Two says, eagle-eyed on Sebastian's ankle. I risk a quick glance. No tinfoil. But just beyond the bright halo of the street lamp, something crumpled and shiny catches the light.

"No, sir. It probably just needs a charge." Both cops snicker the way boys do when they're thirteen and cruel is cool.

"Yeah, yeah. That's what all the sickos say. We'll check it out down at the station."

"This yours?" Cop One holds up *Lord of the Flies*, proud, like it's a head on a stake. In his other hand, he's got the picture, mutilated by Sebastian's hand. "What about this photo?"

"Yep."

"And what about you?" he asks, grinning at me, wicked and wide as a jack-o-lantern. He fingers the envelope, and I'm done for. *Sayonara, Butchy.* "What's this?" His question, not a question at all. An assumption. Of guilt.

I should keep quiet, but fuck it. If I'm going down, I'm going down a smart-ass. "Only one way to find out."

## BUTCH
## MAY 7, 1994
## SIX DAYS BEFORE I KILLED HER

**"YOU** got the scratch fixed." Gwen ran her hand along the side of the 'Cuda, sounding disappointed.

"Not really. I just used a touch-up paint stick. Doesn't it look better?" It still stung to look at the mark Trey left. But I couldn't bear to be without the 'Cuda for a whole two weeks, waiting on a new paint job. No ride meant no Gwen—Butch of the Filthy-Rich Calders didn't do public transportation—and no Gwen meant the end of everything.

Gwen pursed her lips into a totally kissable blood-red pout. "I kinda liked the scratch. It fit you. It was…" *Damaged.* "Tough. Badass, you know?"

I smirked at her trying to look as badass as she thought I was. I definitely had the look. Or I'd bought it anyway, for another five bills at Nordstrom. A black leather jacket that I'd hoped would make Gwen swoon. At some point tonight, I'd planned to drape it over her shoulders, real gentleman-like, and pull her in for a kiss.

But seeing her strut out of the Shaw mansion in her party dress—short and tight and red—I had no intention of covering that up. Unless it involved my body on hers.

"So where does Matthias live?" I asked, opening the door for her and watching, like a total perv, her skirt ride up as she slid inside. *Who says chivalry is dead?*

"Out in the boonies near Pinole. Cherice said it's actually his half-brother's place. He's old, like thirty or something, but I hear he's got the hookup on some E."

I'd never heard Gwen talk about drugs before, and I was partial to alcohol myself, but as usual, I just rolled with it. "Cool."

Once we hit the freeway, she fiddled with the radio until she found a song she liked. And when she belted out Sinead, I started to wonder if she was already tipsy. "It's been seven hours and fifteen daaaaaays since you took your love awaaaaaay..." She leaned in, nibbling my neck, and I caught my answer in a whiff of cognac.

"Did you start the party without me?" I teased.

"Mom and Dad left early for their hoity-toity charity thingie, so I might've had a sip or two. Just to take the edge off."

"Do they know what a lush you are?"

"You're one to talk, Calder. If I remember correctly, you've got booze hidden in here somewhere." Guilt whacked me in the face and called me a moron. She was right. But I'd sucked down that bottle of Jack just before I'd watched Trey have his wicked way with Evie's friend, doing absolutely nothing to stop him. And the filthy thoughts I'd had about Gwen that night—well, at least I could blame it on the alcohol.

"Actually, I think I already..." I went mute when Gwen reached between my legs, gliding her hand down my thigh, my knee, my calf, and searched the empty space beneath the seat. "...drank it."

"It's a good thing I brought this then." She unzipped her purse and plucked out a bottle of Hennessy.

"Your dad's?"

"Nope. I got this one myself." She fluttered her hands at me. "Five-finger discount."

"Geez, Gwen. You really are a klepto." Instantly, I wanted a take back. Her bright eyes dimmed, and she pulled away when I tried to touch her. "That came out wrong. I just meant you don't have to take things."

"Thank you, Captain Obvious. You sound exactly like my ex." *Bingo.* So I'd been right to hate Russ. The infamous ex. The fool stupid enough to let Gwen get away.

"So why do you…take things?"

She sighed and shut off the radio. Then she took a long swallow from the bottle. "My answer or my shrink's?"

"Both, I guess."

"Well, it feels good. When I'm doing it. Like a high. There's this bad part of me, the part that gets off on it. But later, I feel dirty. Like the worst person in the world. So it's this vicious cycle. That's my answer."

"And what does your shrink say?"

Her laugh came out bitter and sharp, and when she spoke, she put on a throaty voice. A man's voice. "Gwen, the reason you feel the urge to steal can be traced to your childhood. To your feeling emotionally neglected and deprived of love. By taking things, you attempt to substitute that feeling of happiness and to express your anger at the people you hold responsible."

"Damn."

"Yeah. I know. I guess that's why I like music so much. When I play, I feel like a halfway decent person, and if I miss a note, it's not the end of the world." I could tell she was fighting tears. "I'm f'd up, Calder. Royally."

If I had been a better man—or a man at all—I would've spilled it right then and there, come clean about everything. It was on the tip of my tongue. "Are you f'ing serious? You play an f'ing viola! How f'd up can you be if you don't even say the f word. F!"

She shook her head at me and giggled. And what did I do? I grinned back, grabbed the Hennessy, and washed down the truth in one stiff gulp.

****

The party was totally wrong. Right from the get-go. After we got off the freeway, already buzzing, we drove ten minutes on a dirt road to get there, kicking up dust and gravel all over the 'Cuda. For this. A sprawling field littered with junk and a ramshackle house barely

**224**

standing at its center. A bonfire licking the sky. Metallica throbbing from a car stereo. And a crowd way older than Gwen and me, milling around dead-eyed like zombies. The whole scene was straight out of a slasher flick. Direct from Charles Manson's compound.

"Hey, man. Nice car." A lanky zombie with a cigarette droned at me as he passed.

"Is he stoned?" Gwen asked.

"I sure hope so. That or we're extras in *Night of the Living Dead.*"

"I think we're gonna need this." Gwen sipped from the bottle, licking a drop from her bottom lip. And I had to fight the urge to drag her back to the car, find a turnout somewhere, and finally make use of the condoms I'd bummed off Wade. A three pack. As if.

"Magnum?" I'd asked him, snorting with embarrassment at the flashy gold word printed on the package.

"Don't worry," he'd said with a straight face. "Half of sex is setting an expectation." And that's exactly what I *was* worried about. Now that she'd coined me a badass, Gwen probably assumed I was experienced. A real ladies' man. Or at the very least, not still sporting my v-card. *Not for long, Butchy. Not for long.*

"There's Cherice. C'mon."

She pulled me along behind her—yanking me straight out of my reverie—pointing toward the fire, where Cherice stood alone.

"This is lame," Gwen said, offering Cherice our bottle. She took a drink and smiled right at me. Like Gwen didn't even exist. And it hit me in an instant. *Cherice digs me.* It must've hit Gwen too—hard—because she wrapped her arms around my waist and squeezed me to her, claiming me. If I could go back, I'd slap myself silly. With my lazy, shit-eating grin, I was happier than a pig in slop. And man, that's exactly what I was. A total swine.

"Hi, Calder. Gwen didn't tell me you were coming." She stepped closer and dabbed at her forehead with the back of her hand. Her whole body glistened in the heat of the fire, her skin shining like she was an Amazonian princess. I glanced away, worried I'd already looked too long.

Gwen dropped her head and sulked like a little girl, muttering. "Didn't know you cared." Soft, as if she didn't want Cherice to hear her. But loud enough that hearing was inevitable.

Cherice rolled her eyes and flashed another smile my way. *Damn.* Two guys would've just duked it out and been done with it. A broken nose seemed like small potatoes compared to girls' two-faced backstabbing. *And they were friends?*

"Where's Matthias?" I asked, desperate for an ally in this vicious game of chess.

"Heck if I know. He ditched me the minute we got here for his sketchy brother. Matthias follows him around like a puppy."

"He never mentioned a brother." Not that I knew the guy. Beyond our shared affinity for cigarettes and alcohol. And girls who ~~liked~~ hated each other.

"Half brother," Cherice corrected. "Apparently their dad was a real skeezball. A girl in every port, you know? They only just met a year or so ago."

"So…" Gwen was all sugar and spice again, fiddling nervously with the choker around her neck. "Does he really have ecstasy?"

"Why don't you ask him yourself?"

"Maybe I will." She untangled herself from me and marched away, the silence reverberating in her absence like the aftershocks of an earthquake.

"Well then," I said, chuckling. "Sorry 'bout that. She's drunk."

"Don't make excuses for her, Calder. She's a spoiled brat. I can't even believe you're with…" She kicked at the dirt with her boot, scattering an empty beer can. "*Are* you with her?"

I shrugged. "Yeah. Kind of. I mean, I guess. But, we haven't really made it official or anything."

"Just be careful. Gwen's a lot like her dad. She'll get bored with you."

My thoughts were a little fuzzy, dulled by the slow burn of the cognac. But that cut fast and deep. "Wait. You know her dad? You know she's rich?"

"Ha! Loaded is more like it. My mom works for the Shaws. She's their housekeeper. When Gwen got in trouble—again—my mom asked me to get her some community service hours at the Port. And then you showed up."

Still reeling, I tried to steady myself the only way I knew how. Another swig of the sauce. I'd been so busy keeping my own story straight, I'd never suspected Gwen lied too. And better than me. "Don't tell her you told me, okay?"

"My lips are sealed. But, Calder?" She leaned into me, until her face was right there. Her scar a brilliant purple that made me want to touch it. "You can do better. We both can."

"Calder!" I jumped back, startled. "Hey!" Matthias jogged toward us, a broad grin on his face. As wide as I'd ever seen him smile. "My brother said he knows you."

In my head, I said every single curse word I'd ever learned, and a few I made up right there on the spot. That must've been the way my dad felt when he'd stared head-on into the jaws of that misguided big rig. Too late to swerve, I had to take what was coming to me. Tagging along behind Matthias was Gwen, as hot as she'd ever looked, her cheeks flushed from the booze and the heat. She stuck out her tongue at me, revealing a tiny blue pill resting at its swollen center. Her eyes sparkled, dared me as she swallowed. And bringing up the rear, backlit by the fire, the devil himself.

"Hot dog, Nobody. If I knew you were comin' I'd have baked a cake." He half-sang, half-slurred the words. But he wasn't as far gone as the other zombies. "Why didn't you RSVP?"

**\*\*\*\***

I sat rigid as a corpse in the driver's seat of the 'Cuda. Top up. Outside, Gwen giggled at me as she held up a red bandana over her head. She stared up at it, eyes glazed over, until someone in the crowd gave her a nudge.

**227**

"Gentlemen. Gentle. Men." Another burst of laughter. "Start your…oh, that's really bright. So bright. So pretty. *We didn't start the fire…*"

She raised a shaky finger at the bonfire, singing Billy Joel to herself until another girl grabbed the bandana and pushed her out of the way. Gwen stumbled against Cherice and nearly fell. This was better (or worse) than a goddamned PSA. *This is Gwen. This is Gwen on drugs. Any questions?* But she bounced right up, like one of those roly-poly toys, bobbing her head to her own music. Then she snatched the bandana with a shriek.

"Start your fucking engines. See, Calder—I *can* say it."

My right foot revved the gas. Left foot held the clutch. Once I released it, I'd be flying. Up ahead, only dirt road as far as I could see. Matthias waited with a flashlight a quarter mile out at the finish line.

I risked a glance to my right. Trey waved at me from behind the wheel of the eggplant. The Grand National was quick, no doubt. But certainly no match for the 'Cuda. He was about to be embarrassed. Humiliated. But he'd insisted. Too high for logic. And I was too drunk and too proud—and let's face it, too stupid—to refuse.

"You got yourself a real looker," he'd said to me, thirty minutes earlier, side-eyeing Gwen. "I'll bet you didn't find her at the Blue Bird." Thankfully, she'd already been too high to notice. "Wanna show her what your whip can do? Let's race." He wouldn't take no for an answer, wouldn't leave me alone. "C'mon. What have you got to lose? Unless you're scared of me."

*You're dead, Nobody. Next time I see you, you're dead.* He hadn't said it again. In fact, he'd been as nice as pie. But those words colored his eyes black when I'd shaken his hand and agreed to his ridiculous terms. Pink slips. Never mind that the 'Cuda was worth forty times more than his beater.

"On your mark. Get set—"

"Wait." Trey smirked at me, shifting to park. "There's somethin' missin'. I think we need a couple shotgun riders. What d'ya say, Nobody?"

"Sure, Trey. Whatever you want."

"Cassie. Get over here, darlin'." Trey curled his finger toward the edge of the crowd, beckoning, and the girl from the motel stepped forward. I hardly recognized her, clad in the outfit of a forty-year-old stripper, her lifeless eyes hooded with heavy makeup. She looked just like the other zombies. Either stoned or lobotomized.

"Ain't you gonna call your girl over?" He jerked his head at Gwen. Who was, of course, blowing kisses to a fence post. "Looks like she met herself a new somebody."

The onlookers laughed, and I felt my face get hot. Until Cherice caught my eye and grinned. "I'll ride with him. Since Gwen's too busy."

"Goddamn, Nobody. Is your pecker made of gold or somethin'?"

"It's Calder, Trey. It's Calder."

**** 

"On your mark. Get set. Go!"

I let the clutch out and floored it, jamming the accelerator. The 'Cuda launched like a rocket ship down the dirt road with Trey just behind me. He'd been slower at the start, and I watched his back end fishtail before he found his groove.

"He's close. He's gonna bump you!" Cherice yelled, her hands braced against the dash.

Trey swerved hard toward the 'Cuda's back end, just as I redlined it and shifted up to second. *Not today, asshole.*

Then, third. Then, fourth. *See ya, sucker!* Engine roaring beneath me, I felt like I could take flight. Like nothing else mattered but crossing that finish line. *Winning.*

"Hell yeah!" I pumped my fist, when Trey spun out in the ditch.

And again, when we flew past Matthias' waving flashlight.

The whole race took less than ten seconds. But something in me changed. Sometimes, ten seconds is all it takes. To make choices you can't take back. To become someone else entirely.

Cherice was laughing and cheering and squeezing my shoulder, KISS blasting in the background, *I Was Made for Lovin' You.* And when she looked at me, I felt like a king. Whatever this was, I didn't want it to stop.

"Keep driving," Cherice whispered, and I already knew that she would be my first.

**\*\*\*\***

When I pulled into the Blue Bird in the wee hours of the morning, I understood Gwen better than I ever had. *There's this bad part of me, the part that gets off on it. But later, I feel dirty. Like the worst person in the world.* Yep, I got it.

Wade was sitting outside on the curb with two red Solo cups, half-filled with the good stuff. Johnny Walker Gold.

"Been savin' this for a special occasion. Let's see it." He held out his palm. As promised, I gave up the proof. Two empty condom wrappers. "Two? Damn. You must've done somethin' right. So who was the lucky lady?"

"Cherice. Her name is Cherice."

"Here's to Cherice then. We'll drink to her." And we did.

I didn't tell Wade the whole truth. Not ever. Didn't tell the parole board either. Or the half-dozen shrinks who'd interviewed me. A boy amped up on adrenaline and still a little buzzed; a quickie in the passenger seat with an older girl, who all but begged me for it; even, six days later, a murder. Those things, they understood. I'd told them I'd driven Cherice home post-hookup and hadn't seen Gwen till the following afternoon.

I'd intended to spill it. To somebody. Someday. I really had. *Tell the story of the crime, Mr. Calder. In your own words.* And I'd start where I always do. The day I bought that godforsaken car. And end where I always did—with Gwen dead and the 'Cuda wrecked. I'd chicken out every time. It was easier to tell it like always. If I'd changed my story then, that late in the game, they'd start asking questions.

**230**

But, honestly, I couldn't tell them who I really was. The kind of guy who wasn't so different from Trey after all. The kind of guy who'd gone back to the party and dropped off Cherice with the cover story that we'd gone for more booze. The kind of guy who told Trey to keep his piece-of-shit car. *The only use I've got for it is scrap metal.* My exact words, before I'd turned tail and run, Matthias barely holding him back, his teeth bared like a pit bull on a leash. I'd left the way I came, with Gwen riding next to me. And she'd been coming down hard.

"I'm sorry," she'd said, sniffling. "I shouldn't have done that stuff." She'd pressed her hand to her heart. "Sticking to booze from now on. I swear."

"Don't worry about it. You didn't miss much."

And when she'd invited me into the Shaw mansion, up the winding staircase to her room where her viola was propped against the wall and into her bed with the softest sheets that smelled faintly of watermelon bubblegum, I certainly couldn't tell them I was the kind of guy who said yes.

# CHAPTER TWENTY-SIX

**I'M** staring wide-eyed at the ceiling with Sammy paperweighted on my legs like a sack of sand. My journal is open beside me, Violet's letter tucked in the back and three, brand-new sentences—memories!—I'd scrawled in ink hours ago.

*He bought us beer and knew my name because Cassie told him. I drank some and Cassie did too. He said the hanging tree would be more fun if we were drunk.*

There's a fourth sentence, a question really, but it's only in my mind. I couldn't bring myself to write it. *Were we drugged?* It would explain a lot. The morning-after wooziness. The nausea. The complete-and-total black hole in my memory.

I turn the question over and over again like a stone, hoping to exhume an answer beneath. But there's nothing. Just the plaintive sounds of the house, the creaks and groans I'm certain are Danny slinking up the steps, trying my door. He knows where I work. *How hard would it be for him to find me here?*

*Easy peasy.* The rasp in my head sounds just like him. *Like mother, like daughter.*

I slide my legs from beneath Sammy's warmth and try the door. Again. It's locked. But I could break it without much effort. Or pick it so quietly no one would hear.

Right after they'd cautioned me about my reckless behavior following Danny—taking matters into my own hands, they'd called it—the cops assured me they'd send a regular patrol past Maggie's driveway. But every time I close my eyes, I see his. Hard and blazing full of hate. I can't shake the feeling that, for him, this is personal.

Trying not to wake Sammy, I contort myself around him, folding my legs like a pretzel. He repositions himself and falls back into a heavy sleep. I wish for that kind of peace. For morning. For breakfast with Calder. For surly Brenda, who'll probably spit in my coffee. Even for my session with creepy Sebastian. For anything but this night that seems as dark and deep and endless as the ocean.

When the phone rings, I'm not sleeping—not even close—but it stops my heart anyway. Because it makes me think of Jared and that feeling of dread from the final days. The brief respites away from the hospital and the shot of pure terror every time the phone rang. Sammy lifts up his head and eyes me like he's thinking what I'm thinking. Nothing good comes from a 4 a.m. phone call. It's a direct line to hell.

There's no receiver in the guest bedroom so I wait for Maggie to answer. But first, her soft footfalls down the hallway. The shrill ringing, expected now, comes again and again, each time jolting as an alarm clock.

"Hello, Maddox residence." Maggie's composure is daunting, her ability to simply keep moving. "Uh, yes, she is. But, may I ask who's calling?"

Me, on the other hand, I do what I always do. I freeze. With my mother. With Cassie. With Butch today in the car. Even with Jared, on the day the doctor told us. *It's cancer.* But not just any cancer. *Glioblastoma.* The worst kind. If only I can be still enough, quiet enough, the curse of Evil Evie will pass over. And the world will be right again. But it never does, and it never is.

Still, I lie stonelike beneath the covers, my skin clammy and my mouth sawdust dry. Sammy jumps from the bed and sits beside it, licking his front paw. He's waiting for me. Maggie calls from outside the door.

"Evelyn. Wake up. Telephone."

She raps softly. Tries the door. And it's inevitable now. I have to move. So I do.

"Who is it?" I ask, forcing the words out. Bracing for the answer. Because even though her mouth is pursed, tight and annoyed, her eyes look worried.

"That detective. They found your driver's license."

****

Twenty minutes later, Detective Munroe is waiting at Maggie's door under the soft glow of the porch light. I watch through the kitchen window as she presses the bell and waits. Her shoulders proud, feet planted firmly. From here, she seems as solid and stoic as the hanging tree. And she's not alone.

Maggie clears her throat. "I think that's for you," she says, lifting her eyes from yesterday's newspaper.

But I wait a little longer. Long enough to size up the man on the doorstep. To notice what needs noticing. Short, squat, and wound tight, like a package of dynamite, the man wrangles with the tie at his neck, grumbling. Like somebody else makes him wear it. Like somebody's made him wear it for the last twenty-five years. He reaches past Detective Munroe and jabs at the bell again.

"Easy there, Macaroni. It's still four in the morning." *Macaroni?*

**234**

He grunts at her and pulls at his tie again, loosening it completely. Balls it up and stuffs it into his pocket. "You're right. It's too early for this noose." Then they both laugh, and in the crinkle of his eyes, I see the shadow of a much younger man. And a memory nearly knocks me over.

****

"How old are you, Evie? May I call you Evie?"

I'd nodded, but I didn't want to answer him. I'd wanted to be badass like my mom. Was. "Twelve," I'd said. Because I wasn't like her—not at all—and he was a cop. The first cop to talk to me, even though I'd been the one sitting there with her corpse. I'd felt rooted to her, like a baby just born. I couldn't cut the cord.

"Well, I'm Officer Maroni but you can call me Macaroni, if you'd like."

*Macaroni?* I'd managed to smile back at him and his pathetic attempt to cheer me up. His teeth were crooked on the bottom just like Mom's. Were.

"Tell me what happened with your mama today."

"I don't know. I was at school."

He wasn't a moron like Trey, so he hadn't bought it. Not for one second. I could tell because he'd glanced real quick at his partner and frowned. "At school? On a Saturday?"

I'd shrugged. "That's how I found her when I got home. She took too much, I guess."

"Does anybody else live here at the Blue Bird with you, Evie"?

"Um, no."

"No? Are you sure? The desk clerk said there's a man who hangs around here? Trey?"

Like usual, that name had made my stomach scramble like a small animal burrowing in its nest, a fox nipping at its heels. "Oh, him. Yeah. He stays with my mom sometimes. But I haven't seen him in a few days."

"Do you know where we can find him?"

I'd shaken my head. Felt my bottom lip start to tremble. Like it belonged to somebody else.

"Are you afraid of this Trey guy?"

Sometimes a minnow of truth makes a whopper of a lie believable. Mom had taught me that one. So I'd looked him square in his face. "Yes."

****

Maggie stands up, her chair scraping against the wood floor like she's determined to drag me back here. To the present. "Don't be rude, Evelyn."

I make my way out of the kitchen, but my legs feel impossibly heavy, the past still grabbing at my ankles. Still wanting a piece of me. Even Maggie nudging me along with a hand at my back doesn't help. She sighs as she opens the door and clears the way for Detective Munroe and the man. This man who saw me on the first worst day of my life. He must remember too. That's why he's here. This is an ambush.

"Dr. Maddox, Mrs. Maddox, I'd like you to meet Chuck Maroni. He's the homicide detective working the Violet Kurchell case." *Of course he is.*

I shake his hand and meet his eyes—still kind, still brown—but I won't let him throw me off balance. I strike first. "I remember you," I say. "Macaroni, right?"

His warm laugh doesn't hide the purposeful look he shoots in Munroe's direction. "I was hoping you'd remember. It's been ages. As this old face will tell you."

"You know each other?" Maggie asks, lurking.

"Detective Maroni—I guess it was Officer Maroni back then—was the first one there after my mom died. He was very kind to me."

"It means a lot to hear you say that. I didn't know squat about talking to kids back then, much less interviewing them. I always

**236**

thought I'd screwed it up somehow." He walks toward the sofa, wringing his hands like two old dishtowels, and takes a seat. "You know, your mom's case is the one that got me into homicide. I just couldn't shake the feeling there was more to the story. Where'd you end up after that?"

"LA. I moved back up here for college."

Maggie's brows lift a little, but she keeps her questions to herself. Instead, she offers coffee and tea and bagels. She even plumps the pillows before Detective Munroe joins Macaroni on the couch. With nothing left to do, she touches my shoulder. "Shall I...stay?"

I'm silently screaming no, but apparently no one can hear me, because Detective Munroe nods. "I think it might be helpful if you did." She gives me a pitying smile. "We have a lot to talk about."

"You found my license. Isn't that why you're here?"

"We did." She puts it on the coffee table and slides it over to me. It looks remarkably unscathed, but I don't touch it. I can't help but think of Danny's greedy hands all over it, all over me. "One of our officers on patrol happened to stumble across it near your office."

"Do you think Danny could've dropped it there last night? Or left it on purpose?"

Macaroni turns to me when he speaks, one hand dipped beneath the table scratching Sammy's head. Sammy leans in, his chest humming like a motor. *Traitor.* "Well, Evie—if I can still call you that—that's the very question we're hoping you might help us with. Do you think Danny knows you?"

*Like mother, like daughter.* There it is again, that rasp. "Do you?"

"Yes, we believe there's a connection." I feel Maggie's eyes on me. Detective Munroe's too. And the whole world shrinks down. To me and my past—as hard and far-reaching as the limbs on the hanging tree. This room is too small for the both of us.

"The license plate number you gave the officers last night... Danny's truck...it's registered to Trey Waters. As I recall, you know him, right?"

I feel the lie on my tongue, the same one I'd told Detective Munroe—"I don't remember Trey Waters." But if I lie again, they'll start to wonder why, what I'm hiding. I let Cassie die. I let her die and I kept quiet. So I give them the minnow and keep the whopper reeled in close where they can't see it.

"Knew him," I say. "I *knew* him." And he nods like he understands. In hell, all roads lead to the devil. All roads lead, have always led, to Trey.

**** 

As soon as the door closes behind them, I'm ready to bolt upstairs and dive under Jared's covers—where if I press my face deep into the pillow, I can convince myself I still smell him—the only place I'm sure I'll be able to breathe again. But Maggie grabs my arm, her long nails closing around it like a steel trap.

"I can't believe you didn't tell us your mother was consorting with a common criminal."

I laugh but it goes nowhere, sinks fast in the deep quiet of the room. "Really, Maggie? You knew she was addicted to heroin. You knew she was a prostitute. I didn't think I needed to tell you she wasn't a card-carrying member of the country club. Besides, I haven't seen the man in over twenty years. What does it matter?"

"It must matter. Or they wouldn't be here asking you questions about him." And I know she's right. Trey's not the sort of animal that stays buried. He's the Stephen King sort, clawing his way up to scratch out your eyes.

"This guy...this Trey...he lived with you?"

"Sometimes."

"And he...was he your mother's...boyfriend?"

I can't stand the way Maggie tiptoes around it, so I hit her with it smack in her well-to-do face. "He was her pimp. They used drugs together. And Detective Maroni thinks Trey killed her. Or at least that's what he thought back then."

**238**

She gasps, and I relish the breathy sound of it. I like that I can shock her even now. Especially now when I don't have to explain myself to Jared. "Did he?"

I dart away from her, but I pause on the first stair, because I want to look at her when I say it. I want to scald her with the truth. But then I see her eyes—Jared's eyes. My anger boils out and cools, until it's nothing but a placid lake of sadness. I can't be angry. Not at her. I feel the tears come before I say it.

"Yes."

# CHAPTER TWENTY-SEVEN

## BUTCH
## JANUARY 18, 2017
## WEDNESDAY

I roll down the window and stick my head out like a hound dog, jowls flapping in the wind. The air of downtown Oakland—exhaust, rain, the faint scent of garbage—has never smelled so good.

Jail had a different odor than prison. Raw and cold and alive. An acrid bouquet of oniony sweat, metal, and fear. Worse. Because they don't even bother to pretty it up with a chemical sheen. Folsom, on the other hand, had always smelled like bleach. That sharp, stinging odor meant to cover up blood, urine, vomit—all the things that come out of a man. Every day, they'd mop down the tiers, slicking the floor, shining it up, ready for the next J-Cat Jimmy to take the leap. As long as I live, I'll never forget that smell.

"Do you want to talk about it?" Mr. Richert asks as he drives us back to the halfway house.

*Hell no.* I could say what I'm thinking, but Richert would pull it out of me anyway. He's one of those. "We just went out for a walk. It was no big deal."

"Hmph."

And so it begins. The litany of cognitive distortions I thought I'd outgrown at Folsom. "I lost track of time." *Denial.* "We weren't even that late." *Minimization.* "It was Sebastian's idea." *Blame.* I scold myself from afar, but I don't take it back. Not any of it.

"I thought you didn't like the guy. A few days ago you were demanding a room transfer and calling him a perv. Now you're breaking curfew with him. Something don't add up, Calder."

"He's not that bad." Sebastian *is* a lying, thieving snake in the grass, and I plan on telling him exactly that when—*if*—I see him again. But, right now, freedom blowing in my face, I kind of love him for it. Because getting rolled up on a curfew violation is one thing. It'll get you a slap on the wrist, a do better next time. Getting caught with the driver's license of an attractive female psychologist, especially one who works in the same building with you, well, that's another animal altogether. I know exactly how they'd spin it. Just like the DA did with me and Gwen.

*Mr. Calder became obsessed with Gwendolyn. Stalked her. Demanded she see him again. When she refused, he couldn't live with it. Or, more accurately, he couldn't let her live with it. And he viciously, savagely, ended her life.*

And what could I say? There was truth there, untruth too. But when you do something as downright evil as murder, you lose your right to clarify.

So when Cop One had ripped open the envelope, practically salivating, I'd had to bite my tongue to keep from laughing. With pure joy. Relief. A goddamned baseball card. Some no-name Yankee from the 1990s. Even now, thinking of it, I cover my mouth to hide a giddy smile.

"This don't have anything to do with that lady doctor, does it?" Instantly deflated, I frown at him. "Don't give me that look, man. You know what I'm talking about."

"How do you know about Evie…uh, Dr. Maddox?"

"I know because it's my job to know. Agent McElroy told me. He's worried about you. And so am I. When you told me you got a lead on a job from an old friend, I was picturing a bald ex-con with a half-dozen tattoos and a beer gut, not a pretty little psych doctor."

"It's not like that." I wish I could sound more convincing. "Seriously."

"Well, since she popped up, trouble's sure been on your tail. Think about it."

"I *am* thinking."

He slaps the wheel and guffaws like I meant to be funny. "Oh, I know that. But are you thinking with the right head?"

****

I've got a confession to make. That first night in the alleyway, I took your license. I don't know why. It was just lying there on the ground—sad, like a dead leaf or a scrap of paper—and then it was in my pocket. But that's not all. I lost it before I could give it back—I wanted to give it back. Why am I telling you now? Because I'm sorry, for starters. And because Danny never had it. He never took it. I think he knows you.

That's the speech I practice on the walk to Chicken and Waffles. It comes easy, because it's the truth. Mostly. And after my two hours stuck in a foul-smelling jail cell—*to teach me a lesson*, Agent McElroy had said—I want to start fresh. Honest.

I tense up when I get close to the restaurant. There's a line of people outside, just milling around in the cold. Waiting. My booth is taken, of course, because every booth is taken. And at the counter, a butt in every stool, half of them gun-toting, backslapping boys in blue. *Just my luck*. Probably finishing up the night shift. At least I don't see the cops who took me in…yet.

*I know a fish out of water when I see one.* Brenda had been right when she'd said it. That's exactly how I feel. A poor fish, flopping

**242**

around, desperate. Just waiting for somebody to clock me over the head and put me out of my misery.

I stop, start to turn back. I can talk to Evie at work. Anywhere but here.

"Calder?"

And now I really am a fish. A hooked one. Caught. I walk toward Evie as she reels me in with her eyes.

"Hey," I say, because it's all I can manage right now. Looking normal takes effort when your brain is hardwired for the big house. I maneuver through the crowd—*why is that big dude with the tats looking at me?*—my shallow breath just marking time till I get the shank in my back. Or a bum rush from the skinheads. Or a solid push over the tier like Jimmy. I know it's not real, but when I get to Evie, smack dab in the middle of the line, I press myself to the wall and suck air into my gills.

"I didn't think it would be this crowded," she whispers, leaning in. Confessing. *I've got a confession to make.* "Or this cold. It's freezing."

My brain goes blank, and her face fills it. Her nose is pink at the edges. Like she's been crying. Or maybe it's just the January wind whipping it raw. Her eyes look tired, a murky seaweed green, but they light when she smiles. And I think of something to say.

"Yeah, me neither. I never come here in the mornings."

"I see why. I'm sorry I suggested it." She joins me on the wall, the sleeves of our jackets almost touching. Like she knows I'm a live wire—sparking and pitching—that needs to be grounded. The line moves on without us. And when the tatted man answers his cell, his hard-as-plaster face breaks into a grin.

I realize I've got her red umbrella in a death grip, and I ease up. Hand it to her. "Thanks for this," I say.

Evie moves closer or maybe I imagine it. And all I can think is I hope I'd scrubbed hard enough to get the stench of jail off me. Sometimes, even before last night, I'd think I still smelled like prison. Despair gets in your pores, you know. Till you start to sweat the stuff out like it's some kind of sickness in your blood.

"Maybe your friend—Brenda—can help us out with a table." Evie's definitely closer, because I feel her elbow nudge me, teasing. "Or you anyway. She'd probably make me sit out here."

"I just remembered Brenda has Wednesdays off."

"Then what the heck are we doing here? I don't know about you, but I came for Brenda." She laughs at her joke, and I feel like I can breathe again. Until she links her arm with mine and points down the block. "There's a mini mart up the street. We can grab a coffee and walk to the office. I'll get Melanie to give me a ride back to the parking garage this afternoon. If that's okay with you."

*I've got a confession to make. That first night in the alleyway, I took your license. And now, I'm thinking with the wrong head.* "It's perfect."

Once we've cleared the Chicken and Waffles' chaos, I swallow hard. *Now's the time, Butchy.* Do it now. I stop moving, and Evie releases my arm. I turn and face her. *Get it over with, dude.* "So…"

"You'll never believe what happened last night after the whole thing with Danny." And before I can spit it out, she's holding up the goddamned license. "The cops found it."

For a ten count I'm pretty sure I'm having a heart attack. Like there's a vice in my chest and it's clamped tight. "They did? Where?"

She shrugs. "Somewhere near the office. They came by this morning…early. That's why I look like hell."

For another ten count, I pinch the skin between my thumb and forefinger, dancing on the ledge of hysterical laughter. Because Evie's hell is a place I want to visit. And because somebody up there is pulling strings for me. Not my dad though. He'd have left me in the slammer last night for my own good. He'd want me to fess up, even now. Maybe it's Jesse. He was always up for a bit of mischief. Like the time we put red dye in the milk carton. Or when we slathered all the doorknobs with Vaseline.

"Just to give you the license? Or did they catch Danny?"

"Neither." And she starts to walk again, pulling her jacket tight to her like a hug. I'm glad not to have to look her in the eyes. They see me, somehow, down to the bones. Down to the part of me that's

**244**

all rust and ashes. "They wanted to talk about the past. My past. You know, you're the only one who could possibly understand."

"The past? What do you mean?"

"Trey." She whispers it like a curse word. And in a way it is. A *cursed* word. "Danny knows Trey or Trey knows Danny. Either way, they're connected. The truck's license plate came back registered to him."

"Why would...? Do you think it could just be a coincidence?"

The mini mart beckons up ahead promising warmth and caffeine—I'm desperate for both—but Evie slows, shakes her head. "I got a note from the dead girl."

**\*\*\*\***

Evie's been tearing at the edge of her empty coffee cup for the last two blocks. I've got this urge, a stirring in my belly, to put my hand on hers, to quiet it. But I don't. I most definitely do not. It's been so long since I touched a woman with intention, it feels impossible. Treacherous. Like scaling Mount Everest or lifting a semitruck. Touch like that—real intimacy—is one of the things I'd learned to live without. Same for privacy, dignity. And cheeseburgers with fries.

"So you don't know when she left the note...and it just said to meet her at Willow Court?" I ask. "That's all?"

"Yes. That's all. I told you already."

I've spouted enough lies to know when I'm being lied to, but I let it go. Because if I didn't, I'd have to officially change my name. Just call me Mr. Big F. Hypocrite, folks.

"I'm sorry," she says. "I didn't mean to snap at you. It's just...it was a long night. And I'm worried. What does Trey want with me?" She looks at me like I might have the answer. Like she trusts me. And that thrills me and freaks me the hell out. "I thought that part of my life was over."

The office parking lot is mostly empty. Just Mr. Vinetti's old work truck and a beat-up Buick. So nobody would notice if I put my arms around her. I imagine how she'd fit perfectly, with her head just under my chin. How her hair would smell—the exact opposite of prison—like hope. But then, I think of Gwen, and the smell spoils. Rotten like my rancid apple of a heart.

"Hey, listen. I'm probably not the best person to be giving advice. But my first night in the halfway house, I totally lost it. Just thinking about all the what-ifs and to-dos and might-have-beens. Mr. Richert told me something that stuck. He said, 'Butch, if it's not happening now, it's not happening.'"

She nods, but her attention is somewhere else. And I hear the soft opening of a car door, the Buick. Even before I see him, there's a shift in the air. A feeling in my gut, like guilt, only darker. Like he's opened a portal to 1994 and let all the ghosts through. I stare at him, wishing he wasn't real.

"Uh, Calder. I think it's happening. Now."

## EVIE
## MAY 8, 1994
## FIVE DAYS UNTIL MY BIRTHDAY

**DISGUSTED,** I stared at myself in the mirror and watched my face frown at Cherice. "I thought you said the eye shadow would make my eyes look less green. But this? Ugh. They're still the exact shade of the Incredible Hulk."

She rubbed my shoulder and shook her head. "Trust me, girl. One day those eyes will be some boy's favorite thing about you. Here, put this on."

I applied the lipstick—Paint the Town Pink—the way I'd seen my mother do it. Bottom, then top. Smack the lips together. And blot with a tissue. "Look at you. You're already a pro," Cherice said, giggling.

My own laugh sunk like a stone, heavy with guilt. Guilty that I was here, primping, and my mom's lips were fish food. That Cassie was holed up with the devil. That I hadn't seen it coming. That there was nothing I could do.

"C'mon, don't be so serious." Cherice tickled my side until my laugh felt light again. "So, do you wanna tell me why you're wearing my makeup to the music hour?"

"There's this boy I like...but he's older, and I think he likes somebody else."

"Does he live here?"

I tilted my chin, raised my eyebrows—the are-you-kidding-me look—because no boy at Port in a Storm would come near Evil Evie. And that was just fine with me.

"But he'll be here today?"

"I hope so. Maybe."

"Alright, since you're not making this easy, I'll play detective. He doesn't live here. He's older. And…Oh! I know." She smiles, soft and secret, the way I do when I'm thinking about something really good. Like the time when Mom had stayed clean for three whole months, and we'd watched *General Hospital* together after I got home from school. "Butch Calder."

My neck bloomed red, and I turned away from the mirror. "It's stupid, right? I mean, like I could ever compete with Gwen. She's perfect."

"Nobody's perfect, Evie. Especially not Gwen."

"I thought you liked her." Cherice wrinkled up her nose at me like she smelled something sour. "But, she's beautiful. Drop-dead gorgeous. And I'm…" I didn't know what I was, only what I wasn't. "Not."

"First of all, that is a downright lie. You know what I see?" She put her hands on my head and gently redirected my gaze to the mirror.

"Long, straight black hair." *That I pull out sometimes.*

"Porcelain skin." *Pale and ordinary as bread.*

"And eyes the color of emeralds." *Creepy, creepy, CREEPY.* "A real beauty. Come to think of it, you remind me of Snow White. And second, it's not all about that anyway. The right kind of boy will like you for the inside too."

"Is Butch the right kind?"

"Absolutely. And he's damn fine. That's for sure." Her grin reminds me of springtime, warm and free and blossoming with life. I can't help but smile back, until she adds, "But he is way too old for you."

\*\*\*\*

When we heard the rumble of Calder's 'Cuda through the open window, Cherice winked at me. I pretended not to notice as I settled into my spot, alone, cross-legged in front of the piano. I didn't look back at the rest of the kids, huddled with their groups, giggling to each other. Hands cupped to ears, whispering. I knew better. Looking only made it worse. I wore lonely like a tattered coat, proud as I could.

Gwen came first, sparkling in the drab room, a pearl in a crowd of oysters. But I barely noticed her. Because, Calder. I can still remember him—KISS T-shirt, brand-name jeans, and black boots, the kind you'd wear if your name was James Dean or you were riding a motorcycle—as clearly as if I'd taken a photograph and kept in my pocket for the last twenty years.

I waited for him to notice me. The moment he glanced in my direction, I flipped my hair and launched Cosmo tip number three. The perfect smile: *Make eye contact for three seconds—one thousand one, one thousand two, one thousand three—smile. Look down shyly. Turn away.* But by that time, he was leaning against the wall, holding Gwen's viola case in one hand, his arm casually draped across her shoulders, as lovely as a mink shawl. And I felt like a colossal idiot.

But the longer I looked, the more I saw. The tension in his jaw. The hunched set of his broad shoulders. The way Gwen kept gazing up at him like a little girl. And his eyes that flitted around the room, unsettled, and landed on Cherice every single time. Gwen seemed to see it too, because she leaned into him, put her mouth right up against his ear, until his eyes snapped back to attention, a dog choked by its leash. He was rapt, riveted by her, and I felt certain I'd imagined the whole thing.

I was so busy staring, I didn't see Officer Maroni arrive in his squad car, didn't see him saunter up the sidewalk and ring the bell. And then, he stood there in the doorway, waving at me while Cherice beckoned me over.

"Ooooh. Evil Evie's in trouble. Popo's here to get her." Bobby Pierce started his singsong mocking, my personal anthem of shame. My head got all fuzzy with panic. Legs so heavy I could barely stand. "She probably looked at somebody again. Turned 'em to stone. Killed 'em, dead."

"Bobby, zip it." Cherice pointed at him, and he went silent. Underground. Simpering at me and widening his eyes with his grubby little fingers. I hated him so much, I wished he spoke the truth. That I could squash his tiny, pea heart with one well-timed glance. Freeze his empty brain and crack it like a block of ice.

I narrowed my eyes at him, conjuring myself as a black cat—back arched, tail puffed—and hissed.

Everybody got quiet. Everybody but Calder. His laugh soothed me like medicine. And then, serious as a heart attack, he turned to Bobby. "Oh my God, dude. There's something wrong with your face. I think it's turning to…no, wait. That's as messed up as it always looks. My bad."

****

"Remember me, Evie?" Macaroni pulled up a child-size chair in the Port in a Storm art room and sat. I nodded, still trying to swallow my tears, a sob stuck in my throat like a hunk of steak. "Sorry I embarrassed you like that. That kid, Bobby, he's a little shit."

That got a half smile from me. "He's the worst."

"Do you want me to arrest him? That would teach him a lesson." The other half of my smile caught up, and I started feeling better. Calder had stood up for me, after all. "Anyway, I just wanted to check in and see how you're doing. It's been what…a couple months since your mom?"

"I'm okay." *One.* I started counting my lies.

"Is school good? You have friends?"

"Yeah." *Two.*

"You ever see Trey Waters?"

I hesitated. "Sometimes."

"Well, if he bothers you, you let me know."

"I will." *Three.*

Macaroni didn't say anything for a while, and I wondered if he was counting too. Trey had told me I had to keep my story straight, that the police would try to catch me fibbing. That they'd try to pin it all on him. "They're just looking for an escape goat, Evelyn. I didn't do nothin' wrong." And when I'd opened my big mouth to correct him, a part of me snickering with glee—"Scapegoat, Trey. Not escape goat."—he'd shut it with a hard slap.

"I'll be honest with you. Evie. I still think that guy is hiding something. Did he threaten you? Tell you to keep quiet?"

"No." *Four.*

"Alright. You can tell me, you know. Whatever you tell me is between us. He'll never find out."

There's no keeping secrets from the devil. That much I knew. But the heat from that slap still radiated in my chest. Just another log on the fire Trey stoked. He'd taken everything from me already. And now, Cassie too. I wanted him to feel it, to burn his fingers, singe the animal hair off his arms. It wouldn't ever be enough—not for my mom—but it was something. I couldn't speak Trey's secrets, but maybe I could outsmart him. For Cassie.

"There is one thing," I said, surprised at the boldness in my voice. And I'm not sure I would take it back even knowing what came after, all the dominoes it set in motion. "He's living at the Blue Bird. You should go check it out. I think he's dealing drugs there." *Five.*

**\*\*\*\***

After Macaroni left, I didn't go back to the music hour. I lingered in the art room, coloring on a sketchpad and picking out the best crayons. Cerulean, my mother's favorite color. Silver, my Dad's ring, the one Trey wanted the same way he wanted everything else. Dandelion, Cassie's dress. Chestnut, Calder's eyes. And the worst too. So many shades of green. Olive and jungle. Pine and asparagus. I slipped them into my pocket for destruction.

When Calder walked in, I flipped my drawing face down as fast as I could. What a baby I was, sitting there coloring. He just smiled.

"You missed my solo." He did a quick tap dance, his boots clunking on the tile floor. "Come fly with me. Come fly away."

"Yeah right, Sinatra. I'm sure I would've heard that from here."

"The singing or the booing?"

I tried to laugh like Gwen, cute and delicate. Mine was more of a snort. "Both."

"Are you alright? I'm sorry about that kid. What a loser."

I shrugged. "It's okay. I'm used to it."

He sat where Macaroni had, just across the table, and peeked at my drawing. I let him. Mainly because I'd stopped breathing and lost all feeling in my body. Except for a slow buzz that crept up from my toes to the heart of me. This liking a boy thing was worse than I'd expected. And better. I thought again of Gwen, how practiced she'd seemed, how composed. Even with her lips so close to Calder's neck. *How did she do that?*

"Is this for me?" He turned it over. The letters *K-I-S-S* spelled out in all the best colors.

"Do you want it?"

He raised his eyebrows. "Well, they're only the best hard rock band of all time."

I pushed it toward him, and he ran his hand zigzag along the chestnut *S*. "Hey, what does your friend Cassie look like?"

My whole body started up again with a sputter and a jolt. "Cassie? Uh, she's got long brown hair and she's a little taller than me. Why?"

"I think I saw her at a party last night with Trey. Is she…okay?"

Naive as I was, I imagined Macaroni speeding to the Blue Bird right that minute, busting down the door and carting Trey off to a jail far, far from here. Bringing Cassie to the safety of the Port, where Trey couldn't touch us. "She will be," I said. "Thanks to me."

Calder frowned, but he didn't push. He took out a crayon—blue violet, a classic—and sketched his name in the corner of the paper. His whole name. *Butch Cassidy Calder.*

I snorted again. "Is that really your middle name?"

"Yeah. Thanks, Mom. I guess she had a thing for outlaws." *I have a thing for outlaws too.* That's what Gwen would've said, all flirty and kittenish.

"And your brother?" I asked.

"Jesse James Calder." When we both laughed, I liked the sound of it. It thrummed in my chest like Cherice's singing. Resonated like a perfect harmony. "But, you're sworn to secrecy, okay?"

I nodded fast, seizing the chance for *Cosmo* tip five. *Create an opportunity to touch him.* "Shake on it." I reached my arm toward him, ready, but it happened so fast. Too fast. His hand was there—warm and solid and electric—and then it was gone.

"Alright then." If I was more like Gwen I could've kept him there, transfixed. If I was more like Gwen, he would've noticed my eye shadow, my pink lips. But, I was me. Evil Evie. Only twelve, almost thirteen. And he stood up. Oblivious. "I'll see you soon, Evie."

*Not soon enough.*

He left, and the 'Cuda growled—louder, louder, then quiet, fading to nothing—before I realized my drawing was still on the table.

# CHAPTER TWENTY-EIGHT

EVIE
JANUARY 18, 2017
WEDNESDAY

**I'D** always told my patients to confront the past head on. No matter how ugly. But I realize now what I'd been asking. The impossibility of it. Because when Trey Waters appears in the parking lot, I only want to run away. As far and as fast as I can. From the wicked smile that spreads like a stain. From his legs clad in black denim, long and spindly as a spider. From the vile sound he makes when he hocks up phlegm from the back of his throat and spits, proud of himself and the thick, stringy glob he's left on the concrete.

The closer he gets, I can see half his teeth are capped in silver, ringed with black at the gums. Like the drain of the grimy Blue Bird bathtub. The TV screen hadn't done him justice. Time had given Trey exactly the face he'd deserved. And if it weren't for Butch next to me, I'd be long gone.

"What do you want, Trey?"

"Damn, Evelyn. Is that the way you greet an old friend?" He stretches out his arms toward me, all scarred and needle-tracked. It's still there. Of course it is. The small tattoo in cursive on his wrist. *RIP Arlene.* "Come here, girl. Give Trey a hug." And I feel like I might be sick.

Butch walls himself between us, and I stare at his back. The rise and fall of his shoulders. He's breathing hard. "I don't think you should be here."

"Oh really. Should you?" Trey cocks his head and squints at Butch. Like he can't quite see him clearly even in the light of day. "You think I don't remember you, Nobody? It's like a goddamn reunion. Let's see. We got the little orphan girl. And the punk-ass bitch who was too big for his own britches. Landed himself in Folsom. Guess the prison's got so crowded, they're letting anybody out these days."

"There's always room for one more." Butch steps forward, calmer than I expect. But when I grab his arm to tug him back, his skin is feverish, simmering to a boil.

Trey stalks in a semicircle, toying with me the way a cat plays with a mouse. Half-bored, half-aroused. "Frankly, I'm surprised to see you consortin' with the likes of him. You bein' a fancy doctor and all. And a Maddox. Damn. Your mama would be real proud."

"Don't talk about her. Ever."

"Oh, c'mon." And there's a hard edge in his voice. Claws unsheathed. "Don't be like that."

"Seriously, why are you here?" I ask.

"Fair question. I just wanna make sure we're cool. Are we cool, Evelyn?" The way he says my name, like he knows something about me, makes me want to slap him. Because he does. He's seen what a coward I am.

"I don't know, Trey, are we?"

"Well, now that you mention it. Seems to me you been stickin' your highfalutin nose where it don't belong."

"What is that supposed to mean?"

"Don't play all innocent with me. Ruby told me you came by askin' questions, bein' real curious. Hey, what's that old saying about the cat?"

"Are you threatening her?" Butch asks. "That's probably not such a good idea for someone in your position."

"And what position is that?"

"Murder suspect."

Trey cackles, but his eyes don't change. They're windows too, like Butch's. Only Trey's lead nowhere. To nothing. "Don't go believin' everything you hear. You should know that, Nobody. Like I heard you killed that rich girl because she wouldn't give it up to you. And then, you waited till she was dead and you—"

Butch flinches, and Trey jumps back, fists up, huffing air through his nostrils, wild as a mustang.

"Relax, man. I'm not gonna hit you. You mean nothing to me. Less than nothing. But, you should leave 'cause I'm calling the police." Butch holds up his phone, his finger on the nine, ready to pull the trigger. And it hits me then how solid he seems. How he's grown into a man, rooted to the earth. How Trey shrinks, small as a mouse compared to him.

"You got the message, right? Stay the fuck out of my business." He turns tail and scampers back to his car. Under the bruised black paint on the fender, I recognize that hideous shade of purple. *No offense, but your car is a hooptie*—I hear Butch's voice in my head. And it bolsters me, knowing Trey is still driving that Buick. That he's just as chained to the past as I am. Maybe more.

"How'd you get my Dad's ring?" It winks at me from his finger—a sterling silver skull with two rubies for eyes. "Real goddamned rubies," my mom had always said.

He grins at it, proud, like he earned it. "Shit, Evelyn. You gave it to me."

"Like hell I did." But I doubt myself.

"This little beauty and the money you owed me. I always knew you'd come around."

**256**

"I don't believe you."

"You really don't remember? It was the last night I saw you. You and that friend of yours. What the hell was her name? Purdy little thing. Anyway, I put you on a bus to LA just like you asked. You were drunk or high on somethin' that night. Hell if I know. But you had a little baggie of powder on ya. I flushed it down the toilet."

One hand on the Buick's roof, he lowers himself to the driver's seat. His arm is inked to the shoulder, as gaunt as a chicken wing. All sinew and gristle. The parts you'd spit out.

I nod at him, savoring the salt of my sarcasm. "Thanks, Trey. I appreciate your stopping by. It's always a pleasure to see you." He snaps his head back like I slapped him. Blinks those empty eyes and smiles so wide I wonder if his jaw has come unhinged. If he'll swallow me yet.

I feel Butch behind me, the presence of him. I wish he would touch me. I need someone to tether me to the present. Because I don't want to remember anymore. But I do.

I'm floating through Willow Court, small and unseen—Cheesy's ghost. I must be dead. Cassie's dead too. And Trey is here. He's a hungry cat, biding his time. Nipping at my tail as I go. Through 136 and past the swing set to 201. "There." I point. And Trey's whiskers start twitching. He makes paw prints on the counter, stretches his long body up to the hole in the ceiling. Grins. "Atta-girl."

The Buick whines and grumbles to a start. Once he's made it to the edge of the lot, Trey rolls down the window and sticks his hand out, middle finger raised. I hear Butch's laugh, lemon-bitter. And when I turn to look at him, the weight of it all—my mother and Trey and Cassie and my own bag of secrets, strapped to my back—pushes me forward and into his chest.

It's like I've split into two Evies.

One is twelve, going on thirteen—*I'm freaking hugging Butch Calder!*

The other, thirty-six and widowed. *He'll never be Jared. No one will. And he's an ex-con. Who killed Gwen.*

Butch stiffens, his own arms straight-jacketed to his sides, freezing the way Sammy does when I pick him up. Embarrassed, I start to pull away. "I'm sorry," I say. "I didn't even think. I—"

He takes a big breath, like he's preparing for something life changing. War. Surgery. A pilgrimage across the desert. Then, his arms move. Cranking to life like a tin man, he pulls me closer.

"What's wrong?" he asks, his chin moving against the top of my head.

"Trey's lying." I don't say the other. That Trey's also telling the truth. About me and the ring and the money. Or the other thing I'm thinking. That it's been two years since I've felt a man's arms around me.

He lets go first, avoiding my eyes, but my skin keeps buzzing. "Well, yeah. Obviously. That's what he does, right? Classic Trey."

"No. I mean, he's definitely lying about Cassie. He didn't forget her name. He's got it tattooed on his arm."

# CHAPTER TWENTY-NINE

**FOR** the first time in years, I've got a goddamned KISS song in my head. *My insulation's gone, girl you make me overload...shock me.* And that's how I feel. Stripped bare, right down to the nerve endings. Shocked.

*Act normal, Butchy.* So I put my eyes anywhere but on Evie. Because I want more. I'm desperate to touch her again. And I know why. Skin hunger. It's what happens when they lock you in a box with other men. When nobody touches you and you touch nobody, you turn into one of Harlow's rhesus monkeys. That, and it's Evie, and she's beautiful.

"What happened to Cassie?" It's the only logical question, even though I'm scared of the answer. Because I had a hand in it. I know I did.

Evie frowns, as if she's measuring the words, snipping them down to something bearable. Just the way I've done—*I killed a girl*—and I want to take back the question. "You don't have to talk about it if you—"

"Cassie's...dead. She died." Like she's testing it out. Like she's never said it before. "Cassie was a real person, right? You remember her?"

It's one hell of a strange question, but I can tell she means it. That she needs an answer. "Of course. I saw her a few times. With Trey." And guilt burns through me like a fever. "How did she die?"

Evie looks up at her office and starts to speak, but the staccato honk of a car horn silences us both. 23A, Melanie's Massage wiggles her fingers through her open window and pulls alongside us. "Good morning, you two." Then, to me. "I don't think we've officially met. Though you did do a bang-up job on my clogged sink."

She's about as subtle as a hammer, clocking me over the head with a coy smile and the most come-hither rendition of "Melanie" I've ever heard. Flattering, I guess. But I'm still not used to flirting. Or hugging. Obviously. I keep waiting for somebody to tell me I'm breaking the rules. Being overfamiliar. A fancy prison word for crossing the line. So, I keep it simple, professional.

"I'm Butch. Nice to meet you."

"The pleasure is mine." Her eyes flit between me and Evie, playful and daring. "Oh. Am I interrupting something?"

*Yes? No?* A total oaf, I watch Evie's face for clues. She glowers, then offers a tight-lipped smile. "Don't you open at 8:30 today, Mel?"

Melanie sticks out her tongue at Evie. But there's something serious and surly in her pretend pout.

"Hmph. I guess Dr. Maddox wants you all to herself." She winks at me, her car inching forward. "Can't say I blame her. Everybody's got a thing for bad boys."

I stare straight ahead and pretend not to hear that part. I should've known there would be talk. But it's not real anyway, the bad-boy thing. It's just a thin coat of varnish. A throwaway line for us screw-ups to make our sins sound good. She doesn't know me—*I killed a girl*—and if she did, she wouldn't be batting her goddamned eyelashes.

When she stops again, I plan to level her with the truth. But, then, she leans her head out the window and calls to Evie. "Hey, did you ever track down your hooker friend?"

****

I trail Evie up the stairs to her office. She hasn't uttered a single word since the parking lot. Since she'd silenced Melanie with a clipped no and shot me a look that urged me to follow her.

For all the ways I'd been left in the dust, prison had earned me a PhD in body language. I knew when shit was about to hit the fan in the chow hall by the way the Mexican Mafia closed ranks, circling up like dogs in a pack. Knew which COs were cowboys and which were old-timers by the width of their swagger. Knew the Tier 1 porter was getting it on with the free staff librarian by the way he hummed Marvin Gaye while he shined the floors.

And right now, I know Evie is about to lose it. Completely. She's advancing up the steps two at a time, a slight tremor in her hands. I get it—maybe better than anybody—and I want to protect her. But I can't. *What protection is there from the past?* It's not a scar like you think it is. Like the one on my neck, smooth and raised and white—a wound in negative. Not for people like me and Evie. For us, the past is a scab. Ugly, tender, and brittle. Easily picked away. And it still bleeds. Boy, does it ever.

At the door, Evie pauses and looks at me. "You don't have to get involved in this…" But I'm already in up to my neck. Not just involved. Complicit. "…in my mess."

I shrug at her. "I know that. But I want to." *I have to.*

She unlocks the door and lets us both into the waiting room. Shutting it behind her, she drops into the first chair like a sack of sand. Her face is pinched, pained. But she doesn't cry. Not yet.

I sit too, nearest the small window, leaving one chair between us. My fists clench in my lap, so I won't be tempted to think with the wrong head again. "You were a good friend to me, Evie. Way back when. Besides, your mess can't be any messier than mine."

She winds a finger through her hair, the black strands coiling like a snake. She pulls the thick strand tighter and tighter until I'm sure she's about to yank it right out. But then, she lets go, and it falls to her shoulder, slightly curled. "I suppose there's only one way to find out."

Her eyes settle on the window. It frames the edge of the park across the street. And I know if I moved closer to it, pressed my nose to the pane, I could see the tree. That tree.

"I haven't talked about this. Ever. With anybody."

She's not looking at me, but I nod anyway, showing her I'm not afraid. Showing myself too. Even though I am. Terrified.

"That night…May 13, 1994. I can't remember a lot of it. Some parts not at all. But Cassie and I were supposed to find Trey. That's why I called you. We needed a ride. But, you…I guess you were…"

*Too damn busy choking the life from somebody. But not just somebody. Gwen.* "I'm sorry." I've said it so many times to so many people. But it always feels the same on my tongue. Heavy, bitter, insufficient.

"So we hitchhiked. Somehow, we ended up at that tree. And I climbed up in it."

I can picture her, crouched in the crook of the branches, lost as a fledgling. Dread owns me then. It cuffs me. Tosses me in a cage. Shuts off the lights. And all I can do is sit, a prisoner to the dark, and listen as my own past comes for me. Ready to slit my throat.

"That's where Cassie died. At the tree. He was on top of her. He killed her. I saw it happen."

"Who? Who did?" My voice sounds strange. Young. Like I'm seven again. Like I'm seven and guilty with that stolen Matchbox Corvette in my pocket.

"I…it's crazy, but I…I can't picture his face. No matter how hard I try."

**262**

"And then what?" I spew it out, hot and insistent. "Did you see anybody else?" I have to know. *What does she remember?*

"I don't know. I don't think so, but I can't be certain. The whole night is a blank. Trey was telling the truth about one thing though. I remember it. I took him to Willow Court and showed him where the money was. And my dad's ring. Why would I do that? Next thing I know, I woke up on a bus to LA."

"Are you sure she's dead?" *Please, God, don't let her be dead.* That night had played again and again and again like a horror film I couldn't turn off, couldn't look away from. But in twenty-three years, I'd never considered that. That Cassie had died. Now, it seemed so obvious. So possible. So likely.

"Yes. I'm sure." But she's asking, not telling.

"How do you know?"

"I just do, okay? The guy—whoever he was—was choking her, and she stopped moving. And...I just know. I've been living with this for twenty-three years. Don't you think I've looked for her? Tried to figure it out? She's nowhere. It's like she never existed at all."

"Well, she existed alright. You said it yourself—Trey has her goddamned name tattooed on his arm." She flinches at the curse word, and I mutter an apology. "When do you think he got it?"

She shrugs, shakes her head, hopeless. Like the answer is unknowable. Or she doesn't want to know. I can't tell which.

"What about the cops?" I ask.

Evie walls herself off from me, turns her whole body toward the door. Still, I can hear in her voice that she's crying. "What about them?" That she's ashamed.

"You didn't tell them?" I already know she didn't. And I already know why. Because there are two reasons people keep quiet. Why I'd kept quiet. Fear and shame. And I'm guessing Evie's two for two.

She looks at me over her shoulder, sweeps her wet cheeks with the back of her hand. "I didn't tell anybody, Butch. Not even my own husband."

What she doesn't say, that's she's telling me now—me, of all the people in this world—scares the hell out of me. "Well, you should tell them about today. About Trey."

The doorknob turns—the real world intruding—and I want to shut it. Lock it. Shelter us both. But Evie stands up, straightens herself. Dabs her eyes and forces a smile. She's good at it too. Practiced. So am I.

"Come in, guys," she says. "Group starts in five minutes."

The men file into the waiting room past Evie, and I slip out. Her arm brushes mine as I go, and the past throbs in my chest, gaping like an open wound.

# CHAPTER THIRTY

EVIE
JANUARY 18, 2017
WEDNESDAY

**THERE'S** one empty seat in the ring of folding chairs, and the rest of the men regard it with watchful eyes. The same way I look at the tree. Vigilant and wary, like it's a rabid animal that could lunge at any minute, sink teeth into flesh and infect us all.

I clear my throat, and they look at me, deferent. To them, I'm still Dr. Evelyn Maddox. I'm still in control. But inside, I'm wriggly as a snake that's shed its skin. *Cassie's dead. She died.* I'd said the words out loud, cast them off of me, set them free into a vast universe where they'd tumble and float with all the other confessions and secrets and black-hearted prayers. I'd shed a skin—brand-new Evie—but this one feels just as rotten. Because I didn't tell anybody until now. Because it was my fault we'd been there in the first place, hitching a ride. Because I'd wanted revenge—not for Cassie, but for myself. I'd wanted Trey dead.

"So where's New Guy?" Vince asks, pointing to the chair. "I figured he wouldn't last long. What'd he do? Get caught at Victoria's Secret with panties in his pocket?"

Tony chuckles. "I heard they snatched him up last night for a curfew violation."

"I knew it, man. I figured that guy had a jammer with his hoity-toity *Not everybody breaks the rules like you, Vince.*"

George sighs and shakes his head. "It's really none of our business." I can always count on him to restore order. "But...he didn't have anything to do with that girl's murder did he, Doc?" Or not.

I fiddle with the binder on my lap. Today's lesson—Responsible Sexual Behavior—tucked inside under the fax I'd pulled off the machine. It had come through at exactly 8:59 a.m. After the men had barged in and Calder had left and I'd fished Macaroni's card out of my pocket, looking hard at the numbers, as if I'd expected them to dial themselves. The fax had arrived with a beep and whir, the paper warm to the touch but cold somehow, like the unrelenting glare of a spotlight. Because sex offenders aren't allowed to keep secrets. Not in here. Not from me. And it strikes me as more than a little ironic. Turning over the stones of everyone else's secrets while my own had stayed hidden under the biggest rock I could find. Until today. Until Calder.

**FROM: DIVISION OF ADULT PAROLE OPERATIONS, HIGH-RISK SEX OFFENDER UNIT**
**TO: EVELYN MADDOX, PHD**
**FYI: Sebastian Delacourt was arrested last night at New Hope Halfway House for curfew violation, suspicion of tampering with a GPS device, and possession of a victim-related photograph. He may be a late arrival to group. Call me to discuss.**

"Sebastian might not be coming to group today. The rest of you'll have to ask him yourself when—"

Vince's guffaw cuts me off. He makes a show of slipping out a silver money clip and peeling off a crisp bill. "I've got a hundo that says he's already on the bus back to the big house on a murder beef."

"I'll take that bet." First comes the voice from behind the cracked door. And the rest of Sebastian follows—scarecrow-thin frame, hunched shoulders, tired eyes, a shock of black hair that hasn't been combed. And most noticeable, his hands. They dangle awkwardly at his sides like he doesn't know what to do with them. The book he'd carried Monday is gone.

He aims a weak smile at me and fills the empty seat. The men won't say it—Tony and George twitter uncomfortably—but his arrival is a relief. Too often they don't come back. I'm relieved too, more than I'd care to admit, and selfishly so. Because as strange as he was, Sebastian had known about the hanging tree, and I'd been hoping our individual session might trigger another memory. Maybe *the* memory. The faceless man, faceless no longer.

"Where were you?" George is pure grandpa again. More concerned than angry. But Sebastian stares at Vince. And Vince stares back, cocking his head in expectation.

"Well? George asked you a question, didn't he?" He's used to getting what he wants. Even the courts had given him a break. Three hundred and twenty-two images of naked teen girls, and he'd wriggled away with probation and house arrest.

"Well, what? I'm here, aren't I? Fork it over, Moneybags."

I frown at both of them. "Put the money away, guys."

With a satisfied smile, Vince slides the bill back under the clip and returns it to his pocket. "Sorry. Doctor's orders," he says.

"Sebastian, would you like to start our check in?"

All eyes on him now, he shrugs. "I'm guessing I don't really have a choice. So here goes. I'm um…" He consults the oversized feelings chart on the wall. "That one. Disappointed. Disappointed in myself.

I'm late to group because I left the house after curfew last night with one of my housemates, and we got caught."

I don't push him further. I just wait. And the sharks begin to circle.

"What were you doing out that late?" Tony asks.

"Nothing really. Just clearing our heads after the police showed up at the house asking us to snitch about that murder."

"I told you so," Vince said. "Where do they look first?" He spins his finger round and round. "Right here. We're goddamned pariahs. I'm surprised they haven't started tattooing our foreheads or some shit. That way everybody can see us coming."

"And they passed out fliers with her picture too. Anyway, after that Butch and I—" Sebastian lifts his eyes right to mine, and I nearly gasp. "We took off." He sits back in his chair, arms folded, looking… smug?

*Yes.*

*No.*

*Maybe.*

Before I can decide, he gestures to Tony. "Your turn."

****

It's just us now, one-on-one. And I still can't tell if Sebastian's half smile is tired or mocking. I notice the twist at the corner of his mouth, the way his head dips slightly, but I don't trust my instincts anymore. "Tell me about the picture," I say to him. *And Butch. I need to know about Butch.* "The one they found in your book." *And Butch.*

I try to quiet my nerves. Maintain my game face. Which means I shouldn't—I can't—I won't—think about Trey. Or Cassie. Or most especially, Butch. And the fact that Sebastian had been telling the truth about him. Agent Hopkins had confirmed it for me after group. *Yep, him and his roommate. Caught 'em red-handed.*

I'd waited twenty-three years to turn my rock—to expose the worms writhing beneath it—and I'd done it for a liar. *I'm sorry, Jared.* Because a lie of omission is still a lie.

"You know about the picture too? I guess they tell you everything."

My nod is curt, sharp as a hatchet. "That's how treatment works. It's called the containment model."

"And I'm the one who needs containing?"

"Well, yes. Considering what happened last night, don't you?"

"It didn't have anything to do with Sasha. Or sex. Or—"

"What did it have to do with then?"

"I told you in group. We just went for a walk. It's not like we were out painting the town…" Something about the slight upturn of his lips bothers me. Like an itch I can't scratch. "Butch suggested it. He said he needed to clear his head, that they never check our rooms after lights-out anyway."

*Game face, Evie.* Game face. "You disabled your GPS device."

"Those things are always breaking down. You know that."

"Your PO said they inspected it down at the station. It was working fine." He shrugged. "And the picture you had? It was of your stepfamily, right? You and Sasha. Your mother and her father."

"It's not what you think."

"Tell me, what *do* I think?"

"Probably that I was up in my room jacking off to teenaged Sasha. That I'm obsessed with her or something."

I held off on confirming his suspicions. But I couldn't *not* think it. I'd seen the letter in his file. The victim statement from Sasha herself. The way he'd followed her around like a puppy. Cute at first, her kid stepbrother. Then, he became something else entirely. Sneaking in and peeking at her in the shower, claiming it was an accident. Dedicating that creepy song to her—Depeche Mode—every weekend. Following her and her boyfriend. Watching her like she was under his microscope, the only one in the room.

"So, what were you doing with it? Your parole agent said it had been partially destroyed." *Desecrated.* That was the word Agent Hopkins had used. Then, he'd added, *I'm no therapist, but the guy's got anger issues.*

"Destroyed?" Sebastian gives a sarcastic snort. "Yeah, like my life. Here lies Delacourt's dignity." He makes the sign of the cross. "May it rest in peace."

*Rest in peace.* The words echoed back, taunting me from the past in Trey's gravelly voice. Just before he'd dropped me at Port in a Storm to fend for myself, he'd caught me staring at his tattoo. At the letters he'd inked above my mother's name.

"You like it? I added it on myself this mornin'. Go on. Touch it." The thought had disgusted me, but I'd figured if I didn't do it myself he'd make me, and that was worse. Way worse. So I'd traced the angry *R* with the tip of my finger, knowing I'd scrub it raw the instant I got inside. "You know she wasn't never at peace. Ain't no such thing, Evie. Not in this world."

My heart thrashes in my chest, beats against my ribs like the desperate wings of a wild bird. Because I know it in an instant. It's not a memory. It's a feeling, an instinct. How wrong I'd been and for so long. I want to scream it until my throat goes numb. Until time shatters and my thirteen-year-old self can hear me. As sure as I'd known Arlene Allcott was dead the moment Trey had coaxed me out of the bathroom that day—*rest in peace, Mom*—I know Cassie wasn't.

# BUTCH
## MAY 9, 1994
## FOUR DAYS BEFORE I KILLED HER

I woke up at one in the afternoon, totally hungover, to the blare of police sirens. So loud and so close, they got inside my head, driving out my eyeballs, splitting my skull in two. I stood up too fast, and the room went spinning like those tops Jesse used to play with. *Round and round and round she goes, where she stops nobody knows.* The rhyme made me think of Gwen—her tongue in my mouth, her hips grinding on mine—and the room got still again. My back ached. Hell, my teeth and skin hurt too. Like I'd slept in a tub of acid. And I nearly bit it on the single Doc Marten I'd kicked off right in front of the bed. Apparently I'd been too drunk to take off the other shoe, because it was still on my foot, unlaced. I hobbled to the window and pulled back the curtain. When the sun streamed in, I felt like a vampire. Blinded and half-dead.

I closed my eyes, and my brain sputtered to the start. Music hour at the Port with Gwen. Getting hammered on stolen tequila. After that, I couldn't remember much. The rest was fuzzy white like an overexposed photograph. Except the one thing. I pushed it away, out to sea like a bloated body.

Lifting my eyelids took real effort—they felt stapled shut—but I did it. I looked outside. And I couldn't imagine a worse feeling—the glare off the sidewalk, the flashing red and blue lights, the goddamned siren nobody bothered to shut off—or a better one. Trey Waters in handcuffs, dancing cheek to cheek with the hood of a cop car.

I put my forehead against the windowpane and stared. It felt warm from the sun. A wave of nausea came and went as Trey writhed and bucked like an animal in a trap, and the officer jostled him to the pavement. I forced my eyes to follow, grating against their sockets. I needed to see more. And when the girl's face appeared on the other side of the glass, I screamed.

"Shh." She held a finger to her lips. "Open your door."

"Jesus Christ, you scared the shit out of me." My voice was too loud for my own head. And that scream. My scream. It might as well have been a bullet.

"Please, Calder. Let me in. I'm Evie's friend."

I unlatched the chain, unlocked the bolt, cracked the door, and slumped back toward the bed, exhausted. The outside air felt cool as a compress. So I lay there, watching the slice of blue sky get bigger and bigger and smaller again as Cassie floated into my room and shut the door behind her.

"Are you sick?" she asked.

I started to nod, but my head was bowling-ball heavy. "Drunk still, I think."

"Do you know who I am?"

"Cassie. Right?" She didn't say anything as she walked over to the window, watching just the way I had. "What happened over there?"

"I don't know. Trey told me to go to room 120…he wanted me to…to see this guy there. But I couldn't do it, so I just hid out behind the motel for a while. And then I heard the sirens, and the cops showed up."

When she turned back toward me, I saw her face in the sunlight. The split in her lip like a furrow in the ground. The blue kiss of a bruise on her cheek. How young she looked, but also how old. And the room started spinning again, so I looked away.

My eyes rested on the flesh-toned wall. It was the exact shade of the peach crayon, and it reminded me of Evie. I'd forgotten to take the picture she'd drawn. I felt impossibly, ridiculously sad. "Did Trey do that to you?"

"What do you think?" Cassie jutted out her hip, rolled her eyes.

"I think you're in way too much trouble to act like a smart-ass."

She paced to the dresser and back to the window again. I realized she was barefoot. "He's gone," she said, finally. "The cops are gone too."

"You can't stay here. Trey will make bail. He'll be back." Evie's words, that cop at the Port—the pieces swam together in my pickled brain—it made sense now. She'd told him something about Trey. "And he's gonna be pissed."

"Who said I want to stay?"

She sits on the bed, and the mattress sways like a ship rocking beneath me. Something warm and sour oozes up my throat, and I swallow it.

"I feel so stupid," she says. "Evie's gonna hate me. She tried to warn me about him."

"She doesn't hate you."

"Did she say that?"

"Trust me. She doesn't."

"Can you talk to her for me? She likes you, you know. She told me you were her boyfriend." Then with a smirk, she added, "You know, you'd make a really sucky boyfriend, Calder."

I laughed at Cassie's remark—and at Evie's crush—to drown out Gwen's shrieking, her finger pointed in my face, but it was too late. The body I'd pushed out to sea had floated back. And it pulled me under…

"I heard you asked Cherice to ride with you at the party. Is that true?" I'd been too drunk to lie.

"You were out of it. Totally whacked. I didn't tell you to use that shit. What was I supposed to do?"

"Oh, gee, I don't know. Not get some other girl—who clearly has the hots for you, by the way—to fill in for me. But I guess that was too much to ask. I get it though. You want to slum it with the hired help." Her lips, loosened, let her lie slip out. But she was too far gone to realize. "Pity screw…poor little Cherice with the scar on—"

"At least she's not a whack job like you."

It had happened so fast. I wasn't sure what had come first. The slap across my face, Gwen's hand hot with shame. The word, thick with spit, hurled from my mouth. *Bitch!* Or the shove. More of a ram, really. And harder than I'd intended. Because it had launched Gwen back against the window of the 'Cuda, the crack of her head terrible and satisfying.

"Butch? Are you asleep?" Cassie tapped on my shoulder, and I groaned. She sat cross-legged on the bed, and the dull drone of the television swarmed like a nest of hornets in my ears.

"Unfortunately not."

"Well, you seemed kind of out of it for a few minutes. I turned on the TV. I hope that's okay. It's my favorite show."

I recognized the theme song, and the blonde on the screen. "*Charlie's Angels?*" I asked.

"My mom and I used to watch the reruns on Saturday mornings. That was before she stopped taking her meds and threw the TV against the wall." Cassie had the gloomiest laugh I'd ever heard. "She thought it was sending her messages."

"That sounds really messed up."

"Who's your favorite and why?" she asked, and I groaned again. "Oh, come on."

"Jill," I said. "Because Farrah Fawcett. Obviously."

"So predictable. She looks kinda like that girl you were with at the party." *Gwen. Oh God. I need to talk to Gwen.* "I like Kelly Garrett. I stole my last name from her, you know." I roll off the bed and to my feet, ignoring the sudden rush of blood to my brain, the spinning room, the sick feeling. "Hey, are you even listening to me?" she asked.

"You've gotta go," I told Cassie. "There's somewhere I need to be." I pulled on my other boot and concentrated on tying the laces.

"Where am I supposed to go?" For the first time, her voice quivered. And my heart seized up. *But Gwen. Cassie's not my problem. I need to talk to Gwen.* "I'm scared of him…He's killed people, I think. Or at least that's what Evie told me."

"Seriously? He's not going to kill you. But I'll drop you off somewhere if you want."

"Will you take me to Evie? To that stupid Ship in a Storm or whatever it's called?"

****

I took a long drag from the cigarette and let the nicotine work its magic. It settled my stomach and tamped down the frayed ends of my nerves until I felt like myself again. Not Hangover Butch, otherwise known as Run Over by a Truck Butch. But the Butch I needed to be— charming and persuasive and knight-in-shining-armor perfect—to win Gwen back. If that was even possible.

I'd dropped Cassie off at the mini mart near Port in a Storm. Truth, I'd practically shoved her out the door and hit the freeway like a bat out of hell, so I could be here for the school bell at three with a dozen red roses on my seat. I'd parked a block from the school so I could feel Gwen out, plan my approach. Because I'd fucked up. Royally. And this had to be good. Damn good.

That's the problem with plans.

They always blow up in your face.

When Gwen walked out the double doors of Berkeley High, I caught my breath. Not because she was smoking hot, which she was. And not because Cassie was right. She did look a lot like Farrah. A blonde goddess. But because there was someone with her. He held her hand, and he smiled at her with the straightest, whitest teeth I'd ever seen. Like a goddamned toothpaste commercial.

*Boom.* That was the sound of my plan blown to bits.

Last night's tequila came back up, and I was lucky to open the door in time, spewing it all on the pavement. A hot puddle of regret.

I leaned back against the seat and wiped my mouth on the sleeve of yesterday's shirt, sizing up the competition. A pretty boy, that's what he was. In a mint-green polo, khakis, and penny loafers. His jet-black hair didn't move, even as Gwen's was tossed by the wind.

In another life, I stayed in the car, reeking of humiliation.

In another life, I let Gwen go.

But in this life, I just couldn't. I had needs I didn't understand, and they demanded action. They drove me the way a parasite drives its host. Toward the only thing, the essential thing.

"Gwen!" I headed toward her, the roses in my hand. "Wait."

"Calder?" Her mouth hung open, those lips that had once been mine parted in surprise. Or was it fear? "What are you doing here? I told you I don't want to see you anymore."

"You did? I—I don't remember. I was so drunk, Gwen. Please. Just talk to me."

I did remember, but I owed it to her to let her save face. After she'd hit her head—*you shoved her, you asshole*—I'd told her to get the hell out of my car. And she did. I'd told her we were through. That I hated her. That I never wanted to see her again. And then I drove away.

"You heard her, man. She doesn't want to talk to you." Pretty boy studied me for a moment, cocking his head at me. Narrowing his eyes. Like he was trying to figure out what the hell I was, the same way you'd examine a specimen in science class. Amoeba or protozoa? "Hey, what's your name? Calder?"

"None of your goddamned business."

"I know you." Then, he spun to Gwen, his horse teeth bared. "Are you kidding me, Gwendolyn? This is who you've been hanging out with? Does your dad know?"

"I met Mr. Shaw. He knows me." Pathetic. I sounded pathetic. So pathetic even Gwen tried to defend me.

"Russ, please. Calm down. You're making a scene." So this was Russ. In the flesh. "His family bought the house on Drury Road," she said. "They're in the oil business."

"Bullshit. My dad's security busted this loser last year for throwing rocks at our house. He's an orphan. And the only money he's got is a handout from a bogus lawsuit against our company."

"Is that true, Butch?"

I had nothing to offer Gwen but the truth, so I ignored her. Instead, I stepped up to Russ, fists balled. "Your dad owns Y-Trax?"

It surprised me how fast the rage came. How it must have been there all along just waiting. The roses dropped to the ground, and I levelled Russ Conway with the hardest punch I'd ever thrown. In juvie or otherwise. His head snapped back, and he fell to his knees. But it wasn't enough. I wanted him to fight back, needed him to. So I stood him up, and I hit him again. And again. And again. For Dad. For Mom. For Jesse. But most of all, for me.

"Butch, stop! Stop! You're gonna kill him." When I saw Russ's blood spatter onto Gwen's white jeans, I fell back in the grass, exhausted. Emptied. Like a party balloon the morning after. Deflated and barely hovering above ground. That's the vessel rage leaves behind.

"I didn't mean any of it, Gwen. What I said to you. What I did. I never meant to hurt you like that. I just got carried away. I…I think I love you."

If there's one face of Gwen's I'll always remember, it's that one. Because it was the worst. Huddled over Russ's bloody pulp, she'd looked only at me. The real me. The real Butch Calder. And I sunk into the blue of her eyes and drowned there in her pity.

# CHAPTER THIRTY-ONE

I wait until Sebastian leaves Evie's office, until he crosses the street. Just in case Young Butch finally wins a round and throws a punch that'll drop him to his knees. If I screw up, I'd rather be here, by the tree—it seems fitting—and not at my workplace, letting Mr. Vinetti down.

Sebastian doesn't know I'm coming, and he's taking his time, so I don't need to run. But I do. It feels good. Way better than it did in prison when I would lap the track for an hour, running with nowhere to go. Like a hamster in a wheel. It doesn't take long before I'm right up on him, breathing hard with the cold air burning my lungs.

I spin him around by his arm. "What the hell, man?"

"I think you meant to say, thank you, kind sir, for saving my ass. Go on. Try it again."

"You weren't saving my ass. You were playing games."

He must see Young Butch in here, chomping at the bit, bucking like a bronc, because he doesn't smirk like I expect him to. "I planned on giving it back to you. I really did. But I must've lost it the day before somewhere between the house and—"

"You couldn't just tell me?"

"Hoping to delay the inevitable, I guess. I was sure you'd look in the envelope. And then, you'd say the deal was off. You'd tell the cops about me."

I shake my head at him, half-disgusted, half-amused. "But a baseball card? Seriously?"

"You have to admit, it was better than the alternative. All things considered."

"Yeah. I'll give you that." As much as it pains me. "Where'd you disappear to that night anyway? You got a secret stash of sports memorabilia buried behind the building?"

He chuckles, proud as a peacock. "Man, I had it in my backpack the whole night. Ever hear of the art of misdirection?"

"I've been to prison, haven't I? Like when the Mexican Mafia starts a whole big ruckus in the chow hall just so they can slice up a guy in the library. Now that's misdirection."

"Exactly. Dissection by misdirection." And creepy as he sounds, I almost laugh.

"So what'd your PO say?" I ask while he twitters to himself.

"Not much. Just the usual threats—one more mess-up and you're back on a bus to Quentin. But they kept my book. Yours?"

"Same." I think of the picture he'd had, the face marked through with the kind of rage that poisons from the inside out. The kind that'll eat you through and through if you let it. Didn't I know. And there I am again, feeling bad for the guy. "Evie got her license back. The cops found it."

"No shit. Well, all's well that ends well. Isn't that what they say?"

As he walks away, I feel unsettled. Because in my experience, when things end well, it's not really the end.

**** 

Since she spilled her guts this morning, Evie's been avoiding me. At least that's how it feels. She must regret telling me, and why wouldn't she? I don't deserve her secrets. *You're not good enough, Butch. You never will be.* Always that thought, always Gwen's voice in my head. Always. But Evie will say it too. Surely, she will. It's just a matter of time.

After lunch, Mr. Vinetti had sent me to repaint the fire lanes in the parking lot, and I'd waved at her when she'd appeared in the window. Like an angel of reckoning, she'd stood there for a heartbeat, judging me with a frown, and then disappeared.

By the time five o'clock rolls around, I can barely keep my head on straight. As in, I reach for the flathead when I need the Phillips. It's that feeling clogging up my brain, my whole goddamn body. The one where I've done something wrong—so many things—and I'm about to be found out for the fuck-up that I am.

"See ya tomorrow, Butch." Mr. Vinetti pats my shoulder on his way out. "Keep your chin up. It could always be worse." He pauses for effect. "Two words, my friend. Projectile vomit."

"Amen to that." I'm quick to fake a smile, a belly laugh. I don't want him thinking there's something wrong with me. That I'm hiding things.

"And Butch?" He pauses at the door, and I wait for him to level me. To tell me I'm acting shady. Like an ex-con. "Don't forget to empty the trash cans before you head out."

I sit there for a minute and gather myself. Picking up my pieces, the ones I'd scattered all day—in the line at Chicken and Waffles, going toe-to-toe with Trey, in Evie's office watching her fall apart—fitting them back together the best I can. Until I resemble a man. A man on trash duty.

**280**

I tell myself not to do it, to go in order, the way I've been taught. First floor, then the second. But my feet don't listen. They carry me straight to Evie's door.

It's locked. My hand knocks anyway, fingers clenched as tight as my chest. And the sound throbs down the hallway, heavy as my heartbeat.

No answer.

I insert the master key and step inside, already feeling guilty. Feeling like a criminal. And that's how I move too—twitchy and wired—like I don't want to get caught. *You're taking out the trash, Butchy. Not stealing trade secrets.*

I dump the waiting room can into the heavy-duty bag I'd brought with me and head for Evie's office. The shades are pulled shut, her computer dark. Her chair positioned to face the window. I breathe in, because it smells like her. Alive and light and faintly floral.

And it occurs to me then how alike we are. That she's here, in this office, because of that tree, not in spite of it. The same way I begged the parole board to let me come back to Oakland. She wants to be reminded. She wants to remember for Christ's sakes.

And me? I'd been relieved that she couldn't, didn't, hopefully never would. *You were selfish, Mr. Calder*—the parole board's perpetual refrain—and apparently, I still am.

Her trash can sits next to the shred bin, but it's already empty except for a gum wrapper. I reach in, grab it. Toss it in the bag.

And that's when I see it, with Gwen in my head, smacking watermelon bubblegum and shoving her tongue in my mouth. With the parole commissioners shaking their heads at me, their distaste apparent.

A fax on top of the shred pile, awaiting destruction.

I mouth the words to myself, horrified. "Sebastian Delacourt... arrested...curfew violation...victim-related photograph..." And then the worst part—because I know now why Evie's been acting funny—*call me to discuss.*

She knows. She knows I snuck out of the house. She knows I got arrested. She knows I never said a word about any of it. Just pretended to be normal, the kind of guy she could trust. When clearly I'm anything but.

I can't get out of there fast enough. I shut the door. Lock it. And shudder. Like there's something demonic on the other side.

"Hey, Butch." 23A—otherwise known as Maneater Melanie—calls up to me from the sidewalk below before I can duck and hide. "Are you looking for someone?"

"Uh…" *Say something. You look suspicious.* "Uh, yeah. Dr. Maddox. Have you seen her?"

"Oh." She sticks out her lip in a pout. "For a second I thought you might be looking for me."

I swallow a lump, and there it goes. My heart, skittering, chattering like a junkie on speed. "No. I need to find Evie."

"You look a little tense in the shoulders, like you could use my services. I give a twenty-percent discount for building tenants…and employees. Deep tissue. If you're interested."

I spin around, sure there's someone watching. And I'll be blamed for whatever this is. I shake my head at her. "Not interested. I just need to—"

"Yeah, yeah. I got it. You need to find Evie. She already left for the day. I drove her back to her car at the garage downtown about thirty minutes ago."

"Did she say where she was headed?"

Melanie shrugged. "I don't know. Pinole, I guess."

"Pinole? Did she say that?"

"No. But she asked me the fastest way to get there. So…"

She probably kept talking, but I couldn't hear her over the roar in my head. A fierce wind of panic. A hurricane, really. Because they give those things names. And this one, I'd call it Trey.

## EVIE
## MAY 10, 1994
## THREE DAYS UNTIL MY BIRTHDAY

**THE** sky was still pitch-black when I nudged Cassie's shoulder. Her body like a small animal curled next to mine, soft and warm. "Wake up, Cass. You've gotta go."

She turned over on her back, mumbling, dreaming. The dark room hid the cut on her lip and the bruise on her cheek, but I knew they were there. As surely as if I'd drawn them on myself in wild strawberry and royal purple. I'd seen Trey's handiwork yesterday in the unforgiving fluorescence of the mini mart. Cassie had been there waiting for me after school, barefoot. And I'd kept my poker face when she'd told me Trey had been arrested. That he'd tried to get her to work for him. That he'd smacked her when she'd refused.

"Cassie. I'm serious. Wake up." Her eyes fluttered open.

"Huh? What time is it?"

"I don't know. Early. But Cherice gets here before the sun comes up. You have to be gone by then."

She covered her face with my pillow and flipped onto her side, nearly shoving me off the bed.

"Unless you want to live here permanently? With all of us other misfits. Because that's what's going to happen if somebody catches you."

She drew the pillow down from her face and groaned. "Alright, alright." Her feet slapped the floor as she gathered yesterday's clothes and the shoes I'd loaned her. She walked toward the window, sliding it open as quietly as a cat burglar. The early morning air smelled fresh. It gave me hope.

"You don't think they let him out yet, do you?" When I caught the tremble in her voice, I wanted to say I told you so.

"No. But don't go over there without me." Like I had power over Trey. Like I could hold back the devil. "I'll meet you after school. We'll get your stuff back."

She swung her legs over the sill and disappeared, and my stomach ached with unease. I imagined her shimmying down the drainpipe the way she'd come up, the way I'd showed her, with Trey waiting for her at the bottom, claws unsheathed, fangs sharpened. I laid back down in the still-warm spot she'd left, shivering.

****

Sometimes, you know you're dreaming. It's not real. Like when you're flying through the sky above it all or when your teeth start to loosen and drop from your gums like Chiclets. Other times, it's not a dream so much as a memory.

"Get in the closet, Evelyn." I hadn't wanted to. The closet at the Blue Bird was tiny, and it smelled like Trey's cigarettes and my mom's Calgon body spray. But I'd listened, because there was a man at the door. And because my mother was sick and angry. She'd needed a fix. I'd pretended to be a cat with black hair like mine. Eyes like mine. And I'd crawled inside, sliding the door shut behind me—not considering how dark it would be, how suffocating.

"Hey, Matty. C'mon in." It hadn't been the voice she'd used with me, all hard and cold. This voice slithered, soft as the belly of a snake.

"I told you not to call me that."

"How 'bout baby? Is that okay? C'mon in, baby."

**284**

"Trey's not around?"

"Don't worry about it. You want to have some fun or not?"

"Yeah. You know I do. I just—"

"You got the stuff? Put it on the dresser. The cash too."

My mother's bracelets jangled.

Bedsprings squeaked.

A zipper, undone. A moan.

I'd cupped my hands over my ears and tried not to listen, but the sounds were so loud. Like they were in my head.

Then, my mother'd laughed. She hadn't laughed in so long, not with me, I'd barely recognized it. And I'd hated that man. Matt. Matty. Whoever he was, I needed to see him. In all his ugliness. So I'd scooted against the wall, tucked my feet under me, and cracked the door until there was a sliver of light.

My heart quickened. I'd sucked in a breath. Held it.

"Evelyn. Goddamn it. Shut the door."

And I had. I'd seen nothing and everything.

"Jesus. Who's Evelyn?"

"My daughter."

"Shit. Trey's gonna kill me."

"It ain't his daughter."

"Still. You know how he is. He's gonna kill me anyway."

"Only if he finds out."

They'd gone on like that for a while. Until the noises had started up again. But worse this time. And then it'd got really quiet. Too quiet. So quiet, I couldn't stop myself from looking again.

My eyes had gone straight to his hands, squeezing her neck like a tube of empty toothpaste. I'd just sat there, wishing to die. Or turn into a cat. Either one.

Finally, Matty left. I'd stayed in the closet, relieved when she yelled at me.

"What the fuck were you thinking? You nosy little perv. I told you to stay in there."

I would've rather she'd slapped me. At least I'd have a good reason to cry. "Who was that guy? How does he know Trey?" I'd whimpered through the closed door. "Why was he choking you?"

She'd shut herself in the bathroom to get high. That had been my answer. And I'd sat there sniveling like a baby. But in my dream, there'd been more. Another pair of eyes pricking the dark, burning red, and I knew Trey had been there with me all along.

****

That half dream, half memory stayed with me the whole day like nightmares often do, clinging to me, charging the air like static. I kept looking over my shoulder for those eyes. Trey's eyes. The kind of eyes that could be one thing—playful and winking and full of promises—and then another thing entirely. My mom had stashed Matty's money before Trey got back. She'd been floating on a heroin cloud by then—"It's like love," she'd told me once, "so good until it's bad"—and she'd slipped the money deep inside the bowels of the torn cushion on the happy yellow sofa, holding a finger to her lips. "Our little secret," she'd said.

But the dream didn't stop me from hitching. Again. This time, a lady in a snow-white Cadillac stopped for me. She had a wrinkled face and hands with skin as thin as crepe paper. When I told her to let me off at the Blue Bird, she *tsked tsked*. "Does your mother know you're taking rides from strangers?"

If it wasn't so sad, it would've been funny. "She's dead, so…"

"Oh, you poor dear. How did she die?"

My mother's face, pale and slack, came to me. "Cancer."

"My goodness. I'm so sorry. I'll bet you miss her terribly."

"Terribly," I repeated. The word drove a sharp stake of guilt through my heart. I missed her. That much was true. But I didn't want her back.

After the woman drove away, pausing at the stop sign to wave at me, I scoured the parking lot for Cassie. And Calder, of course. No sign of either, and already I felt uneasy. I sat down on the sidewalk in front of 145 and picked at the weeds growing up through the cracks in the concrete. The butt of a Marlboro cigarette—Calder's brand—stuck up through the grass like a daisy, and I rolled it between my fingers, knowing it must be his. I studied the end of it. Put it to my lips, and an awful, wonderful yearning feeling gripped me. *So good till it's bad.*

"Evie? Is that you?" Peggy poked her head out and shuffled over, her feet in flip-flops, bathrobe tied at her waist. "Haven't seen you in a while. How ya been, girlie?"

"Alright, I guess." I tossed the butt to the ground, hoping she hadn't seen me.

She rubbed my arm and gave it a gentle squeeze. "They treatin' you alright at that Port in a Storm?"

"It's great. Just great," I said, making a face.

"I wish Wade and me could take care of ya, but we can hardly keep ourselves afloat. How 'bout that weasel, Trey? Has he been botherin' you?" I shrugged. I didn't want to worry her. "You let me know if he needs another knock on the head, okay?"

"I heard he got arrested."

Peggy threw back her head and let loose a throaty laugh. "Sure did. They got him with a little bit of coke and a warrant for pandering. I heard somebody tipped off the cops on him." She winked at me. "You know ol' Peg's got her sources."

My stomach cramped like I'd been sucker punched. "Does Trey know?

"Know what, hon?"

"That I sent the cops here."

Her mouth hung open. "You did? I thought it was Butch."

"Have you seen him? Butch?"

"Come to think of it, I ain't seen him since last night. He was pretty strung out about something." Her eyes danced, mouth twisted to a quirky smile. "Got yourself a little crush, do you?"

I lowered my head and sighed. "Why do I like some stupid boy who'll never like me back?"

She wrapped an arm around me and pulled me in close like she was about to tell me a secret. Her breath was hot and stale. "If you figure that one out, Evie, you let me know."

****

I had to be lightning quick. Nanette was standing outside waiting, and she could get in trouble—big trouble, she'd warned—for letting me in to 157 to grab Cassie's stuff.

*Where is Cassie?* My thoughts raced like rabbits, every trail leading to that one. Dark and thicketed with dread.

I did a quick search of the room and found Cassie's gray duffel in the closet, still stuffed full of the clothes Trey had bought her. Balled on the floor in the corner, the yellow dress. Here in the dank light of the Blue Bird, the color didn't look the same. It was drab—more potato than lemon—like my mom's sofa, and I wondered if I'd misjudged its color all along. Or if it was this place that washed the life out of things. One of the straps was torn clean off. And I shuddered looking at it.

"Almost done in there, Evie?"

"Almost."

I draped the dress over my arm and carried it to the trash can, preparing it for burial. It hadn't been emptied in a while. Knowing Trey, he'd declined the spotty maid service. He'd never wanted anybody going near his things. Just because I could, I rifled through the empty beer cans and a moldy slice of pizza. A condom wrapper and a clump of cigarette ash. These were the things Trey was made of. Near the bottom, an envelope, stained with coffee and God knows what else, a typed address on the front.

> *Arlene Allcott, care of Trey Waters*
> *10 Eagle Pass*
> *Pinole, CA*

I pulled out the crumpled contents. A check stub from Alameda County General Assistance. Money that should have been mine. I tightened my fist, strangling the small slip of paper.

Unbelievable. Rage hissed through my veins, a steaming poison. It demanded release.

"Evie! C'mon."

"Okay. One sec." I slung the duffel over my shoulder and ducked into the bathroom. I grabbed Trey's toothbrush from the edge of the sink. Dunked it once, twice, three times in the toilet and scrubbed once around for good measure, returning it to its resting place.

"Ready," I said to Nanette, slamming the door shut behind me.

**\*\*\*\***

When Wade dropped me off, Cassie huddled on the front steps of the Port, her eyes blurry. I dropped the duffel at her feet. "What happened to you?" I asked, still trying to tamp down my anger. At Trey. At my mom. At Bobby Pierce. At Calder for never showing up when I wanted him to. "Where were you?"

"Trey's here." Together, those words were the worst two I could've imagined. They sobered me, turned the heat of my anger cold and suspended me somewhere between fury and fear.

"Where?"

"Everywhere." She hugged her knees to her chest. "Willow Court, this afternoon."

"And what happened?"

"He thinks we called the police on him. That we ratted him out. Evie, I…" Her eyes welled up. "I told him something I shouldn't have."

She peeled a strip of white paint from the step, the flecks sticking to her fingers, and stared at it. I sat down next to her so she wouldn't have to avoid my eyes. "It's okay." Though I was certain it wasn't.

"When he hit me the other day, it just slipped out. I called him a murderer. I told him what you said about your mom. How he'd killed her. And he didn't deny it."

"Geez, Cassie." When we'd still lived at Willow Court, I'd fallen flat on my back from the monkey bars, the impact so jarring I hadn't even cried. I'd just laid there, eyes fixed to the clouds. Lungs empty of air, wheezing. That's how I felt with Cassie's confession bouncing around in my skull. Like there wasn't enough air. "What did he say?"

She shook her head.

"Tell me."

"That I should stop hanging out with you. Because when you're around, bad things happen...and bad things might happen to me too."

"So he threatened you?"

She shrugged. "What're we gonna do?"

"I don't know." But I lied. Already, I'd gone to a dark place. Darker than dark. To something Trey had asked me once, weeks after he'd started living with us. My mom lay passed out on the bed, and I'd been watching the rise and fall of her chest, so slow I'd wondered if she'd stopped breathing.

"Ever think what life would be like without her?" Trey had sat down next to me, and I froze. I couldn't even shake my head no like I'd wanted to. "I bet you do. My mama was just like yours. And hell, sometimes I wanted nothin' more than to put her out of her misery. Go ahead," he'd said, nodding at the nightstand. The plastic baggie, the spoon, the needle still half-filled with my mother's blood. "I won't tell."

I'd scooted away from him, as close to my mom as I could get, and burrowed into the sickly sweet smell of her. Trey had put his dirty hand against my cheek, caressing it, and I'd clenched my teeth so hard my jaw ached.

Way down, in the dank basement of my heart, I blamed my mother for all of it.

"Think about it, Evelyn."

That's when I knew for sure Trey was the devil. That he could see into me, to the parts I hid from everybody else. And then, when he'd gone and done it himself—put my mom down like an old dog—I knew it was my fault. My curse. Evil Evie.

But sitting next to Cassie, crying on the porch steps, I realized Trey and I weren't so different. How else could I explain the sinister thought that had come to life in my brain? We shared something my mother never had, always thinking she needed to leave him to make her escape. As much as it gutted me to admit, Trey and I had something in common. A wicked imagination.

# CHAPTER THIRTY-TWO

**SOME** places appear exactly the way you'd imagine. Like you'd conjured them in a dream. And if I'd imagined 10 Eagle Pass, if I'd pictured the hole Trey crawled back into, this would've been it.

I follow the dirt road for at least ten minutes before I see it. A turnoff. A mailbox, half-standing, in the weeds. But the fence is in good shape, new barbed wire—not a hint of rust—pulled taut. And there's an iron gate, padlocked shut. I drive past and park on the shoulder a ways up. When I crack the door, the cold rushes in and slaps me to my senses.

*What am I doing here?* At Trey Waters' house. His compound, by the looks of it. And definitely still his. At lunch, I'd searched the address I'd never forgotten on my work computer. But it hadn't told me what I'd find here. Who I'd find. Or what the hell I'd been thinking coming here alone.

I lock the car and slip on my jacket, determined not to be afraid. *I'm not a little girl anymore.* And I need to see Trey again. For closure. For confrontation. Or something in between. Then there's the nagging hope, nibbling at my heart. That Cassie's here. That Trey knows where she is or what happened to her.

I don't bother with the gate. Just maneuver around the barbed wire, slipping through the seams unscathed, except for a tiny snag on my sleeve. Past it, a field stretches as far as I can see. There's a faint smell of smoke from the charred mountain of junk at its center. A recent bonfire, I'd guess. Someone's placed a worn-out armchair at the periphery, and it reminds me of my mother. I wonder if I'd misjudged her, carrying that hideous yellow sofa. Maybe she'd only wanted to make the Blue Bird more of a home. Maybe she'd done it to make me happy.

I'm not a little girl anymore. So I walk on, ignoring the gnawing in my gut.

The house—if you can call it that—has collapsed partway, the wood rotted and bare. All but one of the windows has broken or gone missing, and the door's been stripped from its hinges and tossed on the porch, as if someone or something desperately wanted in. Or out. What sunlight remains burns through the gaping hole at the entrance—so bright I have to look away. Like it's the gateway to hell. And the thought of Trey in there, flames licking at his feet, makes me pick up my pace.

To my right, a semicircle of travel trailers, their wheels removed, their windows curtained with bedsheets. Two poles staked in the earth anchor a clothesline where men's T-shirts and a pair of blue jeans hang stiff as death. Not even a breeze to rustle them. A lacy red bra has fallen to the ground. It looks like something my mother would've worn.

If I listen hard, I hear the murmur of a television. Maybe a sitcom rerun, because the laughter sounds canned. I move closer until

I can make out voices too. Until I can see the space behind the trailers. And even though I'm not a little girl anymore, my blood turns to ice, fixing me in place. Because parked in the high grass, next to a blue pickup truck, I spot Trey's Buick.

*What am I doing here?* The question clung like a wet blanket. Only one answer. *Cassie.*

But now that I'm practically on Trey's doorstep, I can barely breathe. I find a place to hide. To think too. But mostly to hide. I'm good at that, always have been. Near the first trailer, I duck behind a corroded washing machine, grown-up with thistle. And I wait without knowing what I'm waiting for.

Except for the hum of the television, the only sounds out here are wild ones. I focus on my favorite, an owl's soft hooting, soothing as a mother's cooing lullaby—a mother different from mine in every way. Until.

The low growl of an engine, louder and louder still. The crunch of gravel under tires. And my heart, rat-a-tatting away. Someone's coming.

I risk a quick glance and my breath quickens. It's a black jeep with a license plate I recognize. A driver I recognize. Careful to stay hidden, I slip my cell phone from my jacket pocket and snap a photo as Danny climbs out.

He must've been expected, because the middle trailer's door opens before he reaches it. It sticks a little at first, then squeaks.

"Hey, Dan the Man, what's shaking?" Though his face is out of my view, Trey's lilt makes my skin crawl. He sounds too gracious. Like a man ready to stick a knife in your back.

"I'm freakin' out man. I got the cops on my ass, and Matthias said I could hole up here for the night. That you might have a hook-up on crossing the border, gettin' the hell outta Dodge."

"Sure. Sure, buddy. But you've gotta relax. Here. This'll take the edge off." I hear the pop of an opened can, and I picture it on Danny's mouth, the beer sloshing with his chew on its way down his throat. I nearly gag. "Listen, Dan-Dan, they've got nothin' on us."

"You mean they got nothin' on you."

"If you'd have done exactly what I told you, we wouldn't be in this mess."

"Yeah, well, I keep tellin' you that guy showed up outta nowhere. What was I supposed to do?"

"Well, first off, not use your goddamned real name from the get-go. And finish the job for two." *Finish me.* That's what Trey means. "Should've done it myself when I had the chance."

"I don't get what your deal is with her anyway. She doesn't know nothin' about it. Nobody does."

"You don't know what she knows. She's too smart for her own britches. Me and her, we got history. And it ain't purdy."

"You think she talked to Violet?"

"Keep your mouth shut about Violet. She was stickin' her nose into things. And that's the sort of trouble you find when you stick it where it don't belong." He shrieks with the kind of laughter that stains your soul. "But you know all about that, don't you, Dano? Get it? Stick it where it—"

"Alright. Alright. I get it. I ain't tryin' to overstep. I just wanna get out of here. Start fresh."

"Sure thing, man. You just sit tight and let me take care of everything. Don't worry. I got your back. We'll get you on your way to Mexico in the mornin'." Trey had told my mother not to worry once. After a guy had stiffed her. He'd been found the next morning in the Blue Bird parking lot, naked and beaten to a pulp with a tire iron.

"Thanks, Trey. I guess that means we're square, right? It means—"

The sudden sounds are the worst I've ever heard. A cry—"No!"— part groan, part wounded animal. The gun blast, the bursting apart of flesh that I can't unhear. There's no end to it. There never will be.

Even after I cover my ears.

Even after the memory explodes like a flashbulb. *Cassie had said no too.* And I'm back there again, newly thirteen and staring up at the hanging tree.

I'd started to feel funny like my legs had gotten too heavy to move. Like I might fall down.

"This is the hanging tree, ladies. Spooky, right? Who knows, you just might find the noose up there."

Cassie's laugh had sounded far away, tinkling like the highest note on the piano. I'd pressed my hand inside my pocket, reminding myself. The plan. We had a plan.

"We're in Oakland. You said you'd take us to Pinole. I want to go there now." It had taken so much energy to say, I'd leaned against the tree, exhausted. No way I could have made it back to the truck, though I'd seen it there, parked at the blackening edge of my vision.

"Your friend wants to hang out here for a while. Don't ya, Cassie?" And when I'd looked, his back was to me, his arms hanging down thin and white and bony as the branches of the tree. Cassie had nodded, leaning around him to stick out her tongue at me.

My head had felt cottony, stuffed like an old toy. "How 'bout if I climb it?" I'd asked. "Will you take me then?"

But the faceless man had never answered. His mouth was busy with Cassie's. And I'd started climbing, slow as a sloth. Only stopping to look back when I'd heard her say no. Her voice as clear and bright as a bell.

Just like Trey's now. "Is he dead?"

And another man's voice I don't recognize. "Deader than a fuckin' doornail, man."

"You did good, brother. Help me drag him outta the goddamned front yard."

I only realize I'm shaking when I lift my phone and hit *camera*. I force myself, by sheer will, to lean my head ever so slightly to the right.

*Breathe, Evie.*

I point the lens. Hit record. And then, only then, I look up. My heart stills.

The men are already gone. A small patch of grass in front of the trailers is flattened and darker than the rest. I wonder if the blood will seep into the soil. What will grow there.

**296**

# CHAPTER THIRTY-THREE

**BUTCH**
**JANUARY 18, 2017**
**WEDNESDAY**

**I'M** going to regret this. And soon. That much I'm sure of. I've been hawk-eyeing the speedometer the whole way here, never pushing Melanie's Mini Cooper more than five miles over the limit. Because, drumroll please, I'm driving without a license. In a car I don't own. In a car I'd borrowed in exchange for a ninety-minute rubdown by Melanie herself on a date yet to be determined. I've stooped to an all-time low, selling my body for a foreign car the size of a goddamned matchbox.

But it's a pretty sweet ride, and now that my heart has stopped racing, I'm almost enjoying the drive up the freeway. Even if the powder blue paint job doesn't say *Butch Calder*. Even if I don't think I'll remember how to get to Trey's. I've only been there once. And right now, I am definitely lost. In the dark, on a dirt road in the middle of nowhere, Pinole.

I fumble around for the brights, praying for a sign. But with the road lit up, I'm just as clueless. Fields and fences on either side of me and beyond, the night spilling out for what seems like forever.

I'd turned off on Eagle Pass Road at least ten minutes ago. And I haven't seen any signs of life since. No cars. No joggers. Not even a damn raccoon. So it jolts me when I spot Evie's car in the ditch. I pull up behind it and get out.

It's so quiet out here. The kind of quiet a man can only dream about in prison, where the sounds—whispers and whistles and moans and curses—never stop. But it unnerves me, and I keep waiting for the ghosts of the past to arrive. For the 'Cuda to blaze past on a victory lap. With Gwen in the passenger seat, high on ecstasy. Cherice, sucking on my neck. And me, selfish and smack-dab between them, having my cake. Eating it.

Evie's car is empty, and the hood is cold. I walk along the fence line toward the only light I can see—distant, but steady as the sun—until I reach a gate and a dilapidated mailbox. A set of new tracks on the dirt road. This is it. 10 Eagle Pass.

Fear can be a friend. Or a foe. I'd learned that in Folsom. When you feel it nestle against your breastbone, nudging you like a dog's nose, you'd better pay attention. Show it some respect. Because if you don't, sooner or later, it's gonna bite. And I'm not ashamed to admit, working my way through the fence, I feel it. I'm afraid.

So I do what any self-respecting ex-con would do. I look for a weapon. At the edge of the bonfire, I find a rusted metal pipe that'll do the trick. I hold it in my hand, feel the weight of it. It could dent a skull with a single swing. I drop it, pick it up again, drop it, and move on. If it comes to it, I'll fight fair. With my fists.

Hard to believe, but the place hasn't changed much. It's like Trey in that way. Still broken down, burned out, fit for condemnation. The trailers are new though, and there's a light on—the light I'd seen from the road—so I head toward them.

When I see the black jeep parked out front, fear turns rabid and gives me a good chomp right in the gut. The cops had been right. Danny knew Trey. Trey knew Danny. And Evie's here alone.

I circle around back, past Trey's Buick. And I crouch in the tall grass, listening. The TV's playing inside, faint. An owl is doing his thing, making the whole scene a little more Vincent Price than I care for. *I should've brought the damn pipe.* And there's a rustling to my right, a delicate chattering. With my eyes, I follow the sound to the washing machine.

"Evie." I say it so soft I'm sure only the weeds brushing my face can hear me. But the chattering stops.

Just then, I hear Trey, the unmistakable rasp of the devil, coming from the trees and getting louder. Closer. "It's fucking freezing out here, man. I'm takin' my beer inside. We'll finish up later."

"What about the jeep?"

"Not now, dude. You're killin' my buzz."

"Alright. We gotta get rid of these clothes. You got the gasoline?"

"It's in the house. But chill, man. You're making me nervous."

Certain now my hunch is dead on, I make a run for it, crawling behind the washer where Evie sits, wide-eyed and cold. Her teeth knocking against themselves. I put my finger to her lips. Even though it seems like she's gone mute. Like her voice has turned tail and taken off without her.

I wait for the trailer door to open and shut.

"We've gotta get out of here," I whisper, shrugging off my jacket. "Put this on. You're freezing."

Her mouth opens slightly. She's about to say something. But then she closes it again, takes the jacket, and slides her arms inside. I grab her hand and help her stand, her legs as wobbly as a newborn fawn. Then I tug her along behind me.

We make it as far as the jeep, when the trailer opens again. The pool of light I'd welcomed from the road now sends me scurrying for cover like a cockroach, dragging Evie with me. We duck behind the wheel and watch. At least I do. Evie buries her head in my shoulder.

A man—not Trey—staggers toward the pile of burned rubbish, carrying a bag and a gas can. He tosses the bag at the edge of the refuse, douses it, and strikes a match. The flames burst up, alive and hungry, and he stokes them briefly with the pipe I'd left there. Satisfied, he turns back toward the trailer, his face awash in firelight.

*I know him.*

*I knew him.*

And fear takes another snap at me, its teeth sinking in deep. *Matthias.* After he disappears inside the trailer, the TV gets louder and Evie croaks something quiet against my upper arm.

"They killed Danny."

I hear it, but I don't take it in. I don't let myself feel it. Not yet. "Can you run?" I ask her, and she nods, clutching my hand.

I don't look back. And I don't slow down until I see the Mini. Powder blue is my new favorite color.

****

For the second time today, Evie's in my arms. And damn, I'm starting to get used to it. But then, she wriggles away like I'd been holding her hostage. She pushes me back, shoving her hands against my chest. "Why didn't you tell me you got arrested?"

I liked it better when she wasn't talking. "Let's get in your car. We'll discuss it in there."

"Hell no. I'm not going anywhere with you." She stares at the Mini, as if she's seeing it for the first time. "Is that Melanie's car? Did you steal it? Jesus, Butch, I trusted you."

*Trusted.* The past tense hurts. "Melanie let me borrow her car. When she mentioned Pinole, I told her you might be in trouble. And I didn't say anything about getting arrested because I was embarrassed. I didn't want you to think I'm some screw-up. That I haven't changed. And it's no excuse—I was wrong to miss curfew—but I had a good reason."

"To clear your head?"

"No. Who told you that?" *That lying little punk.*

No answer as she walks to her car. And I stay put, rewinding, replaying my conversation with Sebastian. He'd sold me out, and the whole time he'd known. "I'm sorry I didn't tell you."

"Thanks for coming here," she mutters, almost to herself. "I don't know what I was thinking. I just...I thought maybe Cassie was...still alive. Is that crazy?"

"No." Our eyes meet, and I look away. "What happened out there?"

Quiet again, she unlocks her door, shakes her head and sighs. "Get in," she says, gesturing to the passenger side. "But just to be clear. This doesn't mean I forgive you."

At least she doesn't hate me. Not completely anyway.

I nod and climb inside, where she cranks the heat, thawing us both. "I wanted to confront him...Trey. About his tattoo. About that night when I gave him the ring and the money. About everything. But I got scared. And then Danny showed up all freaked out, and Trey sweet-talked him, telling him he'd help him get to Mexico. There was some other guy too. I didn't get a good look at him, but Danny said the name..."

"Matthias," I finish, not wanting to. Scared that if I say it he'll show up, knocking at the window. Summoned like that Bloody Mary game kids play.

"Yeah. How did you—"

"He's Trey's half brother. I met him with Gwen. Him and Cherice, they were dating back then."

She shivers even with the heater on blast and my jacket still draped around her. "He shot Danny. And then they dragged the body somewhere. And...you know the rest."

"Did anybody see you?"

"No. And I...I took pictures." She checks her pockets, frowning. Then rifles through them, her face stricken.

"What is it?"

"I think I left my cell phone behind the washer."

## BUTCH
## MAY 11, 1994
## TWO DAYS BEFORE I KILLED HER

**"WHERE** you been, man?" Wade asked, peering up over the top of his dime-store sunglasses.

I joined him on the lawn chairs he and Peggy had set up on the sidewalk outside their room, the door slightly ajar to let out a stream of the cool air. Wade rested his beer atop his paunch, bare and reddening in the sun. Sweat trailed from his forehead to his pecs, little rivers of heat in the sparse forest of his chest hair. The guy had no shame.

"I just had some stuff to take care of." And by that I meant getting drunk alone at Grizzly Peak, blasting KISS till my brain went numb, and sleeping it off in the 'Cuda.

"Want one?" He pointed to the half-open cooler, stocked with Coors. "You look like you could use a little hair of the dog."

I laughed, but damn, he was right. "Nah. I can't. I've got an appointment."

"With that shyster attorney? Is he houndin' you again?"

I nodded and slipped off my own shirt. Because what the hell.

"C'mon, man." Wade swatted at me. "You're making me look bad."

"He sure is, honeybun." Peggy winked at me as she perched on the arm of Wade's chair. "You drank the only six-pack you're ever gonna have."

"Damn. That's cold, woman. Cold, but true."

Peggy planted a kiss on Wade's forehead, leaving her mark in red lipstick.

"Heard Trey got out yesterday," she said, shaking her head. "That guy is as slippery as an eel. Them cops can't hang on to him no matter what he does."

"One of these days…" Wade took another long swig from the bottle and wiped his mouth. I wanted a drink so bad it scared me. So bad I lit a cigarette to distract myself. "He's gonna mess up. And they're gonna have themselves a real good time with his scrawny ass in the big house."

Peggy chuckled, but it didn't quite make it to her eyes. "Hey, Butch. Have you seen Evie? She was lookin' for you the other day. Seemed like she was worried about ya." Wade squirmed in his chair, wriggling like a worm, but Peggy stilled him with a hand on his shoulder. "We're all a little worried."

I choked back the urge to snap at her, to curse Evie. That little girl had latched herself to me like a flea. I couldn't shake her. *At least somebody cares about you, Nobody.* I sat up, frowned, and put out my cigarette, trying to look as pulled together I could. "About me?"

But Peggy never answered. And for a split second I thought I was dreaming. That I was still in the middle of a hard sleep in the front seat of the 'Cuda. Why else would Cherice be there?

"Hi, Butch." If I was dreaming, she sure looked real. Brown skin shining in the sun, just like that "Boys of Summer" song. Flaunting it in short shorts and a tank top, and I couldn't help but think about the world I'd seen beneath them. Yep, she looked real. And sexy as hell. And pissed.

"Cherice."

Wade jumped up so fast I thought for sure he'd spill his beer. "So you're Cherice? *The* Cherice?" He snickered under his breath. "Pleased to meet you."

Cherice barely looked his way. "Can I talk to you? In private?"

"Uh-oh," Wade said, before Peggy jabbed him with her elbow. She dragged him back inside their room, but I knew they were listening.

I stood up and put on my shirt, intent on taking her somewhere private. Not my room though. I didn't trust myself. And if I had any chance with Gwen I had to keep it in my pants.

But she launched right in. "Why didn't you call?"

"I don't have your number."

"Really, Butch?" Her voice, and the truth behind it, hit so hard I wished she would've just smacked me. "I wrote it on your arm. Remember?"

Of course I remembered. I'd scrubbed it off with my own spit before Gwen got back to the car. "I'm sorry, Cherice. I don't know what to say. I've been kind of busy lately. Besides you're with Matthias, right?"

She shook her head no. "Not anymore. Not after he—"

"And I'm…"

"You're what? With Gwen? You don't even know, do you? She told me she was done with you."

"Yeah. Thanks to you. Why'd you tell her I let you ride with me? She was so out of it, she'd never have known." As soon I said it out loud, I realized how bad it sounded. Like a total cretin. A pig.

"I didn't tell her."

"Well, who did then?"

"Matthias more than likely. They—"

"You probably told her about the other thing too."

"The other thing. You can't even say it? God, you're such a child. I should've known better. I thought you were…"

"Well, I'm not."

"Not what?"

"Whatever it is you thought I was."

"I was going to say a good guy. I thought you were a good guy, Butch."

I had this crazy urge to grab her and mash my tongue down her throat. But I just shrugged at her. Like whatever I was, it couldn't be helped.

**\*\*\*\***

When I got back to the room that night, about as far from sober as I could get, the lawn chairs had been folded, the empty beer bottles stacked by the door. Wade and Peggy's lights were out.

I stumbled inside. Collapsed onto the bed. The red message light blinked at me.

"Mr. Calder, this is Simon Merriwether. We had an appointment scheduled for today at…"

I let the receiver drop. *Shit.*

The last thing I thought before I stopped thinking altogether: *She's not worth it.* And even now, I'm not sure if I meant Gwen or Cherice.

## EVIE
## MAY 12, 1994
## ONE DAY UNTIL MY BIRTHDAY

**ONCE** I'd decided it consumed me. *Isn't it always that way?*

The thought became a spark.

The spark caught fire.

And the fire burned everything clean.

Except for the thought.

And so it went. Over and over again. The whole night before, the day before I turned thirteen.

"I've got an idea," I whispered to Cassie that morning. She was poised on the windowsill of the Port, halfway between it all. Between here and there. Between sleep and waking. Between girl and woman. "What if we get Trey to admit to it? To everything. On tape."

I felt bad, lying. But I couldn't say aloud—not to anybody— what I really had planned for Trey. How I needed her help. "And then what?" she asked, skeptical.

"I'll take it to that detective. Macaroni. Then he'll be out of our lives forever." That was the truth, at least. I pictured Trey dangling over the pit of hell, clinging to a rope with all his might, clawing his way back up like only the devil would. The other end, anchored to me. And I had to cut the rope or we'd both fall forever. "We just have to figure out where to find him. Didn't you say he had another party planned for Friday?"

She shrugged. "You make it sound so easy, but Trey...he's..." Her eyes drifted to the ground, wary, like she saw him there, his mouth a gaping hole of fire and brimstone.

"I know, Cas. I know what he's like. I know better than anybody."

She swung her other leg over the sill and began the two-story climb to the ground below. Midway, she looked up at me, searching. With the sky moonless, her face was lost in the dark, her bruise hidden by shadows. "Do you?"

Scolded into silence, I watched until she disappeared over the fence at the back of the Port. I knew where she was headed. Yesterday, I'd shown her my hideout, my secret spot. An abandoned drainage tunnel, surrounded by a clump of trees. Only to be used in case of emergencies. In other words, Trey. He definitely qualified as an emergency.

As soon as the first ray of sun pierced the gauze of morning, I padded downstairs to the empty kitchen and opened the drawer to the right of the fridge, retrieving the old dishrags we used to clean the counters on chore days. I turned the faucet to hot and waited until the water steamed. Then I bit my lip and stuck the dishrag beneath it. Scalding. But perfect.

Upstairs, I climbed back in bed with the rag pressed to my forehead. I kept it there until I heard Wally tramping up the steps like an elephant. At least I wouldn't have to lie to Cherice. She had the day off.

"Get up! Now!" he boomed, his voice rolling down the hallway, noisy as a bowling ball. And the pins scattered. I closed my eyes and hunkered down, perfecting my act.

I heard the door open as Wally looked for stragglers, that last lone pin he needed to down. "If you're not up in one minute, Evelyn, you've got bathroom duty tonight."

"I don't feel so great, Mr. Wally." I added a groan for dramatic effect. "I think I have a fever."

He touched a finger to my forehead like I might bite. "You are a little warm. But your education is very important and—"

"It could be cramps. Leftover from my period. That happens sometimes, you know. It just goes on and on for the whole month and there's blood—"

"Enough." His face paled. "It's fine. You can stay home." Wally shot for the door like he'd been launched from a cannon, leaving me alone.

I peeled back the covers and snickered to myself. Cassie had been right. The older they get, the dumber they seem.

****

With the house cleared out, I made my move, creeping back down the stairs to the sofa where Wally snored in front of the television, a bowl of popcorn precariously balanced on his belly. I snagged the keys he'd left on the coffee table and headed down the long hallway, past the laundry room to the supply closet.

The Port had never been so quiet. Like the whole place held its breath. But I kept calm. I knew which key to use. It had a cluster of scratches on the bow where I'd stepped on it a few weeks ago. I'd dropped it accidentally, my foot grinding it against the concrete floor. Cherice had sent me down here to get the bleach—one of the little kids had thrown up again—and I'd been fine, totally fine. Until the door had shut behind me. Until the pitch black had become a thing of its own, slithering around me like an asp. In the scramble of my own fear, the key had fallen. But I hadn't screamed. I'd been determined not to. It's funny how the eyes adjust to darkness, the heart too, and I'd finally calmed a little. Enough to have found the light switch. Then, I'd heard Bobby and his little band of merry fools giggling outside the door. *Do you think her eyes glow in the dark?* And I'd been steeled by hate.

The key slid in without effort. *It can't be this easy. It shouldn't be.* But it was. I flicked the light first thing and scanned the shelves, finding what I needed. I wondered what it meant that I felt nothing when I slipped the box under my shirt and turned off the light. Maybe I was evil just like they said.

**308**

Footsteps shuffled behind me, and I froze in the dark, thinking it had to be Wally, nudged awake from his nap by some nagging feeling.

"Whatcha got there, Evil Evie?"

But no. Not Wally. "None of your business. And shouldn't you be at school?"

Bobby cocked his head at me and flashed a grin—I wanted to slap it off his face. "I got to skip today. I had an audition."

"Audition?"

"With a real family who wants to adopt me. You wouldn't know about that though. Nobody wants you. And who can blame them?"

The words tore at my scabs, ripped them right off. And I scratched back. "Audition's the right word for it then. Keep up the act, Bobby. You'll blow it if you show them what an asshole you really are."

"Well, you're a freak. And a thief." He pawed at my shirt, grabbed the hem and twisted until the box tumbled to the floor. Tiny pellets of rat poison scattered like rice.

Our eyes met, and for the space of a lightning bolt, I saw he really was afraid of me. Impossible as it seemed, I used what I had.

"Don't forget murderer. You were right, Bobby. Dead right. I killed my mom." It felt like the truth even if it wasn't. I picked up a handful of pellets and walked toward him, looking as properly evil as I could. "What makes you think I won't kill you too?"

Bobby skedaddled, leaving me alone to gather my poison in peace.

# CHAPTER THIRTY-FOUR

**EVIE
JANUARY 18, 2017
WEDNESDAY**

I follow Butch's taillights the whole way back from Pinole to the office, trying to shut off my brain. Because the things growing there are vicious and unwieldly. Like the creeper vines that choke out all other life.

Butch said we couldn't go back for the phone. That it wasn't worth the risk. Anyway, Trey would never find it. I'd switched it to silent. *Hadn't I?*

He said he'd go with me to the police station. Tonight. And tell them what we saw.

He said he'd lied because he didn't want me to think he was still a screwup. And I believe him—*I do*—because I get it. I understand the pivot point. How one day, one moment, one decision can change the course of an entire life, the way a fallen tree redirects a river.

*May 13, 1994.* Everything I'd been since, good and bad, led back to it.

We pull into the lot just after seven. And Butch gets out, signals to me. *One minute.* He disappears into 23A. I don't consider going in after him. The thought of Melanie—her lecherous smile draped all over him, her questions—makes my stomach turn.

So I sit and breathe. Slowly reclaiming my sanity.

"Sorry it took so long," Butch says, cracking the passenger door. "She's relentless."

I nod. "Are you sure you want to go to the station? I can drop you back at your place."

He climbs inside, and the air shifts. Calms, tenses. Both at the same time. "I'm coming with you."

I know he's probably just trying to prove himself, but I'm grateful anyway. Not to have to go alone. "Before we leave, can I borrow your phone? I need to call my mother-in-law. I told her I'd be back early tonight."

His phone is warm from his pocket. "The dinosaur is all yours. Do you need...privacy?"

"No. It'll be quick." *I hope.* I flip it open, peck at the keys. Maggie answers on the first ring, the worry darkening her voice. Like she's expecting the worst. But not *the* worst. She's already lived through that.

"Hello?"

"Hi, Maggie. It's me."

"Evelyn, where are you? Why aren't you answering your phone? I've been worried sick." I imagine my phone lying in the grass, the screen lighting up again and again. A beacon that surely would draw Trey in as a moth to a flame.

"I'm okay, but I lost my phone. Just call me on this number if you need to reach me. I'll be back soon."

"But—"

I hang up on her mid-protest—there'll be hell to pay for that later—and turn to Butch. He's staring straight ahead, fiddling with the air vent. And I expel it all in one breath. "Trey is going to find the phone. He'll see the pictures. He'll know I was there."

"Even if he does find it, the cops will be swarming his place before he can figure out what to do about it."

*You don't know Trey. You don't know what he's capable of.* I almost say it until I remember he does. He does.

✳✳✳✳

We'd caught Macaroni readying to head home on his night off. His tie already gone, probably shoved into the backpack he carried, and his top button undone. Halfway out the door, he'd made an exception for me. Evil Evie.

"I can't believe you went out to that place on your own," he says, shaking his head at me the way Maggie would. "You're lucky you got out of there. Especially if you heard what you think you did."

"If?" Butch asks. He's been quiet until now, subdued like the first night I saw him again. One word answers and only to the questions asked. Nothing more. "With all due respect, sir, are you saying you don't believe her? Because I heard them too. And we saw Matthias burning those clothes. I'd say that's pretty undeniable evidence of wrongdoing."

"Of course I believe her. I'm just saying Evie's been through some heavy stuff. Probably even more than she lets on." He sighs and offers a doleful smile. "Sometimes trauma can skew our perception of things. Turn rhinos into unicorns, if you know what I mean."

Butch doesn't respond even when I laugh. He stays contained. Like he's back in a cell. "Is Trey supposed to be the unicorn in that analogy?" I ask, still smiling.

Macaroni chuckles, but it doesn't last long. His face stiffens again. "Listen, Evie. Go home. We'll send a unit out to Trey's place to check it out. And I'll be in touch first thing in the morning."

I nod, mainly because going home—even if it means to Maggie's home—sounds like a relief. I might even consider letting her cook for me. But I can tell Butch isn't satisfied. He's eyeing Macaroni the way I do when I know a patient is lying to me.

"Do you know something we don't, sir?" Macaroni raises his eyebrows at Butch's insinuation, but he doesn't deny it.

"Well, do you?" I ask.

"Mr. Calder, would you mind if I spoke to Evie alone for a few minutes?"

"He can stay."

Butch is on his feet and at the door before I can launch a proper protest. "It's okay, Evie. I'll be outside."

Macaroni scoots his chair closer to mine. "You didn't hear this from me, okay? Danny had a hangout. Merchant's Saloon in Oakland. Goes there every night around seven. Well, somebody called the station right before you got here. They spotted Danny milling around outside. And when we got there, we found the jeep. No Danny, of course. But there was a note to his mom saying sorry, telling her he had to get out of town."

For a split second I doubt myself. My mind *is* cracked after all, a fissure so deep a whole night fell right through. But then, I close my eyes. I hear the gunshot. The slump of his body when he'd hit the ground. *Real.* "I know what I heard. Trey and that other guy... Matthias...they probably called in the tip themselves."

"It's a possibility. I agree. We'll dust the jeep for prints."

"I'm not crazy." *But aren't crazy people always saying that?* "And I'm not a liar. Butch isn't either." *Debatable on both counts.*

"Speaking of Mr. Calder..." Macaroni raises his eyes to the door, the little window at the center. Outside, Butch leans against the far wall, forlorn. Like an old dog passed up for adoption. Again. "I understand you feel you know this man. That he was a part of your life at one point. But I'm a cop, an old cop, and I can't *not* ask you. Has he told you why he went to prison?"

Whatever he's about to say, I know he's right. And still, my heart stings, indignant. "Murder."

His mouth twists, and I feel him readying a blow. "I know Mr. Calder too. From a past life when I was a lowly beat cop, the one you remember. I was on duty that night. I responded to that scene. Gwendolyn Shaw, strangled. Evie, it was awful. One of those that sticks with you."

I glance at Butch, and he half-smiles back before I can look away. Back to Macaroni and his hard glare. I make a sound of understanding, hoping he'll stop. He doesn't.

"Do you know how long it takes to strangle someone to death? A good three to five minutes. Think about that. And be careful. That guy's got a thing for you."

"Okay," I say, feeling sullied and slimy. Like I've done something wrong. "I'll be careful. If you tell me you believe me about Trey and the murder."

He cocks his head at me, brows knitted. "Well, you'd have to specify exactly which murder you're referring to. Then or now?"

****

We trudge back to the car, wordless, both of us weighted by things we don't say. I turn down the radio and leave it in park. Turn to Butch and his sad eyes.

"Why did you kill Gwen?"

I expect him to say, "Where did that come from?" Or, "I don't want to talk about it." But it's almost like he's been expecting it, waiting for it. The way you feel when you get a bad grade on a test you didn't study for. Like you deserve that big red *F*. "Do you want the easy answer or the hard one? The insightful one or the bullshit? The long or the short? Because I've got them all."

"I want the truth. The honest one."

And I watch his hands. Strong, capable hands. Capable of ending life. Of saving it too, though. He had saved me more than once. "Evie, I...whatever he said about me, it's probably right."

**314**

His phone buzzes then, and we both stare at it, startled. Like it's the past calling to explain itself. He turns the outer screen toward me. "Is that for you?"

I recognize the number. "It's Maggie."

"Go ahead."

I take it, flip it open. And already, I'm uneasy. *Why is she calling?*

"Maggie? Is everything okay?"

"Why aren't you answering your phone?"

My unease curdles, sours, and I snap. "I told you already. I lost it."

"Then why did you call me?"

"I didn't."

"Yes, you did," she insists. "While I was in the shower. Your name showed up on the screen, and you left a message."

I'm nearing full-blown panic, but I manage to speak. To deny. "That's impossible."

"Hmph."

"Fine. What did I say?"

She lets out an exasperated breath. And my own breathing gets shallow, my stomach a pit of snakes, writhing. "You didn't say anything. You just hung up."

# CHAPTER THIRTY-FIVE

**EVIE'S** talking fast. Ninety miles a minute. Something about Trey and her mother-in-law and the cell phone, but I can barely keep up. Because I'm stuck on this: *Why did you kill Gwen?* And my pathetic non-attempt at an answer.

"Uh, Butch? Hello?" She touches my forearm, and I blink up at her and her bottle-green eyes.

"Sorry. What?"

"I need to go to my office to get my laptop. Then I can use the app, the *find phone* one. I can show Detective Maroni exactly where Trey's at."

"Sounds like a good idea." She's already pulled away from the curb, her face pinched with focus. "What's an app again?"

We both laugh a little too hard—clipped and nervous—like we need it to ease the tension. After, the silence is strange, an awkward third wheel between us. "I haven't forgotten your question," I say, finally.

"Oh. You don't have to—"

"I want to answer it. Properly. I'll tell you the whole story when you're ready to hear it."

Her eyes are fixed on the road, impossible to read.

"But till then, I'd have to say the short answer is all the usual reasons. I'm one of *those* guys. Control. Fear of abandonment. Rejection. The whole nine." I tick them off one by one, each word thrumming with truth. "I'd like to tell you I was a different person back then, but that's bullshit. The truth is I don't really know who I am now. I know who I was in prison. And I know who I want to be. But the psych doctors were right. I haven't really been tested. Out here. In the land of the living."

I've been talking forever—that's how it seems—and I force myself not to fill the quiet. This nervous chatter thing is new. *It's an Evie thing*, I remind myself. No wonder she's a goddamned shrink. She's used to this. She's probably diagnosing me right now.

"Okay," she says, Switzerland neutral.

"Is that a good okay or a bad okay? Cause I can't really tell."

She smiles. "What time is your curfew?"

"1 a.m. Why?"

"Do you want to come back to the office with me? Help me with the app? I don't want to go alone."

I take that as her answer—a good okay—and I give her a nod. "Sure. But I won't be much help. Unless you need to rewind a VCR. Or make a mix tape. Or find something in the yellow pages. Then I'm definitely your guy."

**\*\*\*\***

I sit on a folding chair while she powers up her laptop. "So, Dr. Maddox, this is where the magic happens, huh?" *Shut up, Butchy.* You sound like an oaf.

But she laughs while she types. And it warms me. That she still laughs a lot. As much as I'd let her down, not all is lost. "I wouldn't call it magic. More like trudging through…"

"Excrement?" I ask, grinning.

"Wow. You remember that conversation?"

I shrug it off, but I feel proud. Because she seems impressed. And I'll take what I can get. "Two things you're never short on in prison—regrets and time. So you tend to spend a lot of it reliving the past."

"Oh my God." And right away, I check myself. I've done something, said something. Screwed it up somehow.

But it's not me. I breathe out, relieved, even as she panics.

Evie motions me over, pointing to the map on the screen, the flashing circle. "That's my phone. And that's my address. My new apartment."

"Are you sure?"

She nods fast, already dialing the number on the card she'd pulled from her pocket. Detective Maroni. And just like that, I'm a lowly ex-con again. Because that guy doesn't like me.

****

Evie twists her hair with one hand and drives with the other. It's making me nervous. Because Trey is messing with her. That and the thought of the cops meeting us at her apartment, scrutinizing me. Maybe it's my imagination, but it's like they just know—*ex-con, parolee, murderer*—the way a dog can sniff out a tumor.

"Can I ask you a weird question?" I try to distract us both.

"Shoot."

"Why'd you buy this car?"

"Seriously? With everything that's happened today, that's your question?"

"I'm a car guy. You know that." In a flash, I see the 'Cuda on my last day of freedom. The decimated passenger side. Crumpled like it

**318**

had been made of paper, not steel. "It's just that I don't really see you as a Prius kind of girl."

"A Prius kind of girl?" She smirks at me. "It sounds like you've put time into developing this theory."

"A fair bit. Think about it. Doesn't Melanie strike you as a powder-blue, Mini Cooper gal? And Mr. Vinetti, he has Chevy pickup written all over him."

"I see. So silver Prius doesn't say Evie?"

*Hell no.* "Well, the theory is a work in progress, so..."

"I didn't buy it, if that helps with your research. It was Jared's. I always took the BART to work." I keep my mouth closed. No way to stick my foot in it. "But now you've got me curious. What sort of car did you see me driving?"

*Uh oh.* "Hmm." I put on my thinking face, but I'm just buying time. This answer I know.

"C'mon. Spit it out."

"A black Corvette." The burst of her laughter is contagious, and I chuckle even though my face is burning. "Black because of your hair, of course. And a Corvette for the look of it. It's tough but also..."

"A gas guzzler?"

"I was going to say elegant." And just like that, I'm doing it. *Hold the phone, Butch Calder is flirting.*

But I'm not even sure she heard me, because her frown is back. She hits the blinker and points to the gated complex on the right. "That's my building." As if I didn't know it already, with the red and blue lights flashing out front. Total buzzkill.

"I figured."

Evie maneuvers the car into the first open spot, waving at Detective Maroni. Then she turns to me. Lays a casual hand on my knee. "Hey, Calder, thanks for distracting me."

Evie gets out, swallowed by a swarm of cops, before I manage to mutter *sure*, my knee still slightly electrified. I go after her, trying not to act like myself. Maybe I can throw them off the scent this time.

"Did you find it?" I hear Evie's voice and follow it to the curb. Her and Maroni.

With a gloved hand, he holds up a cell phone. "Is this it? It was sitting on your welcome mat."

She nods, reaching, but he pulls it back. "We'll need to get prints first. But, didn't you say there were pictures? Of Danny's jeep?"

"And a video. Just after they…" She doesn't finish, probably worried he'll doubt her again.

I take a step toward them. Then, a few more, testing my luck. Maybe he won't notice me. "Mr. Calder. I didn't expect to see you here. Don't you have a curfew?"

The officers lingering at their cars turn their heads to look at me. With *that* look. Like I'm the tumor. Like I need to be excised. Burned away.

"Yes, sir. It's not for a couple more hours though. And Evie asked me to—"

"I asked him to come." She motions me over.

Maroni gives a single nod—all the approval he can muster, but I'll take it—and powers up Evie's phone. "Well then, let's have a look."

Evie stands over his shoulder, directing him, a caveman like me. He follows orders, and I watch her face. Because it tells me everything I need to know.

"He erased them," she says, lifting her eyes to me, her voice quavering. "Trey erased them."

\*\*\*\*

Evie slogs up the stairs to check her mailbox, a uniformed officer trailing her. Which means I'm left alone with Maroni. I start to pace, the way I did the first few months in Folsom. If I'd added up the steps I'd taken in that six-by-eight box, they would've sent me around the world and back. But like any captive animal, I'd grown placid over time. Adjusted to the size of my cage.

"How long did you say you'd been out?" Maroni asks. Like I hadn't already faced his inquisition at the station. Like he's just making small talk.

"About five months, sir." I give him my best free-man smile—small and polite—hoping he'll back off, at least take pity on me.

"Did Evie tell you I warned her about you?" Or not.

"No, sir."

"You might not know this, but I'm familiar with your case. That was my beat back then. And some cases, they stick with you forever. My partner and I got the call that a homeless guy had found a body over at the Port. A dead girl."

I try to go somewhere else in my mind, back to the car with Evie's hand on my knee. Back to the first day I met Gwen, her sundress and her watermelon bubblegum. Back to my bedroom, before my world got smashed, with Jesse and me playing cops and robbers. It doesn't work. His voice is more powerful than all of it.

"That's a scene I'll never forget. Such a young girl. A beautiful girl. Her whole future ahead of her. Just dumped out there on the pavement like a sack of trash."

I wish he'd cuff me, tase me, throw me to the ground. Anything but this. Hell, I'd rather he shoot me. I would deserve that. But this, this is just cruel. "Her neck was broken. I imagine you know that. Did you do that with your hands or when you ran—"

Evie is my angel of mercy. Because when he sees her, he stops.

"You okay?" he asks her. Meanwhile, my whole heart is shredded to ribbons. But what can I say? He's right. He's right about all of it.

"Yeah. Just tired."

When he turns his back and walks ahead, I finally look at her. And I see why he asked. She's gone faraway. Miles from here. Her hands hold a stack of mail, an opened letter on top marked with a bright yellow FORWARD sticker.

She moves like a ghost. Like she could pass through walls.

She stops. Whispers. "It's from Cassie."

**EVIE**
**MAY 13, 1994**
**MY BIRTHDAY**

# THIRTEEN steps to the gallows.

Thirteen knots in a hangman's noose.

Thirteen feet before the guillotine falls.

And thirteen days of May when Arlene Allcott became a mother. My mother. She'd told me the story once. Only once. Like she'd rather it never happened.

"It was the longest I'd ever gone without using," she'd said, pausing, probably waiting on me to thank her. "Your daddy too. Both of us, clean as a whistle." I couldn't say if I believed her, but I'd wanted to. "You would've been real proud of your mama."

*Anyway, your dad was real antsy, waiting on you to come out. So he took me to one of those carnivals. Wasn't my idea, I'll tell you that. I was fat as a tick and ready to pop. My ankles all swollen, thick as ham hocks. Worst nine months of my damn life.* Another pause, and I'd almost laughed. And cried. Seeing how she'd wasted away to nothing.

"Right off the bat, your daddy had taken me into one of those cockamamie fortune-tellers with the cards. Who knows why? More than likely, he'd been checkin' her out. In fact, I'm sure of it. Cause he'd kept givin' her the eye. And she'd been givin' it back. Your daddy was a looker alright with those same unnatural green eyes that you've got. And I'll admit I'd been jealous. Especially on account of you

**322**

fattening me up like a cow for the slaughter. And do you know this skank—in her rickety old tent and spooky black veil—she'd had the nerve to pull out the death card?"

I'd sucked in a big, audible breath, felt a chill work down my spine.

"Exactly. What a bitch, right? Messin' with me like that."

My mom had put her arm around me, skinny and pasty and scarred by a thousand needles, but I'd leaned in, desperate for her touch. "My water broke not more than fifteen minutes later in the middle of the damn house of mirrors. Imagine that. Your daddy carried me out of there, right past that hoochie and her tent. And if I hadn't been feelin' the throes of hellfire comin' out of me, I would've made him stop just so I could have told her to go fuck herself." A tired laugh had hauled its way up my mother's throat. "Pardon my French, but it's true."

"Turns out she wasn't too far off the mark. But it was your daddy that card was meant for. Not you and me, baby girl. We're survivors."

*Survivors*, I think, watching the ebb of Cassie's chest, the soft push and pull of her breathing from the pillow next to mine. It would be time to wake her up soon. I counted her breaths until I reached the magic number. *Thirteen.* My first birthday without my mother. And I couldn't stop myself from wondering if that fortune-teller had been right about all three of us. Our little family. We were all cursed.

**\*\*\*\***

It goes without saying, I skipped school that day. Heck, I figured if I planned to kill somebody, truancy was the least of my sins.

After breakfast, I slipped out the back door and made my way into the trees, hoping no one had been watching. The drainage tunnel was a short walk, but time stretched out, lazy as a cat, and I started to think I'd missed it somehow. The trees watched me with their identical faces, until I'd spun around so much I felt dizzy. I picked a direction and kept walking, sure now I was lost. Until I heard a low whistle.

Cassie sat at the tunnel's entrance, poking at the ground with a stick. When I got closer, I saw what she'd written in the dirt. *Happy Birthday, Evie.*

"So I guess you're officially a teenager now, huh?" Her smile had a tinge of melancholy.

"Thirteen going on thirty," I teased, just to watch her brighten. But she didn't. "Exactly like you."

"Here." She handed me a paper bag, my name written in marker on the front. "I made this for you."

I joined her on the concrete lip of the tunnel and opened it, spilling her gift into my hand. "You only used good colors," I said as she looped the friendship bracelet around my wrist and tied it tight. Not a trace of green in it. Her face scrunched in confusion, but she didn't ask, only nodded as I held it out for both of us to admire. "Thanks, Cas."

"There's one more thing." She produced a pink-swirled birthday candle and a lighter from her pocket. I suspected she'd stolen it from our Wal-Mart, slipped it out of the package when no one was looking. I'd seen her do that before with other things. Gum, cookies, makeup. "I don't have a cake, but I figure you should still get a wish."

She held it between her fingers and lit the wick. As I closed my eyes, the flame licked upward. And I thought of the twelve birthdays before this one. The wish I'd made since I'd been old enough to make wishes. *Please let Mom get clean.*

I needed a new wish now. I tried them on one by one.

*Please make Bobby leave me alone.*

*Please give me some friends at school.*

*Please let me move out of the Port to a real home.*

*Please let me kiss Butch Calder.*

*Please kill Trey so I don't have to do it myself.*

"Geez, Evie. C'mon. My finger's about to burn off."

**324**

I stared at the flame with an aching in my stomach, because none of those wishes by itself would give me what I really wanted. *Please, please, please, just let me be happy. Someday.* I breathed deep and blew out the candle in one puff.

She gave it to me. "For luck. So your wish comes true."

I held it in my hand like it was worth something, like it had the magic she'd claimed, and motioned Cassie deeper into the tunnel, where the moss grew thick and slimy on the walls, and a small pool of brown water buzzed with mosquitos.

"Did you think about it, Cas?" I swatted one on my arm, leaving a freckle of bright red blood. "Are you gonna help me?"

"I don't know. Can't you go without me?"

I sighed, guilt sucking me dry just like that mosquito. "We've been over this. He'll never admit any of it to me. It's gotta be you."

"I don't think I can do it."

I grabbed her arm, squeezed it. "Of course you can. Listen to me. Trey is never gonna leave us alone. You or me. We have to do this. Together."

"How are we even gonna get there? Trey's place…it's out in the sticks. Way out. I don't even remember where."

I patted my pocket. "It's in Pinole. I have the address. Just leave the transportation to me."

"What if Trey's not there? Then what?" She picked up a rusted beer-bottle top and tossed it into the water. The mosquitos scattered, droning.

"You said yourself he talked about a party on Friday night, right? This Friday. Just before he got picked up by the cops…"

She made a noise that sounded like a whimper. It echoed through the tunnel, louder than the hungry mosquitos, louder than our voices. Impossibly loud. "But I…I just wanna leave here. I don't even care what happens to Trey. I never want to see him again."

"Then do it for me. And if you really want to leave, if you want to find your dad, I'll give you the money I hid. The money Trey's looking for. All of it."

"You'd do that?"

"It's yours." I couldn't even look at her when I said it. Because I knew she'd agree. Because I'd stooped as low as Trey, paying her to turn a trick. Because I owed her the truth. Somebody should know when they've agreed to be an accomplice to murder.

**\*\*\*\***

I laid in bed, the blanket pulled over my face, pretending to sleep. Beneath it, I wound a small strand of my hair around my finger and pulled until I felt the relief and the pain of separation. In a few hours, I'd be thirteen and a day. And a cold-blooded killer. *Evil Evie through and through.* Trey would be out of my life—but not just that. In a hole in the ground, rotting or burned to ash like Mom. Either, far better than he deserved.

I'd made a list and checked it twice. Literally, two checks. But only two.

One mini tape recorder. *Check.* I'd swiped it from the music room that morning.

One small plastic baggie of rat poison, ground myself with a rock from the backyard. *Check.* I'd planned on dumping it into Trey's beer while Cassie had him distracted, confessing his sins.

A ride to Trey's place, 10 Eagle Pass in Pinole, courtesy of Calder. *No check...yet.* I'd called his room at the Blue Bird, but he hadn't answered, so I'd left a message, nervous and rambling.

*Hi, Calder. It's, uh...Evie. I know you're probably really busy, but I was wondering if you could maybe give me and Cassie a ride. It's kind of important. It...uh...it has to do with Mr. Excrement Face himself. Anyway, we'll be waiting at the underpass by the mini mart near the Port around ten. If you can make it. Okay? I hope to see you. Bye.*

After Cherice finished bed checks, I waited for Cassie's whistle and whipped off the covers. I stuffed my pillows under the blanket, molding them to the approximate shape of me. Then I slung my backpack over my shoulder and climbed out the second-story window, shimmying down the drainpipe like I had nine lives.

Somehow, Cassie looked fearless and unpredictable. *Real purdy*, to hear Trey tell it. Exactly the way I needed her, and I bit back my jealousy. And my regret. Her brown hair glinted against her bare shoulders, her legs tan and lean in the cutoff shorts I'd loaned her. "What's the plan?"

"I asked Calder if he'd give us a ride. But…"

Cassie rolled her eyes. "But what?"

"He didn't answer. And he never called back. Still, I think he'll be there."

"You think?" I shrugged at her, embarrassed. "Where?"

She followed my gaze as I pointed up ahead, past the gas station to the underpass. "We can get Slurpees while we wait," I suggested.

"Fine."

Twenty minutes later, wild cherry coating the back of my throat like cough syrup, I finally said it out loud. "I don't think he's coming." The disappointment clung there too, in my throat, and I thought I might cry.

"Of course he's not coming. He's not your boyfriend. You realize that, right?"

"I know."

"Because you said—"

"I know what I said."

"So what now?"

I took a step toward the road and stuck out my thumb. "I guess we'll just have to hitch a ride."

Cassie stayed in the shadows, pressed flat to the wall like a lizard. When I turned back to look at her, she'd crouched to the ground with something in her hand.

"What're you doing?" I asked her. Like a big dummy, a clueless kid. Not thirteen at all. As soon as I got close enough, I answered my own question with another. "You're popping pills now?"

"If you want me to do this, I'm gonna need a little help." She put one in my hand, the tiny *M* mocking me. I threw it as far as I could into the nightmare end of the underpass, dark and crawling with God knows what.

"Do you know what that is?" The noise from the highway swallowed my shout, turned my fearsome yell into something small and meaningless. "Where did you get it?"

"Where do you think?"

"It's methadone, Cassie. It's made from the same stuff as heroin. He wants you to end up just like her."

She cocked her head all sassy. "I'm not your mom."

"Yeah, well, I didn't know you...did that."

"There's a lot of stuff you don't know."

"Such as?" But I didn't want her to answer. Not really.

Her eyes narrowed. "Such as, I lied to you about that last day at the Blue Bird. I did what Trey wanted me to do. I had sex with a guy—a grown man—for money. For only fifty freakin' dollars on account of it being my first time. When he was done, I left the room and I saw Trey getting arrested so I hid. I pretended it never happened."

She tossed down the pill, chasing it with her Slurpee, gulping it so fast I knew she'd get brain freeze.

"You need a ride?" The voice came, disembodied, from behind me. It sounded harmless. Like no one I knew. No one I'd remember. *And wasn't that the truth?*

Cassie nodded, pushing past me to talk to him, the swing of her hips meant to wound me. Anger burned my eyes as I watched her, and the man's face blurred in the tears I blinked back. But I nodded too, somehow already knowing he was the one who would take us where we wanted to go.

# CHAPTER THIRTY-SIX

**ALL** day, I dream of Cassie. Only Cassie. In my dreams, she's dead. Pale and cold and stiff. And every time, upon waking, I startle with the thought of it.

Cassie is alive.

I pull Jared's comforter over my head, leaving a space for the sunlight to seep. Cocooned in near darkness, I read the letter again.

The letter Cassie had written and mailed about a month ago. To my old apartment. It didn't seem fair that it had to travel for weeks. After twenty-three years.

The letter I'd first read quietly in my apartment, police lights strobing outside. And next read aloud in the car outside the halfway house, with Butch coaxing me through it. We'd sat there until his curfew when I'd assured him I'd be okay—Macaroni had dispatched a patrol unit to Maggie's—and watched him go inside, his steps stuttering and reluctant.

Now I can practically recite the letter from memory, but I hold it open anyway. There's something comforting about seeing her handwriting, looping and bold and messy on the page. A little like Cassie herself.

*Dear Evie,*

*I'm pretty sure this letter will be a big shocker for you. But I hope it'll be a good surprise. Like the time we found that twenty-dollar bill underneath the overpass. It was so long ago that we knew each other and for such a short time, but sometimes it feels more real to me than anything…you and me. I saw it in the paper when you got married—eloped! And I cried for you when Jared died. And you're a shrink now—damn, girl. You really did it. In some ways, I guess I've been living through you. And I wonder if you ever wonder about me. I wanted to call you so many times, but I didn't want to drag you back there. To the past. And I figured you'd hate me for that night. You have every right to. Because I hate myself.*

*If I had listened to you, my whole life would be different. Trey would be rotting in prison—where he belongs—not here in the next room, drunk and passed out on the sofa. I wouldn't have gotten hooked on dope, and clean again, and hooked again, and clean. Clean just over a month now. But also, I wouldn't have a daughter. And that's the only saving grace. Violet. That's her name. And yes, Trey is her dad. A sorry excuse for one. He won't even admit it, so I gave her my last name. My real one.*

*I hope you know how brave you are. Totally fearless. But me, I just didn't have enough guts that night. And then Matthias pulled over out of nowhere to pick us up—I couldn't remember his name then, but I'd seen him before at Trey's party. He'd been nice to me. And I was such a fool, I thought he liked me, that maybe I could stay with him. Or he could help us. So I agreed to go to that stupid tree. The last thing I remember is seeing you up in it. Crouched in the branches like a little squirrel. But a safe one. I hope that wasn't a dream.*

*When I came to, we were both in the back of Matthias' truck, and you were totally out of it. He was freaked out too. Crying and blubbering and slapping my face. I guess he thought I was dead. Then Trey showed up—real angry. And you begged him to send you somewhere. Anywhere. You told him you'd give him the stuff he wanted, and I guess you did. Because I never saw you again. But one of us had to get away. And I'm glad it was you.*

*But now, it's my turn to be brave. I'm done with this life. Done with Trey. Last week, I decided. But not for me. For Violet. She's back living with me again. And that sick SOB said she should start earning her keep—you know what that means. Anyway, I couldn't help but think of you and your mom. That's why she wanted out, Evie. To protect you from him.*

*Nobody should have to go through what we did. So I'm going to the police. With all of it. And I've been hiding away my money, and Violet and I are taking off as soon as it's safe. When we do, I'll come and find you. And I hope you'll forgive me.*

*Friends always,*

*Cassidy Kurchell (that's my real name)*

I cancel my clients, spend half the day that way. In Jared's room with Sammy purring at my side. Sleeping. Dreaming. And reading the letter, awakening to my new reality. *Cassie is alive.* Knowing that, I feel better, but somehow worse. As if I've failed her—and Violet and myself—in a colossal way. Because it didn't matter what happened in the past. What matters is what you believed happened. And everything I'd believed was wrong. But it had marked me, stained me. Like a water ring on an otherwise flawless mahogany table. Regrettable. And completely and utterly permanent.

Maggie stays away. Until the doorbell rings.

She raps on the door gently. Like there's a monster in here with me that we shouldn't disturb.

"Go away," I mutter. Barely loud enough for her to hear.

"Those detectives are here."

"I don't care. Tell them I'm sleeping."

"Evelyn. They're here. Right outside the door with me."

I sit up too fast, blood whooshing to my head and making me dizzy. "One minute," I say. My voice sounds rusty and stiff, like it hasn't been used in a while.

Sammy launches a few protest meows before he relents, jumping from the bed and slipping beneath it. Hidden from the world. The way I wish I could be.

My robe is right where I left it, discarded in a heap at the foot of the bed. I slip it on, secreting Cassie's letter in the front pocket, and fling open the door without as much as a glance in the mirror. They wanted me, they've got me. And I hope I look as bad as I feel.

Macaroni and Munroe in the flesh. Right there in my face. But I turn to Maggie first. She shrugs, almost apologetic. As if she'd had no choice in the matter. "I tried to tell them you were...tired. But they need to talk to you. They told me it was important."

Detective Munroe speaks first. "Could you join us in the living room?"

I follow them out into the world of the living, the rich hardwood awash in sunlight. I squint against the harshness of it. Macaroni pats the seat next to him, and I sit with Maggie on the other side. Too empty, too exhausted to think for myself.

"We checked your phone. There were no prints. None at all. It was wiped clean. And we sent a few units out to Trey's early this morning."

"And?"

"The property appeared deserted. Trey was gone. His car too." He's measuring his words or measuring me. Seeing how much I can handle. I'd done that before with Maggie when Jared got sick. Only telling her the moderately bad. Saving the unspeakable. With my patients too.

"What about Danny?"

**332**

There's no missing the look exchanged between the two detectives. "You were right. We found the body newly buried in the woods behind the house. He'd been shot."

Feeling vindicated, I crow over Maggie's gasp. "I told you."

"We also found another grave nearby. Another body."

My thoughts begin to gather speed. Then, to race, breakneck. Until there's only one way to end it. "Who?"

"A female. She was known to us as a prostitute and heroin addict."

My brain comes to a firm stop. Frozen. And in the quiet space, an image. A memory. Cassie at the base of the tree, wobbling on shaky legs, scrambling away from the faceless man—he had a name now. "Climb higher, higher." Her words, slurred. "Don't come down." He'd shoved her to the ground and smacked her face hard, stunned her. Then he'd unbuckled his pants, shoved them down to his thighs, and pressed himself on top of her.

"How did she die?" Maggie asks, and I realize she's holding my hand. Patting it.

"Too early to tell. There was no obvious trauma, and the body had been there a while. The coroner said at least a couple of weeks. Could've been an…" Macaroni swallows hard, clearing the way for whatever nasty word he's about to cough up. "…overdose."

My head bobs up and down, nodding at him. It feels disconnected. Like it might float away. "What was her name?" Because I have to hear him say what I already know.

"Cassidy Kurchell."

Cassie is dead. Again. And it's still my fault.

There's nothing left for me to do but this. I take out the letter, hand it to Macaroni.

"I need to tell you something. Everything."

# CHAPTER THIRTY-SEVEN

**AFTER** Mr. Vinetti gives me my assignments, I check Evie's office—still locked—and I hole up in the bathroom for a good hour. It feels safe in there, compact and contained. Predictable. The kind of world I'd grown accustomed to. Not this one.

Sebastian had been asleep last night when I'd returned, worried sick about Evie. Punch-drunk on Evie. And I hadn't planned on waking him. I'd deal with him in the morning. With a level head.

"You barely made curfew, huh?" He'd looked wide awake, like he'd been playing possum. I'd shrugged, pulling back the covers and climbing in. Staying mute. "Cat got your tongue, Calder?"

I'd stared up at the ceiling, steadying my breathing. But it didn't help. This guy got under my skin like a goddamned ringworm. "And what about you? Did you take the night off? Or did you just finish up the vandalism portion of the evening early?"

"Ouch. Why so hostile? I thought we were cool, man. All's well that ends—"

"Yeah. I hate that saying. And that was before you ratted me out to Dr. Maddox. You made it sound like it was my idea."

"Relax. She likes you. She'll get over it."

I'd turned toward the wall. Better not to look at him, even in my peripheral. "You seem pretty confident for a guy with nothing left to lord over me."

I hoped he'd leave it alone then. But hope is the thing with feathers, and it had flown right out the window. "I got audio, you know. That night. Had my cell phone in my pocket the whole time. It's one of those fancy ones with the video recorder. Not like your relic. You say anything about anything, and you're going down with me."

"Good night, Sebastian." And I'd spent the next five hours and forty-five minutes listening to him listening to me.

Peeking out the door first—coast clear—I sneak out of the bathroom like a common criminal. Evie's still not here, and my stomach is a pit. I head down the first floor and try to focus. One minute at a time. One hour at a time. One day at a time. Just like in Folsom.

I hang a few pictures in the waiting room for 16A. And clean up a toilet overflow in the clinic. Mr. Vinetti left a couple sacks of garbage for me to lug to the dumpster, so I head across the parking lot, dragging the bags and myself. My legs, heavy, weighted with the heft of the last few days. My head, spinning in the clouds.

I toss the trash over the side and sit on the curb behind the dumpster, flipping my phone open and closed, open and closed. I can call Evie at her mother-in-law's. The number is still in my phone from yesterday. In fact, I'd spent ten minutes at breakfast trying to figure out how to save it before I'd just jotted it on a scrap of paper. Like we did in the days of old.

But I don't want to overstep. Especially after last night. When a line had been crossed and not by me. At exactly 12:45 a.m.—I'd seen it on the dash clock—I'd opened the door of the Prius. Evie had gotten out too, and we'd met in the middle. I'd felt like a kid on a first date. If your first date involves witnessing a murder. She'd closed the distance between us herself, taking me by surprise. And then: *You know I had a huge crush on you back then, right?* The words alone would've been one thing, but the way she'd said them, her lips right there against my cheek, so close they'd brushed it by accident. That had been another thing entirely.

*What did I do?* What I always do. Run. Well, not run exactly, but stutter step back to the house, glancing over my shoulder to be sure she was real. Because I will mess this up. Whatever *this* is. I already have. Thanks to Sebastian, I'm skating on thin ice, and I haven't even told her the whole truth. Yet.

Nope. Can't call. I pocket the phone and get to my feet, cursing Sebastian again. And that's when I remember.

He'd snuck back here that night, gotten his hands dirty. "Misdirection," he'd said. But his whole shtick seemed an exercise in it. One move to cover the next, to avoid capture. Like pawns on a chessboard.

Sure that no one's looking, I slink behind the dumpster and into the small wooded area in the back of the building, the leaves crunching under my feet. There's a spot by the bushes where the ground is different—smooth, like it's been swept clean—and the leaf cover, less dense. I kneel down and start digging, pawing the soil away like an old hound dog, sure there's a bone underneath.

And I'm right.

My bone is a metal lockbox. But with a few solid hits against the nearest tree trunk, it springs right open. *What have you been up to, roomie?* Besides graffiti and destroying my life.

Turns out a helluva lot.

## BUTCH
## MAY 13, 1994
## THE DAY I KILLED HER

I needed to get plastered. Wasted. Totally shit-faced. I gazed with longing at the bottle of Jack, stolen all by myself this morning—*fuck you, Gwen*—in the glove box. I could already taste that first swig, feel the bite of it at the back of my throat. But it would have to wait.

I locked up the 'Cuda, dropped two quarters in the meter—this would be quick—and walked the block to Simon Merriwether's office.

"Mr. Calder, glad to see you could fit me into your busy schedule." Mr. Merriwether smoothed the edges of his gray mustache and gestured to the chair in front of his desk. Since I'd seen him last, he'd shrunk like a prune, smaller and more wrinkly.

"I'll stand."

"Suit yourself." He cleared his throat the way Mr. O'Shaughnessy always did just before he'd start in with a lecture on my unruly behavior. And by the way Mr. Merriwether's throat rattled, this lecture was going to be epic. "You missed our appointment on Wednesday."

"I forgot."

"And you haven't been returning my calls."

I shrugged. "Been busy."

"Well, yes, I'd say you've been very busy." He opened a file folder I could only guess bore the label: *Stupidest Client I've Got.* Or maybe *Lowlife Loser.* "Let's see. In the span of less than one month, and following your release from juvenile detention I might add, you've spent roughly $210,000. A two-hundred-thousand-dollar car. Nordstrom. Neiman Marcus. Autographed memorabilia from that vulgar rock band. And the list goes on…and yet, you're living in one of the seediest motels in Oakland."

"It's my money, right? I can do what I want with it."

He sighed, and I caught a glimpse of my reflection in the law school diploma framed over his desk. My complete and utter indignation writ large on my face. And I actually felt sorry for the guy. That he had to deal with screwups like me. Until. "At this rate, you'll be penniless by the end of the summer. Homeless too. What would your parents say, Butch?"

Like a cloud passing over, I watched my expression darken in the glass. Of the fancy diploma from the fancy school I'd never get into. His whole office—the leather, the mahogany, the perfect pictures of his perfect family lined up in a straight little row—a study in all the things I would never, could never, have.

"My parents are dead in case you didn't notice. So, they'd probably say to live it up. Go wild, son. Because you never really know when a doped-up trucker is going to smash your skull to bits."

Mr. Merriwether's eyes bugged, and I waited for him to tell me to get out. That's what I wanted actually, what I'd been aiming for. "I'm sorry. I know this hasn't been easy for you. But I'm concerned about your future. Remember, I'm on your side."

*My side, my ass.* "But it's my money."

"Yes. And no."

"What do you mean?"

"The judge made it clear the money was to be spent in your best interests. Now, I've given you ample leeway—probably too much—but I have to put my foot down before you blow it all. If you can't act responsibly I'll have no choice but to suspend your access to the account until you demonstrate the type of sound decision-making that comes with being an adult."

Heat crept up my spine. I could feel the beads of sweat pricking at the back of my neck and along my forehead. My bones felt like hot coils, rigged for explosion. "Screw you. If you call this stick-up-your-ass routine being an adult, then you can have it."

He raised his eyebrows, slightly offended, but there was fear there too. And I liked it. "My point exactly," he said, pretending I hadn't scared him. "Someday, Mr. Calder, you'll have to grow up. Whether you like it or not."

"You can't touch that money, you prick. And I'll grow up when I'm damn well good and ready." I grabbed the first thing I saw, a golfing trophy perched on the edge of his desk, and I hurled it at the wall. The thud pleased me, but not as much as Mr. Merriwether's flinch and cower. *Damn, that felt good.*

I stomped out, high on rage. Anything seemed possible. Even winning Gwen back. And one thing, certain. Butch Calder knew how to make an exit.

****

What goes up must come down. And by the time I'd started the 'Cuda, feeling that low growl of the engine in my belly, I knew I'd messed up. Big time. I washed down my regret with a long swallow of Jack and hit the highway doing ninety-five. I figured I had at least a few hours before Mr. Merriwether made good on his threat. And I knew what I needed to do.

Twenty minutes later, I strutted into Tiffany in San Francisco, determined to buy my way back to Gwen. The oversized door was heavier than I expected. Like I needed a couple of servants to open it for me, to announce my entrance.

Inside, I tried not to gape. But, the cases, the diamonds, the goddamned brightness of it all—I felt like a deer in the headlights, startled, right before impact.

"Can I help you, young man?" A woman appeared in a black skirt suit, her hair twisted into a tight knot at the base of her skull. So tight, it explained her pinched smile.

"Uh, yeah. I mean, yes, ma'am. I'm looking for a present for my girlfriend." *You wish, Butchy. You blew it. She's probably banging Russ Conway right now.* "She's actually kind of upset with me, so it has to be really special."

The woman nodded like I wasn't the first total lame duck she'd seen. Like we came in here all the time, guys like me, ready to cough it up—whatever it cost—for one more night with her. Who knew? I was Everyman.

"I'm sure we can find something that will make her forget whatever it is you've done wrong." Another plastic smile. "Now, what sort of jewelry would she like? A bracelet, perhaps?" She directed me to the first case. "We have a lovely silver charm bracelet. Simple, but exquisite. And it's quite… affordable. If that's a concern."

*Bitch.* "It's not."

"Oh. Well then. How about a necklace?"

"This one," I said, peering into the glass at the sterling music note. I imagined it resting in the hollow of Gwen's throat. How I'd kiss her there. How she'd let me. "She plays the viola."

"A beautiful choice." She plucked the charm from its cushion and set it atop the case, glancing up at me as she checked the little price tag and pecked at the register. "It's two hundred dollars."

Her pause seemed deliberate. Like she knew. But how could she? I looked over my shoulder, wary, as if Simon Merriwether waited behind me, grinning, broken golf trophy in hand.

"How would you like to pay, sir?"

"Personal check."

"Alright." But a tiny wrinkle appeared in the center of her forehead as I filled in the amount, scrawled my signature. "One moment, please."

She disappeared into the back of the store—my check held captive between her manicured fingers—leaving me standing there,

340

pacing like a desperate fool. I tried to act normal, but the other Tiffany robots clad in the same, bland uniform kept swiveling their heads in my direction.

And suddenly, I felt drunk. Impossible, because I'd only had a few swigs. Four. Or five. Ten at most. But my feet swayed beneath me, and I grabbed onto the counter to stay upright.

"Are you alright, sir?"

I nodded. *I should leave now. Before I embarrass myself.* I didn't belong there anyway, and no amount of blood money would change that. I took a wobbly step toward the door, but—

The necklace. The music note. Gwen would love it. She would see how thoughtful I could be. How sincere. She would let me fasten the clasp, sweeping her golden hair to one shoulder. And I would linger there, fingers on skin. Lips too.

No, I couldn't leave without it. Then I'd be empty-handed. Hopeless. With nothing to give but myself. So less than nothing then.

When the saleswoman returned, the wrinkle in her forehead deepened, and I wanted to smooth it, to smash it down. To flatten it with a hammer. She spoke in a hushed tone, but in the Friday morning quiet, everybody heard. Everybody. "There was a problem with your check, sir."

"What kind of problem?"

"Apparently, there's a hold on your account."

"A hold. Weird." *Shit. Shit. Shit.* "I can pay cash."

I pulled out my wallet, counted the bills out loud, and prayed. *Please, God. I need this.* "One ninety-seven. One ninety-eight. One ninety-nine...I've got some change in my pocket."

I shoved my fingers down deep and tossed a handful of change on the counter. As she picked through it, I leaned in, nearly knocking our heads together. She gasped and wrinkled her nose.

"Sir, have you been drinking?"

"No. Of course not." *Act sober, Butchy.* "Do I have enough?"

"Two hundred on the dot. With a couple pennies to spare. But—"

I smacked my palm against the glass, rattling the case. "Then what's the goddamned problem?"

Finally, I'd gotten her to look alive. "I'll wrap this up for you, sir. Right away."

She backed away slowly, leaving the pennies—five to be exact—on the counter. One-by-one I placed them in my palm, balled them tight in my fist. I would've thrown them at her, but they were all I had left.

****

The message light accosted me the moment I got back—its steady blinking like a constant tap on my shoulder. Probably Merriwether calling to rub it in.

*I'm broke. Penniless. Except for those five.* The thought kept creeping up, pushing its way through. If it came to it, I'd have to sell the 'Cuda. Let go of the only good thing I had left. Except for Gwen, of course. That's why I had to stay focused.

On her. My lifeline.

I took my time in the shower. And I spent at least fifteen minutes perfecting my shaggy mane. Dressing for the job I wanted. Gwen's boyfriend, of course.

I stood at the door, armed and ready. Tiffany box in hand and looking damn good. Like a guy about to win the girl. But that red light kept insisting. *So what the hell. It can't get any worse.* I held the receiver to my ear and pressed the message button.

*Hi, Calder. It's, uh…Evie. I know you're probably really busy, but I was wondering if you could maybe give me and Cassie a ride—"*

I hung up. Evie would find another ride. I didn't have time for distractions. Not now. Not tonight. Because tonight was going to be epic.

****

The little blue box mocked me from the passenger seat, its haughty white bow winking at me. Judging me. Like it knew what I was.

Who I was. Who I would be.

I covered it with my jacket. I expected Gwen soon.

And I'd be waiting. Watching from a turnout three houses down, with a clear view of the Shaw mansion.

Already, I'd been there for hours.

Long enough to see her prick dad come home with that mobile phone glued to his ear, the one I'd like to shove right up his ass.

Long enough to sober up...mostly.

My legs were cramped. My back ached. But inside, I felt alive. I had the feeling that something good—one good thing—could still happen to me. Even with five pennies in my wallet and the Tiffany box pronouncing me an impostor, that feeling burned at the center of my chest like a lit match. I guess you'd call it hope.

And Gwen had given it to me with one sentence. "I think I should talk to him at least." That's what she'd said to Dickface Russ—who was sporting a pretty impressive black eye, courtesy of yours truly—when he'd dropped her off after school in his 911 Porsche Carrera Turbo. Red. He didn't deserve that car. And definitely not a girl like her.

"I don't want you seeing that guy again," he'd said, loud enough for me to hear. "I don't trust him."

But Gwen. Sweet, perfect Gwen. She hadn't fallen for his macho bullshit. "He seemed really sorry. I think I should talk to him at least."

"Are you kidding me? He broke my nose. That asshole's lucky I'm not pressing charges."

"He's been through a lot. He lost his whole family, Russ. Cut him some slack."

"Whatever, Gwen. I'll see you tonight. Seven, right?" And then, he'd tried to kiss her. To kiss *my* girl. But Gwen, amazing, beautiful Gwen. My Gwen. She'd pushed him away.

"Eight. And don't be late."

Now, it was well past eight. Of course Dickface was late, and Gwen had already come out to the front steps. Seeing her, my heart always raced but that night...wow. It wasn't the knockout black dress or the heels or the sparkly bag she'd probably stolen. In the dusky light, she practically glowed, her skin radiating stardust. And the way she stood there, vulnerable and uncertain, like she doubted he'd come, like any guy in his sound mind would stand her up, that's what really got me. I wanted to march right up to her, sling her over my shoulder, and carry her away. Neanderthal style.

Gwen's face shifted in the last rays of sunlight, and I wondered if she'd heard my car door open. If she knew I was coming to rescue her. If she wanted to be rescued. *By me.* I hesitated.

And that's when Dickface finally rolled up. I had to hand it to the guy. His timing was impeccable.

He had the nerve to honk. Can you believe it? Didn't even bother to open her door. I shook my head in disgust and waited until the brake lights disappeared around the sharp curve at the top of the road. Then, I followed.

Everything I knew about tailing a mark came from the movies. Lesson one: Drive a car that didn't stand out. *Total failure.* My 'Cuda was a head turner…like Gwen. Which meant I had to go overboard on lesson two: Stay a few lengths back. On the freeway, that was easy. I didn't speed, didn't signal. Just coasted behind them, my mouth dry with anticipation. I felt calm. Singularly focused. Like an arrow, perfectly aimed and whizzing toward the heart of its target.

Fortunately, Russ's ride was no wallflower either. Even the worst spy couldn't lose a cherry-red Porsche. When it glided off at the Twelfth Street exit in Oakland, I slowed, allowing a truck to move between us. The sedan behind me laid on the horn. And I held up my middle finger in the rearview mirror. The lady driver returned the gesture, and I felt the rage swell.

"Go around me!" I yelled, fist pounding the steering wheel. As if she could hear me, she zipped past, pausing to flip me the bird one more time. I swerved into her lane, ready to give chase. But—Gwen.

I'd nearly blown it. Russ's car had snuck a light ahead of me.

"Fuck it," I muttered, plowing right through the red. So much for laying low. I needed to get hold of myself. And fast.

I inched forward till I could see Gwen in the passenger seat. Her hair fell over her left shoulder in waves. Soft waves that always smelled like too-sweet watermelon. I thought of the night of the party. Of burying my face in her neck.

Focused again—*nothing else matters*—I drove on.

At the second stoplight, I watched Russ extend his scrawny octopus arm across the center console, seeking his prey. Gwen didn't stop him.

At the third, I didn't look at all. I cranked up the music. "Love Gun"—Gwen's song.

The Porsche cruised down Broadway and turned into a parking lot near the water. I drove past and circled back. By that time, they were walking, Gwen a few steps behind. And I could see where they were headed. A banner hung from a white tent.

**Congratulations Berkeley High Class of 1994! Welcome to Your Future.**

I stared at the red-and-gold letters until they blurred together. Until the truth of them hardened in my stomach, a bitter kernel. And when I called Gwen's name, all I felt was a yawning emptiness, so deep and wide nothing could ever fill it. I wished I was still drunk.

"What the hell is he doing here?" Russ's face got red fast. Red and blubbery. Like I'd already hit him again.

"Nice shiner, Dickface."

"Did you invite him?"

Caught in the middle, Gwen shook her head, her eyes wide and ricocheting between us.

"I just want to talk, Gwen. Please. Just give me five minutes."

Russ grabbed her hand and tugged her toward him. "Did you follow us here?" he asked me.

"Five minutes, Gwen. Then I'll be out of your life forever. If that's what you want."

"Of course that's what she wants. You're a loser, dude. You'll be cutting our grass someday."

"Why don't we ask her? Gwen?" Her eyes met mine, watery blue. And about to spill over. In them, I saw her answer, and my heart soared.

"Five minutes, Russ."

**** 

Five whole minutes. *I could change her mind in five minutes.* Hell, as unfair as it seemed, sometimes five minutes could change your whole life. I'd lost my whole family, my whole world, in less.

"Let's take a drive," Gwen whispered, back where she belonged. With me. In the 'Cuda. Sitting shotgun.

"Seriously? Are you sure?"

She unzipped her sparkly bag, whipped out a miniature bottle of Jack, and downed half in one swallow. "Here," she offered.

And I drank the rest. It sloshed into the empty core of me with a satisfying burn. I half-smiled at her and shook my head, firing up the engine. "You came prepared, didn't you?"

"How else am I supposed to get through grad night?"

I drove us less than a mile to the Port of Oakland. The fog had rolled in from nowhere, misty and cold, and I shivered, cursing myself for leaving the top down. I tossed Gwen my leather jacket from the back seat—the Tiffany box hidden in the pocket—and she curled beneath it like a blanket. Maybe it was the fog, or the quiet, or the memories, but the whole place felt haunted. And I thought about turning around.

I hadn't been there in years, but I remembered the way. Every Monday after school, my dad had taken Jesse and me here to watch the cargo ships unload their freight. And I'd held my breath, watching those beastly bodies navigate the narrow channel. Sure that one day, a ship would sink. And all those containers, filled with riches, would tumble into the sea. Sometimes, I wished for it. At twelve, it had felt like an adventure. But I saw now, taking Gwen here, it was the kind of thing you do with your kids when you're poor. So poor you can't even afford the movies.

"I can't believe you punched Russ," she said, after we'd parked. The fog was so thick, the whole world was a whiteout. It was just us.

I shrugged. "He deserved it."

"You broke his nose." She touched her own, adorable and sprinkled with cinnamon freckles.

"Improved it, if you ask me. But, I'm sorry you had to see it."

I sucked in a breath and reached under my jacket, searching for her skin. I needed to touch her. "You're freezing," I said, cocooning her hand in mine.

"Why did you lie to me, Butch?"

I tightened my grip on her and summoned my courage. "I didn't intend to, but that first day...you just assumed I was rich. So I went with it."

"Not about being rich." She pulled away, and the whole world felt colder. And me, more desperate.

"About what then?"

"Russ's dad told us everything."

"Us? Everything?"

"Me and my parents." *Oh God.* "He said you'd been in and out of jail. That you're a criminal. That you wasted all your settlement money."

"Not all of it."

"So you have been to jail?"

"Juvenile hall. There's a difference." A flare of anger shot up from the hollow space inside me. Lit me up. "Besides, you're just as bad as I am. Worse even."

"Worse? Really? I've never been to jail. Or juvenile hall."

I started to argue, but her eyes iced over, and I knew I'd lose. Even if I was right, goddamn it. "Okay. Okay. I don't want to fight. I just want..."

I kissed Gwen. And she kissed me back. A kiss unlike any other. Because it felt wrong. And necessary. The way a vampire must feel sinking his teeth into a perfectly good neck. Sucking out the life force with all his might, filling himself with it. Knowing it would never, ever be enough. Nothing would. "I love you, Gwen." Killing the thing at the same time, ruining it for all eternity.

She pulled away—"Don't say that"—and I winced.

"Why not?" Though there were a million reasons, least of all I had no freakin' clue about love. Not even the iceberg tip of it. What I did know: Girls liked it when you said it. Usually.

"Because you don't mean it. Not really."

I swallowed hard, dousing another flare. Cherice *had* told her. I knew it. "Is this about Saturday night?" I asked.

The question, spoken aloud, froze us both. We stared at each other—two statues of ice—until she blinked first, in surprise. Her face, ghost-white like the fog. "Cherice told you?"

"Told me? Told me what?"

"Uh…" She bit her lip and looked down all innocent.

Was this the sort of face she gave her dad? The judge? Russ? Well, I wasn't about to join the line-up of other suckers who'd fallen for her doe-eyed bullshit. "Told me what, Gwen?"

"That she and Matthias broke up."

Thoughts flitted through my mind too fast to hold onto. I couldn't make sense of it. And the alcohol wasn't helping. It coated everything in a slick veneer of confusion. And beneath it, a dull rage that throbbed like a toothache. "What does that have to do with anything?"

"I sort of hooked up with Matthias while you and Cherice were getting beer after the race. I don't even remember it really. You know how out of it I was." She sighed and turned away, broken. Her shoulders hunched and quivering like a drowned kitten. I knew exactly what she wanted. What she expected. And I knew I couldn't give it to her.

"And then you slept with me? And you gave me shit for lying? For letting Cherice ride in my car? Jesus, Gwen." It all spewed out—hot

**348**

and slimy and wrong. Vile. But I couldn't stop it, even if I wanted to. "Did you already screw Russ too?"

She whipped around, her wet face darkening in hurt, in anger. But, God, she was beautiful still. "Did you really think you were my first? Russ and I have been together since freshman year. We make sense. You and I both realize what this is. And what it's not."

"Am I not good enough for you? Is that what you're saying?"

No answer. Only her eyes, wavering between yes and no. Between frost and foam. Steel and the open water of the ocean.

"Say it." There was a hardness in my voice I didn't recognize. "Say it, Gwen."

Steel, it was. Then, ocean. Then, steel again. And her uncertainty goaded me like a finger to the ribs. Because she was better than me. "I won't mean it. I don't want to."

My whole body tremored with sheer fury, and it scared me. "Yes, you do. Fucking say it, bitch."

Her slap stung, burned. Seared flesh, really. Her words too. "You're not good enough for me, Butch. You'll never be good enough." True or not, I needed them. They honed me, sharpened me to a point. A keen and fearsome blade.

Right then, I'd decided. *I'm going to kill her.* Less a thought than a fact, already written in the stars. A punishment I had to dispense, a debt owed to me, a sacrifice I deserved. Like a god. *The* God, maybe. Or just a man, who was barely a man, who thought he was a god.

And I had to throw a lightning bolt.

And Gwen just happened to be there.

Sitting in the 'Cuda, in the passenger seat, at the point of inflection. The last one. And no matter what had happened before, all the roads chosen and unchosen, I'd ended up with my hands on her neck.

Lovely, delicate as a stem under my fingers. Her fists beat against my arms like a million butterfly wings—frantic and futile. And my thumbs rooted into the small hollow above her clavicle. I thought of the necklace I'd wanted to put there. Of the five pennies. And the

**349**

three graves. And all the world had robbed me of. Of all she'd robbed me of, this girl with so much life ahead of her. While mine had ended years ago. Before it even started.

What I couldn't have burned through me, hot and sick. A fever.

And I squeezed.

Until there was nothing left.

# CHAPTER THIRTY-EIGHT

**EVIE**
**JANUARY 19, 2017**
**THURSDAY**

**THE** detectives left hours ago, and Maggie's dozing on the sofa, the television droning. Trey had been on the news. Armed and dangerous, they'd said. A wanted man now. And not just by the police.

Because Trey deserves to be punished.

For my mother. For Cassie. For Violet. For all the girls whose names I didn't know. Hell, even for Danny. I name them off like a rallying cry.

But most of all, for me. Because I had to keep living without all the things he'd taken from me.

I've laid down his sentence. Quick or slow, hard or easy, I want him dead. And I want to be the one to do it. Even if it means we both end up in hell.

After twenty-three years, the ember is still hot.

And the thought is a spark.

The spark catches fire.

And the fire burns everything clean.

Except for the thought.

And so it goes. Over and over again. Until it isn't just a thought anymore. *It's never just a thought.* I tell my patients that all the time. A thought leads to a feeling leads to an action. A thought is the first step across the line between doing and not doing. And don't I know it? I'd been thinking about slipping back into Butch's arms all last night—how safe I'd felt there—and then I'd done it. Embarrassing myself, admitting my schoolgirl crush.

I dress and pad down the hallway to Jared's room. Open his closet. Push aside his clothes, not breathing them in like I usually do. There's no time for that, for sentimentality. Back here, in the bowels of the museum of Jared, is where Maggie keeps the gun she bought after Bill died.

I don't know much about guns, but an internet search tells me enough. It's loaded. And how hard can it be? Point and fire. The best part—it's small enough to fit in my coat pocket.

I give Sammy a quick rub behind the ears and leave a note for Maggie.

*Gone to the office. Be back soon.*

Then, I snag the keys and go, heading out the driveway in the Prius that should have been a Corvette. And as of right now, it is one. And I'm Evil Evie. Tough and elegant. Dangerous too. Because how do you destroy a devil without becoming one?

I stop by the patrol car, and the officer lowers his window. Young and bored out of his mind. Now that I can see him up close—the drooping of his eyes—he might have been sleeping.

"I'm just heading to my office to grab a few things. I'll be quick. I don't need anybody with me."

"You sure?"

I shrug, nonchalant. "It's still business hours. I won't be alone."

**352**

"Alright. Call if there's any trouble." And he settles back into his seat, too comfortable. I think of Maggie. And how Trey could break her without even trying.

I reach through the window and smack his door. I like the way it sounds, the way it jolts him. "Do me a favor? Stay awake, alright?"

He's wide-eyed now, looking at me like I'm unhinged. Off the rails. Just like Bobby, running from Evil Evie and her rat poison. The gun sits hard and heavy in my pocket. He doesn't know the half of it.

**\*\*\*\***

It's a long wait, but it's worth it. At 9:05 p.m., I spot hair the color of fire, legs white as cleaned bones. Wearing the same black stilettos. The same oversized sweater, falling from a gaunt shoulder, the strap of a hot-pink bra exposed. And the snake tattoo slithering across her chest.

I wait until Ruby sits on the curb and puts a cigarette between her lips.

"What the fuck do you want?" There's a new bruise—a nasty one—on her cheek, covered in makeup two shades too dark for her pale skin.

"To make a business deal."

"I already got my own business. And I don't do chicks."

My bitter laugh surprises her, because she sits up straight, takes me in.

"Not that kind of business," I say, flashing the wad of money I'd withdrawn at the ATM. "This kind."

"Lemme see it." Her fingers are tentacles, latching onto my arm, squeezing. I shake her loose and step back, a little afraid of her. The intensity of her desire. *I've gotta get paid, baby.*

"You can look. But you can't touch. Unless…" I count out the bills for her. Five hundred smackaroos, and I know she wants them by the way she stares.

"Unless what?"

"I need to know where Trey is."

"Who's Trey?"

"Alright, then. I guess you don't want my money." I call her bluff, turn away. Walk toward the Corvette, grinning. Because I know, it's just a matter of—

"Wait." Time.

She toddles across the empty street, like a newborn colt in those heels. And I see my mother in her. And Cassie. I feel disgusted all over again, using her like this. But it doesn't stop me.

"He can't know I told you." Her whisper was as fragile as a dream.

"He won't."

"He's at the Blue Bird. Room 157. His usual. But he's not alone."

"Matthias?"

She raises her eyebrows at me, twists her mouth. Like she can't believe I had the nerve to ask. "I told you what you wanted, so…"

The money disappears inside her bra, and she starts back in the direction she came. Down the long stretch of road that leads to nowhere.

For Ruby too.

✳✳✳✳

The Blue Bird isn't blue anymore. It's mustard. A dirty canary. Almost as bad as the color of the sofa my mother had dragged in. But I guess *yellow bird* doesn't have quite the same ring, the kind that sticks in your head like a one-hit-wonder pop song. Even a head like mine where things disappear. Because the name is the same, spelled out in big letters. *VACANCY*, flashing beneath.

I park near the office and sit, watching 157 in my rearview. The curtains are pulled, but I know Trey's here. Or close by. Because I spot the blue pickup from his place, parked at the fast-food joint across the street. No license plate.

I hold out my hands. They're steady, solid. Ready to act. But my mind is shifty, unreliable as quicksand, sucking me back to the past. To two days before my mother had died.

**354**

I'd been asleep on the hideous sofa, my mother wrapped around Trey in the bed like a spider with a fly. Somehow the fly broke free and buzzed away, leaving her limbs stretched empty across the sheets. He'd stumbled toward me, and I'd shut my eyes fast and hard. But that hadn't stopped him. His breath, hot on my face, and reeking of alcohol. His hand, that devil's claw, slipping beneath the blanket.

"What're you doin' to her?" my mother had asked.

He'd rubbed his hand across my chest, my barely there breasts. It was the first and only time he'd touched me like that, but it felt like he'd been doing it all along. Forever. Like he owned me. Like it was nothing, and I was nothing.

"Nothin'." Exactly.

My mother had called his name then, beckoned him. And little by little, I'd felt him withdraw, his evilness getting farther from me. Until the air above me felt cool and empty again.

When I'd opened my eyes, he'd gotten back in bed. Mouth on my mother. "Don't you think it's about time she started earnin' her keep?"

# CHAPTER THIRTY-NINE

**"WHERE** did you say you found this?" The question is mine to answer. But I stutter. Like I did something wrong.

Mr. Vinetti and I sit side by side in the office, Detectives Munroe and Maroni perched on the metal folding chairs we'd brought in from the storage room.

"Go ahead, Butch. Tell 'em where you'd found it."

"Out behind the dumpsters. I think it belongs to my roommate."

Maroni studies me, nods. "And how did you know exactly where to find it?"

*Here we go.* "The other night we'd left the house, and he went back there to get something. I'd forgotten about it until today."

"So, you just decided to have a little look-see, huh? Go diggin' through the dirt?"

"Yes, sir. I thought it might be important, what with the murder of that girl and all. Violet." Goddamned right, it's important. Critical, even. Because when you find a few barely legal porn mags and a pack of condoms in a lockbox, it's probably a clue. But add a cell phone with a dead girl's name scrawled on the case—*if lost, return to Violet Kurchell*—you've got a smoking gun.

He narrows his eyes at me. "How do we know this stuff doesn't—"

Maroni's phone buzzes at his hip—saved by the bell of modern technology—and he answers it, excusing himself. With him gone, the air lightens and I can breathe again.

Mr. Vinetti clears his throat and turns to Detective Munroe. "Should Butch have an attorney? Your partner is on him like white on rice."

"It's alright," I tell him, the back of my neck burning hot. "He's just doing his job."

"No, it's not alright, Butch. They're treating you like a suspect." He scowls at Munroe, but she's distracted, probably listening to Maroni like I am. I can hear him, his clipped voice, outside the door.

"Okay…I'm sure it's fine, Mrs. Maddox. Let me check."

He pokes his head in. "Have either of you seen Dr. Maddox this afternoon? Or heard from her?"

I shift in my seat, worms of worry squirming in my belly. "No. Her office has been locked all day."

I curse myself as soon as I say it. I sound like a stalker. Just the sort of guy who would bury a lockbox behind the dumpsters.

# CHAPTER FORTY

I knock on Trey's door, already knowing. One way or the other. Him or me. It ends now. Today.

No one answers. I press my ear to the door, half-expecting to hear his heartbeat on the other side. To feel the wood warm from the fire of his breath. But Trey's heart is a stone. And the door is cold.

"I know you're in there, Trey. If you don't open the door, I'm calling the police."

The door opens. Just a crack. A slim gap held in place by the security chain. And the barrel of a gun points through it. "You'd better take off. Skedaddle. Trey ain't here."

"Matthias?" He has a name *and* a face. I'd googled him this afternoon on Maggie's phone—Matthias Granger—and stared at his

Facebook photo until my eyes blurred, picturing him there that night. In the truck. With Cassie under the tree.

And now, he's real. But I can't quite believe it. For half brothers, they don't look a thing alike. It must be the devil inside that binds them. Matthias is younger than Trey. With broad shoulders and meaty bones and hair so blonde it's white, framing his face like a halo.

"I said leave."

"Not until I talk to Trey."

He nudges the barrel of the gun through the gap, closer to me, and fear zips like a cattle prod at the back of my neck. It stuns, even though I'd expected it.

"Go ahead. Threaten me. I've got a gun too."

I reach into my coat, tasting my own arrogance. Bold and bitter, it quells my fear. Until from behind, a hand shuts my mouth.

I squirm against it, tasting sour skin now. Cigarettes and filth and the metal of my father's ring. Trey is all hands. Like he's got more than two of them. With one, he tightens his grip while greedy fingers search my pockets, my skin crawling beneath them.

"Talk, talk, talk. That's what they pay you shrinks for, huh? Personally, I've always been of the mind that talkin' is overrated." The gun—my gun—is mine no longer. "But you wanna talk, Evelyn? We can talk. We can talk all night. Ain't that what you always wanted? To find out what makes ol' Trey tick. What gets me hot and bothered."

Trey's strength surprises me. Rail-thin but all muscle, he drags me into the room next door and tosses me onto the bed, pinning me on my stomach with his knee. Matthias laps at his heels, eager as a puppy.

My face rubs against the bedspread, and I turn a single eye to the room. A row of beer bottles stand watch on the dresser, guarding a thin line of white powder at the edge. Above it all, a mirror shows me half my face. Half a grimace. The other half hidden in cheap linens.

I try to move. Can't. And the backside of Trey's hand makes a sickening thwack against my skin, so hard my teeth rattle. Now, I taste blood. My own.

"That's me talkin'." He pokes my leg with his finger. "Just like you wanted."

"You killed Cassie."

He hits me again, even harder this time.

"And Mom. And you scammed her government money. The money that should've been mine."

Another strike. And this is the Trey I remember. Vicious, red-faced, and frothing at my mother on that day. Her first and last minutes of freedom.

"You killed your own daughter. Violet."

With the next blow, the room goes dim and starry. A whooshing in my ears like I'm sinking underwater. He puts a gun—*mine?*—to my temple. It's cool and hard with no life of its own. But in his hands, it's greedy. And vicious. And ready to take whatever it wants.

"Talk," he says. "C'mon. I can't hear you."

It wants me.

✳✳✳✳

I must be dead. And this must be hell. Because Trey's still here, prowling circles around the bed. Matthias too. Four black eyes, hungry and fixed on me.

Wakefulness is gradual, a slow tunneling to the surface. But my situation comes to me—sudden—like a flash of sunlight on the water. A shark fin piercing the blue.

My hands are tied together and secured to the bedpost, makeshift, with a ratty T-shirt. A towel from the bathroom bunched in my mouth like a fist. And the mirror reflects an *other*, a *not me*, a misshapen image.

I find my gun on the dresser, gaze at it with longing.

"Told ya to leave." Matthias snorts at me, taunting. And now that I know his face, I can't stand it. I want to scratch it, strip it, tear skin from bone. Until it's gone again.

*Fuck you.* I spit it at him. But only in my mind, of course. Out loud, it's gagging on my own saliva, the towel already soaked with it.

Trey leans over the dresser, sucking up the line of powder in his nose. He sniffs, shakes his head.

"Damn, Evelyn. Look what you made me do. You got me all worked up." I jerk my arms forward, bucking against the ties, and the bed creaks. "Easy, girl. Don't go breakin' anything. They charge for that shit."

Matthias cackles with delight. "So what now?" he asks.

"Go get the truck."

The front door opens for an agonizing second, and I kick at the bed, scream into the towel. Exhaust myself.

Matthias is gone. And somehow that's worse.

Trey wastes no time. Yet, he's unhurried. He slithers to the bed and backs me up against the headboard. Until he's right there, his tar-pit pupils big and black, his stringy hair falling against my knees. Silver teeth bared, crooked as old headstones sunk into the earth. And the smell of him is in my nose.

"That's what you came here to talk about? All the wrong I done to ya?" He runs a finger down my cheek, and it hurts. My skin hurts. Traces a line to my mouth and pulls out the towel in one vile, wet clump. "What do you want from me, Evelyn?"

I gag. Cough. Move my mouth, my aching jaw. And sounds come out. But words take longer. *Everything you took. Priceless things. Things you can't return.* "I want you to admit it. Admit something."

He sits back on his haunches, slips my father's knife from his pocket and sets free the blade. Perfect and ruthless and pointed at me. I can't look away.

"Cassie and your mama, they were a lot alike. Loved 'em both. Took care of 'em. Hell, I even let Cas and that bastard kid of hers live with me. Even after she started makin' accusations, threatenin' me. Threatenin' to get you involved, to dredge up the past."

"She wrote to me, you know. Is that why you sent Danny after me?"

His smile is a wound—raw and red and festering. I take it as an answer. Yes.

"And they both loved somethin' else more. You know that. Your mama, she loved dope even more than she loved you. Her own flesh and blood."

Then, his shirt comes off. He's all ribs and ink and hair. And the sight of it—what it means—knocks the wind from me.

"As far as I see it, I did you a favor. I set you free. And look how damn good you turned out. Real, real purdy. Hell, you're beautiful."

"Thanks, Trey. That's sweet." It comes out right. Soft and unexpected. "I need to ask you something." His hand rubs my thigh, and it feels like the devil's kiss, but I simper at him.

"Don't play games with me."

I shake my head. "No games. I swear. I just want to know what happened the night you sent me to LA. Did you tell Matthias to find us?"

The key turns in the lock, and I think about screaming. But Trey's even closer now, running the tip of the blade down the seam of my blue jeans. Lightly. Like a promise broken. And I know for certain he's planning on getting rid of me. But not here. Too much to explain. He'd made that mistake before.

Matthias stares at us. "Guess I'm late to the party."

"Naw, man. You're just in time." Trey moves away. Sits at the edge of the bed. And that's when I see the butt of a gun at the small of his back. "Evelyn was askin' about ya. About the mess you made that night at the hangin' tree."

They share a look, both sets of lips parting in the same grin. That's what they share. A wicked smile. The kind that would rob you blind. The kind that would kick a dog when it's down. The kind that would stab you in the chest with your own knife—or in my case, my father's—and twist it a little deeper.

"What do you wanna know?"

"You raped Cassie that night, didn't you? Did Trey tell you to do it?"

Matthias takes a gun from his waistband, sets it with mine on the dresser, and unbuckles his belt. "Information like that is gonna cost ya. What are you willin' to give me for it?"

**362**

The belt swishes through the loops, menacing. Like the tail of a snake disappearing in the underbrush. "Whatever you want. I need to know."

"Trey didn't know nothin' about it...till later. You remember Cherice?" I nod, transfixed by his fingers on the button of his pants, the roll of fat still concealed by his shirt. "She paged me to look for your ass after you snuck out again. So if we're layin' blame, I'd say it's on you. And her. Besides, I didn't do nothin' to Cassie she didn't ask for."

Trey shrugs at me, grinning, but there's tension in his shoulders. In the way he grips my father's knife. He's watching Matthias just like I am. "I told ya so," he says. "I'm not the bad guy you think I am."

"I heard Cassie say no. I saw you choke her, Matthias."

He pushes Trey out of the way and latches on to my ankle. Drags my legs toward him, my arms stretched overhead and straining against the T-shirt. Hung up to dry like an animal carcass.

"C'mon, Matty. I got dibs on this one. You wait your turn, little brother."

Matthias' jaw works like he's got a mouthful of something thick and bitter. And I notice. Because that's my job. "How many goddamned times do I have to tell you not to call me that?" To notice. And to remember. To make meaning.

"Choking. That's your thing, isn't it, Matty? Your little fetish?" I feel the power in my words. Even here, beat up and flat on my back. "You knew my mother, right?"

His mouth pinches tight. And his laugh comes out high and breathy. "Everybody knew your mama. Ain't that right, Trey?"

Trey stands, and they face each other. "As I recall, you never met Arlene."

"Did you ever wonder where Mom got all that money she had? The five thousand dollars she stole right out from under you. That was supposed to be your money. You were the one providing for her. Feeding her habit. Taking care of her when she got dope sick."

Trey nods, proud. Like finally—*finally!*—I got it right.

"I remember one time when you were gone, this guy came over, and I had to hide in the closet while Mom did her thing. Funny when you think about it. That guy was into choking, too. I know because when I peeked out—"

Matthias lunges for me—and Trey for Matthias—his fleshy arm smacking against the headboard, slackening my ties.

Trey swipes at him with the knife, slicing a gash through his T-shirt. It turns to a blood river—deep and wide and flowing, and Matthias' eyes darken. He's a wounded animal—a bear to Trey's winter-starved wolf. And one wallop of his angry paw sends the knife flying.

They wrestle onto the floor, Trey on top, then Matthias, rolling toward the dresser as I struggle to get free.

The gun at Trey's waist slides across the floor. And he scuttles for it. Fast like you'd expect. No matter how quick you are, the devil is always faster.

But Matthias is part devil too. And he scrambles to the dresser, to the gun he'd laid there.

I make one last jerk, and my hands come loose. I scoot off the bed and crouch beside it. "He was choking her. And I saw his bright blonde hair. And do you know what she called him? Matty. She called him Matty, and he didn't like it."

Both guns pointed at the other, nostrils flaring like wild mustangs.

"He gave her a wad of cash that she stuck in the sofa. And told her you could never find out."

"Lying bitch." Matthias' eyes are fire, and he wants me to burn. I look back at him—at his face—and pretend it's scribbled over in black crayon.

"I'm not lying. And I can prove it."

The room is still. The air electric. I'm holding a grenade. And all that's left to do is to pull the pin. To launch it. "He has a tattoo on his back. An iron cross."

I duck down from the spray of bullets, head between my knees. Legs pulled in close just like that night at the tree. And it's Cassie's voice I hear over the pings, the cracks, the sounds of flesh exploding. *Climb higher, higher.*

****

Matthias slumps near the dresser, blood pooling around his head. He hasn't moved.

The shattered mirror reflects Trey in pieces. Fragments. He writhes, and I watch him, transfixed.

I stand up, my legs tottery beneath me. They'll be here soon, so I take my gun from the dresser, wipe it on the sheets. And return it to my pocket, unused.

Trey moans. Says my name. And I go to him. I want to be closer.

The hole at the center of his chest is small, but the floor is soaked with blood. He coughs, sputters. His breathing is shallow. Stops and starts. Stops and starts.

He says my name again, in a way that's asking a question. The only question that can matter to him now. To either one of us.

*What kind of person am I?*

I kneel across his bony thighs, pinning him like a tack, and they give under the weight of me. His hand reaches, outstretched, but I brush it aside like a withering vine. It's too weak to pose a threat. His eyes are open, glassy and wet. And that feels right, because I want him to see.

I put my hand over his mouth, his nose. Count to one hundred. Slow and unwavering. With each number, I steal back what I'm owed.

Until there's nothing left.

****

I sit on the curb at the Blue Bird between two patrol cars and watch them wheel the bodies out. One long black bag, then another. So

**365**

I can't tell Trey from Matthias. One devil from the other. But not devils at all, apparently. Just men. Mere mortals.

Detective Maroni nods at me from the door and gives a sympathetic smile before he ducks under the crime-scene tape. He's heard my story, written it on his little notepad and tucked it in his pocket. He believes me. I am Arlene Allcott's daughter after all.

The body bags disappear into the coroner's van, same as my mother's all those years ago. I wonder if she's here. If she passes through these walls, a restless ghost. If she'd watched me slip Dad's ring from Trey's lifeless finger. What she would say now to her baby girl. "We're survivors, Evelyn." And I'd nod, but I'd tell her I don't feel satisfied, satiated the way I'd always expected. Instead, I'm emptied. Razed. Like a forest slashed and burned, the ash fertilizing the soil beneath.

I run my hand along the cold sidewalk and my finger grazes the butt of a cigarette. Marlboro, Calder's old brand. I smile at the memory, at the girl I was then. At the woman she grew into. I pluck the cigarette from the sidewalk crack and hold it with tenderness and awe. Like a daisy that's sprouted against all odds.

# CHAPTER FORTY-ONE

*WHEN* *it starts to get hairy—and it will—stick to the basics. The routine.* They'd told us that in the reentry prep class I'd taken six months before I'd walked back out into the free world. And, right now, I'm clinging to it like a goddamned life raft.

I sit in my usual booth way back in the corner. Sip my usual coffee, lukewarm and black and slightly better than dishwater. And Brenda's here, of course. With her pushed-up cleavage and her crooked smile. But she can tell I'm not right. Even though I keep telling her I am. *Fine.* That word you use when you really mean anything but.

I ask Brenda to turn the TV off, because I've already seen it. And once was enough. Mr. Vinetti and I had watched it on the set in his office after Maroni got the call. He'd been in the middle of Shake Down Butch Calder, Part Deux, when his phone had buzzed again.

"Shoot-out at the Blue Bird," he'd told Munroe. "Multiple victims." And then they'd left like somebody lit a fire under them, taking the lockbox and my dignity with them.

*Stick to the routine.* So I force a bite of the waffle before it goes cold. Chew, swallow, and repeat, eggs this time. Ignore the rubbery taste of worry that coats my tongue and makes everything bitter.

She's alive. I know that much. And only thanks to the Channel Five news.

**The victims have been identified as Oakland natives Trey Waters and Matthias Granger. Both men were wanted in connection with a recent homicide, after two bodies were discovered on their property in rural Pinole. A female at the scene was reportedly held against her will and suffered minor injuries. Police have not released her name.**

After the report, I'd broken down and called Evie's mother-in-law. No answer. And I wasn't brave enough to leave a message.

Brenda tops off my cup and lingers. "You sure you don't want to talk about it, Butch? You seem troubled."

I shake my head. But then, I reconsider. *Don't be afraid to ask for help.* Per reentry prep, lesson two. *Throw out a lifeline.* "You said your dad went to prison?"

"Sure did." She slides in the booth opposite me, her smile tinged with sadness. Just like I'd expect. "Armed robbery. He went in when I was two. By the time he got out, I was seventeen and pregnant. Can you imagine?"

Actually, I could. Whole lives stopped and started. Wars were fought and won. Trends came and went and came again. And all the while, I sat in a box, waiting for my second chance. And now that I had it, sometimes it felt wrong. Like more than I deserved. "So how long before he felt normal again?"

**368**

"Normal." She tosses her head back and laughs. A little rusty. Like it's the first time in a while. Like she's forgotten what it feels like. It's infectious, so I laugh too. "Ain't no such thing, hon. No such thing. But you've got a great laugh. I'd like to hear more of that."

Behind her, the door opens. And Brenda can see it on my face—excitement or elation or just plain relief. Whatever it is, she turns to look. Then she scoots out of the booth and pats my shoulder. Gives a soft sigh. "Guess this seat's taken."

Evie heads for the table. For me.

I take her inventory—a nasty cut on her lip, a bruise on her cheekbone, hands that won't stop shaking, and the ring Trey stole on her finger. But she's okay. She's safe. And that's my one good thing.

Before I can decide what to do next, my feet carry me up and out of my seat. Arms invite her in, and somehow—standing there, holding her—this ex-con in the Chicken and Waffles feels brand new.

"I knew you'd be here," she says, a faint lift of her lip. Barely a smile. But then, it broadens. "And by the looks of Brenda, I got here just in time."

"Evie." I pull away and meet her eyes—green as the first patch of grass I'd walked on barefoot. I'm not sure where to start. *With the license? The lockbox? The tree? Cassie?* And I know there are things she wants to say too. Her face is full of them.

It's like the last scene in a movie when the music kicks in. And I know just the right song too. KISS, of course. *But every time I look at you, no matter what I'm goin' through, it's easy to see. And every time I hold you, the things I never told you, seem to come easily.*

So, I need to go first.

Before the credits roll and I lose my nerve.

"I have a confession to make."

**369**

## BUTCH
## MAY 13, 1994
## AFTER I KILLED HER

*HOW* *did you feel right afterward?* A psych doctor had asked me that once.

*Bad,* I'd said. *Really bad.* And then I'd wanted a take back. To say instead, *What kind of a stupid, goddamned question is that?* Because, when it came to Gwen, to what I'd done, words were empty shells, hollow husks.

I could have said I felt nothing—just static in my head—but that wasn't right either. Finally, I'd settled on it. *It was like a power surge,* I'd added, prompting an encouraging nod from the shrink. As if she understood. As if she could ever understand. *Every emotion all at once. Full bore, full blast. A total blackout. And then, panic. Only panic.*

*Tell me more,* she'd said.

Gwen slumped in the passenger seat, so still, head leaning against the window. Her strapless dress, gone askew in the struggle. One side of her bra exposed. Black lace. I tugged her dress back up. Righted her. Put two fingers on her neck. *Don't look, don't look.* Because my hands had left marks, raw and red. Gentle this time. *Gentle, Butchy.* Hoping—*no*—begging. The soul-on-its-knees kind.

*Please, God.*
*Please, God.*
*Please.*

**370**

"Gwen. Wake up." I shook her by the shoulders. Limp as a rag doll. "Gwen."

Tapped her face. Still warm.

Uncurled her fingers, balled in fists.

Said her name a hundred times. Wailed it, sobbed it until my throat hurt. Nothing changed. Nothing fixed.

Imagine the worst mistake you've ever made. Multiply by infinity. Start there.

****

*I am so fucked.*

Russ knows Gwen left with me. My prints, all over her. Hers, all over the 'Cuda. My skin started to buzz. Like I'd touched a live wire. All the feeling coming back.

*I've gotta get out of here. I've gotta get rid of it.*

And by it, I meant her. Gwen. Rid of it. That's what I needed to do. And now.

*I could put it in the water, sink it. Yes.*

I drove up, as close as I could get to the water's edge. Flung open the car door, got out, and went to the other side.

I pulled it out like a sack of cement and dropped it there.

And the water lapped, black as oil. But cold, so cold. I knew it would be. Deep, maybe. But not deep enough. Not nearly deep enough.

*I am so fucked.*

I squatted down to drag it to the water. To let it float away. And I wanted to float away with it. To lie on my back in the ocean and stare at the sky. To feel the water cover my face. To anchor to the bottom. Both of us, at peace.

A sound pricked my ears, paralyzing me. A car, coming down the road. This way.

*Leave it. Just leave it.*

And I did. Backed up, peeled out. As fast as I could. As fast as the 'Cuda would go. So fast, I barely felt the bump.

Later, they'd ask me, *Why did you run her over?*

****

The idea came to me—a revelation, really—as soon as I hit Broadway, doing seventy in a thirty. It flashed bright, urgent as a stop sign. And I wondered why I hadn't done it before. Before tonight. Before this. I'd thought of it. Of course, I had. But I'd been too chickenshit to pull the trigger.

*I want to die.*

Four words. And I couldn't get them out of my head. They demanded action. Compelled it. It needed to happen. Now.

I sped up a little, revving the engine. Unbuckled my seat belt.

*I want to die.*

Aimed the nose of the 'Cuda at the nearest utility pole. That would do the trick.

*I want to die.*

Let the clutch out and floored it. At the last second, just before impact, three things happened.

I saw my Dad's face. Mom and Jesse too.

I closed my eyes.

I changed my mind.

****

That's where I'd always stopped the story. It seemed as good a place as any. But, you already know, it wasn't the end. There's no such thing.

My head had split in two, right down the middle. That's how it'd felt. When I'd touched it, my fingers had come back wet and red. And my vision had blurred. Adrenaline had spiked my blood, and my hands had begun to tremor with the shock of it all.

*I'm alive.* There was no joy though.

I'd swerved, hit the brakes last second. And the whole right side of the 'Cuda had taken the blow. The door had bent inward. The

**372**

utility pole had cracked. Electrical wires had drooped toward the road, sparking.

Sirens—behind me, inside me—even in the beat of my heart. So I'd had to hurry.

*To what? To where?* I didn't know.

I'd pushed open the door, surprised at my body. The strength of it, still.

"Are you alright?" A man's voice. A voice I'd ignored, because he couldn't have helped me. No one could have. Even as every part of me, right down to the cells, screamed no.

I'd climbed out and started running, and the voice had yelled after me. It'd felt good to run. Lungs puffing, heart pounding, just like always. Same old Butch Calder. Like nothing had gone wrong. Like I hadn't gone wrong. All the way wrong.

Down Broadway, I'd hung a right on Jackson. Without thought or reason. Just legs carrying me away. The street had been near perfect—deserted and dark. I was nobody, just like Trey had said. Just a man in silhouette. Faceless.

I could've kept running forever on a street like that.

But forever doesn't last. A park up ahead. Noise and shadows. So I'd sprinted to the other side and drew my jacket up over my face, hiding. Thinking I could still get away. That there could be life after this.

The shadows had taken shape like the beginning of a dream. A man straddling, his back strained with wanting. A body struggling beneath him. A tree with a girl in it. Not a dream after all. A nightmare. Mine.

"Hey, mister! Help us, please!" By the voice, I'd known it was Evie. The girl who'd already lost so much. The girl I'd made promises to. "Please!"

A choice had been made then. I'd made a choice. To stay hidden—shrouded in my jacket, with the Tiffany box rattling like a millstone in my pocket. To keep running. Running. Running.

Hoping maybe, just maybe, someday, I'd be fast enough to outrun myself.

## SEBASTIAN
## JANUARY 23, 2017
## TEN DAYS AFTER I KILLED HER

I arrive early for Monday's group, skin throbbing. Practically aroused. Because Butch found the lockbox last week. Dug it up like a good little boy, just like I'd expected him to. And mum's the word—he hasn't said a thing about it. As if I don't know. He thinks he's so clever. Poor sap.

Now that I'd told them what I'd seen last Friday—*who I'd seen*—it will happen soon. "I'm sorry, Detective. I was too scared to come forward. I thought I'd get in trouble." It could even happen today. It could happen here. But that almost seems too much to hope for. And I'm not greedy. I only take what I need. What I absolutely need.

The others arrive—all of them—and fill the chairs in the waiting room, but I keep my head down, afraid I might get a fit of giggles and give myself away. If I still had my book, I'd open it and stare at Sasha for a while. Let the longing feelings come and go, come and go, like the ebb of the tide. I wonder if she still feels it too. She must.

Dr. Maddox opens the door, invites us in. I take the seat next to her, across from the window, with a view of the parking lot and that tree she's obsessed with. She nods at me, and I nod back. Her blouse is open—two buttons undone today—and sheer enough to see the line of her bra strap across her shoulder. Her makeup is different too.

Heavier on her cheeks. Like she's hiding something. I look without looking. Careful not to get caught.

I'm always careful. Except when I'm not. Some things are meant to be, urge card be damned. And some things just can't be helped. Like with Roland, for example. Sasha's prick boyfriend. He'd walked in on us, Sasha and me. He didn't understand. No one did. I would never hurt her. I hadn't expected to hit him so hard, so many times. Hadn't expected his soft skull to crack and open like an eggshell. But it had. And what else could be done? He'd been beyond saving. Humpty Dumpty. His pieces wouldn't go back together, even if I'd wanted them to.

"Good morning, guys." I smile at Dr. Maddox as she greets us. It is a good morning. An especially good one. "I'm sorry I missed last Friday, but I hope you enjoyed Dr. Richards." I stifle a scoff. Dr. Stick-up-the-Ass is more like it. A total stuff shirt. "Should we start with check-ins?"

I fucking hate check-ins. But I feel generous today. "I'll go first," I say, savoring each word as it leaves my tongue. "The cops came by the house on Friday night. Apparently, they found some new evidence in the murder of that girl and wanted to question a few of us." *A few, meaning me.* "At first, it made me nervous. Then I realized I have nothing to hide."

An accident. A total misunderstanding. That's all it was. Scout's honor. From behind, she'd looked exactly like my Sasha, lithe and auburn-haired and shimmering in the light by Dr. Maddox's office.

"What're you doing?" I'd called to her, knowing I'd caught her at something. *Bad girl.* And she'd cursed, scampered down the steps like a scared little rabbit. Though she wasn't scared of me. Yet.

"Wait." And she'd stopped and turned to me. I'd been disappointed. Not my Sasha after all. Just a cheap replica. Worse. I know a hooker when I see one. But I was hard up. And she would do. "Are you looking for Dr. Maddox?"

She'd nodded her head and came closer. Licked her red lips like she'd been daring me to cover them with my own, just the way Sasha used to do. "I need to talk to her."

"I know her. Maybe I can help you." I'd smiled at her. My Piggy smile. Sheepish, nervous. Jack, well-hidden underneath.

And she'd relaxed. I had posed no threat. "Maybe."

"You remind me of my girlfriend." It just came out. I hadn't meant to say it out loud. "Ex-girlfriend, I mean."

"What's her name?"

"Sasha." A name that belonged only to me. It had sounded wrong to say it out loud, to give it to her.

And worse out of her filthy mouth. "Sasha," she'd repeated. "It's a pretty name. Why'd you break up?"

"Extenuating circumstances." Like she'd know what those big words meant. She was probably a high school dropout. "Her dad didn't approve."

She'd made a pouty face, and I had to pinch myself. Slow myself down. Because she looked so young and pliable. She'd do whatever I wanted. "Why are you looking for Dr. Maddox?"

Oh, my fault for asking, because she'd gotten all teary-eyed. Killed my buzz like a wet blanket. "It's a long story. My mom knows—knew—her. And there's this guy. Well, he's my dad actually, and I'm kind of—"

Blah, blah, blah. "Do you think maybe I could kiss you?"

She'd blinked up at me, surprised. Disappointed. That whore was disappointed in *me*. Like she was a prize.

"I don't think so," she'd said. "I only just met you."

And then my stepfather had started talking in my head, the way he always did. How I'd never get a girl as good as his Sasha. How I'd better toughen up, buck up. Stop being such a pussy.

"You don't get to say no." My voice is hard, and so am I. "You're a fucking prostitute."

Alright, maybe it hadn't been a total accident. But I'd never meant to take it that far. And she'd been just as much to blame, running like she did.

Dr. Maddox moves to the whiteboard, starts writing. I settle in and watch. Thirty seconds of obstructed viewing time. I'd missed the other check-ins. A damn shame because I'd wanted to hear his last. If it happened today. Which it might.

"We're going to pick up where we left off on Wednesday. Responsible sexual behavior."

The way she says it you can tell she's hot for someone. Maybe another shrink like her or a lawyer. Definitely an asshole. Because chicks like her dig assholes, even assholes that smack them around a little. That would explain Friday's absence. And the makeup.

I feel sorry for Butch. It's pathetic how he thinks he's got a chance with her. A woman like that needs to be wined and dined before she puts out. *Chicken and Waffles ain't gonna cut it, buddy.* But, hey, maybe she'll give him a pity lay. Either way, I'm glad I didn't pin it on him like I'd planned. Because I'm actually starting to like the guy.

Butch and me, we're a lot alike. We both got a raw deal. Wasting our best years in the clink. And we don't deserve to go back. We've done enough time. More than enough. Good thing there's more than one way to skin a cat.

"Sebastian? Responsible sexual behavior? Can you give an example?"

*Shit. Busted.* "Uh...I'm sorry, Dr. Maddox."

"Get your head out of your ass, New Guy." Vince winks at me, smirks. And my chest flares. I swear he looks just like my stepdad, puffed up and laughing at my expense.

I wink back, and he frowns. He doesn't understand. He doesn't see what I see. Or know what I know.

Cop cars in the lot. Today. It's happening today. I want to shout it, wave my hands. But, I sit on them. Clamp my mouth shut. And look without looking again. So careful. Like wearing a condom with Violet. That careful. The rain washed the rest away.

Detective Maroni is right where I want him to be. At the trunk of a black Mercedes. He'll find Violet's leggings, the ones I'd strangled her with, and her necklace inside the pocket of the monogrammed golf bag—exactly where I'd put them last Friday—some of her hair still caught in the chain. A nice touch, don't you think? The way I'd led them right to him.

I'd heard him yammering on his headset last week before group. A trip to the range with his frat-boy buddies. So I'd followed him there on Friday and waited until he was three sheets to the wind on gin and tonics. Until he wouldn't notice a guy in a stocking cap and sunglasses. A guy who knew how to blend, how to move unseen. A chameleon. A Jack and a Piggy, both.

Dr. Maddox groans at us, irritated. It's throaty and sexual and kind of a turn-on. Enough to stop my reverie. "C'mon, guys. Does anybody else have an answer?"

Luckily, good ol' George pipes up. Model sex offender, that guy. "I've got one, Dr. Evie. Using a condom. That's an example, right?"

And the irony of that. Damn. Who knew I was so responsible?

Of course, Dr. Maddox eats it right up. "Good," she says. A pat on the head for Georgie.

"What about you, Tony?" He balks right away. And it's so obvious he's guilty. He's an amateur, and I can't stand to look at him.

"I thought of one," I offer, just so he'll stop wriggling like a worm. "Having sex for the right reason."

"And what would that be?" She's teasing me. We both know the answer.

*Because you fucking want to. Because it feels good. And you can.* "Love. Procreation. The progression of intimacy. To name a few." *Damn, I'm good.*

I wonder if they'll knock first. I doubt it. But sure enough, a rap at the door. And that bitch detective, Munroe, comes in first. Before she's invited. And it gets me all riled up, in the best way, that she's the one who says it. That she's the one who cuffs him up. Ruffles that fancy suit, disturbs the tie I'd like to choke him out with.

I take it all in. The shock and awe on their faces. It reads like applause. A standing ovation for yours truly. The crescendo builds to this moment. The moment I created.

**378**

"Vince Kincaid, you're under arrest for the murder of Violet Kurchell."

And that face, *his*, the best of all of them. *Who's the hot shot now, asshole?*

I show them what I want. An open mouth, wide eyes, a tiny gasp. But inside, way down, where no one else can see, the curtains open and I take a bow.

*Now that you've finished The Hanging Tree, please consider leaving a review. Reviews and star-ratings may not seem that important, but to an up-and-coming author, they are essential. They help readers like you discover my books! And they give an author a little "street cred" for those browsing for their next read. So what's the best way to feed an author? Leave a review, of course. You can find all the links to review The Hanging Tree on my website ellerykane.com.*

# ACKNOWLEDGEMENTS

**ONCE** again, I owe an immense debt of gratitude to the AnnCastro Studio team—Ann Castro and Emily Dings— who provided all editing services for The Hanging Tree, including developmental editing, manuscript evaluation, line editing, copyediting, and proofing. Ladies, your work is invaluable! And to Giovanni Auriemma—who always amazes me with his artistic talent and creative vision.

In order to tell this story—especially Cassie's experience—I relied heavily upon the insights of Rachel Lloyd, a survivor of commercial sexual exploitation, and her fascinating memoir, *Girls Like Us*. Girls like Cassie disappear every day into the seedy underbelly of the world that most of us never see. If you suspect that someone you know is a victim of human trafficking, call the National Human Trafficking Resource Center hotline at 1-888-373-7888.

And finally, we all have a space inside us that we keep hidden from the world, a space we protect at all costs. So many people have allowed me a glimpse inside theirs—dark deeds, memories best unrecalled, pain that cracks from the inside out—without expectation of anything in return. I couldn't have written a single true word without them.

# ALSO BY ELLERY KANE

**THE** Hanging Tree is the second in the *Doctors of Darkness* series of psychological thrillers by forensic psychologist and author, Ellery Kane. Look for the next book, The First Cut, coming soon. If you want to be the first to know when new books are released, sign up for Ellery's newsletter at ellerykane.com.

If you enjoyed The Hanging Tree, look for these other great reads from Ellery Kane.

## Doctors of Darkness Series
Daddy Darkest
The Hanging Tree
The First Cut (coming soon!)

## Legacy Series
Legacy
Prophecy
Revelation
AWOL
The Legacy Series Boxed Set

# ABOUT THE AUTHOR

**FORENSIC** psychologist by day, novelist by night, Ellery Kane has been writing--professionally and creatively--for as long as she can remember. Just like many of her main characters, Ellery loves to ask why, which is the reason she became a psychologist in the first place. Real life really is stranger than fiction, and Ellery's writing is often inspired by her day job. Evaluating violent criminals and treating trauma victims, she has gained a unique perspective on the past and its indelible influence on the individual. And she's heard her fair share of real life thrillers. An avid short story writer as a teenager, Ellery recently began writing for enjoyment again, and she hasn't stopped since.

Ellery's debut novel, Legacy, has received several awards, including winning the Gold Medal in the Independent Publisher Book Awards, young adult, e-book category, and the Gold Medal in the Wishing Shelf Independent Book Awards, teenage category. In 2016, Ellery was selected as one of ten semifinalists in the MasterClass James Patterson Co-Author Competition.